FEAR
Is A Killer

Sixteen Stories of Crime
and Punishment

WILLIAM · BANKIER

EDITED BY
PETER · SELLERS

F E A R
Is A Killer

Sixteen Stories of Crime
and Punishment

WILLIAM · BANKIER

EDITED BY
PETER · SELLERS

MOSAIC PRESS
OAKVILLE, ON. - BUFFALO, N.Y.

Canadian Cataloguing in Publication Data

Bankier, William
    Fear is a killer

ISBN 0-88962-553-0

I. Crime - Fiction. 2. Detective and mystery stories, Canadian
(English).* I. Seller, Peter, 1956-   . II. Title.

PS8553.A56F4   1995   C813'.54   C95-931466-0
PR9199.3.B35F4   1995

Published by MOSAIC PRESS, P.O. Box 1032, Oakville, Ontario, L6J
5E9, Canada. Offices and warehouse at 1252 Speers Road, Units #1&2,
Oakville, Ontario, L6L 5N9, Canada and Mosaic Press, 85 River Rock
Drive, Suite 202, Buffalo, N.Y., 14207, USA.

Mosaic Press acknowledges the assistance of the Canada Council, the
Ontario Arts Council, the Ontario Ministry of Culture, Tourism and
Recreation and the Dept. of Canadian Heritage, Government of
Canada, for their support of our publishing programme.

Book design & illustrations by Susan Parker
Printed and bound in Canada
ISBN 0-88962-553-0

In Canada:
MOSAIC PRESS, 1252 Speers Road, Units #1&2, Oakville, Ontario, L6L
5N9, Canada. P.O. Box 1032, Oakville, Ontario, L6J 5E9
In the United States:
MOSAIC PRESs, 85 River Rock Drive, Suite 202, Buffalo, N.Y., 14207
In the UK and Western Europe:
DRAKE INTERNATIONAL SEVICES, Market House, Market Place,
Deddington, Oxford. OX15 OSF

Table of Contents

SONGS IN THE
KEY OF DEATH:
THE FICTION OF
WILLIAM BANKIER
by
Peter Sellers

A man hears a woman operator's voice on the phone and, attracted and intrigued, he makes an appointment to meet her. Three questions spring to mind. What drives a man to ask? What kind of woman responds? And what godawful things are going to happen?

That basic premise, from William Bankier's story *Her Voice On The Phone Was Magic*, is typical of his work. Acts committed on whim or on the basis of incomplete or incorrect information lead, invariably, to nightmare. But the characters involved aren't often given the blessed relief of waking up. At least, not in time. Also typical of Bankier, and evident in that outline is the recurring theme of relationships as destructive and a breeding ground for all manner of evil.

Bankier himself is no stranger to acting on a whim. In 1974, having grown as he describes, "incurably dissatisfied with life as it stood", Bankier and his wife Phyllis packed up their two daughters, packed in his career in advertising, and headed for London where he was to live for ten years, much of it on a cramped houseboat moored on the Thames. Bankier left England after PhyLlis' untimely death. He now lives in West Hollywood with his second wife, editor and gag-writer Felice

Nelson. His daughters, Heather and Amy, continue to live and work in London.

Prior to his move, Bankier had published sporadically. He sold his first story to *Liberty Magazine* in 1954. A few years later, two horror stories appeared in the *Magazine of Fantasy and Science Fiction*. Then in 1962, *Ellery Queen Mystery Magazine* published *What Happened in Act One*, Bankier's first professional crime fiction sale. Over the next ten years, he sold seven or eight more crime stories to the major mystery magazines. But once he left the advertising business in which he'd laboured for 25 years and became a full time writer, the floodgates opened. There were over 45 romantic "nurse" novelettes under a variety of women's names, and a steady stream of increasingly assured crime fiction.

That assurance has been reflected in Bankier's status as one of the most frequent contributors to *Ellery Queen Mystery Magazine* over the past two decades; an Edgar Award nomination in 1980; two Crime Writers of Canada Arthur Ellis Award nominations, and the 1992 CWC Derrick Murdoch Award for his lifetime of achievement.

Bankier started writing crime stories as a child in his native Belleville, Ontario. "A brother and I used to write a story together often on a Sunday afternoon, one writing a paragraph, the other coming along and reading it and adding the next paragraph. We killed off each other's characters and left the plot in impossible situations."

Decades later and three thousand miles away in LA, the killings continue. And characters are still thrust into impossible situations.

In Bankier's world, families aren't just unhealthy, they're dangerous. He doesn't always restrict himself to dysfunctional relationships between husbands and wives, or parents and children. Siblings, as in the deeply unsettling *The Prize In The Pack*, included here, or the wonderfully titled *How Dangerous is Your Brother?*, have their moments, too.

Titles and first lines are a Bankier strength. Richly evocative, the names of his stories often hint strongly at his underlying themes. *Girls, Like White Birds. By the Neck Until*

Dead. Only If You Get Caught. And the opening lines (Darius Dolan climbed the iron stairs with another beer for his wife's lover) reinforce the menace and the message. Relationships don't work. Happiness is not a realistic goal. Shocking violence appears when you least expect it.

Despite the violent death in many of Bankier's stories, his work is not about bloodshed. His concern is motivation. What drives people to the actions they ultimately take? In stories such as *What Really Happened?* he goes so far as to apply that concern to real life, offering his solution to one of history's most fascinating murders, the Lizzie Borden case.

Although he played detective himself in that case (as well as later in *Death of a Noverint*, about the killing of playwright Christopher Marlowe) Bankier has written about detectives only infrequently. Bankier's sole entry into the detective pantheon is Professor Harry Lawson, known as the "Praw", a former professional stage magician who specializes in finding people and objects that have disappeared. He, along with his voluptuous wife Lola and her slightly thick brother Al, made his first appearance in *The Mystery of the Missing Penelope* in December 1978. *The Mystery of the Missing Guy*, included in this volume, followed the next year. However, after his third case, *The Missing Missile* in February, 1980, Praw Lawson himself disappeared without a trace. Lawson could possibly have stepped into the guild of detective magicians peopled by the likes of Clayton Rawson's Great Merlini, but whodunits are neither Bankier's interest nor his forte. They lie elsewhere: in Baytown, in sports, and in music.

In the geography of longitude and latitude, Baytown lies on the north shore of the St. Lawrence River, a little less than halfway along the main highway between Toronto and Montreal. In the inner geography of the soul, however, it lies about equidistant between despair and tragedy.

The people of Baytown are Bankier's true recurring characters. People who drift in and out of the ongoing series, changing, aging, gaining a promotion or losing their hair, giving the series a ring of truth beyond the emotional, forming a consistent backdrop for the action, occasionally stepping to centre stage. Radio station personality Clement Foy. Sammy Luftspring, the bellboy at the Coronet Hotel. Police chief Don Cleary. Coronet owner Jack Danforth.

In the Baytown stories, Bankier explores all his recurring themes. And the presence of Baytown colours most of his other fiction as well. A story may take place in Montreal or London or Los Angeles, but chances are at least one of the characters will be from Baytown. Creating unhappiness seems to be the towns' largest industry; killers its biggest export.

Many of those characters, whether at home or abroad in the Baytown diaspora, are performers and the action is centered around the arenas in which they perform. Invariably, the arenas are ones in which Bankier himself has held a long and active interest. Amateur theatrics, in which he has been a keen participant, are the basis for this collection's *The Last Act Was Deadly* but also show up in other tales such as *Rock's Last Role* and *Is There A Killer in the House?*

Bankier is an avid sports fan. "A sports watcher," he says, "not much of a doer." His particular passion is for baseball, a common theme most notably in the loosely connected Jonathan "Johnny Fist" Fitzwilliam stories. Other sports that come up include boxing in *The Dreams of Hopeless White* where a security guard's vision of a career in the ring ends in tragedy. Bankier's Canadian roots show in his use of hockey in *The Missing Missile*, in which the star player of the Montreal Canadiens is kidnapped, which would be sort of like snatching the Pope out of Vatican City.

Television and ad writers abound. Radio station DJ's show up frequently. The hero of *Funny Man* yearns to be a stand-up comic. Professor Harry Lawson is a retired stage magician. And then, of course, there are the musicians.

Ellery Queen once wrote, "No one in the genre writes about music better than William Bankier." Several stories in this collection bear eloquent testimony to that. Bankier's life-long love affair with music is reflected in some of his finest work, including his 1980 Edgar Award nominated masterpiece *The Choirboy*. In occasional pieces such as *Murder at the O'Shea Chorale*, the tone is comedic. Most often, however, music forms the soundtrack of a tragedy. Each musical story becoming a song in the key of death.

The types of music involved, each described with passionate understanding and palpable affection, range from jazz to pop, classical to chorale. "Music has always been important to me... I sang in church choirs for many years...I love jazz and taught myself to play the clarinet and tenor saxophone, but I let them slip. Today, I play recorder by ear. My big number is *I Can't Get Started.*"

The diversity of Bankier's stories is as impressive as the output. Humour and suspense, whodunits and character studies, historical recreations and contemporary shock endings. The real mystery is why, with almost 200 stories to his credit, this is the first collection of Bankier's stories to be published. Welcome then, to the world of William Bankier. A world where nightmare comes silently, in the dead of night. Where the last act is often deadly. Where fear is a killer. Now turn the page and enter a bar where the patrons demonstrate Bankier's finely tuned ear for the lyrical, almost musical way people speak. Listen and find out what happens in Act One...

Toronto, Ontario, Canada
March, 1995

Ellery Queen Mystery Magazine, July, 1962

WHAT HAPPENED
IN ACT ONE

Come in and take a chair and watch it all happen, the way I did. Sit right up there at the bar, beside the head of creamy cheddar cheese and the bowl of fist-filling pretzels. Eat as much as you want and have several cold seidels of lowenbrau, the best Munich can brew.

Oh, refreshment, oh, satisfaction, oh, exhilaration! This is New York in the summertime -- and anything can happen.

Keep your eye on the door; somebody is about to come in. Not now, but very soon. This is a playback. I am going to rerun it for you the way I saw it happen the first time.

Why are you here? Please share my excuse. You have been sent to New York by the Head Office to study the organizational setup of the main Accounting Department. When you have it all filed and tabulated in your mind, you will go back to the mid-West and install an identical system in the regional office. Time allotted for this project: one month. Actual time required: one week. Expense account: generous in the extreme.

And so, as I did, you have spent several evenings visiting the various tourist attractions -- enjoying, for example, the Metropole bar, chuckling at the droll monologue of the guide on the Day Line Cruise around the island, knuckling the glass to arouse the pigmy marmoset in his modest enclosure at the Bronx Zoo. All this done, you have now settled down to some serious drinking.

It is an intoxicating bar. The warm brown wood and red-leather interior, the dim glow of sepia light always in the semidistance, the slow and hypnotic sweep of the second hand on the illuminated clock -- all these are quite enough to make a man forget home and wife and job and other responsibilities...

Okay, then: join the rest of the lotus eaters and wait for the arrival of Agnew Plover. By now you are studying the faded photograph hanging over the bar, sipping your beer, and wondering idly who that young man is in the boxing trunks, standing with his arm raised in victory, the blood from his nose and the ugly cut over his eye unable to mask the glow of sheer triumph shining on his face. Could this be the man who now tends bar? Terry O'Biggo, the lard-cheeked, dull-eyed gentleman who smiles with china teeth and corduroy skin as he mops bottle rings from the mahogany?

No matter, for old Terry and the boy boxer have nothing to do with our story beyond the fact that they were there when it happened.

But hush -- I can hear a gay step on the walk outside and a creak from the ebony door. This is how it began -- the first entrance of Agnew Plover. Bartender, would you please reduce the volume on the Muzak system? I love the way Charlie Parker plays *Everything Happens To Me*, but we must concentrate on the center ring.

Correction. I said a moment ago that this would be the first entrance of Agnew Plover. To be more accurate, I would say that this was his first arrival in my presence, but I was a newcomer and Agnew Plover had been in this bar several times before.

It is a large bar; they call it Act One. The bar itself seems miles long, covering the total length of the west wall except for three feet of doorway leading into the Men's Room.

The rest of the room is occupied by small round tables, none larger than a barrel head. The decor in Act One is limited mainly to bottles--bottles that make people drink. What subtly seductive shapes the glass blowers have contrived, and how suggestively the labels wink and leer, some garish, some sophisticated, some bizarrely European, others as American as Kentucky corn. Whatever your personality, at Act One a bottle beckons.

Wait now. Spring doors flutter, conversation falters. All eyes focus on the door.

Agnew Plover is here.

Disappointed? Well, there he is. Some might call him effeminate, that being invariably the first impression: green corduroy trousers, yellow shirt with tails knotted about the waist, large head capped with yellow hair close-cropped and carelessly combed, ringing his skull like the curls of a childish Nero. And the face of Agnew Plover: eyes, two brown caramels, mouth protruding in a perpetual pout, chin thrust forward inquisitively.

Queer? I can still see the rowdy who took out his handkerchief and whipped it across Plover's path as he made his grand entrance. With a lightning gesture, Agnew seized the fluttering linen in both hands, reversed their position, and drew the cloth around the hoodlum's throat. Then, with no perceptible effort, he raised the lout off the floor and bore him, legs dragging, to the front entrance where he flung him through the doors and into the street. The thug tried to return and Agnew hit him -- not *in* the face, but (and this is the only time I have ever seen it) Agnew Plover hit his man *through* the face and put him flat on the pavement.

No, Agnew Plover is a man -- make no mistake about that.

On the first night I saw him, he walked in off 48th Street, waved to several of the Act One habitués with a modest smile, and nodded his head at Terry O'Biggo behind the bar. Terry poured four ounces of straight gin into a glass, dropped a wedge of lemon into it, and carried the glass across the room to Plover's table. Plover drained the glass, then popped the wedge of lemon into his mouth, chewed it and swallowed it, skin and all. Throughout this procedure there was almost complete silence in the place except for the hum of an exhaust fan near the door.

His drink finished, Agnew Plover smiled again, drew a book from his pocket, and calmly began to read. O'Biggo went behind the bar and a dozen conversations chattered back to life. I was soon to learn the reason why this little community took time out whenever they were joined by this curious fellow.

Perhaps half an hour passed. I had three beers and went back to the Men's Room. On my return, I saw Agnew Plover leaning back in his chair, his head slumped forward on his chest, his body swaying back and forth in rhythm with a low crooning.

"The drink seems to have disagreed with our friend," I began.

"Shush," Terry O'Biggo said. "It's the possession. It comes over him every now and then."

"The possession?"

"That's right. The spirit of a dead person enters his body and takes over. It only lasts a short while. We've seen it before."

"I've never seen anything like..."

"Well, you're seeing it now. Just hush up and don't disturb him. It could kill him if he's disturbed while he's under the possession. Watch now."

I watched. After a few minutes the convulsive movements stopped and Plover sat up. He seemed to be himself now and yet there was something different about his face -- a commanding, imperious expression.

Then he spoke, but not in any language that I had ever heard before.

"What's he saying?"

A man at the end of the bar said, "It sounds like Polish to me. He asked where the piano is."

For the first time I noticed an upright piano at the far end of the room. The keyboard was covered and it had an air of disuse about it. At the same moment Plover -- or whoever now inhabited Plover's body -- saw the piano and walked over to it.

Silence came over the bar as he sat down, stared at the instrument for a moment, then began to play. If I live on into the two thousands, I never expect to hear anything like that again. The flow of music from that piano was like the spray off Niagara Falls. It hit us in a million cool drops, but there was muted thunder in its sheer power. I tried to place the composer; it sounded like Chopin though I could not be sure.

It was not a long performance -- perhaps five minutes. As the last brilliant chord echoed through the room, Plover lowered his forehead to the backs of his hands. Then he shivered, raised his eyes, turned, and looked at us.

"Did I just play?" he asked.

A chorus of delighted affirmation flowed about him.

"I've never played a note," he said. "I wonder who it was this time?"

"You spoke Polish. You asked for a piano in Polish," said the man at the end of the bar.

I volunteered, "I'm not sure, but the music sounded like Chopin to me. Chopin was Polish."

A murmur of excitement passed through the crowd. Plover stood up yawned, and stretched his arms.

"It always takes a lot out of him," the bartender whispered to me.

Plover joined us, dropping a bill on the bar. "My tab, please Terrence," he said. O'Biggo tried to push the money back to him. "Please Terry," Agnew said, "I'm not an itinerant minstrel. I pay for my drinks."

The bartender made change and Plover went away into the night, leaving a generous tip on the bar. When he had gone, conversation rose in a flurry to a peak of excitement.

"You've seen all this many times?" I asked.

"A few times," Terry corrected me. "See that painting over the bar?"

I glanced up and saw a brilliant orange-and-black poster done roughly in oils. There was no mistaking the posturing figure in the foreground, the rakish top hat, the elongated jaw in profile.

"He began to speak French one night. Lucky we had somebody here could make it out. He asked for paints, so a lady who lives next door ran upstairs and got her oils. He dashed that off in ten minutes."

So "Toulouse-Lautrec" had been here on 48th Street in the body of this unbelievable man. And unbelievable is the word. I could see his painting, I had heard him play.

"You must consider yourselves lucky," I said, "falling heir to all this free entertainment."

Oh, it isn't always so pleasant. One night he came up Hitler." I almost choked on my drink.

"He stood up here by the bar and he almost looked like him. And when he spoke, there was no doubt. He gave us a real harangue, just like in the old newsreels."

"That must have been a treat."

"Like I said. There was this guy in here that night, Sol Bloom. Drives a cab and comes in here on his free nights. He took offense and threw a punch. It was a glancing blow but Agnew kind of stiffened and his eyes almost came out of his head and he threw up right here on the floor. It was messy for a few minutes."

I shook my head in sympathy and understanding.

"It was after that Agnew told us how dangerous it was for him to be brought out of it sudden-like. He has to be left alone. Like sleepwalking."

My own sleep that night was broken, not by an ambulatory excursion but by visions of a man whose body seemed to act as a living receiver, picking up transmissions from some celestial tower where the spirits of good and evil dwelt -- the famous and infamous.

I was unable to visit Act One on the following night owing to an unexpected dinner invitation from the personnel chief of the Head Office. But the next night found me at my accustomed spot at the head of the bar. I was half full of ale and overflowing with anticipation when Agnew Plover finally arrived about 11:30.

We were all to be disappointed. Nothing happened that night. Plover merely had two of his gin and lemon specials just like any other barfly. And so, home to bed.

But the following evening was something else again. The procedure was the same: a drink, a short period of reading, then head on chest, then moaning and swaying. When he sat up and faced the expectant room, a frightening change had overtaken his features. His face was pale, his cheeks seemed hollow, and his eyes burned with a feverish fire. Then he spoke. "What place is this?"

A sigh crossed the room. "Ah, you're English-speaking, sir," Terry O'Biggo said somewhat unnecessarily. "My name is Terence O'Biggo. Delighted to welcome you to the Act One bar."

"Poe is my name," Plover said. "Edgar A. Poe." He coughed into his handkerchief. "Have you anything for a man to drink? A brandy? God, I don't feel well."

Made brave by beer, I ventured, "Would you be Edgar Allan Poe, the writer?"

He glanced at me and then away. "I write some, but I did not realize my fame was widely spread."

The bartender brought a generous glass of brandy to Plover-Poe's table. The man drank it and Terry refilled it from the bottle he had carried with him. The liquor seemed to revive the fellow's spirit for he took his glass to the bar where he sat down beside me.

"So you're familiar with my work. I'm flattered, sir." He smiled at me and raised his glass.

"I've read *The Fall of the House of Usher,*" I said, "and *The Pit and the Pendulum*. And of course, *The Raven*."

He nodded at each of the titles, sipping his brandy. Then he said, not so much to me as to the room, "I've just finished a story. Perhaps you'd like to hear some of it and I can profit from your reaction."

We chorused our approval.

"Very well," he said. "This story is called *The Murder in the Rue Morgue*."

I don't know if you have ever read that great classic, but it is a story that lifts the reader to a pinnacle of horror and fascination. Plover now began to deliver a portion of it in a moody recitation so grandly in character with the subject matter of the tale that an audible sigh hissed from the rapt gathering. At the conclusion there was the beginning of applause but Terry raised his hand and said, "Hush...don't disturb him."

This time Plover did not resume his own personality in our presence. Instead, he downed his drink, nodded casually to me and O'Biggo, then strolled, as Edgar Allan Poe might have done, out of the bar and into the hustle of 48th Street.

"He left like that," the bartender said, "when he was John Barrymore. That kind seems to favor the dramatic exit."

Three days went by before we saw Plover again. It was Saturday night and the Act One was crowded with the old clientele, all getting a good start on the week-end.

Perhaps only now, in retrospect, does Saturday evening seem to have had an air of finality about it. Indeed, I was finished with my research at the Head Office, and the end of next week would surely see me back home in the middle West. But this feeling of termination went beyond the boundaries of my own mood -- it permeated the whole bar.

Agnew Plover arrived about ten o'clock, and half an hour went by before the possession overtook him. I didn't see it happen. One moment he was glancing around and munching his lemon section; the next time I looked, his head was slumped forward on the bar, and as slow tremors shook his body, a high keening moan arose from the mound of white shirt and yellow hair.

Silence eddied out quickly as everyone in the room concentrated on Plover. They had not long to wait. Suddenly he sat up, turned his head, and looked slowly around the room. There was something menacing about the strangely altered features and a steely glint of malevolent purpose in his eyes that killed, almost as soon as it was born, the speculative murmur that usually accompanied one of Agnew's periods of possession.

One circuit of the room by his frozen eyes was enough. Plover licked his lips which seemed now thinner and paler than before. With a graceful movement he slipped from the stool and swaggered to the middle of the bar. As he walked, he held his arms stiffly out and a little back from his body, fingers spread wide a few inches from his thighs. His heels clumped a hollow march on the wooden floor.

When he reached the place along the bar where Terry O'Biggo was standing, he stopped and said, "Now, they ain't *nobody* goin' to move a muscle."

A gentleman at the far corner of the room began to snicker and choked it off in mid-breath. Like a jungle cat, Plover spun toward the sound, crouching, knees bent. At the same time he brought his right hand along his trouser leg in a whipping motion and then held the hand extended, the index finger pointing menacingly at the man who had dared to laugh.

"What's so funny, mister?" he said, his voice touched with a slight drawl. "You see anything here to laugh at? 'Cause if you do, I wanna tell you, mister, 'tween these two guns I got seventeen notches. And they is room for plenty more."

Sitting near O'Biggo, I turned my head to the bartender and raised my eyebrows. Terry's face was pale but he frowned and shook his head in warning: Leave him alone.

Now Plover -- although this rigid animal was surely not he -- turned to O'Biggo and said, "And now you, friend, take off that apron and spread it on the bar."

"Anything you say, mister," Terry replied, slipping out of the white linen and clearing away glasses to make room. "By the way," he added, "who might I have the pleasure of serving?"

A faint smile twisted one corner of Plover's pale mouth. "The name is Bonney," he said. "Most folks know me as Billy the Kid."

"All right," he said when the apron was spread, "you'll oblige me, bartender, by puttin' the night's takings in that apron."

Another gasp arose from the room and this time O'Biggo cut it short. "Quiet," he shouted. "I want you all to do exactly as Mr. Bonney here says. Don't nobody try to lay a hand on him or interfere in any way. If anyone needs an explanation, he'll get it later." And with that he opened the cash register, scooped out its contents, and dumped the money into the apron.

"Bartender, you got sense," Bonney-Plover said. Now he turned and swept the pointing finger in a slow trajectory around the room. "One at a time now," he said, "come on up here and leave your wallets on the pile."

The outcry this time was immediate and prolonged, and spiced with such phrases as, "A joke is a joke," and "Going too far."

Again O'Biggo shut off the uproar. "I told you people to cooperate. I won't have this man disturbed. Just do as he says and nobody will lose a thing."

Well, the unburdening lasted about five minutes. When my neighbor at the bar came back from leaving his wallet he muttered, "I'm just glad that finger isn't loaded."

It was a stimulating little scene and it ended with Billy the Kid gathering up the ends of the apron and leaving the bar slowly, walking backward, his cocked finger aimed here and there, and carrying our wealth with him like a sack of laundry.

After the doors banged shut behind him, there was silence for a full half a minute, broken finally by the voice of Terence O'Biggo who said, "He'll be back soon."

So we waited. And we talked.

Midnight came and went, and conversation rose and fell away. Terry refused to call the police. "I'll not cause trouble for my good friend Agnew," he said.

We were all back in the Act One by opening time Sunday afternoon. When he had come to open up, Terry had found a well wrapped parcel jammed in front of the doors. Inside were all our wallets, our papers, our snapshots, our drivers' licenses.

But our money? Not a nickel of it.

We compared notes, padding a little for the sake of pride. It looked as if Agnew Plover had got away with about $3500 in cash.

In a sense, none of us felt too bad. After all, it was a unique experience, one to talk about all our lives. And we *had* been treated to some rare entertainment.

As for me, I finally understood the true meaning of "possession." It was not so much the entering and inhabiting of a living body by spirits from the past. No, indeed. In this case it was the expert, professional way in which Agnew Plover, conman par excellence, had "had" the whole crowd of us, had us and owned us for almost a month back in that hot New York August a couple of years ago.

Ellery Queen Mystery Magazine, September, 1967

TRAFFIC VIOLATION

Through the open Police Station doorway Don Cleary saw Billy Kemp leading the prisoner across the deserted market square. The man had white hair and was well dressed in a black suit that glistened in the light of the late August afternoon.

Cleary said into the phone, "Billy Kemp is bringing somebody in."

"Do you want to call me back?" Marney said. Her voice had the flat, tense quality that raised pointless anger in Cleary whenever he heard it. Maybe it was just the way he handled his own fear.

"No, I can talk for a minute. What's Pete's temperature...a hundred and what?"

"Almost a hundred and three." Cleary could see her pale face, her dark eyes frowning at the threatening silver thread. "The doctor is coming over."

He waited, watching Kemp and the stranger approaching across the square, listening to his wife's prolonged silence. Then --" Are you thinking what I'm thinking?"

"Polio?" she whispered.

"We should have taken him for those shots. All the other kids were getting them."

"I was going to. Don't put that on me, Don."

"Nobody's putting anything on you." He added, "It probably isn't that anyway" -- but something told him it very well could be.

The man came in arguing and Cleary disliked him instantly. "I'll have to hang up now," he said. "When the doctor has a look at him, call me right away."

Her goodbye was cold and Cleary wondered how much of it came from her anxiety and how much from his abrupt dismissal of her. He supposed he should have said he'd get

Kemp to take over for him so that he could come home. But what good could he do there? The doctor was on the way.

"Okay, you've delayed me, you've put me behind schedule. Let me guess what happens next." The prisoner spread his hands. "There's no judge available till tomorrow, so either I pay my fine now or I spend the night in jail."

"You may spend the rest of your life in jail, depending on what you did," Cleary said harshly. "Sit down. What's the charge, Billy?"

"He made an illegal left turn at the four corners. When I made him pull over he chewed me out. Must have been ten people listening."

"Why did you have to give the constable a hard time when he was only doing his job?"

"I'm in too big a hurry to waste my time listening to some hick cop lecture me to impress his friends. Now how do I get out of here? I plead guilty to an illegal left turn, okay. Now how do I get out of here?"

The last thing Don Cleary needed on a Sunday afternoon -- on this Sunday afternoon in particular -- was an out-of-town detention. When Marney called back he would want the place empty and his mind clear. If this bird had only kept his mouth shut he would have been able to send him away with a reprimand.

Cleary thought he would do that anyway, but he heard himself saying, "Now just a minute here, let's not be in too big a hurry. You just have a chair and we'll look into this. What's your name?"

"My name is Sieberling and you're going to be very sorry you ever heard of me."

"Mr. Sieberling, let me see your identification."

The man took out a wallet and began to extract his driver's license from a plastic envelope.

"The whole thing, please."

Sieberling paused, then tossed the wallet across the desk. Cleary could not help noticing the sheaf of paper money in the bill compartment nor could he stop himself from glancing up into the arrogant eyes watching him, registering his discomfiture.

"Don, there's nobody up at the intersection. Maybe I should get back up there."

"Anything else you should tell me about what happened?"

"No. Will you be okay?"

"I don't think Mr. Sieberling wants to get into any more trouble. You go on back."

Constable Kemp walked out of the station and headed back across the empty square. Cleary checked the license: it identified Alvin R. Sieberling, 19 Sun Crescent, Montreal, Canada. The plastic sleeve was one of a dozen joined end to end in an accordion fold. The other sleeves were filled with assorted cards.

"Look, there's just the two of us here and I'm really anxious to get going." The man's sarcastic whine was gone and now his voice vibrated with common sense. "And I'll admit I've put you boys to some trouble. That's my nature, I can be a damn fool but it doesn't mean anything. Now why don't you just take out one of those twenties and give the wallet back to me. Then I'll go on my way and we'll both be better off than we are now."

Cleary felt the blood infuse his cheeks and the moisture rim his eyes. He tried to keep his voice steady. "Mr. Sieberling, just you pretend you never said that and I'll try to forget I heard it."

"Well!" The little laugh put Cleary in a category by himself in Sieberling's experience.

Unable to look up until his composure had returned, Cleary riffled through the chain of cards listing credit facilities, airlines, club memberships, and insurance plans.

"Those are credit cards, son. They'll get me just about anything I want, anywhere on this continent, and no questions asked."

"They don't get you the right to drive dangerously in Baytown."

"Dangerously? Come on , you heard what the man said. All I did was make a left turn."

Cleary was fingering the cards. One of the sleeves felt fatter than the others. He pinched it open and found two cards back to back, and between them a folded slip of paper. This proved to be a driver's license in the name of Emery Disco.

"Two drivers' licenses, Mr. Sieberling?" Cleary could hear in the silence the other man's apprehension. He looked up now into the gray eyes and saw no more arrogance there. "That's a bit unusual, isn't it?"

Sieberling's smile returned. "The other one belongs to my partner. Em flew out to his island last week and he forgot some things. Asked me to bring along his license, figures he might rent a car."

"You had it packed away very carefully."

"Well, where else could I put it and not lose it?"

A Colonial bus from Toronto pulled up in front of the Coronet Hotel and a couple of passengers got out. Cleary watched them perform the slow confused movements of travellers unaccustomed to dealing with luggage and bellboys and strange, heavy doors. The bus hissed and rolled away.

"Disco. Emery Disco." Cleary fingered the license. "That name is sort of familiar. Disco..."

The man said nothing.

"I've seen that name in print somewhere not long ago." Cleary turned to a stack of newspapers on the side table and shuffled through them. Then he stopped. "That was it, sure. The promoter who disappeared last week in Toronto. Started a pig farm and lined up investors for a year and then vanished. A quarter of a million bucks invested and not a sty to show for it."

"You didn't read far enough. There was no evidence against Disco at all."

Cleary got up and went to the doorway. He closed the door. Then he crossed the room and opened the barred enclosure that occupied a corner of the small room. "I'm going to have to detain you. Would you go in here, please?" It was Cleary's first arrest apart from an occasional drunk-and-disorderly and one shoplifter. He found himself sounding excessively polite.

The man got up. "My name is Sieberling, son, I can swear to that. And you are making a big mistake."

"I can always apologize."

With the barred door locked, Cleary went back to his desk, picked up the phone, and dialed. "Is the Chief there, Mrs. Kalb? I see. Well, when did he say...? I see. Okay, I'll be here till midnight when Ed comes on, so if he comes in have him call, please. Have him call even after then because I'll brief Ed. Thank you." He hung up the phone and sat down in the swivel chair.

The prisoner took off his jacket and folded it neatly on the end of the cell cot. He came to the barred door in his brilliant white shirt. "Okay," he said, "let's get down to business. Let's straighten this thing out while there's still just the two of us in it. You got insulted when I offered you twenty dollars. Now I'm offering you twenty thousand. Cash."

It was hot in the station with the door closed, but suddenly Don Cleary's damp shirt felt cold against his back.

"Don't say anything," the man went on, "just think about it for a minute. You didn't look closely at the money in my wallet. If you do, you'll see that a lot of those bills are thousands. And I have more in my pocket and in my belt. My friend, I have a hundred and twenty-five thousand dollars on me and as much put away where I can reach it. Twenty grand is yours, right now, if you just open this door. That's all you do. Take twenty thousand out of the wallet, then open the cell and turn your back. Your buddy brought me in for a wrong left turn. He doesn't expect to see me again."

There was a fly in the room. It was restless; *zzzzzz*, silence, *zzzzzzzz*, silence.

"What do you say?"

Cleary picked up the phone. He dialed. "Operator, I want Toronto, Provincial Police headquarters." He gave a number. He waited.

"You're crazy! Throwing away twenty thousand bucks."

"This is Sergeant Cleary, Baytown Police. I've just apprehended a man who may be Emery Disco. He has a driver's license in that name and another with the name of Sieberling. About forty-five, I'd say, chunky, white hair, well dressed. Yes, he's in the cell now. No, I don't think there's any doubt. Okay, I'll hold him. Right, I'll expect you around nine -- three hours from now. Not at all. Thanks." He hung up.

The prisoner said, "The funny thing is , you're doing this for nothing. I'll offer those guys the same twenty thousand on the way back to Toronto and they'll let me disappear when we stop for gas. Or if they're crazy like you, I'll pay a guard up there. Or if I come to trial, I'll buy the judge. A man with a quarter of a million dollars in cash doesn't go to jail."

In the next hour Cleary ignored the prisoner who stood behind the door or sat on the cot. After further attempts at conversation had failed, Disco became silent. Cleary put his hand on the phone a couple of times, but took it off again. He wanted to call Marney and ask about Pete, but he felt uncomfortable with the other man breathing behind him. The doctor should have been there by now; of course, doctors were hard to pin down on Sunday.

At seven o'clock Cleary telephoned for sandwiches and coffee. When the boy from the Paragon Restaurant delivered the food, Sieberling wanted to pay.

"Keep your money," Don said. "You're a guest of the city of Baytown."

Sieberling insisted on tipping the boy anyway. Then he ate standing at the cell door. "When those cops from Toronto come and take me out of here at nine o'clock, I guess you'll feel pretty good, won't you?'

"I want you gone, sure."

"You're the only man I know who doesn't need money."

"I need money as much as the next man."

"But you don't want my money."

"I want it."

"Then why don't you take it?"

"Because I can't!"

The prisoner heard the high ring of impatience in Cleary's voice. He took his coffee and moved to the back of the cell.

The Paragon always made Cleary a good sandwich and this was one of their best. But it tasted flat in his mouth and he had trouble swallowing. There was nothing wrong with the prisoner's appetite; the wet sounds in the cell were like animal noises from a cave. Cleary put the sandwich aside and drank black coffee.

Marney telephoned at a quarter to eight. "The doctor just left. He says Pete has to go to the hospital. They'll do tests tomorrow and see what it is."

"It's the best thing, honey. They'll take care of him there. How are you getting him to the hospital?"

"He called the ambulance from here. They have to be paid right away don't they?"

"I think so. There's two ten-dollar bills in the cuff-link box on my bureau. It shouldn't be more than that."

"All right. Don, he's asking for you. When can you get over and see him?"

"I'm not through here till twelve. You know that."

"But Billy Kemp comes in to check out at eight, doesn't he? You could ask him to sit in for you."

"I can't tonight. There's something I have to attend to."

"Can't Billy do it?"

"No. Tell Pete I'll see him tomorrow." Marney didn't understand and he couldn't explain with Sieberling listening. The conversation ended on a hostile note.

Ten minutes later Billy Kemp came in to end his shift. He was delighted when he learned he had apprehended a wanted man. He stood for some minutes at the door of the cell looking in. The prisoner ignored him and after a while Billy turned in his gear and went home.

With him went Cleary's last chance to bring in a substitute and get over to the hospital. He should have asked Kemp to stay. Marney would be alone now. Once he could explain, she'd probably understand and forgive him. Or would she? He was assuming that Billy Kemp would be a sucker for Sieberling's offer--$20,000!--accepting the money and putting it away somewhere, and then taking his chances with the authorities later. Could he think that little of his friend's moral fiber? Apparently he could. But meanwhile, Marney was sweating it out by herself.

"Sickness in the family, son?"

"It's under control."

"I know what it's like. I'm a lot older than you are. Thirty-five years ago we didn't have the medical facilities you have now, and I couldn't afford what there was. Daughter of mine got sick and I didn't even have taxi fare to get her to the hospital. I carried her in my arms and she was dead when I got there."

Was it phony or straight goods? Cleary looked at the broad ruddy face beneath the even white hairline. The gray eyes were level with no sign of sentiment. "I'm sorry to hear that."

"Well, it was a long time ago. I made up my mind then that no child of mine would ever lack for money again. I started getting my hands on money and I haven't stopped since. Only thing is, I never had another child. I guess there's a moral in there somewhere."

Cleary checked his watch. In less than an hour the Toronto police would arrive and he'd be off the hook. His thoughts went back to Pete. Maybe he should phone the hospital, but he didn't like to do that either with Sieberling listening. It could wait forty-five minutes.

"Why do you want me in jail so badly, son?"

"The law wants you, and I work for the law."

"But let's drop the textbook interpretations and be human beings. What did I do that was so bad? Did I kill somebody? Did I take bread out of a hungry child's mouth?"

"It's possible. You stole a lot of money."

"Let me tell you something. The people who put in that money were looking to be taken. They listened to me spin them a fairy tale about profits a hundredfold. It was nonsense and they believed me. Instead of putting their money in sensible investments where it would do the economy some good, they were greedy. It's the old story -- they wanted something for nothing, something they hadn't earned."

"I suppose you earned it?"

" Matter of fact, yes, I did. I worked damned hard for a year promoting this thing. But the point is, the money I got was lying around in socks and mattresses, hoarded by a lot of mean little people who didn't need it and weren't using it. Now does that make me such an evil man?"

The telephone rang and Cleary picked up the receiver. It was one of the Toronto detectives. They were in a garage in Cobourg having some motor trouble attended to. Would he be okay for another hour?

It seemed like a long time and Cleary said so. No, he wasn't having any difficulties but he wanted this man off his hands. And he didn't say so, but he wanted to be alone to call the hospital and have a doctor tell him first-hand that the early fear was wrong, that Pete just had the flu, and he wanted to call Marney and tell her why he wasn't up there with her. Most of all, he wanted to hear her tell him he had done the right thing.

The phone call ended with the Toronto detective saying he would do everything he could to get there sooner.

Cleary put down the phone and listened to ten minutes tick by on his wrist watch. He got up and opened the station door. It was almost dark in the market square. The orange light from the Coronet Hotel lobby spilled through the front window onto the street. He could see the bellboy leaning on the glass counter talking to the desk clerk. A lone car cruised down Front Street toward the Bay. Cleary turned back to his desk.

"I guess you'll have a lot of doctor bills to pay next month."

"Will you shut up about that?"

"No, son, I won't. I'm trying to get myself out of a jam and the only way I can see is to talk some sense into you."

Cleary opened his desk drawer, looked at the forms and paper clips and a broken stapler. He slammed it shut again.

"Now it's true we're not alone in this any more. Those boys from the city will be coming here looking for me, but we could handle that. I'm a pretty husky guy. Suppose I wanted to go to the john and when you let me out of there, I jumped you and clobbered you. We could make it real, I'll give you a good one you won't be ashamed of. When you come to, I'll be long gone. First, of course, you'll have to take the trouble of hiding the twenty thousand."

"Save your breath, Sieberling."

The prisoner laughed again, the short rising laugh of disbelief. "You just don't make any sense! Somewhere, somebody is going to take the payoff and let me go. And he won't be half the man you are. Believe me, as long as I have to spend the money, I'd rather see you get it. You need it."

Cleary got up and went to the cell door. He stood looking into Sieberling's eyes. He was having trouble breathing steadily. "Maybe you'd like to go to the john," he said. "You're welcome to take that shot at me on the way."

The prisoner laughed. "Without the fix being in? No, thanks, you look too serious."

The detectives arrived half an hour later, two of them. One of them went directly to the cell and looked in. "This is him all right. Nice going."

The other detective said, "Can I use the phone?"

"Go ahead."

He began dialing the Toronto area code. "Hello? This is Donovan. We're here and we're picking up Disco right now. We'll drive straight back without stops and we should be there before midnight. Okay, Inspector. Right."

The first detective had his handcuffs out. When Cleary opened the cell door, the detective stepped in and snapped one band around the prisoner's wrist, the other around his own. Then he walked him to the door.

"We're not stopping on the way back because we don't want to take any chances with this one."

Cleary knew what he had to say, but it wasn't easy. He stood in the front doorway, blocking the exit. He took a deep breath and ran his tongue across his teeth.

"I'm going to say something. I hope you won't take it wrong."

"Go ahead."

"Well, this man has been offering me twenty grand all night to let him go. He said he's going to offer it to you guys on the way back. So if he escapes, you'd better have a real good story ready."

The detective handcuffed to the prisoner stared hard at Cleary, his face coloring. Then he glanced at his partner and grinned. "Well," he said, "there goes our chance to get rich."

When they were gone, Cleary telephoned the hospital. Pete was resting and they could say nothing more until after the tests tomorrow.

Next, he called Marney. She sounded cold. "I went in the ambulance with him and hung around the hospital for a while. Another doctor spent some time with him and he said he doesn't think it's what we're worried about."

"God, I'm glad to hear that. What do they think it is?"

"Maybe some virus or other. He may even be home tomorrow." She paused. "So you don't have to go to the hospital if you don't want to."

Cleary spent the next few minutes explaining about the prisoner. When he was finished, she said softly and with a trace of her old warmth, "So we could have had $20,000? Honey, rich you'll never be."

"Did I do the right thing?

"You did the only thing. How could we ever spend that kind of money?"

It was ten minutes later when Nick Pappas from the Paragon Restaurant came in with the delivery boy in front of him, stumbling before Nick's outstretched arm.

"Don, I think this dumb kid I hired has done a bad thing. I found him counting money, twenty bucks. I thought he stole it from the cash register but there was none missing. So I twisted his arm a little and he gave me this note. Says a man in the cell gave it to him with a ten dollar tip."

Cleary took the note. It was written in ballpoint pen on a page torn from a pocket notebook. "This $10 is yours. Phone 639-8001 in Kingston, ask for Donovan and say Disco is in Baytown jail. If you do this fast, he will come and give you another $10."

Cleary read the note again. Then he said, "I'll have to keep this as evidence. I won't lock the kid up if you'll promise to keep an eye on him. He'll have to face charges."

"Okay, Don. I'm sorry about this."

"Not your fault, Nick. Thanks for coming in."

As they were leaving, Cleary said, "Why did you do it, son? You knew he was a criminal."

The boy looked him right in the eye. "Twenty bucks is a lot of money," he said.

They went away and Don Cleary sat down alone to wait for the Toronto detectives to arrive.

Ellery Queen Mystery Magazine, July, 1976

WHAT REALLY HAPPENED?

Margaret came into my study talking. I had heard her grumbling approach up the back stairs from the kitchen, the signal that my eleven o'clock mug of tea was on the way. The price I would have to pay was a certain amount of inattentive listening, a smile or two, and a couple of noncommittal ahums.

She bodied open the door and there was the radiant little girl's smile in the 60-year-old face. "I thought you'd like a cup of tea" -- as if the idea was new that morning instead of a time honoured tradition.

"Thank you, Margaret." It was one of my standard lines; most of the improvised script would be hers.

"I'll dust in here when you're out for lunch. The vacuum cleaner needs bags but I can get those when I go downstreet tomorrow." Downstreet. After half a lifetime in the city Margaret retained many of the small-town locutions she had learned as a child.

"They have the oil tank leaking across the road. It's gone and drained itself during the night and now they've got no heat and no hot water till somebody comes and fixes it. Have you noticed how the blossoms are out so early on the chestnut tree, they'll all be nipped off if we get a late frost, and then..."

Old Margaret regularly began talking the minute she entered the house at 8:30 in the morning and her monologue continued uninterrupted throughout the day. You might call it an unacceptable distraction for a writer, but she has been with me for 15 years as a housekeeper, and her nattering drone is as much a part of the pulse of my existence as the hum of the central heating. Besides, she is as solid as an NFL linebacker and has a mad focus to her eyes -- not the sort of person to be dismissed lightly. What's more, she knew my father and always speaks well of him.

"I'll take it here, Margaret," I said from my armchair, and she turned from the desk and brought me the steaming mug. "I'm reading this morning, not writing."

She glanced at the cover of the book spread open on my lap and I suppose the name Lizzie Borden in the book's title caught her eye. Her lips formed the name silently, then she said aloud, "Not much of what they say about that poor woman is true. It was a blessing they never convicted her, but still most people go along believing she really did kill her mother and father. Of course Lizzie wanted it that way instead of having people know what *really* happened."

I was so intrigued that I found myself encouraging a conversational exchange with Margaret. "I've never read anything to that effect," I said.

"And you wouldn't. It's never been written down. But I got it through my mother who knew the Bordens' maid, Bridget Sullivan. My family lived in Butte, Montana, where Bridget ended up. Bridget promised Lizzie she'd never tell a soul, but as she got older she felt she had to share it, and my mother was her closest friend. I was just a wee thing then, so I suppose they thought they could talk in front of me and it would all go over my head. But I've always remembered the story."

"I'm fascinated. Sit down, Margaret, and tell me what really happened between Lizzie Borden and her parents." If there was a trace of sarcasm in my tone, it either escaped her or she ignored it.

"I will, then," she said. "I'll just go and fetch my tea first." And she was gone, pounding down the back stairway, her voice fading into the distance as she trailed her cloud of words like smoke from a thundering locomotive.

I waited, reminding myself that any story that Margaret could tell would be hearsay twice removed, and after a blurring separation in time. The events that took place in the Borden home in Fall River, Massachusetts, on that oppressively hot day in 1892 had been well documented at the time and studied ever since. But the book I was reading made it clear that Lizzie had delivered conflicting testimonies at the inquest and subsequently. The author took this to meant she was guilty and trying not very skillfully to cover her tracks. Now here was Margaret suggesting that Lizzie had indeed fabricated a story to hoodwink the authorities and the public -- but for some other reason.

Margaret came back into the study with her double-size tea mug and a plate of jam turnovers, my favorites from the pastry shop on the corner. I placed a second armchair near mine and moved a small table to take the pastries and our tea. Margaret sat down, drew the skirt of her flowered smock across her knees, and picked up her tea, holding it quite elegantly as she turned her head this way and that, seeing my familiar workroom from a new angle. Watching her, I realized that the woman had not spent her whole life waxing floors and scrubbing bathtubs.

"This is very nice," she said. That was all. She sipped her tea and the room tingled with silence. I wondered if the cat had got her tongue on this one occasion when I was eager to listen to her. I decided to set the stage.

"All right now. The book I'm reading tells us that Lizzie had a motive of sorts for killing her stepmother, a woman she had never cared much for. Five years earlier, Mr. Borden, whom Lizzie loved very much, had signed over one-half of a house he owned to Mrs. Borden. Lizzie looked on this as a betrayal and ever afterwards there was hostility between her and the older woman. Adjoining doors were kept locked. Harsh words were exchanged.

"Then," I continued, "just before the murders Mr. Borden prepared to make the same mistake again. He arranged to place in his wife's name a farmhouse in Swansea, a summer residence Lizzie had loved to visit as a child. This was said to be the last straw. And on the morning that Mrs. Borden was to leave the house and go to the bank where papers would be signed, Lizzie Borden, it was alleged, took the axe and gave her mother forty whacks. In fact, it was more like eighteen. Then when her father came home to see why his wife had not shown up at the bank, Lizzie murdered him too."

Margaret was regarding me sceptically with her fine Irish face. Drops of perspiration, caused no doubt by the hot tea, beaded her broad forehead. I added, "Of course, Lizzie was subject to attacks of epilepsy during which she could have performed such an act and scarcely remembered doing it."

Margaret set down her mug. "Well, it's a great mishmash of misinformation you've gotten hold of. I don't know about the attacks, but as for the rest of it, about the only true thing you said was that Lizzie Borden loved her father. And he loved her. Did you know she gave him her school ring when she was a little girl -- girls usually give it to a boy friend -- and he wore it for eighteen years. Had it on his little finger when he died. Now there's a sad thing."

"Yes. I read that in here."

She sneered at the book. "Then it has *some* truth in it. Myself, I never read much, if at all."

"I'm ready to hear your version."

"It's not a version. It's what Bridget Sullivan herself, Lizzie Borden's maid who was the only person in the house with her that day, it's what she told my mother."

"Yes."

"You have to realize that the stepmother was a great, fat, lazy creature who scarcely went out of the house. She just sat around inside and ate herself huge. Weighed two hundred pounds or more when she died."

I nodded. "She's described in the book as a compulsive eater."

"That's a fact. It's also a fact that Lizzie didn't like her. But she never killed her. All that nonsense about houses being signed over -- well, it may be true. But Lizzie was missing nothing. There was plenty of money and she had her share. No, there was a much more obvious suspect around but everyone overlooked him."

"Uncle John?" I asked, recalling the visitor in the house, the original Mrs. Borden's brother. "John Morse had been considered a suspect by the police at first but was exonerated when his alibi checked out."

"Gracious no. Much closer to home. Who kills wives anyway? Husbands do. Mr. Borden was a fastidious man, and frugal. The sight of this great bloated creature occupying his house must have eaten away at him. Anyway, he was the one who took the axe to Mrs. Borden that morning. For no other reason than that he wanted her dead."

"And then," I said, "I suppose he struck himself with the axe several times, thereby committing suicide."

"Of course not. That's where Lizzie comes in."

"She killed her father? You said she loved him. Her ring on his finger --"

"Don't look so baffled. A writer should appreciate how people act. Picture it. Borden kills his wife in the morning. Then he goes out and visits the banks to establish *his* alibi. That was what the signing was all about -- it put him in the clear. Why would he be suspected of killing a person he was so generously giving a house to?"

"It's a theory."

"It's a fact. While he was out, Lizzie discovered the body. Bending over it, she got blood on her dress and had to change it."

"The dress she burned in the kitchen stove later."

"If she burned a dress, that was it. Then she waited for her father, knowing that he must have done it and that he could never get away with it. The police would question him, he would be arrested and tried. And even if he got off, his reputation in the community would be ruined. Lizzie had plenty of time to consider the shame the family would have to bear. And in those days, in Fall River society, this was unthinkable."

I shook my head. "So she killed her father. Even though she loved him."

"*Because* she loved him. Loved him so much she could not bear the idea of people knowing he was a murderer. *One* body meant Borden had killed his wife. *Two* bodies would allow people to believe a maniac had gotten in the house."

"So Borden killed his wife and Lizzie killed him."

"Exactly. Which I call justice." Margaret got up, loaded our empty mugs on the pastry plate, and went to my study door.

"But in seeking to avoid a scandal," I said, "a blot on the family name, she created a worse one."

"She never dreamed people would suspect *her* of doing such a terrible thing," Margaret said. "But they did, and there's the pity of it."

Alone again, I thought of this new scenario. It was entirely circumstantial, of course. But so was the original case against Lizzie. I picked up a pen and began scratching on a piece of paper.

> Andrew Borden took the axe
> And gave his woman forty whacks.
> Then loving Lizzie, like as not,
> Hacked out justice on the spot.

Later in the day I went out into the back garden and moved a deck chair into the rectangle of spring sunlight near the wood shed. As I placed myself, I heard the familiar thump and clatter which told me Margaret was splitting firewood on the other side of the shed. She came by and stood over me just before I closed my eyes.

"You aren't going to go writing down any of what I told you, are you?" she asked.

I only wanted to fall asleep in the sun. "Don't worry about it, Margaret," I said.

"But I do worry. It was a secret Bridget told us. And I am sworn to protect it on the grave of me own mother."

She said this in a heavy voice and then she walked away with a pile of kindling clutched in one massive arm and the hatchet hanging from her other hand.

Be damned, I'll write the story anyway. I won't be subtly threatened by my own housekeeper. Besides, I have it on Margaret's own word: she never reads much, if at all.

Alfred Hitchcock Mystery Magazine, August, 1977

WEDNESDAY NIGHT
AT THE FORUM

The Quebec referendum was only two weeks away and you could feel the tension in the Montreal population, even in a neighborhood so dedicated to drinking and relaxation as Crescent Street. Argentina Carr sat in splendid isolation at a small round table snug against the brick outer wall of El Diablo, well in the canopy's shade and as far as possible from the pedestrian flow, drinking Irish coffee and waiting for Bosco Latourelle.

Argentina loved the sensation of getting high early on a Thursday afternoon. Especially when the air was tingling with anticipation, a sort of suppressed scream in the city as if a carnival crowd was watching a jammed ferris wheel teetering and about to fall. With no program to do this afternoon at Radio-Canada, she was free to sit and drift and take whatever the rest of the day had to offer. The premier of the province was in Montreal doing an all-afternoon open-line show which was pre-empting her time. So the listeners were getting Yves Baril instead of Argentina Carr. And Argentina Carr was getting high.

Bosco Latourelle arrived with his customary flair. Brakes squealed on Maisonneuve Boulevard, tires ripped the pavement, and then voices rose in theatrical dispute, full of thunder but without much conviction. After all, metal had not been bent nor any glass broken, and who really minded the excuse to sound off?

Argentina could see her friend's chestnut head, large and smooth from recent attention at the stylist's, moving above the roofs of parked cars. He was doing everything at once; paying the taxi, tipping to compensate for the sudden command to stop, shouting down the offended motorists, greeting friends at El Diablo's ringside, placating the laconic cop, and then, with the immaculate timing of the successful advertising man, leaving the meeting while he was still ahead.

"You're going to get killed one day," Argentina said as
Bosco manipulated a couple of Steinberg wrought-iron chairs
to make a place for himself.

"No way," Bosco said. "I cause other people's deaths, not
my own. I'll die in bed."

"Sounds a lonely way to go."

"Who said I'd be alone?" His mildly accented English was
a sound Argentina never tired of. Latourelle -- articulate as any
man in Canada -- knew the good thing he had going and made
no attempt to lose the vocal evidence of his Gaspé origins. He
sat down, the jacket of his dark-blue summerweight suit
unbuttoned, his white shirt taut across his generous chest and
belly. His glossy tie was loosened at the unbuttoned collar and
hung like a striped flag. *"Fait chaud,"* he said, swabbing his
clean-shaven face with a balled handkerchief, his pale-blue
eyes never leaving Argentina's. "If June is like this, we'll roast
in July."

"The long hot summer," Argentina said meaningfully.
Like everyone else these days, she seldom got the referendum
out of her mind.

"What's that you're drinking?" Bosco asked her. "Irish
coffee? Today? Only the English." To the waiter he said, *"Un
autre café comme ça pour ma'm'selle, et moi, je veut prendre
une grosse Canabrau."* Latourelle preferred whisky to beer
but he served his brewery clients in public by always keeping
his table covered with their bottles.

"I'm mystified, Bosco," Argentina said. "Why the phone
call? Why the insistence on meeting me?"

"You should always keep your shoulders and arms
uncovered like that," he said. "You gleam."

"Thank you." The light cotton frock, dotted like confetti
and held at the shoulders by two ribbons, was one of her own
favorites. Argentina was very aware of the slope of her arms,
the tanned skin and the gold dusting of tiny hairs where a shaft
of sunlight was penetrating the shade. "Is this courting day? It
sounded very urgent on the telephone."

"Courting can be urgent, Argentina."

"As I remember, it was anything but urgent last time. Measured and contemplative would be more like it. Not that I'm complaining."

The drinks came and Bosco put down half the glass of beer at one draft, his broad muscled neck pulsing slowly. He set down the glass and wiped his mouth with the back of his hand, the sophisticated man of commerce retaining his farmer charm. "O.K., my love, I need you. This is the time."

"Are we still on that subject?"

"I need you to help me bring off a coup." He lowered his voice and his eyes went flat. "A political adventure, old girl. A kidnapping."

"I don't get it."

"No joke. You and I and a few others are going to make the big move. We're going to get involved. That's if you'll agree to go along." He looked at her, measuring her. "And I hope you'll agree, because if you don't this whole population is due for the cruelest blood-bath our native land has ever experienced."

"Bosco, you don't sound like yourself."

"I don't? Well." He put the glass to his lips but set it back down, this time untasted. "Changed times, Argentina. Means people have to change too. I've been thinking for a week, ever since a piece of information fell into my lap. Never mind how. And I've decided I have to act, before it's too late. While we still have a little freedom."

Argentina's mind was racing, stimulated by her friend's electric mood. "Are you talking about the referendum? Is this to do with Yves Baril?"

Latourelle looked at his watch. "Dennis Masterson is supposed to join us by two-thirty. We have to persuade him to come in too."

"We? How can I persuade him when I'm in the dark?"

"O.K. You're right, it's Baril. He's the man we have to kidnap."

It was hard for Argentina to know which way to look. Madness. "Kidnap the premier of the province? You have to be joking, Bosco. Come on, even the FLQ never went that far.

They snatched poor Pierre Laporte and even then they ended
up murdering him and getting caught and going to jail for life.
Don't suggest to me that you're heading down that road. Why?"

"To prevent a civil war. Separatists fighting
confederationists. Concentration camps in the Laurentians.
Maybe something like Lebanon here in Montreal."

"Bosco, are you smoking something? What kind of
dreams are these?" Argentina saw heads turn at other tables and
she lowered her voice. "The referendum has ground rules to
prevent any of that. It would have to be at least 85 percent in
favor of an independent Quebec before separation would be
considered. Even then it would be a slow procedure."

"That was René Levesque's policy. He was moderate.
But when that plane went down at Noranda, Levesque died and
so did moderation. Baril is another kettle of piranhas."

"Everybody knows Baril was an extremist but when he
took over the party, he had to cool it. That's part of the job.
You've heard what he's been saying."

"What he says and what he means to do are not the same
thing. I've seen the document." Latourelle sounded thoroughly
convinced and, knowing his reputation for common sense,
Argentina felt icy claws close to her heart.

"Baril plans to act if the referendum is 51 percent to 49
in favor. He's got the contingency plans all set. Quebec will
separate overnight -- a fait accompli. Quebec flag, Quebec
currency, Quebec customs and immigration -- the lot."

"But he couldn't. The people wouldn't stand for it."

"The people will never know what hit them. Unless we
tell them about it before it happens."

Dennis Masterson was threading his way between tables.
Tall and broad-shouldered, in a double-breasted blazer and
grey slacks, he looked as though he had just stepped off a yacht.
Masterson's clothes were expensive but square; shoes, for him,
had to be black and fitted with laces. Argentina could recall his
friend Johnny Fist from The Ninety-Seven club teasing Dennis
about it, kicking at them and calling them policeman shoes.

"*Salut*, Denny," Bosco said, half rising and indicating the
chair beside him. "What are you drinking?"

"Just a lemonade, I've got choir practice at six o'clock." Squeezing past Latourelle, Masterson pulled out the chair beside Argentina. "Two more Sundays and they close the church for the summer. Then I can get bombed on Thursdays like the rest of you." He sat down and put an arm around Argentina's bare shoulders. "How's my favorite radio commentator?"

"Fine. How's my favorite radio singer?"

"Not bad, except I'm a little hoarse from rehearsal." Putting on another voice, the singer asked himself, "Where did you say you're from? Nnngaaannnng, nnngaaanng..." Masterson had become hooked years ago on the routines of Bert Lahr and he still salted his conversation with echoes of the old comedian's vaudeville laugh.

Latourelle was watching Masterson with mixed feelings. He liked the singer for the decent man he was, but he doubted the tensile strength of his moral fibre -- a serious drawback now that he needed him to help make the plot work. And then there was the singer's manicured hand on Argentina's upper arm, pressing hard enough to give the tanned skin a white border around his fingertips. He said, "I'm glad you could make it, Dennis. I'm trying something big and I need you to help me."

"Pitching for another account, Bosco? Count on me. I'll sing your presentation jingle for nothing." He winked at Argentina. "As long as you pay me double scale when we do the finished job."

"It isn't a pitch," Latourelle said.

For the first time, Masterson felt the tension. Still, he tried to keep it light, to postpone the threatening discussion that seemed to be shaping up. "You're divorcing your wife for Argentina. Man, she isn't worth it. Just a pair of pretty arms."

Nobody was laughing. The waiter brought the lemonade Latourelle had ordered. As Masterson sipped, Argentina said, "You're going to wish that was mostly vodka."

"It's a desperate situation." Latourelle said. "It has to do with the referendum and what Baril is up to and what's going to happen to all of us if somebody doesn't get in his way." Then he explained, enlarging on what he had told Argentina and ending up with his plan to snatch Yves Baril, to hold him in non-violent detention and thus to get the media involved in alerting Quebec and the rest of Canada.

Masterson listened with his lean face set in a rather prim frown, his lips a tight line. It was as if he was in a cramped studio auditioning a mediocre singer with bad breath. When Latourelle finished, Masterson shook his head and filled his lungs with a long intake of air.

"I think you're out of your primitive French-Canadian mind, Bosco. I've never heard such alarmist claptrap in my life."

"I can show you a copy of the document I got from my friend inside Le Parti Québecois. This is happening, my old friend -- not next decade or next year but in two weeks, after the referendum. That's why we're taking Yves Baril -- tomorrow, at the Publicité Club luncheon."

Masterson blinked. "I'm singing at the luncheon tomorrow."

"That's why you're in the scheme."

"No way, Bosco. Guns and masks and speeding cars are not my specialty."

"Guns are not involved. There will be no violence in this gig at all. It's a peaceful detention. Baril will be detained while we get the television cameras focused on what he's planning."

"How will you take him without guns? He never goes anywhere without all those wrestlers around him. It's like Wednesday night at the Forum"

"I've got a plan. But I want to tell everybody at one time. Tonight."

"Nope." Masterson stood up. "I've got choir practice."

Latourelle had to laugh at that. He looked at Argentina Carr with his round blue eyes screwed up in delight and they both started laughing. Here he was, planning to kidnap the premier of Quebec in an effort to head off a civil war and his key man could not attend the briefing because he had choir practice.

"Come after practice," Latourelle said.

"Never in a million years."

Bosco stood and faced Masterson. "Go and talk to Johnny Fist," he said. "Walk over and see him right now. He's in on it. In fact, the meeting's at his place, upstairs over the club." By invoking the name of Jonathan Fitzwilliam, Latourelle as good as put Masterson in the bag, and both he and Argentina knew it. The singer and the giant club owner were inseparable and had been for years.

"Will you go and talk to Johnny?" Argentina put in. Without any conscious thought she seemed to have become Bosco's accomplice.

"All right." Masterson's consent sounded as grudging as a rusted gate. " I'll go and talk to Johnny." And he left El Diablo, proud-backed, one arm trailing, the other held across his chest, a headwaiter making an exit in a 1940's movie.

For a few seconds, Argentina and Bosco looked at each other, blank as portraits in a gallery. Then she said, "He's going to give you trouble, Bosco."

"The whole scenario is flimsy and full of holes," Latourelle conceded. "But the advantage we have is that it's unpremeditated and it's quick. Give us six months to prepare and we'd get arrested on our way into the hotel. But this thing is all whim and impulse, and it *might* work. It's my forte, girl -- the advertising business couldn't function any other way."

They drank up and Bosco, edgy and more electric than before, checked his watch. "Coming with me? I've got to run over and see Eloise Carpentier."

Argentina had met Eloise once or twice at jazz shows down in the Old Town. Everybody knew everybody, she realized, but why was Latourelle visiting the poor little rich girl in the middle of the afternoon? With four Irish coffees in her, it was no trouble for Argentina to put the question to Bosco.

He said, "I want to tell her the time of the meeting tonight. Can you imagine? She has this lush pad on Sherbrooke Street and she won't have a telephone put in."

Tell her the *time* of the meeting. That meant she was already in the picture, that Bosco had recruited her before Argentina. This bothered Argentina and she strode in silence beside Latourelle as they headed east on Sherbrooke; bare-shouldered and grim-faced, her sandals slapping the pavement, she was like a mythological warrior woman going into battle beside her man.

They passed elegant boutiques set well back from the sidewalk and up flights of stairs, then the new glass towers that had replaced nineteenth-century homes, then the McGill campus with a few lads tossing a football on what was left of the grass after the new library claimed its space and, after crossing Bleury Street, a succession of weary restaurants and shops leaning on each other in the heat, their doors hanging open, gasping for air. Finally, surprisingly, they arrived at a solitary residential tower thrusting high among the flat roofs like the first stone in a new cemetery.

As they approached, Latourelle's tumbling thoughts settled down and he heard Argentina's silence for the first time. "Are you all right?"

"I'm fine."

His ability to read people was the characteristic which, more than brains and a willingness to work hard, had made Latourelle the head of his own advertising agency at 42. He stood with Argentina in the lobby waiting for the elevator, watching her face, doing a low-profile tap-dance on the marble floor. "Having a remote place to take Baril was the foundation of the plan. Eloise has that crazy farm she bought in the Eastern Townships. I had to get that buttoned down before it made sense to talk to anybody else."

"I understand."

"*You*, gleaming woman, are the one who moves and acts and speaks in the piece. Without you, it wouldn't happen."

Feeling better, she said, "Nobody is indispensable."

"Wrong," he said. "Yves Baril is indispensable. No villain, no plot."

The elevator lifted them twenty stories into the air, silently, with only an alarming shudder at the end and a long three seconds while it decided to open the door. Eloise was in apartment 2020, not far down the dim corridor. Bosco pressed the buzzer and a chain rattled immediately on the other side.

She opened the door and they heard a recording of Miles Davis down the hall playing "Bye Bye Blackbird," muted, wistful. Fragile as smoke, Eloise drifted aside to let them come in; a simple kiss on the cheek for Bosco, an elegiac smile for Argentina. She pushed back a curtain of long silver hair with a hand holding a tiny glass. "Let me get you both a drink."

They followed her into a living room that smashed at them with one glass wall framing roofs, steeples, towers of windows, the sky, the river, and bridges vaulting away to the South Shore. On the horizon, the green hills of Vermont had decided to be late-afternoon blue. It was the sort of view you admired and edged away from. But even this panorama could not blind Bosco to the annoying fact that Tancrede Falardeau was in the room.

"You both know Tancrede, don't you?" Eloise was at a cherrywood cabinet, adding water to Pernod.

They exchanged three-way greetings. Argentina realized it was at The Big Bang, Falardeau's club down in Le Vieux Montreal, that she had met Eloise. But the girl had been different at that time, admittedly a couple of years ago. What was it?

Stalling, hoping Tancrede might be on his way out, Latourelle said, "I'm glad to hear you still dig Miles."

"After Otto, he's the greatest."

It was a sign of the remarkable progress made by Eloise Carpentier in picking up the pieces of her life that she could mention Otto's name as casually as this. When Otto Grant, the black man from Philadelphia and trumpet soloist in Tancrede's house band, was accidentally killed in a foolish struggle over some rare phonograph records, Eloise nearly cashed in. In those days, she weighed even less -- a mere suggestion of a girl -- and she was supporting a pernicious heroin habit. Otto was her lover and, so everybody believed, her strength. When they buried him, Eloise put her head down and waited for the world to roll over her.

Then a remarkable thing happened. She got up one day and signed herself into a sanitarium, where she cold-turkeyed the drug addiction. She came home, kept it to cigarettes and

liquor, dated now and again, and seemed to be like thousands
of pretty girls who come out in Montreal when the sun goes
down; but wealthier, of course. The visible difference in Eloise
now was a capability to hate. In the past, she was totally
involved in what Otto and the heroin were doing to her
sensations. Now she had neither and was left with time to be
as hostile as anyone else.

"How do we stand?" she asked Latourelle as she handed
a glass of the cloudy liquor to Tancrede.

So Tancrede was staying, as Bosco had feared. During
her hard times Falardeau had been Eloise's guardian angel and
he still was. There was no way she could embark on a trip like
this one without the advice and guidance of Father Superior.
But Latourelle tried anyway.

"I really think the fewer people in this, the better," he
said.

Tancrede sat behind his drink, fat, prematurely bald, his
gold-rimmed glasses far down his nose. "From what Eloise has
told me," he said, "I think *no* people would be best of all."

"You think the best idea is to let this happen?"

"O.K., let's talk about that," Falardeau said. "You claim
to have some document that says Baril means to separate the
province on a 51 percent vote in favor."

"I don't claim it. I've got it."

"Right. Then call a press conference. Tell the reporters.
You'll achieve the same thing with no risk."

Latourelle tossed down the dreadful drink and shook off
Eloise's sign suggesting another. "Tancrede, how can you be
so naive? For one thing, half the reporters are in Baril's pocket.
And even if some take me seriously, Baril comes out next day
with one of his plausible denials and that's the end of that. The
hungry press rushes on to the next course. So where am I?"

"Nowhere," Argentina said. "He's right, Tancrede. This
thing is big enough and sinister enough; we have to make a
large wave."

"Be careful you don't drown yourselves."

Latourelle was working at containing his irritation.
"Tancrede, I don't really care if you're with us or not. All I ask

is that you keep quiet for a couple of days till it's over, and that you don't discourage Eloise -- we need her."

"You need her? *I* need her." Falardeau shouted this and Eloise showed surprise. For years their platonic friendship had gone along without demonstrations or declarations. "Not shot or in prison, I need her just the way she is now."

"There won't be any shooting. And not much prison for anybody except maybe me. This thing is peaceful, a unique action for a unique situation. If we confound Baril the moderates will give us medals."

"Yeah, sure."

"I wouldn't expect you to agree, Tancrede. You've got your big club down near Place Jacques Cartier where all the revolutionaries hang out. Hell, if Quebec separates, you'll be doing just fine, *merci beaucoup.*"

"I never said I was a separatist."

"No, and you never said you were for confederation either. Stand up, Falardeau. That fence must be starting to hurt."

Tancrede did stand up and he approached Latourelle who squared off to meet him. But neither of them was a fighter by nature and there was about as much menace in the situation as in a collision of two old women in a supermarket. The girls noticed it together, glanced at each other and shared a smile. Then Eloise let them off the hook.

"Come on, Tancrede. Cut it out, Bosco. Go outside if you want to fight."

"I'm leaving," Bosco said. "I only came to tell you the time of the meeting tonight. Can you be at The Ninety-Seven club any time after nine? We'll be in Johnny Fist's place, upstairs."

Falardeau clucked his tongue. "You're working with that ruffian? And you say this will be a peaceful affair."

"Johnny's no ruffian," Argentina said. "Just because he's big, people think he's tough."

"No, it's because he takes the law into his own hands. You can believe that."

Plunging back to earth in the elevator with Argentina, Latourelle put an arm around her shoulder. She could feel the sag in him and it occurred to her that he needed whatever she could supply just then. "I've got some cold white wine at my place," she said. "We can rinse away the Pernod."

Latourelle should have accepted, should have realized that there might not be a surplus of pleasant hours from here on. But his work habits were too rigid to be set aside. "Another time, Argentina. Thanks. I've been out of the shop most of the day and there's a recording session tomorrow morning at Daisy Studio. I've got to go through the copy so the client will think I was in on it."

"If you're recording in the morning, will you be all right for Baril at the Publicité Club lunch?"

"I'll be there. Don't worry, we'll set the timing at Johnny's place. Are you O.K. for nine o'clock?"

"I may go there early and eat. That's one good thing about Jonathan Fitzwilliam's place -- you can always read a book."

When the elevator door opened they were embracing. The deserted lobby watched in silence as the door counted its slow three and closed on them again. By the time they woke up, they'd been transported to the penthouse and had to ride down again, whispering and laughing under the disapproving eyes of an elderly resident.

As soon as he opened the street door of Club Ninety-Seven, Dennis Masterson was reminded of what it had been before Johnny bought it and turned it into a bar and restaurant -- the smell of old bookbindings was unmistakable. Fitzwilliam had cleared out the center but kept the wall shelves in place and loaded with volumes. A couple of library ladders were in position and there were books resting on many of the small tables and leather armchairs.

By this hour, the luncheon crowd had gone and there were only a few regulars in attendance. Dallas was behind the bar engaged in a game of chess with Lucien Lacombe. They made an amusing contrast: the bartender looking like an

Indian with his long hair held by a cotton headband, Lacombe in his square suit looking like what he was, a former Police Constable promoted to plainclothes division because of his good work a few years ago in finding the body of a New York millionaire's kidnapped son.

"One Guinness, coming up," Dallas said when he spotted Masterson approaching.

"Not today, Dallas. I've got choir practice."

"Let's all sing like the birdies sing..." the bartender droned. He had no ear.

"Is Johnny around?"

"Upstairs counting his money," Lacombe said.

Masterson began to climb the spiral iron steps, his clanging tread giving his old friend plenty of notice of his arrival. In the big open-plan apartment with its large window overlooking Stanley Street, Jonathan Fitzwilliam was watering his potted plants, looming in silhouette over the row of foliage on the window ledge, the long spout of the watering can poking and prying among the leaves.

"Right with you, Den," he said, and he went on muttering to the plants, "Hey, you've got a new leaf. Lovely. Look at all that gorgeous stuff." He set the watering can on the floor and turned to look down on Masterson who had lowered himself into the corduroy bean-bag chair. "Want a beer?"

"No, thanks. Choir practice."

"Well, I will." Fitzwilliam moved into the kitchen end of the area, opened the refrigerator and took out a brown quart bottle that looked like a pint in his massive hand. He thrust the cap into a wall opener, snapped it off with a hiss and a clatter as the cap bounced on the counter, took down a huge glass shaped like the face of a smiling gnome on a Doric column, and brought both into the main room where he sat on the sofa opposite Masterson. As he poured, he kicked off his sandals and sat bare except for denim shorts.

"Here's looking at you," he said, raising the glass. It held the whole quart of beer and the gnome's face was amber now with a foam crewcut. "You're worried to death, aren't you?"

"What's going on, Johnny?"

"Bosco said he was going to talk to you."

"He did. But all I've got is some crazy stuff about kidnapping the premier at the luncheon tomorrow. And I'm supposed to be part of it."

"I thought it was crazy myself. But then I thought about it. Bosco may just be the right guy at the right time. For the future of this country."

Masterson struggled up out of the shapeless chair and walked to the window. "There's no future in kidnapping. Anybody but you would see that. I'm talking to the wrong guy."

"What do you mean by that?"

"I haven't forgotten Linda Lennox."

"That's good. You keep remembering her. But don't forget Disco and Kingbright and Cleary, and how she would have gotten away with all those deaths if it hadn't have been for me."

A couple of years back, Linda Lennox, an American copywriter, had surged through Johnny's like a tidal wave. It was a complex summer, full of jealousy and ambition, and when it was over Emery Disco and Noble Kingbright were dead. For a while it looked as if Fitzwilliam's old Baytown friend, Don Cleary, was the killer and when Johnny went after him, Cleary directed a bullet into his own head. Then, just as Linda was about to fly off to California, Jonathan put it all together. It had been the Lennox woman all along and the only way to stop her, since there was no proof, was to pitch her from the roof and let it look like suicide. It was swift brutal justice and Masterson had swallowed it. But ever since, he had experienced difficulty in keeping it down.

"You could have given Linda to the police," he said.

"We've been over that, Den. They'd closed the case with Cleary. And she'd have denied everything. It was my word against hers."

Masterson struggled out of the past. "And now you're going to help Latourelle go the same way with Yves Baril. Hell, all Latourelle has to do is blow the whistle. Let the public in on what he knows."

"Half the public wants Quebec to separate and the other half would never believe Bosco's story."

"Snatching Baril will make them believe?"

"It will concentrate attention on him. Long enough so that he can't smooth it over with a fast answer."

"Just supposing somehow he brings it off, although I swear to God I don't see any way."

"That's what he'll tell us here tonight."

"Then what happens to us? How do we go on living here after a thing like that? We'll be jailed. We'll have to be."

"Bosco says nobody will get hurt. He believes the moderate politicians who take over will go easy on us."

"He believes! He's wrong."

"If he is, then maybe we just have to be ready to pay a price. If the alternative is no more Canada."

"Listen," Masterson said, "if they want their own country, let them have it. They can build a monument to Charles de Gaulle at the corner of Peel and Ste. Catherine. All I have to do is get on a train to Toronto."

"You think it's that easy?"

"Why not? I've sung on CBC network shows, I'm known up there. I could be working in a matter of weeks."

Fitzwilliam had finished the beer. He set the glass on the floor, the gnome face transparent again and curtained with foam inside. "Don't talk about jobs. How long have you been in Montreal? Twenty-five years? All your working life? Your roots are here, and so are mine. I could sell The Ninety-Seven and open a club in Toronto or Vancouver or anywhere. But it would never be the same. This is our city, man, and some ambitious bastards are trying to take it away from us. Without a fight, they *think*. Hoo-boy, have we got a surprise for them."

This was exactly what Masterson was afraid of. Maybe the civilized Bosco Latourelle meant to carry out a symbolic kidnapping, a sort of street-theater happening with nobody getting hurt, but Johnny Fist was another breed. He was ready to punch heads and he didn't mind suffering bruised knuckles or even a broken hand.

"And I've got a surprise for Latourelle," Masterson said.
"I'm not going along with this."

"Denny, I know you better than you know yourself.
Beneath that cowardly exterior beats the heart of a true fellow
traveller."

"That's a rotten thing to say."

"Come to the briefing tonight, hear what's expected of
you. You'll feel different, I guarantee it."

"You're like a bunch of school kids scuffling on the
playground." Masterson stomped across the room and began
to descend the winding stairs.

"Go to choir practice. I'll see you here after nine."

"Maybe. Maybe not."

"And the glory of the Lord shall be reveal-ed," Fitzwilliam
chanted in a fair tenor.

Bosco Latourelle felt safer in his office than anywhere
else in the world. The wall-to-wall carpet, the gleaming oak
furniture, the clean desk surface, his view from corner windows
of Mount Royal and the Cross, not yet illuminated at 5:30 on this
early summer evening -- everything around him was comforting.
He had worked with paper and the telephone for an hour after
leaving Argentina Carr outside Eloise Carpentier's building.
Now, cooling off his mind after intense concentration, he found
his eyes drifting, as usual, to the carved wooden anchor
hanging by its wooden chain from a hook in the painted wall.

The anchor, a fine example of some Gaspé carver's
craftsmanship, had become a talisman for Latourelle. He
looked at it several times a day and occasionally, when alone,
he took it down and caressed it. He dated his current run of
almost-uninterrupted good luck from the day he purchased the
anchor last year during a motor trip home to Rimouski. It had
not escaped his notice that the anchor was a cross of sorts with
its horizontal bar near the top of the central shaft. But he would
not have identified himself as a religious man.

A knock at the door, it opened, and John Keeley stuck
his head inside. Speaking in his quite good French, he said, "I
hope I'm not bothering you, Bosco. May I speak to you for a
moment?"

"Come in, John. *Je t'en prie.*"

The copywriter came in and sat in the chair facing the desk. The sleeves of his striped shirt were rolled just below the elbows, and his tie, neatly coiled, was tucked inside his shirt pocket. He took out a cellophane package of bubble-gum balls and offered one to Latourelle, who refused it politely. Keeley popped one into his mouth and held another ready in his hand.

"I was wondering if you're going to be doing anything in a recording studio in the next week or so," he said, still talking creditable French.

Keeley was a rarity in the agency or anywhere else in Montreal. He was an Ontario native who had taken the trouble to master the second language. He did it the only sensible way -- not by enrolling with Berlitz or by listening to records. Keeley simply talked French every day to as many people as possible. At first it was painful, his speech halting and three-quarters English. But gradually he improved, reading *Montreal Matin* aloud to himself at his desk in the mornings and *La Presse* silently to himself on the bus going home at night.

Now he was, in effect, bilingual. Latourelle wished he could afford to have him on staff, but Keeley worked for Bosco's affiliated English agency down the hall, R & M Advertising.

"I have a session at Daisy tomorrow morning," Latourelle said. "I booked an hour and a half, from ten to eleven-thirty."

"Think you'll use every minute of it?"

Bosco grinned. "Debbie wants another chance?"

"She knows she can do better; she was nervous as hell the first time. I said I'd ask."

A couple of months before, Latourelle had allowed Keeley to bring his girl friend, Debbie Thielmanns, to an agency session. She was a semi-professional folksinger who worked in clubs around town but she had never made a recording. The hope was that the session might run short and she could slip behind a microphone with her guitar and lay down a track. There was time, but the results were disappointing -- almost embarrassing. However, she wanted to try again and Bosco gave her credit.

"Bring her along," he said. "We're bound to have lots of time tomorrow."

"Thanks, Bosco." Keeley put the other gumball into his mouth and began to grind it in with the softened gum already there. "They tell me we're getting seven hours off work on Referendum Day."

It seemed like a lot of time and Latourelle raised his eyebrows. "Is that right?"

"Yeah. Three hours to vote and four hours to pack."

They both laughed and Latourelle said, switching to English, "You don't have to worry in any case. If all the blokes were like you, Baril wouldn't have a leg to stand on."

Keeley chewed thoughtfully. "I worry anyway," he said. "I know I can hack it in French. And I love this city and the people in it -- I really do."

"It shows."

"But if Quebec separates , then I wouldn't want to stay. I'm Canadian inside, Bosco. Can you understand?"

"Certainly, I'm the same way. But you don't have to worry about the referendum, it's going to come out fine."

"There's a funny buzz in the air these days, as if something is going to happen. Don't you feel it?"

"Yes. But it's going to be O.K."

"How do you know?"

"I just know."

Keeley slapped the arms of the chair and stood up. "O.K., papa. I feel better." He went to the door.

"Besides," Latourelle said, "you could never leave Montreal. We've got the best hockey players."

Keeley put on a public address voice and chanted, "*Le but du Canadiens conté par Rocket Richard!*" As he walked away, both he and Latourelle were making hoarse roaring crowd noises into their cupped hands.

Keeley had to cab all the way down to Le Big Bang in the Old Town to see Debbie because she was intermission singer at the club this week and, although not on until nine o'clock, she liked to be there early and get the feel of the room. As

Keeley entered the club, he passed Tancrede Falardeau and gave him a greeting. The owner was usually buddy-buddy, but something was on his mind tonight and he seemed not to see Keeley.

Debbie was out back in a room piled with soft-drink cases, tuning her guitar. Her chestnut hair hung down both shoulders, front and back, smooth as a waterfall before it hits the riverbed. Keeley kissed her cheek and got one back on the lips. "Good news," he said. "Bosco has a session at Daisy tomorrow. Says we can come around eleven."

She hunched her shoulders and made a little-girl grimace. Debbie was 26, almost Keeley's age, and her experience growing up in Detroit had made her a far more worldly person than the young adman from small-town Ontario. But she wore no makeup and her expressions and her voice were those of a teenager.

"Hey, man," she said, "you just scared me to death."

"I thought you wanted to get a good track down."

"I do. But I can still be scared, can't I?" She played a couple of minor chords, then progressed to a vamping strum and sang.

"I'm going down this road feelin' bad ..."

The voice was tiny and clear, as if a bell had taken lessons from a bird.

"Listen, when do you want to eat?"

"Never again, since you gave me the news."

"Come on. Something from the kitchen here or do you want to go out?"

"Give me twenty minutes and we'll go out."

"O.K." In the doorway, Keeley said, "What's the matter with Tancrede tonight?"

"Tancrede is Tancrede," Debbie said. "What do I know from Tancrede?"

He left her vamping.

Latourelle was surprised that everybody turned up. Looking around Johnny Fist's apartment at the expectant faces, he experienced a crushing realization that tomorrow lunchtime they would make a crazy attempt to alter the course of history. He started by running over the background so that everybody would be in the boat together. When he finished with Baril and his illegal takeover plans, supporting this by reading from the secret document provided by his Parti-Québecois friend, Latourelle said, "Any questions so far?"

"I've got one." It was Tancrede Falardeau, the man Bosco least wanted at the briefing. But Eloise was there, so the portly clubman had to be by her side. "How come you have to use Eloise's farm?" He was jumping ahead, using information he must have been given by her. "That means transporting Baril all the way to the Eastern Townships. Why not stash him some place here in the city?"

"O.K., let's deal with that," Latourelle said. "This is a peaceful detention, remember. No ropes, no gag in the mouth. If we keep Baril in town, he'll scream and be heard. Eloise's farm is remote -- only the chickens will hear him."

"But if he isn't bound and gagged, how are you going to persuade him to leave the Publicité Club and take an 80-mile drive with you on a Friday afternoon?"

"That's part of the plan. I'm coming to that."

"I can't wait."

Eloise Carpentier spoke. "Baril is a monster," she said. "We ought to kill him and be done with it."

"And make him a martyr," Bosco said. "His radical friends would love that. They'd turn Quebec into a police state before you could say hello."

"It would be justice. How do you think he got to be premier? The plane crash that killed René Levesque at Noranda, that was too convenient to be an accident."

"We've all heard the rumors, Eloise. Maybe they're true. But that's beside the point right now. Our job is to hold Baril for a couple of days while we tell the world what he means to do. Then he won't be able to do it. Simple as that." Latourelle glanced at Masterson. "Are you with us, Denny? I hope your presence means you are."

Masterson had gone home from choir practice and changed into black slacks, black turtleneck, and black suede shoes with crepe soles. He was no longer dressed like Xavier Cugat, he was dressed like a cat burglar. Bosco's question made him stiffen. With everybody watching him and waiting, his tongue froze.

Fitzwilliam made up his friend's mind for the hundredth time in their relationship. "He's with us," he said.

Without denying it, Masterson was now free to express a little individuality. "Hell, I could move to Toronto next week," he said. "They pay singers more up there anyway."

"If you're thinking of the CBC," Argentina said with quiet authority, "forget it. I just saw a memo about the new budget cutback. Toronto will be firing, not hiring. You'd better hang onto what you've got."

There was something disquieting about this emphasizing of Dennis Masterson's vulnerability. It would be damaging to let it hang there. So Latourelle went right on, deliberately involving Dennis in the first stage of the planning. "O.K., let's get down to details," he said. "You're the guest singer at the club luncheon, right? Any idea how that will work?"

"Just that I'm to do two songs. One in English and one in French, of course."

"If he gets an encore," Johnny Fist said, "he's going to do 'My Yiddishe Momma'."

The laughter that followed was what was needed to clear the air and bring them all together. "Right," Bosco said briskly, and went ahead to explain what each of them would be expected to do tomorrow.

The client was still hanging around the control room at Daisy Studio and Bosco Latourelle, appearing impatient, had to wait and make conversation. Max Acton was at the console, preparing to get a test level on Debbie Thielmanns, who was sitting on a stool in the big studio, her guitar across her knee and a boom mike suspended in front of her. Finally, Bosco referred to his committee duties that day at the Publicité Club, the client realized he was not going to free-load a lunch, and he left, thanking Bosco and Max for a great session.

Bosco hurried into the studio and told John Keeley, who was hovering anxiously, "I've got to go to the Publicité Club lunch. The studio is yours till eleven-thirty. Max knows."

Keeley said, "I'm disappointed. I thought you'd stay and hear my song."

"I didn't know you write songs."

"If this one works, it'll be the first. Go ahead, Bosco. I'll bring a dub to the shop so you can hear it."

When Latourelle was gone, Debbie went right into a rehearsal while Keeley returned to the control room to sit in the vacated producer's chair beside Acton and hear the song on mike. In her clear, sweet voice, Debbie sang:

"I came from Trouble City
To a younger, happier place
Where people walk the streets at night
And no one hates my face.
I've got a man who leads me
Where I don't mind being led -
But still I go to sleep at night
With a handgun by my bed..."

Max Acton listened to the song, adjusting levels, watching the VU meter. As Debbie played some chords and tried a new introduction, Acton said absently, "I heard you say you wrote this."

"Yep."

"Mmmmm. Very nice." Acton was so drugged from his daily exposure to trashy commercial music and so dedicated to telling his clients it was all great that not even he believed in his judgment anymore. They put down three takes in the half hour and kept two of them. Debbie was much more relaxed than she had been the other time and while Max was making a dub from the master, Keeley went into the studio and embraced her. She was still euphoric from the playback of her performance which Acton had enhanced with a bit of echo.

"It sounded good," she said. "I couldn't believe it was me."

"You were fantastic."

With the tape in his pocket, Keeley drove his car slowly through heavy midday traffic along Ste. Catherine Street toward the office. Then, suddenly, he darted through an opening and headed down MacKay toward Dorchester Boulevard.

"Where are we going?"

"To the Queen E. I want to tell Bosco about the session --I can't wait." Approaching the Queen Elizabeth Hotel, Keeley turned off Dorchester and found parking space in the Central Station lot. "We have to eat somewhere," he said, "we might as well attend the Publicité Club lunch."

"Don't you have to be a member?"

"I am."

They were unable to get close to Bosco Latourelle before or during the lunch. They were there a bit late and only managed to find seating at the end of a table near the door. Attendance was exceptional today because everybody wanted to hear the premier of Quebec with Referendum Day only a little over a week away.

Keeley and Debbie ate their consommé and crusty roll while chatting with the executives on either side of them, Keeley rattling on in his loose accented French, which amused Debbie because she had never heard him use more than a couple of sentences to a waiter or a cab driver. Another thing that changed him slightly in her eyes was the plastic name-badge on his lapel. Debbie Thielmanns had gone through her teens and early twenties developing a strong disdain for the establishment. Now here was her writer of hard-core folk music looking like a Kiwanian.

"There's Bosco at the head table," Keeley told her, "and one over from him is Yves Baril." He pointed out a wedge-headed man with gleaming black hair and rimless glasses. Baril was so short his head was six inches lower than all the others along the row. "Bosco's agency does some advertising for Le Parti Québecois. That's why Latourelle is so close to the Premier." What Keeley did not know was that Latourelle was preparing, if Yves Baril should remain party leader, to resign the account.

The food served and cleared away, waiters now doing coffee, the club president stood at the table lectern and read some announcements, then said that prior to the guest speaker they were going to have something nice to listen to. This unintentional faux pas drew laughter. He was referring to the famous singer of CBC Radio, Dennis Masterson, who would now favor the meeting with a couple of songs.

Masterson went to stand beside a grand piano on the dais and sang a Broadway musical hit followed by a French-Canadian folk song delivered with more grace and feeling than Debbie Thielmanns had ever heard. She whispered to Keeley, "There's a guy who doesn't have to worry where his next meal is coming from."

Everybody thought Masterson was finished, but he walked from the piano to the head table and stood behind Yves Baril, raising his hands for silence. When the applause faded, he called, "We all know our premier has a reputation as a singer." It was true. Before the political career took over Baril had been active in club singing around the city. Now he kept his baritone in shape and still performed whenever he was asked.

"I promise you, Monsieur Baril knows nothing of this," Masterson went on. "But I have a duet all set up on the piano, and I know he reads music..."

It was all he had to say. The applause rose to a crescendo and Yves Baril, beaming and nodding, waved a linen napkin over his head as he arose and followed Dennis to the piano. The duet was called "Tenor and Baritone," a comic song based on the operatic aria, *"La Donna e Mobile."* It was new to Baril, but he knew the tune, and with his training he was able to give a creditable performance. The few breakdowns were used by the singers for laughs and the result was a sensation. Any politician would have paid dearly for the image of warm honesty, the willingness to allow a chuckle at himself, that Baril got across in those impromptu five minutes.

His speech, which occupied the next half hour, was not so entertaining. Once a prepared text was placed in front of him, Baril became didactic and his head appeared snakelike as it scanned the room, cold eyes glittering. The words were harmless enough, the usual fuzzy generalities delivered mostly in French with the occasional sentence in flawless English inserted glistening and whole and appearing to the drugged audience like a sausage in a Yorkshire pudding.

When it was over and the membership was milling about, many of them heading for the hotel bars because it was Friday afternoon, Keeley told Debbie, "I'm going to try to speak to Bosco. Hang on."

They were not the only ones pressing through the crowds surrounding the guest speaker. There was Bosco Latourelle holding Dennis Masterson in one hand and Argentina Carr in the other. Keeley did not know the lady by sight but he got close enough to hear Latourelle say to Baril, "Monsieur Baril, this is Miss Carr from Radio-Canada. She does an afternoon commentary show on the network."

"Ah yes, Miss Carr, *enchanté*." Baril shook her hand. "I listen to you whenever I have the opportunity." In fact, he had heard her name but never her program.

"Thank you," Argentina said. "I'd like to use that fabulous duet on my show next week and I wondered if you and Mr. Masterson would agree to record it, just the way you sang it now."

The premier looked pleased. "*Avec plaisir*, but I'm afraid my schedule..." He gave that eloquent shrug, making himself even smaller.

"We could do it in half an hour. I just made a phone call, so the engineer is standing by in a studio. Dennis has agreed." Argentina looked very feminine. "Won't you please say yes?"

Bosco clinched it. "Just a quick ride down Dorchester Boulevard. Then I'll deliver you to your next appointment."

Baril considered then threw up his hands. "For such a charming lady, how can I refuse?"

John Keeley heard all this and said to Debbie, "We're not going to miss this. Come on, let's get the car."

Yves Baril was not alone when he accompanied Latourelle and Masterson to the car park, guiding Argentina by the arm as if she were his lady. Three huge, neckless men floated beside

the party, moving with astonishing agility; Wednesday night at
the Forum.

Outside, the group gathered around Argentina's small
sportscar, a convertible. The movements were confused but
quickly accomplished. "Sit by me, Mr. Premier," Argentina said
as she got behind the wheel. His eyes on her tanned legs below
the hoisted skirt, Baril did not have to be told twice. He
dropped into the passenger seat beside her while Latourelle
and Masterson climbed into the narrow back seat.

One of the bodyguards said something in French and
Baril told the three of them, impatiently, to follow in the other
car. They ran and began piling into a black sedan a few ranks
away. Argentina turned the key, gunned the engine, and pulled
out fast into the exit lane. She turned two corners quickly, tires
squealing, and then the bodyguards' car was out of sight.

As the black sedan moved into the exit lane and headed
for the first corner, a station wagon pulled out at speed and took
its bumper on the left front fender. Headlight glass rained on
the pavement, car doors opened, voices shouted in French and
one replied in English.

"What the hell!" Johnny Fist said. "Didn't you guys see
me pulling out?"

"Get that car out of the way!" one of the wrestlers,
crewcut, with boiled blue eyes and a cylindrical face, said.

"No way. We're waiting for the cops. You guys were
driving like maniacs. Are you drunk?"

"Move it!" The man leaned against the station-wagon
fender and his companions took up positions at the hood and
began to push. Metal screeched as the prang was separated.

Johnny Fist could not have been more delighted. An
explosion of adrenalin in his veins almost blinded him, his
heart pounded, and he felt a sensation of massive expansion
inside. He clapped both hands on Crewcut's shoulders, spun
him around, and drove the crown of his head into the man's
face. As the wrestler fell, Fist had a glimpse of his smashed
nose and blood streaming. Now it was not anything like
Wednesday night at the Forum.

Now came the other two, knees up and elbows out. Johnny kicked at one's crotch and missed, but landed his boot damagingly on the man's thigh above the knee. This left him a few free seconds to face the third. They squared off like boxers but quickly closed, punching together. Johnny took a couple on the face but his blows overpowered and battered down the other's, leaving an opening for him to drive a punch against the side of his head. The wrestler stumbled back and sagged to his knees; Fist took two steps at him and put the boot into his stomach.

A knee caught him punishingly in the small of the back. He ducked and spun, saw an opening, drove his fist up and into the second man's throat just below his chin. The man sat down, fell over onto his side, hands to his neck, making swallowing sounds.

It was very quiet after the brief battle. A few observers were standing well away. The first wrestler was sitting on the pavement with his back against the side of the sedan, his hands catching the blood from his smashed face. He made no attempt to continue the fight.

"Who paid you, you bastard?" he said.

"Nobody. I do this because I like it," Johnny Fist said.

"We'll find you. And next time, we'll know what to do."

"I doubt it."

But as he left on foot, Johnny knew that they probably would find him soon enough. The car was not his -- he had chosen it at random and jumped the wires to start it so they could not trace him that way, and the denim work clothes and boots he was wearing were not his style -- but they would describe him and he was not exactly an invisible man about town.

Crossing Dorchester and heading for his rented tourist room to change out of the bloodied clothes, he concentrated on getting used to the new life he had just advanced into. His back was numb, his hands were aching, and his face felt marked in a couple of places. Maybe Denny was right, he told himself. Perhaps the time was right for a fast move to Toronto. Or Ultima Thule.

Argentina wheeled the convertible into the parking area beside the tall new Maison Radio-Canada. Masterson and Baril had been singing "Tenor and Baritone" all the way down the Boulevard, rehearsing their act. The truth was, the premier was a little high, having put away two double scotches before lunch and a whole bottle of wine during.

With the engine dead, Baril reached for his door handle when Argentina said, "One moment, Mr. Premier." She was fumbling in her giant handbag on the floor beside her. She brought out a chrome flask. "A little cough medicine to help the performance. And so we don't lose that lovely glow."

Baril accepted the large capful she poured, raised it and said, "You think of everything, Miss Carr. Will it always be this way?"

"*Santé, monsieur*," she said and watched him drink it down.

She had closed the flask and put it back in her bag when Masterson said, "Don't I get any?"

"Yes, why not see what the boys in the back seat will have?" Bosco said.

Argentina feigned beautiful embarrassment as she fumbled in her bag and brought out the second, identical flask, the one with the undoctored brandy. "I don't know what I was thinking of," she said.

By the time the two of them had taken slow drinks, Baril's head was beginning to sag. "Don't know wassa matter..."

"That's all right. You just put your head back," Argentina said soothingly. "Plenty of time."

Baril's eyes closed and his head turned, one cheek on the leather upholstery.

Masterson was staring at him, his eyes filling with apprehension. " He's going to be very mad when he wakes up," he said. "We must be crazy." Until now, everything had been harmless. But now they had committed a crime, they had drugged the premier of the province.

"Don't be silly," Bosco said, climbing out of the car. "Everything is working like a charm. Quickly, help me put up the top."

From his car across the lot, John Keeley and Debbie Thielmanns watched the whole scene. They had arrived early and, seeing the convertible pull in, had decided to let the official party enter the building before approaching Bosco with their tape. Debbie said, "They've put him to sleep."

"I don't believe it," Keeley said.

"What do we do?"

The convertible was enclosed now, and driving at speed from the parking lot. Keeley started his car. "I don't know. I've got to follow them. I've got to find out what Bosco is trying to do."

The farm had never been a success for any of its owners down through the years. Situated on high rocky ground a couple of miles from Lake Massawippi, its paint-peeling clapboard walls and tiny windows presented a dismal appearance to visitors approaching along the narrow, pine-lined dirt road.

The convertible was parked in the yard now, the party inside, and Masterson had not stopped moaning. "This is going to blow up in our faces," he said, looking out one of the windows, afraid to face Baril who had come round but was sitting head in hands, claiming to be sick.

"Dennis," Argentina said, "will you shut up?"

"Yeah, come on, Den. Give it a rest."

"It isn't too late. We can apologize and drive Mr. Baril back to Montreal. He'll let us off easy if we do that."

"The singer is right," Baril said through his hands. "Any other way, I'll throw the book at you."

"You aren't going to do anything, Yves," Latourelle said. "By the time I go on television and expose your takeover document, you'll be out of a job. The moderate wing of the party will take over again, and we'll be laughing."

"That's naive," Masterson said. " A hundred things can go wrong. And even if it all works, we'll have made an enemy of this man. He's got friends, powerful friends. He'll never let us walk away from this."

Baril looked up. His eyes were black pits. "You really should listen to him, Bosco."

Eloise Carpentier said, "The answer is to kill the bastard. Right now. Then at least we'll have done some good." She went to a cupboard, opened it, and took down a rifle. "This is loaded."

Latourelle started toward her. "I told you, Eloise, no violence."

But Argentina stopped him, whispered to him. "The rifle is a good idea, Bosco. You and I have to go back to the city. And Denny is weak. The rifle will keep Baril quiet."

Latourelle hesitated. Then he said, "All right. We're leaving now. Eloise, you keep him quiet. And Dennis, keep your cool. You're in this now and the only way out is to see it through and come out the other side. Yves, there's steak in the kitchen, good wine, your brand of cognac. Relax, get happy, nobody wants to hurt you."

Baril's laugh was bitter. "No, you just want to end my career and you'd like me to hold still."

In Montreal that night nobody talked of anything but the kidnapping. Special editions of the daily paper were on the streets. All four television channels had gone over to continuous emergency programming. The police were keeping quiet, but the names of Bosco Latourelle, Dennis Masterson and Argentina Carr were being used. They had taken the premier away in their car and none had been seen since. Had underworld forces or some political activist unit snatched the lot?

And what about the bodyguards? Three of them were badly beaten in the parking lot and eyewitnesses said there had been at least seven men in the fight.

Then, at nine o'clock, the real bombshell exploded. There, on all screens simultaneously, was Bosco Latourelle, explaining that he had arranged the kidnapping, that Baril was alive and well and would remain so, but that his place of detention could not be revealed until an opportunity was provided for him to publicize the premier's secret plan for a takeover after the referendum. And he was ready to prove the charge with documentary evidence. Nor would he say where Baril was being held until moderate politicians -- and he named a couple -- would agree to step forward and put the party platform back in order.

At The Ninety-Seven club as elsewhere, the patrons were watching the telecast in tense silence. Johnny Fist sat at the bar, raising a glass of bourbon to bruised lips. Dallas could not even bring his eyes back to his interrupted chess game.

Latourelle had just read the incriminating document and one of the moderate politicians, quickly and triumphantly on hand, had verified its authenticity.   Dallas said, "Can you believe a thing like that, Johnny? It's fantastic. A private army, concentration camps in the Laurentians -- they were going to take over."

"I believe it," Johnny said. "And I suggest you believe it."

Somebody eased onto the stool beside him. It was Lucien Lacombe in his cheap dark suit, and he was reading the bruises on Jonathan's face. "Been in a fight?"

"A disagreement. Nothing serious." They both looked at Dallas. He took the hint and moved down the bar.

"I heard it was a war," Lucien said.

"Who says?"

"The three guys you hammered." The detective nodded silently. "I'd give anything to have seen it. How'd you manage the three of them?"

"I still don't know what you're talking about, old friend."

Lacombe turned over one of the bigger man's hands, saw the swollen knuckles. "That won't help you catching a baseball," he said.

"The ball team's pretty far from my mind at the moment, Lucy."

Lacombe stared at the television for half a minute. Then he said, "That's what I can't understand. Why'd you get mixed up in a thing like this? You've got this club. We've got the ball team all summer. The fun we have -- it's so sweet. And what's it matter what these stupid bastards do at the parliament buildings? Or who ends up in charge? Nothing would change for us. We could go on just the same."

Jonathan thought about that. He knew the answer but he did not want to say it to his friend. Lacombe waited and then sighed.

"I knew it was you as soon as they described the man in the fight. But they don't know your identity yet. So I'm giving you till tomorrow afternoon, Johnny. Pack your stuff, take your money, and run. Go somewhere you can't be extradited. Otherwise you come back here and those guys are going to hurt you."

"Thanks, Lucy. I appreciate the warning."

Lacombe slid off the stool. "I still don't see why you did it."

"I know you don't, old friend." Jonathan put an arm around Lucien's shoulder and hugged him hard, the way they did when one of them got the hit that drove in the winning runs. "And you will never see it the way I do. Because I'm English and you're French."

Lacombe left the club and Jonathan sat alone at the bar, staring at the television screen, wondering what to do. How the hell could he flee the country and leave his life here? The intention had been to stay and brazen it out, backed by the moderate politicians. But now, with the beaten bodyguards somewhere in the city brooding about the big stranger who had taken them apart, it seemed a different ballgame. Jonathan listened to Latourelle on the TV, wishing he would tell him how to play it now. But Bosco was indulging in abstract political rhetoric and he appeared quite pleased with himself.

Down in old Montreal, they were watching at Le Big Bang too; Tancrede Falardeau, his waiters, his musicians, his customers. No jazz tonight -- music would have sounded inappropriate. The little girl from Detroit he had hired, Debbie Thielmanns, had been hovering around all evening, looking as if she had been shortchanged at the bar and was trying to psych herself up to complain. Falardeau had too much on his mind to consider her but now here she was, confronting him.

"Tancrede, can I talk to you?"

"Sure, go ahead."

"In your office?"

"O.K." He led the way out of the dim club and into the bright atmosphere of filing cabinets, typewriters, and a crowded bulletin board. "What is it?"

"It's about this kidnapping." Debbie paused.

Falardeau said nothing.

"Johnny and I happened to see the whole thing. You'll never believe it." And she went on to describe the events up to and including their encounter on the dirt road with Bosco and Argentina as they drove down from the farm. Keeley's adman friend had levelled with them and asked him not to say anything for 24 hours, claiming this was all the time he needed.

"Then why are you telling me?" Tancrede asked.

The girl's face looked older now, and harder. "Because I've been part of the movement. I know what it's like to try to fight the establishment and turn things around. I think Baril has the right idea. If he wants Quebec for the French, he has to take it. They'll never get it by negotiation."

Tancrede almost smiled. "What sort of revolutionaries were you involved with?"

"The Weathermen," Debbie said. "In Detroit, and out on the Coast for a while after they killed my friend."

"Who killed your friend?"

"The FBI. They shot him in his bed. Because he was with the movement. And because he was black."

"Well, right now," Tancrede said softly, "we don't have that situation here. What we have is a politician, not much different from the other ones, trying to take a shortcut to power. Because he knows he can't get it any other way."

"What does that mean?"

"That Baril is no idealist working for the benefit of the French-speaking population. He's out for himself."

"So you won't call the police?"

"Why don't you call them?" Tancrede had, in fact, been thinking of blowing the whistle, saying Eloise had been coerced by Latourelle.

"They'd believe you better than me." Debbie's eyes shifted. "Besides, I don't like dealing with the fuzz."

The door opened and John Keeley looked in. He sensed from the abrupt silence what had been going on. He came in and closed the door. "You told him."

"Yes, I did. If he doesn't call the police, I will."

Keeley advanced on her. "No way, Debbie. We promised Bosco."

Debbie Thielmanns always carried a large denim shoulder bag. Now her hand flashed into it, and came out with a snubnosed pistol which she levelled at Keeley. "Don't look so surprised, John," she said. "I told you about it and you put it in our song. Go ahead, Tancrede," she added. "Dial. Tell them Latourelle is holding Baril at Eloise Carpentier's farm. Johnny can tell you the way."

"I know where it is," Tancrede almost whispered.

"Then call!"

"In a minute. Maybe. I haven't made up my mind yet."

At the farm, Baril was on his feet, walking around. Masterson was lying on the sofa, his eyes closed. Eloise was sitting crosslegged on a table, the rifle across her knees. The television set was on and they, like almost everyone else in Quebec, were watching Bosco Latourelle make his astonishing accusation.

Eloise said, "Wake up, Dennis, I have to go to the john." She got off the table, handed Masterson the rifle as he sat up, and said, "Never mind what Bosco said. If he makes a move, blow his head off."

When they were alone, Baril turned to Masterson and said, "We don't have much time. Listen. You're the only sane man here. Believe me, *you* are not in trouble. I've heard you doing everything you can to dissuade Latourelle. It isn't too late. Let me go and your future is guaranteed in Quebec, whatever happens politically."

"How can I let you go? There's no car. You're miles from a road."

"Just give me the rifle. I'll find my way out. Quickly -- there's no time."

Masterson wavered. How in hell had he gotten into this? Argentina was right, they'd never accept him in Toronto. And the public would never again believe in him as a singer of romantic ballads. He was a kidnapper now, a desperado.

"Come on, Dennis.   One singer to another."   Baril grinned.   "Tenor and baritone."

Masterson blocked out his thought processes.   He handed over the rifle.   Baril had time barely to heft it in his hands when the door opened and Eloise Carpentier walked in, carrying three opened bottles of soft drink.

Baril swung round and fired.   The sound in the room was deafening.   Eloise was thrown back against the door frame, the bottles caroming off the wall and falling to the floor where they rolled and lay, spilling and foaming.   Blood gushed from her chest.

"Good Christ, no!" Masterson screamed as Baril stepped over to the girl, cranking another bullet into the chamber.   He hung the barrel straight down and shot her again in the head.

Masterson was weeping so hard he could not answer when Baril asked about a telephone.   Baril found it himself and began dialing.

The police, having been called by Tancrede Falardeau, were on their way to investigate the farm when the confirming message came in.   Baril was free and in charge.   Other calls were made and the premier's private bodyguards got onto the highway.

The police arrived first, saw the dead girl, interviewed Baril briefly, then turned to the silent Masterson, who seemed to be in shock.   "Is this the brave kidnapper?"

"He's all right.   He's with me now," Baril said.

When his fleet of bodyguards arrived, Baril sent the police away. He would drive back to Montreal himself, with his cortege, free and in triumph.   As the blue-and-white vehicles left, the premier took Masterson into a bedroom.

"Listen, my boy.   Listen.   Can you hear me?"

Masterson nodded and mumbled something.

"Take this.   It's all the money I have on me.   Three hundred dollars.   Here are the keys to the black limousine. Take it and drive.   Go into Ontario.   I can protect you legally here, but I'm not sure about some of these hotheads of mine. Stay out of sight for a few weeks.   Then call me and we'll set up something permanent for you.   Got that?"

"Mr. Baril, I really haven't -- "

"Not now. There's no time. Just go!"

Masterson left the farmhouse, stumbling into the cool night, almost falling off the porch. He found the black limousine, got in under the eyes of the watchful men, started up, and drove away haltingly. The car smelled new inside. Was all this really happening to him? Was this really the end of it?

Back on the porch, Yves Baril waited until the limousine was on the dirt road. Then he hurried and spoke to his biggest bodyguard, a crew-cut man with a smashed face.

"Catch that bastard and kill him," he said flatly. "He stole my money and my car."

The appearance of Yves Baril on television side by side with Bosco Latourelle was a media coup that newsmen believed would never be surpassed in Canada. Many people said that the whole thing was a put-up job, an elaborate public-relations dodge to convince the part of the population who suspected the premier's motives and methods that he was really a good guy.

Anyway, here they were, flanking each other on the flickering screen, kidnapper and victim. Latourelle made his accusation face to face and then he held up the memorandum which outlined the 51-49 percent takeover plan. Baril listened to it all, nodding encouragement to Bosco as he spun it out. Then he said,

"My old friend, if only you'd come to me with that piece of paper. You are holding one of several scenarios which I and my advisory committee worked out as possible courses of action, post referendum. We considered every possibility, everything that could take place. It goes without saying we rejected that particular scenario out of hand. As we rejected several others."

"Mr. Premier, that isn't the information I was given."

"Then you were given incorrect information." And now Baril turned to the camera and looked down the lens. "In any case, my promise to all Quebecers now, my absolute guarantee, is that after next week's referendum we will only consider setting up a separate Quebec if the vote is at least 85 percent in favor."

Bosco said, "Well, you heard him, ladies and gentlemen. I'm sure, after all that has happened, you'll be on your guard."

The politician had the last word. "And I'd just like to say, Bosco, that I intend to see no charges are pressed against you and your associates in this action. Some would call it a crime. I see it as the efforts of a group of public-spirited citizens to head off what they sincerely but mistakenly believed to be an undemocratic action. In truth, we are on the same side. I only regret the deaths of the young woman and the young man at the farmhouse who made the mistake of holding me at gunpoint and were accidentally killed during my release."

Watching in The Ninety-Seven, Jonathan Fitzwilliam was shaken. Woman and man killed at the farmhouse? That must have been Eloise and Dennis. Dennis!

He went up the iron stairs to his apartment and after some trouble got through to Lucien Lacombe. Lucien had the information. It was secret under threat of dismissal, but everybody was whispering and he was ready to tell his friend. Baril got a rifle somehow and shot the girl. Then he let Dennis drive away in a car and sent his boys to kill him.

There was a lot of silence now on the line. The detective coughed. "Are you still going to cut out, Johnny? Baril said you're off the hook legally. But those three guys may still try to get you in an alley."

"The three guys don't concern me," Fitzwilliam said.

"What, then?"

Johnny's thoughts were not very admirable but he was stuck with them. It was sinking in that his best friend was also the only one who knew he had thrown Linda Lennox off a roof. Dennis's death left him feeling free and lonely at the same time. He said, "I've got to decide whether I'm supposed to do something about Mr. Baril."

Leaving the television studio with Argentina beside him, Latourelle ran into the premier coming down the same corridor.

There were so many big men around Baril now he could hardly be seen. But he broke through the cordon and stepped into an alcove, drawing Bosco and the girl in with him.

"That was good brandy, Miss Carr," he said gleefully. "Where do you get that stuff?" he was exuberant, wide-eyed as a child on Halloween.

"I should have given you the whole flask," Argentina said bitterly. "It would have killed you."

"Save it for yourself, dear. You may need it."

Bosco put his arm around Argentina. He said, "Well, we won anyway. You came out smelling like a rose, Yves, but at least you can't take the province on a moonlight flit after the referendum."

"No, not next week." Baril's grin widened. "But there's plenty of time. You haven't stopped me, Bosco. You've only delayed me. I'll be back on the track soon enough. And listen, old friend --" his smile died like a lamp going off " -- once Quebec finally separates, you'd better get onto Highway 401 that same day and drive to Ontario as fast as you can. Because if you try to live in my country, you'll have no advertising agency. You'll be lucky if you're allowed to sweep streets in Rimouski."

Bosco and Argentina went to her place, where they drank the brandy in the second flask and finished the bottle it had been filled from. Then, just before they went to bed, Latourelle said, "Be sure you spill out the flask with the dope in it. You don't want anyone drinking it by mistake."

Argentina said, "Right," and went into the kitchen to attend to it. But she thought for a minute and then stored the flask of doctored brandy, still almost full, on a high shelf.

She kept waking during the night, her mind full of Eloise, whom she never much liked, and of Dennis, whom she admired in spite of his weakness. And she knew Bosco Latourelle was thinking of his dead friends too, because she heard him quietly weeping.

Alfred Hitchcock Mystery Magazine, June, 1978

THE LAST ACT
WAS DEADLY

The rooming house stuck away on a back street in Brighton had nothing going for it, not even a view of the sea. But it served meals all day, something rare for English eating places, and the front door had a homely appeal, so Eric Tennyson walked under the enamelled sign advertising "Bed and Breakfast," pushed open the lace-curtained door, and went inside.

He knew it was a good choice the minute he entered the vestibule. The cooking smells, the fringe of tattered carpet meeting a crust of worn linoleum, the thickly overpainted woodwork, and the patterned wallpaper populated with framed faded photographs all reminded him of the house he had grown up in back in Vermont. He chose a table in the empty dining room and sat down on a hard caneback chair. The table, covered with a flowered cloth, teetered under his elbows.

A tall grey woman in a black-and-white uniform under a thin cardigan came into the room and stood over him with tiny fists clenched against her chest. She looked at him fondly and Tennyson was ready to be asked if he had done his homework and to get his skates off the kitchen floor. He glanced at the menu and ordered cod and chips.

"Do you want that with bread and butter and a cup to tea? You get cod-and-chips-and-bread-and-butter-and-a-cup-of-tea, 85 pence."

"Lovely," Tennyson said. "I'll have that." He had been long enough in London to learn to say "lovely."

The food came and the crisp brown slabs of breaded fish were quite simply the most delicious he had ever tasted. He soaked on the vinegar and salt, took a bite from a triangle of buttered bread, slurped a swallow of strong tea, and began really to enjoy himself.

It was a perfect example of the rewards that can come from obeying an impulse. The idea of taking this day-trip to Brighton had only occurred to him at breakfast. The sky was clear, Capital Radio said no rain all day, and his writing schedule was up to date, so he was free to walk to Wimbledon Station, take a train to Clapham Junction, and transfer there to the Brighton express. One hour later he was at the seaside -- in June, before the main press of tourists.

Tennyson could hardly stop congratulating himself. His main venture during the afternoon had been a walk along the cliffs to the village of Rottingdean, three miles away. Here he drank lager in a couple of pubs, wandered the tidy streets, and spent an hour in and around a church that dated back to the Saxons.

Then he bussed back to Brighton and roamed the Palace Pier, dropping pennies into the sweeper machines, hoping to cause a penny avalanche over one of the ledges, eating licorice allsorts from a bag in his pocket, lying in a deck chair with his face to the sun.

He even entered the little toy house of Eva Montenegro, the famous Romany clairvoyant, and paid £3 to have his fortune told. She sat opposite him, grainy-faced and clear-eyed, warning him not to put his hands where she had just spilled her tea. Then she nattered on with a stream of consciousness that could have been about him, reading his reactions he supposed, shaping her talk according to the way his shrugs or eyebrows guided her.

One thing she said surprised and pleased him. "You do some writing -- you are a clerk?"

"Not a clerk. I do write."

"Ah. You will write a good story. A big story will be a big success."

Tennyson wandered on the seafront afterwards with eyes half closed, his mind floating on her prediction. The dramatic society in Wimbledon had agreed to perform his play in the fall. It was only an amateur group, to be sure, and there would be no money in it. But he didn't require money. What he craved was success and here was the gypsy telling him he would have it.

Empty plates were taken away, the woman brought him a dish of apple pie with hot custard, and the delightful supper went on.

Then everything crashed as Tennyson looked up through the doorway into the vestibule and saw Meredith Morgan. He wanted to hide beneath the table. Of all people -- the one member of the Hartfield Dramatic Society who really put him off -- and here she was, not ten feet away. Fortunately, she had not seen him yet.

And what was this? She set a large suitcase at her feet and, raising her voice, she called straight ahead into the body of the house, "Hello? Anybody is at home, yes?"

Tennyson stopped tasting what he was eating. The accent was pure German, strong and true. Could it be Meredith Morgan's continental double? No, it was herself -- it had to be. He had seen her only last week at a cast reading.

An invisible landlord made terms for a single room and Tennyson could hear Meredith hissing her stagey German as she signed the book. Then she reappeared beyond the dining-room doorway to claim her suitcase and Tennyson turned his head hard away. When he looked again, she was gone and he heard footsteps on a stairway.

There was absolutely no doubt in his mind that this was the Morgan girl and here she was in Brighton pretending to be a German tourist. Tennyson was intrigued now that the immediate danger of having to spend time with her was past. Not that there was much chance of her trapping and boring him; she was surely less anxious to meet him than he was to meet her.

But what was she up to? Tennyson finished his pie, scraping the last of the yellow custard from the dish, and considered the possibilities. The most preposterous occurred to him first. She was some sort of a spy. But that made no sense at all. If she did some work for M15 or whoever, she might end up in Berlin playing the part of a German. But in Brighton?

Perhaps it was a romantic involvement. She had a boy friend who, for some reason, thought she was from Germany

and she was here for a liaison, carrying on the charade. But
Meredith with a boyfriend, secret of otherwise, was hard to
swallow. She was the least-liked individual in the Hartfield, by
both men and women, and she took no pains to make herself
more appealing.

Then Tennyson thought of a far-fetched notion that
might explain her behavior. Somewhere down the road the
Society was going to do a play in which there was a female part
demanding a German accent. Meredith wanted the role so she
had come here to live for a few days as a German, getting
dialect practice all day long. Possible but, on second thought,
doubtful. She could do this in London -- no need to come to
Brighton.

Tennyson paid for his supper and went outside. He had
gone a dozen paces down the cobbled lane when the impulse
hit him and he returned, entering a pub opposite the rooming
house, ordering a pint at the bar, and taking it to a table near
the front window. He sat down and began watching the
painted doorway. It had become very important for him to
learn why Meredith Morgan was in Brighton, pretending to be
Marlene Dietrich.

As he drank his beer, Tennyson remembered his early
days in England, over a year ago. He had settled in Wimbledon
simply because the name of the place meant something to him
from years of following tennis. And it had lots of Underground
and British Rail trains to and from London. Since his aim in life
was to become a successful playwright, now that he was
financially independent for a few years thanks to a state lottery
win, it made sense for Tennyson to become involved with a
theatrical group. The West End was beyond him at present, so
it had to be an amateur society.

That was how he came to seek out the Hartfield. They
were a friendly group and apparently happy to accept a good-
looking, 28-year-old American, although his accent certainly
did not blend with theirs onstage. Now, after playing small parts
in three productions, Tennyson had made the breakthrough
he was seeking; they were going to do his play, *Call It Love*, as
their September production. It was a romantic comedy, set in
Wimbledon, with a tennis background.

As a group, the Hartfield could only be called jovial. They kidded Tennyson about some of his pronunciations, praised his forceful acting style, and waved to him on the street. He was on a cheek-kissing basis with most of the girls. But not with Meredith Morgan. At first, he took the conversational initiative with her and attributed her monosyllabic replies to shyness but after a while he tired of it and stopped speaking to her -- let her make the effort.

Onstage, at the close of one play, he found himself placed next to her in the curtain-call lineup. Automatically, as they bowed, he took the hand of the person on either side of him. Meredith's hand, cold and claw-like, tore itself free and he did not touch her again.

There was movement in the doorway across the street. Meredith emerged dressed in shades of blue--a tight T-shirt, short skirt, and plastic boots. This was nothing like what she wore back in Wimbledon and Tennyson felt a quickening of his heartbeat as he finished his beer and left the pub.

She turned left at the main road and wandered down the hill towards the seafront. It was becoming dark and strings of lights sparkled along the broad walk. Beyond, the English Channel, flat on this calm night, was fading to black. Tennyson was not surprised to see pedestrians, men and women, turning to look at the attractive girl in blue as they passed her.

This new style of hers puzzled Tennyson as much as anything, because at rehearsals Meredith was a mouse. His impression of her there, whenever he bothered to look, was of furtive brown eyes, unwashed short brown hair, hungry cheeks, and sloping posture, usually with an inch or two of unstitched hem at the bottom of her skirts.

Now she swaggered ahead of him, swinging a red plastic handbag, trailing her fingertips on building fronts -- arrogant, provocative. Tennyson worked to control his breathing as he followed her into a pub called The Cutlass. He used his head and came in right after her, reasoning that given time she would be seated and possibly watching the door.

He was able to watch her order a gin and tonic and carry it to a table in an alcove. Tennyson brought his beer with him and sat on the other side of the upholstered parapet where he could see and hear the girl without being seen, unless she turned fully around.

The action was not long in starting. Meredith finished her drink quickly and set down the empty glass. A middle-aged man, heavy-set and grey-headed, took his own glass and reached for hers. "Same again, love?" he said. His accent was from somewhere up north.

"Thank you, you are very kind. It is gin and tonic."

He returned with the refills and hers looked like a double. "Cheers, love," he said, and after they drank he went on, "Well then, how do you like our country?"

"I am only here one day but it is very good. The people are so friendly."

"Famous for it," the man said. "And where's home?"

"I come from Hamburg. That is in Germany."

"I know where Hamburg is."

"Ah, you have been there?"

"Yes, but not to stay. I flew over in a Lancaster, long before you were born. All I saw was a lot of fires burning." He was well away on the beer and the effect of it could be heard in his voice.

Meredith paused, looking at her hands. Then she said, "It was, as you say, before I was born. But I find it hard to believe that our people could be enemies."

"My dear," the man said, "you are not going to find *anybody* to be *your* enemy."

She laughed at that and their foreheads almost touched as they leaned close together. Tennyson listened to a lot more of the same and then, when the two of them left the pub, he was relieved. The situation was obvious enough; the Morgan girl was one of these shy people who like to get away and play games under the protection of an assumed identity. So be it, and more power to her. Anyway, Tennyson had to hurry to get a late train back to London.

Next day, he worked all morning at his romantic comedy. Now that the group had agreed to perform the play, Tennyson was scared to death; it was simply not good enough. At half past one, he went out to his local for a pint and some food, picking up a newspaper on the way. He took a Ploughman to his favorite corner table and began enjoying the tangy cheddar cheese, pickled onion, and crusty bread and butter washed down with cool lager.

Then he saw the photograph on page three and the food went sour in his mouth. It looked a lot like the man who was buying drinks for Meredith Morgan last night. But it was the caption under the photograph that shook Tennyson --

BRIGHTON VISITOR STABBED TO DEATH

He read the story and learned the Leeds businessman had been found a few yards from the entrance to a culvert under one of the piers, dead of multiple stab wounds. Robbery was not a motive -- he still had his money.

Tennyson stopped reading and stopped eating. He had to make a decision. The obvious thing to do was to go to the police. But there were unanswered questions that impeded him. First, what if the girl was not Meredith? He was ninety-eight percent sure, but that left a devilish two percent.

Worse still, what if it was her, and the man had been bushwhacked after he left her? By setting the police on her, Tennyson would be causing the girl all kinds of trouble for nothing.

For nothing? She might be able to tell the police something that would help them find the killer. That was worth a little inconvenience. Tennyson tossed that problem back and forth in his mind till three o'clock closing, by which time he was three pints further along on the day's high, but no closer to a solution on Morgan.

So he decided to visit the girl and give her a chance to explain. In German or otherwise. He left the pub and wandered on down past Ely's display windows, past the station, and on along the Broadway to the entrance to Meredith's flat. Months ago, after a rehearsal, they had dropped her here from a crowded jolly car and Meredith Morgan, typically, had ducked out with a glum goodnight.

Later that evening, over brandy at his flat, Tennyson had gotten Tony Bastable, the director, to open up about Meredith. Tony was an accountant in real life, a theatrical man only in his spare time. He was one of a type who abound in England, actors with enough talent to be only a shade or two below the Oliviers and Richardsons but who can not make it in a professional system that is grossly overcrowded. So they teach school or balance books and, making it look very easy, put on in church halls productions of a quality to stun visitors from across the Atlantic.

That night he had sat with his thin legs crossed at the ankles, his pink face wreathed in a beatific smile, sipping his brandy and talking of wartime years in India where he and a group of Air Force friends performed Shakespeare for a rajah. Then, prompted by Tennyson, he talked about Meredith Morgan.

She had been a rich girl once. She actually attended Roedean, which explained the plummy accent when she deigned to speak. Then, when she was around eighteen years old, her father managed to pull the set down around her ears.

What Mr. Morgan did was to embezzle money from his stockbroking firm in the city. The reason he stole was to meet gambling debts incurred in a casino in Grosvenor Square. One thing they frown upon in the City of London is embezzling. Not done. So Meredith's father locked himself in an air-tight room wherein he opened the gas valves without igniting a flame. Worse, he persuaded Meredith's mother to join him in this one-way ramble to eternity.

It was then that their daughter's nickname of "Merry" became permanently inappropriate. She stopped attending the prestigious private school, stopped smiling, stopped going out of the house, even stopped eating for quite a while.

It was tough going for a couple of years and, in the end, all Meredith Morgan could afford to offer the world was the cold, quiet robot so thoughtfully tolerated by the Hartfield Dramatic Society.

"Why does she go on with the acting then?" Tennyson asked.

"I suppose because she was a member before the fall," Tony said. "And today, it's her one avenue to the world."

Now, standing on the Broadway outside her door with the big red busses grumbling by and people queuing at the fruit stall in the lane, Tennyson wondered whether to ring Meredith's bell. Go ahead, he told himself. She's at work, she won't answer.

He stepped into the entrance and pressed the button. There was a click from above and the door fell ajar. Tennyson shrugged away a chilly, instinctive warning and went inside. A crumbling flight of steps led upward into a thick smell of animals and soup and rising damp. He trudged upwards, hearing a door creak open above him.

Meredith met him on the landing dressed in threadbare slacks and a sweater coated with cat hairs. A pair of ripe quilted slippers bloomed on her bare feet. "Oh, hello. Have I missed a rehearsal?"

"No. I was just walking by . There's something I have to ask you about -- to settle my mind."

She drew the door almost shut behind her and stood small, the way she did onstage, with those thin arms hanging lifeless behind her back. She was not going to ask him in.

"Can we go inside?" Tennyson asked. "Just for a minute, I can't stay."

She led him in then. Tennyson was not able to look but he received an impression of twisted bedclothes, newspapers and magazines on the floor, used cotton swabs on a dresser, a mottled grey washbasin, and a pot full of something brown on top of a cooker. From the midst of all this, a heavy-eyed cat watched him with contempt.

Meredith said distantly, "I'm not well today. I couldn't go to work."

Not knowing where to begin, Tennyson said, "Where do you work?"

"The Education Authority, typing and filing. It's worth it being a civil servant; they can't sack you." Her tone of voice, the surroundings, cried out with self-pity.

Now, beyond her in a corner beside the bed, Tennyson saw the suitcase. Its shape and color, even the type of handle, identified it positively as the one he had seen in the Brighton vestibule. This made up his mind.

"Ach zo," he said thickly, "did ve haf a gut time by der zee?"

He saw no change in her but he felt a new current in the room, a slightly higher vibration. "Sorry, I didn't catch that."

"Meredith," he said, "I saw you check into that rooming house in Brighton. I heard you using a German accent, quite a good one. And I saw you pick up that man in the pub."

"What has any of that got to do with you?" It was her first speech with any fiber in it.

"Just that I saw his picture in the paper today. Somebody murdered him, Meredith. And since I know about it, and you haven't denied you were with him, I'm going to have to decide what to do with what I know."

She walked past him into the kitchen area and Tennyson had a terrible feeling she was going to offer him a cup of something. Even the thought of the utensils in this place... But she turned and said, "You'll go to the police."

"I don't want to. I don't want to make trouble for you. But that was very suspicious behavior."

"I know." She backed against the counter and turned her face in profile, and he wondered how this sad wraith had converted herself into yesterday's provocative tourist. "You know how shy I am, I can't help it. The only way I can let go is to become somebody else. That's what you saw in Brighton."

"But the murdered man. I'm right, he was your companion, wasn't he?" Her silence was enough. "So what happened? You did kill him, didn't you? I can tell."

Meredith's face crumpled and she wept like a child. Bits of explanation came through. "It was never like that before. He was cruel. He didn't want to make love, he wanted to hurt me. I had no choice. I had to defend myself."

"But he was stabbed. Do you carry a knife?"

"It was his knife. He was forcing me, on the beach by that terrible sewer. I pretended to cooperate and when he wasn't alert I grabbed the knife."

It could have been true and it could just as well not have been. But for a moment or two, Tennyson was touched by something in the girl's fierce loneliness. He remembered Tony Bastable's outline of her tragic background and saw her now as the bereaved teenager whose parents had taken the easy way out. He was not about to add to her misery.

"All right," he said, "all right, don't cry. I'm not going to the police." He found himself putting an arm around her shoulder and felt her stiffen and move away. "It's all over and done with anyway. We can't bring him back."

So Eric Tennyson took his secret away with him and carried it through an exciting summer, during which rehearsals for his play got under way. But his imagination would not let go of the material, and he found himself working it into an outline for a drama that the society might want to stage at a later date. In the play, a shy girl from an amateur theatrical group makes regular trips to seaside resorts, assumes another character, picks up interested men, and then stabs them to death.

It was during the final week of rehearsals for his romantic comedy that Tennyson stumbled on an example of life imitating art that shook him to the ground. He was sitting alone in the dressing-room backstage at Marlborough Hall, waiting for a lighting adjustment to be made. Bored, he picked up a copy of an old newspaper left there months ago by a member of some other company using the hall. The headline on page two caught his eye.

BRIGHTON STABBING FITS PATTERN

He read on and learned that the police had linked the murder of the Leeds businessman with two others committed within the year at other resorts along the coast -- Bournemouth and Ramsgate. They were working on the theory that someone connected with yachting or coastal fishing was involved.

Tennyson tore the page from the musty tabloid, folded it small, and tucked it into a pocket. He was dizzy with apprehension and guilt. He should have gone to the police right away. How would he justify himself if he called them now, months after the fact? Still, she had not been active again -- if, in fact, the other cases had to do with her at all. She had admitted the first killing, in self-defense, she said. The police might be wrong in linking all three.

Tennyson was looking glumly at the floor when Tony Bastable put his ruby face through the doorway. "Come along, author. You're wanted onstage." Eric had given himself a small part in his own play, to share the praise or the blame, whichever it might be.

He followed the director up the narrow steps and was able to lose himself in the make-believe action, to put off the troublesome responsibility, at least until he could talk to Meredith Morgan again.

But she was elusive during play week, vanishing after each performance, so he decided to show her the clipping at the cast party on the Saturday following closing night. It was a triumphant week for Tennyson because the audiences loved the play. A woman with West End connections asked him for a copy of the script and said she was sending it to a chap who was always looking for comedies. Tony Bastable was ebullient and asked Tennyson what else he could give them. Eric said he had something on the fire, a thriller, and promised to show Tony an outline.

By party night, the euphoria had faded enough for Tennyson to be concerned again about the secret he was carrying. He waited for Meredith to show and when midnight arrived without her, he asked around. One of the cattier girls rolled her eyes at a friend and said, "She must have gone off on one of her trips"

"Trips?"

"Yes, didn't you know? Meredith is a loner. She saves her money and then sneaks off someplace were she can get drunk and let her hair down."

Tennyson did know. And his knowledge went further than theirs. If Meredith Morgan was about to do her thing again, he, Eric Tennyson, would be morally if not legally guilty of aiding and abetting.

He left the party and walked to Meredith's rooming house. The idea of calling the police still did not appeal to him. He was terribly late with his information and the story would be hard to follow. His best bet would be to follow the girl and head her off.

His fears were realized when she did not answer repeated rings of the bell and heavy pounding on the door. But a tiny bird of a woman did appear from another doorway on the ground floor. She was in a wheelchair and held a large cat on her lap. Tennyson knew that contemptuous look -- it was Meredith's cat.

"Good evening," he said, putting on his brightest and best transatlantic voice. "I'm sorry to trouble you. I know Meredith Morgan has gone away, but she has a few pages of script in her flat and we need them for a reading. I wonder if I could just dart up and fetch them?"

"You're the lad who wrote the play."

"Yes I am."

"I didn't go. I can't go anywhere. Congratulations, I heard it was smashing."

"Well, thank you." It was a chance, so Tennyson said, "Did Meredith say where she was going this time?"

"Never. That girl comes and goes as she pleases."

"Yes. Well then, if I might have a key..."

The landlady creaked away backwards on her giant wheels. A minute later, Tennyson was on his way up the stairs. It was a blind chance; he would have to be lucky. There were no travel folders on view in the dismal room so he busied himself nosing about the telephone table. Here he saw a directory with a lot of numbers scribbled on the cover. One looked fresher than the others, and its four-digit prefix indicated it was outside London. Taking a chance, Tennyson picked up the phone and dialed the number.

After a few rings, a cheerful female voice answered and said, "Good evening, The Cliffs Hotel."

"I'm sorry to trouble you. I have a silly question. Could you tell me where you're located?"

The girl laughed. "Last time I looked, we were in Penzance."

The first train he could catch was out of Paddington Station at 9:30 in the morning. Tennyson settled himself for the six-hour trip west, down through Devon and into Cornwall. He knew he was being shown some of the most beautiful countryside in the world but his mind would not let him enjoy it. He had to find Meredith Morgan fast. And then he had to decide what to do with her.

Penzance, the end of the line, came up a little after half past three. A stretch of sea on the left dazzled Tennyson -- it was an indescribable blue and there was so much water he felt dizzy and had to grasp the rough train seat. There was no end to it -- the sea was freedom, the sea pulled you away from the land.

The Cliffs Hotel was only a five-minute walk from the station. Tennyson went and stood outside, not knowing what to do. Meredith would not be registered under her own name. Would she be pretending again to be German? Perhaps, but not necessarily. Even so, how could he inquire without a name?

He began to feel the pressure of time. She would probably not be in her room on a sunny Sunday afternoon. But supposing she followed her Brighton pattern and chose a pub -- Penzance had pubs on every corner.

Tennyson turned from the hotel and started walking. After all, Meredith was a visitor too. She could only have drifted down this hill and onto the main street, working up the other hill past the station. And he was in luck with English pub hours; they were all closed till six so she had to be circulating.

It was almost six o'clock when he saw her. She was standing with a man outside a pub called The Turk's Head, the red plastic bag hanging over her shoulder, her hip cocked in a coquettish pose. The man was portly, his face florid in a frame of curly grey hair.

As Tennyson watched, the pub door was opened from the inside and the couple went through, ducking their heads under the low lintel. Not wanting to waste a second, Tennyson hurried across the street and stepped down into the entry. There were two doors, the Saloon Bar and The Snug. He tried the latter and found Meredith sitting alone on an upholstered bench. Her eyes widened.

"Where's your friend?" he said.

"In the loo."

"Good." He produced the newspaper story and showed it to her. She only glanced at it. "You admitted the Brighton killing and here are the police saying it's one of a set. How do you explain that?"

The portly man was back. Meredith spoke first, her German accent sounding impeccable. "I'm sorry, I lied to you. I am not alone. This is my husband, he has found me, and I am a bad girl."

Portly gave a gallant bow. "You could never be a bad girl, my dear. Sir, you are a lucky man." He insisted on buying them drinks and departed, wishing them years of happiness, hinting they needed babies to turn their marriage to gold like his.

Alone now, Meredith lowered her voice and dropped the accent. She admitted the crimes and said, through tears, that she could not help herself. Leaning close to Tennyson, taking his arm, she was everything the Meredith back in Wimbledon was not. He found himself feeling very sorry for her while an inner voice told him they were in this together -- which, after his months of silence, was true enough.

"Look," he said during a second round of drinks, "we don't have to be Freudians to see the problems you've had to cope with. I heard about your parents' suicide and how that turned your life around."

"My life was miserable before that. They never loved me. They only loved each other. Oh, they gave me clothes and money and private schools. But that was to shut me up and keep me out of their sight." Her voice was flat.

Tapping the message out with a fingertip on the back of her hand, Tennyson said, "It can still be all right. You've got your whole life ahead of you. I know you're broke now but we can get you into some sort of psychotherapy on the National Health. Or I can pay for a specialist -- I've got money. No, listen to me. You can talk out this hostility and not have to go after older men."

"But after what I've done..."

"I've never believed in punishment for its own sake. Those men can't be brought back to life. The thing is to salvage *your* life."

He spent the night with her in her room at The Cliffs. A wind blew up and brought rain to lash the bay window, and beyond that sound breakers pulsed and crashed against the shingle beach. On an impulse, he asked her to speak to him in her German accent. She did, crooning romantic syllables in a husky voice, and he was overcome with desire for this strange, dangerous woman.

In the morning, the sky was blue again, the sea choppy under a brisk wind. Their best train to London was at four o'clock so they were left with hours to kill.

Meredith said, "Let's take a bus to Land's End. As long as we're here, it's a shame not to see it."

So they boarded a green coach and drove along winding country roads, the drystone walls ablaze with gorse in golden bloom. At Land's End, the wind was fierce and the mass of tourists headed for the safety of the hotel with its bars and lounges.

"Can we survive this hurricane?" Tennyson said, holding Meredith by both arms, finding it difficult to catch his breath.

"Don't be a coward," she said.

They walked round the hotel and crossed a dry decline to where an outcropping of eroded rock marked the southwestern tip of England. A white signpost indicated mileages to places like John O'Groats. The wind was incredible -- Tennyson had never experienced anything like it. It was more than a movement of air; it had substance, as if they were standing in the rush of an avalanche.

"A little of this goes a long way!" he shouted.

Meredith was looking around. "We're the only brave ones," she said. "I love it." She moved from his side and ventured across a sloping rock, sitting down on it, bracing her feet, then peering over at the sea. She looked back over her shoulder and he was struck by her childlike beauty. With her hair streaming flat across her cheek, she looked twelve years old.

"Come and see the color of the water!" she shouted. "It's unbelievable!"

He crept over the rock and edged to a position beside her. She was right, the water below was churned to an electric foam, boiling and reaching upward with sheets of spray.

Then her foot was kicking at his and her hand was in the small of his back and he felt himself sliding forward over the edge. In that last moment, he saw her eyes and noted that they were intent, filled with a fierce determination. And he thought of his success, of all the plays he was going to write, and there ought to be something he could do but he was head down now and screaming as he fell.

Tony Bastable was astonished and saddened by the tragedy at Land's End. Imagine old Eric being involved with Meredith like that. The American had never said anything; he didn't even seem to like the girl particularly. A faint whisper of suspicion sounded in Bastable's mind but he could not link it with anything.

As for Meredith, she had been a sad enough figure up till now. How could they possibly cope with her after this?

However, life must go on. More particularly, the life of the Hartfield Dramatic Society. Pity they had found a local playwright only to lose him after one success. Still, Tennyson had offered them his new play, so Bastable felt no qualms in rescuing it from his flat. If the outline had merit, another writer could develop it and they would have a nice newsy production, a posthumous premiere!

He settled into his armchair, stretched his legs, and began to read. Then Tony Bastable's intelligent eyes began to widen perceptively as he learned about the unloved actress who travelled to seaside resorts and killed strangers, and who was found out by a writer who pursued her, which left her with no choice but to kill him.

Ellery Queen Mystery Magazine, December, 1979

THE MYSTERY OF
THE MISSING GUY

There were three little boys lurking outside the entrance to the Covent Garden underground station. The smallest of them confronted Professor Harry Lawson as he walked past on Longacre Street. "Penny for the guy, sir?"

Lawson looked down and saw the effigy of Guy Fawkes propped against a brick wall. It was a standard sort of Guy -- an old suit knotted strategically and stuffed with rags. Beside it on the pavement was a cloth cap filling nicely with coins.

"All ready for the fifth, boys?" Lawson said. He fished ten pence from his pocket, gave it to the lad, and saw his eyes widen at the sight of the silver coin. The generous donation went with the accent -- lucky to find an American in London in November.

"Yes, sir. Thank you, sir."

Lawson walked on with the relaxed stride of a man accustomed to crossing stages in front of attentive audiences. In rhythm with his pace, he recited to himself the familiar rhyme:

> "Remember, remember the fifth of November,
> Gunpowder, treason, and plot.
> I see no reason why gunpowder treason
> Should ever be forgot."

Guy Fawkes Day was a colorful and happy event with its fireworks and bonfires and carnival atmosphere. It reminded Lawson of the Fourth of July back in his native Detroit but, typical of the English, theirs was a more theatrical affair.

He arrived a minute later at The Fallen Arches pub, entered the narrow door around the corner, and trudged up three flights of stairs past the photocopy shop to his office under the sloping roof. His wife Lola was on the telephone.

"Wait a minute," she said, "he just came in. Did you want to speak to him? No? All right, I'll tell him." She was nodding and smiling with that large beautiful face of hers as if they owned one of the first videophones.

Lawson stood in the doorway admiring his wife. Years ago she had been at least one-half of the cause of his success when he performed a magic act and she was his assistant in sheer body-stocking and sequins. Not surprising that the bookings ran out when Lola became sensitive about her weight and refused to go on stage any more. These days she limited herself to fascinating smaller groups of men as she walked down the street.

"All right, Mr. Gill," she said. "I'll see you get your pen back." She put down the phone. "That's marvellous, Praw," she said. "You go to the bank to see about extending our overdraft and you walk out with the manager's pen."

Praw Lawson reached into an inner pocket and produced a silver ballpoint pen. His flourish suggested that paper roses might sprout from the tip. "How about that," he said, using the pen to comb his thatch of red and gray hair. "He must have planted it on me." He dropped the pen on the desk beside Lola.

Professor Harry Lawson's nickname came to him years ago when the act was touring America. A carnival announcer introduced him with the words, "And now let's hear it for the Praw-fessah!" He became Praw Lawson from that day on.

"Was Mr. Gill okay about the overdraft?"

"He's given us another three months' credit. I'm a terrible risk but he loves me since I traced that girl who stole the money from the bank and then pretended to commit suicide by jumping out of a moving train."

"That was long ago," Lola Lawson said. "Who have you traced lately?"

"Your brother Al," Lawson said, peering down into the street. "Here he comes with a potted palm."

"Very funny."

"Wait."

Minutes later Lawson opened the office door, allowing his brother-in-law to struggle inside with the biggest aspidistra in the world rising from a large clay pot. "Thanks, Praw," Al said. "Look what I've got." He set down the pot with a thump that must have sent a cloud of plaster dust filtering down onto the Xerox machines in the room below.

"For heaven's sake, why?" Lawson said.

"Come on, Praw, it's just what we need."

"In this broom closet of a room?" Lola said. "If a client comes in, one of us has to go out."

"You have thirty seconds to explain why we need that vegetable," Lawson said. "Starting now."

"Because you're always looking for a place to hide the key to the petty-cash box," Al said. "I've been working on this in the coffee shop so I could surprise you. Look." He knelt and lifted the mat of artificial grass surrounding the narrow trunk. This exposed a hinged metal plate which Al lifted to reveal a metal box beneath. "I got the box at the hardware store. Isn't it neat? The key goes in here, or anything else we want to hide."

Praw Lawson watched as Lola brought the petty-cash key from the desk, dropped it into the box, closed the lid, and lowered the grass mat. "Congratulations, Al," he said. "A lot of your ideas are crazy. This one is only childish."

"Don't listen to him, Al," Lola said. "If it keeps us from being robbed, he'll say it was his idea."

Actually Lawson was more entertained than bothered by Al's eccentric imagination. Anything could happen. Like the day Lawson came in and found several ping-pong balls cut in half and taped to the wall, each one containing a tablespoon of earth and a bean sprout. Al watered them daily with an eye dropper and some of them were doing quite well.

The telephone rang and Lawson made his customary remark. "That may be the phone," he said.

Lola answered it. "Lawson Foundry," she said. The name was another of Al's ideas. In an obscure way it seemed to suggest what they did, so Praw went along with it. "Hello, Helmut. Yes, he's here." She listened. "Well, send him up." More listening. "Okay, Mr. Lawson will come down." She put down the phone. "Somebody to see you in the pub. He can't handle the stairs."

"I wish him no grief," Lawson said as he left the office, "but I hope he's an oil sheik and has lost his harem."

Helmut Dorf was the publican of The Fallen Arches. In 1942 he had made one visit to London at the controls of a Heinkel bomber, was shot down, and spent the war in a camp. Here he learned to speak English and to like the food and the guards. When peace came, he went home, worked hard, and saved enough money to return to London where he bought the Red Lion pub and changed its name. His intention was to commemorate the historic archways destroyed in the deplorable bombing to which he was a reluctant party. Lawson had tried more than once to explain the new name's double meaning, but the Teutonic landlord lacked a sense of humor. Or perhaps he was so subtle that the joke worked best for him if he insisted on not seeing it. Either way, Lawson loved him.

"Morning, Helmut. Where's my man?"

"Corner table. The usual for you, Praw?"

"Please."

Dorf drew a pint of best bitter and Lawson carried it to the table in an alcove beside a leaded casement window. "I'm Harry Lawson," he said to the young man sitting there, looking sharp in a three-piece gray flannel suit.

"Max Trelawny," the man said. "Sorry to bring you down the stairs. It isn't bad heart or legs. It's claustrophobia. I stay at ground level and away from enclosed areas as much as possible."

"No problem. Worse places than a pub table for a meeting."

Trelawny was holding what looked like a gin and tonic. He sipped from the rim of the glass creating the narrowest possible bridge of lip for the liquor to flow across. His head was a loaf, the shape emphasized by short fine hair the color of ashes. His eyes had heavy lids above and pouches below which came together in the middle. He had a sleepy, wistful smile. "I understand you're good at finding lost people," he said.

"Or people who disappear." Lawson told quickly the story of the carnival owner who absconded with the receipts, leaving his performers stranded in Paisley. He went after him. Tracked him the length of England, and found him finally in a bar in south London. Back wages were paid and Harry Lawson moved into a new career.

"My case is a little different," Trelawny said. "It isn't a person who's missing. It's a suit."

The Praw looked baffled.

"Let me explain," Trelawny said. "The suit in question is an old garment of mine, brown tweed with a bit of yellow in it. Patch pockets. Belt in the back. Horrible, I know -- I haven't worn it in years. So I came home last night and found my wife had given it away."

Lawson began to feel uneasy. He could accept a client with claustrophobia but this was beginning to sound like a case of scrambled brains. "Surely you can simply approach the person she gave it to."

"If only I could. You see, it was a couple of little boys who came to the door asking if we had any old clothes they could use to make a Guy -- for Guy Fawkes Day. She gave them my old suit and some rags to stuff it with."

"I'm getting the picture," Lawson said. "But if it's just a suit you've lost, and an old one at that, I'm afraid my fee would make a search uneconomic."

"Ah. Well, now we come to it." Trelawny took a felt pen from his pocket and began to doodle on the back of his bar mat. "The suit is old. But it has great value. Because sewn into the jacket lining are several jewels of considerable worth. Diamonds."

The wind began to rise and Lawson felt the sails billow and fill as they got under way. "I see. And you'd like me to locate the lads, wherever they may be, and reclaim your old suit. Giving them a few quid, no doubt, for their trouble."

"Exactly." Trelawny finished drawing one perfectly faceted diamond and went on to do another. They looked fat and delicious, like the gems sticking out of the wall of the mine operated by the Seven Dwarfs in Disney's marvellous film.

"You'd probably like to know how the diamonds happened to be sewn into that lining," he said.

The information was not essential to his search but, with beer in his glass, Lawson saw no reason not to listen. "I'd like to know that, yes," he said.

"They were bequeathed to me by my father," Trelawny said. "He smuggled them out of Czechoslovakia in the lining of *his* suit before the Russians got established. I remember when I was a little boy in Brataslava, Papa used to spread out the diamonds on a square of black velvet on a table in the big house. To us they represented the future. Then, after supper we'd go outside and watch the American bombers pass over on their way to bomb the oil fields in Rumania. We survived the war, even managed to escape from behind the Iron Curtain. My father risked his life to bring out those diamonds. Then just before he died he gave them to me. And now they're gone." Trelawny threw back his gin with a bitter gesture.

Lawson made a noncommittal noise. His show-biz instinct rejected this romantic story and he made a mental note, if ever he and his client sat down to drink again with at least an hour on their hands, to tell him the one about the Bessarabian Cream Pie. "I'm curious," he said at last. "Isn't Trelawny an unusual name for people who come from Czechoslovakia?"

"We took the name when the family settled in England. Our Czech name has three syllables and no vowels. You'd get a hiatus hernia if you tried to say it."

Lawson finished his beer. "Mr. Trelawny," he said, "it's an interesting case. The missing person I'll be seeking is Guy Fawkes in the shape of your old tweed suit. He'll be in the care of a boy or boys unknown. Where were they last seen?"

"In Wimbledon. That's where I live, and I reckon they'll be local kids." Trelawny pressed a button on a quartz watch that could display more data than the big board at the stock exchange. The date flashed up green on black. "You've got a deadline, Mr. Lawson," he said. "Today is the second. Guy Fawkes night is Saturday, the fifth. On that night a lot of Guys will go up in flames on the big bonfires."

"You're right," Praw Lawson said. "There isn't a moment to lose -- we'd better discuss money."

Upstairs in the office, Lola Lawson counted £5 notes with the dexterity of a bank clerk. Her husband watched the plump flashing fingers with as much pleasure as if he were attending a performance of the can-can. He finished telling the story he had heard from Trelawny.

"Question," Lola said. "Why would his wife be so stupid as to give away a suit with diamonds in the lining?"

"Because he was not so stupid as to tell her the jewels were there. I asked him that before we broke up."

"Nice man."

"One of nature's noblemen," Lawson said. "He pays cash in advance. Actually he explained the secrecy. It seems his wife is one of those mental cripples who believe you should enjoy life while you're young. Trelawny, on the other hand, is a receptacle of that fundamental belief shared by humans and squirrels."

"Which is?"

"It's better to hoard your assets so you can be buried on the better side of the graveyard." Lawson was feeling expansive now, pacing the tiny office, one step this way, one step back. "That," he said, "is known as the wisdom of W.C. Fields."

"Well, I'm going to hoard our fee in a tin box where I can get at it to pay rent and buy food." Lola was thrashing about in the desk drawer. "Who stole the key to the petty cash?"

Al lifted the grass and the metal lid under the potted palm. He tossed the key to his sister. "So what's the first move, Praw?" he asked. "Where do we go from here?"

"I suggest we go to lunch on the credit card." Lola said. "We can afford it now."

"No," Lawson said. "We're going to Wimbledon on the District Line. This case requires legwork and lots of it. For once I'm going to get some mileage out of you lazy sods."

They began by visiting Max Trelawny's house in one of Wimbledon's more modest streets. Here, property prices were merely exorbitant instead of outrageous, as they were up the hill in the Village. Mrs. Trelawny had been notified by telephone that the well-known investigator had been engaged to find the missing Guy. She invited Lawson and party into her kitchen and served coffee. She volunteered that her name was Crystal.

"Describe the suit, please," Lawson said, and they all listened carefully while she talked about a gingery sort of garment that would have kept her husband out of most clubs and restaurants in the free world.

"Now the boys who took it away."

As near as Crystal Trelawny could remember, they were under ten, one fat, one thin, one fair, one dark, one silent, one verbose. She had never seen them before around the neighbourhood. "I feel so vile. I'd never have given away the suit but Max never breathed a word about the diamonds. All that wealth -- if I'd known, we could have been on Lanzarote this weekend."

"Save your money," Al said. He was a frequent visitor to Ascot and Epsom. "Lanzarote hasn't won a race all season."

"Al," Lawson said patiently, "the horse was named after one of the Canary Islands." He turned back to their hostess. "If we spot a likely suit, I'll ring you to come and identify it. Thanks for the coffee."

Mrs. Trelawny saw them out and as they walked down the footpath, they met a bald-headed man coming in through the gate. Behind him, Lawson heard the front door close hard and the mortice lock go clunk. The bald man hurried to the door and rang the bell.

"Wait a minute," Lawson told his companions, loitering within sight of the house. The bald man used the bell again, then began hammering the knocker. Nobody home.

"Why doesn't she answer the door?"

"She doesn't want to see him." As the man came away and got into a yellow sedan, Lawson walked on. "It's all part of the mystery," he said.

"What mystery?"

"Trelawny is up to something. I don't believe the diamonds were smuggled out of Czechoslovakia by his father. I'm not even sure there are any diamonds."

"There must be something valuable in that suit," Al said. "Otherwise he wouldn't be paying us to find it."

Lawson shrugged. "I don't believe he changed his name, either. Czechs are proud people -- they retain their names. Or else they knock off a couple of syllables. But Trelawny? I might believe Smith or Johnson."

"Then what is he up to?" Lola asked.

"I don't know yet. All I'm sure of is that he has an enemy with no hair." Lawson thought again. "Or maybe Crystal has an enemy. Never mind. Let's look for that suit while we have some daylight."

He produced a Wimbledon street map from an inside pocket. "Tada!" he said like a fanfare of one trumpet. "I'll go this way to Wimbledon Park station and the shops along Arthur Road. Lola, you take the far end of the Broadway where the cinemas are. These are places where there are crowds. Kids collecting money for the Guy would hang out here. Al, you take this end of the Broadway and the railway station."

"They might be up the hill in the Village," Lola said. "Good pickings up there."

"We'll try there if we strike out down here. Carry on. And let's meet in an hour in front of the Town Hall."

Three weary searchers came together on the steps of the Town Hall just as the sun was disappearing behind the ironmonger's Tudor facade. They had seen a number of Guys with teams of ambitious lads collecting pennies but none fitting the description given by Crystal Trelawny.

"Nothing," Al said.

"All my Guys were in blue jeans," Lola said.

Praw Lawson had seen one of the wonders of the world. "I went into Wimbledon Park," he said. "They've erected the bonfire ready for Saturday night. It's incredible. The pile of stuff must be thirty feet high." As he spoke he was peering around the corner at the side entrance of the railway station where commuters were queuing at a newsstand. Beside the stand but out of the way, a blond boy and a dark-haired boy stood guard over Guy Fawkes in ginger tweed. "Well, I'll be darned," Lawson said. "The suit exists."

Crystal Trelawny arrived in a taxi ten minutes after the phone call announcing the suit had been found. She looked extremely nervous.

"Cheer up," Lawson said. "Your troubles are over." He led her to within a few yards of the boys and their Guy propped like a scarecrow against the station wall. "Just as you described it."

She stared, chewed her lips, and hugged her handbag. "No, I'm sorry. It's close but not the one."

The Lawson team were stunned. "But surely --"

"No. Max's suit is quite different really."

Deception was heavy in the air. Praw Lawson had lived on it long enough to know when it was being practiced on him. But tact was required. He held Crystal's arm and drew her forward as he put a coin in the cap. The boys recognized her. "Hi," said the dark one. "Thanks for the suit. Do you like the way we stuffed it?"

"I'm sorry, boys," she said. "You must be mistaking me for someone else." She turned to Lawson and forced a smile. "I'm afraid I've got to run, my taxi is waiting. Thanks for trying."

Lola and Al were relieved to be back at The Fallen Arches before all the sausages were gone. They settled down at the table by the gas fire and began wolfing the huge bangers with mashed potatoes and sprouts all covered in brown gravy and piping hot from a few minutes in Helmut's microwave oven. Lawson himself was staring into the blue flames, eating crackers and cheese and looking austere, turning to the table only to take an occasional pull at his pint. All the way back from Wimbledon through a night turned chilly after a fine clear day, the Praw had been silent.

Now Lola tried once again to open him up. "What about tomorrow, then?" she said. "Do we search up the hill in the Village?"

"Waste of time," Lawson said.

"We have to find the suit."

"We already have. But Crystal won't admit it. Something is going on. Somebody is joshing with the old Praw-fessah."

"The joke is on them," Al said. "We're being paid for no reason."

Lawson said, "That would be okay except there *is* a reason. And I'm going to have to find out what it is."

Lola glanced at brother Al and made a monster face. Daddy was provoked and they were going to have to go along with him, whatever the mad adventure.

The next day was Friday, the day before the 5th when huge bonfires would light up the sky throughout greater London. Praw Lawson left Lola and Al in charge of the office and went alone to Waterloo Station where he caught a Southern Rail train to Wimbledon. He strolled the short distance to the Trelawny residence. Max was in. When he saw who it was at the door, he threw on a coat and came outside. "Let's walk," he said.

"It's answer time," Lawson said as they moved along the narrow street between rows of terraced houses.

Trelawny looked embarrassed. "You found the suit, right?"

"Right. But your wife said no, even though the kids thanked her for giving it to them."

"Don't blame Crystal," Max said. "I didn't deal her a full hand. She's covering up because she only knows part of what is going on."

"That's one part more than I know."

A man with a fibre broom pushed yellow leaves beside the curb. On the pathways of a small park children raced their bikes, using as a starting point the painted words: No bicycles. Max Trelawny was thoughtfully silent until they reached a corner. Then he said, "I wonder how much I can tell you? As the one and only Daffy Duck says in my favorite cartoon, there are legalities involved here."

"Think of me as a father confessor," Lawson said. If Trelawny gave information connecting him with a crime, would Lawson go the police? He was not sure -- such a situation had never happened.

Nor did it happen this time. A yellow sedan pulled up, parked, and a bald-headed man got out quickly. He took Max Trelawny by the arm and drew him to the other side of the car. They began a hurried, whispered conversation. Lawson heard his name mentioned by his client. Trelawny was obviously using the detective as some sort of antidote to the other man's poisonous anger. It didn't work.

There was a brief struggle. A fist landed. Trelawny ended up in the back seat and before Lawson could intervene, the yellow car was racing down the street. The Praw was left with no client and more unanswered questions.

He rang the office and told Lola what had happened. "You'd better get back to Mrs. Trelawny," she advised.

"No. You're going to call her but not until tomorrow morning. I have a feeling she'll have been without her husband overnight and she'll be ready to cooperate."

"But what will I say to her?"

"Say precisely this." Lawson went on to give his wife detailed instructions about the message he wanted her to convey to Crystal Trelawny.

"And when will I see you?" Lola asked.

"Not tonight. I have work to do. Look in the phone list and give me the number of Achilles Healey."

Lola moaned. "Whenever you get involved with Healey, things become dangerous."

"Not really. Just spectacular." Lawson explained to Lola what he and Achilles were going to do. He had not been in touch with the former carnival strongman in several months. It was short notice, but Achilles liked the Professor. Barring family emergencies, Healey would make himself available. "So have you the instructions straight?"

"Yes. But you be careful, Harry."

"I will, love. See you tomorrow night beside the bonfire in Wimbledon Park."

The park was crowded with parents and children and young couples all enjoying the finest Guy Fawkes weather in years. Over beside the embankment where the District Line trains rattled by, the light on a small midway made patterns against a dark sky. Loudspeakers poured out pop music played to death on the radio but given new life here by the open air. The smell of boiling wieners indicated the English were trying to make hot dogs.

At eight o'clock, on the other side of the park, the first rocket lit up the sky. It was a splendid display of fireworks and Al joined the crowd in every "Ooooohhhhh!" and "Aaaahhhhh!"

Lola gave her brother a sarcastic sideways look. "You don't have to enjoy yourself so much," she said. "Nobody's showing up."

"Are we in the right place?"

"He said beside the bonfire." Lola looked across an open space at the huge mound of debris that would later be ignited as the climax of the festivities. It was at least 30 feet high.

"Then all we can do is wait," Al said. He looked up at the spectacular burst of silver stars that cascaded down like a candelabra. "Ahhhhhhhh!"

As the fireworks were ending with a static display of Catherine Wheels, three people arrived and stood beside Lola. "Hello, Mrs. Lawson," Crystal Trelawny said. "This is my husband. And this is his colleague, Dickie Kirk." The bald head gleamed in the shadows.

Hands were shaken and Al was left with an instinctive urge to check his pockets. There was an uncomfortable pause which Lola felt obliged to fill.

"Mr. Lawson will be here any minute," she said.

"What's this all about?" the man named Kirk muttered. "Max, if this is more of your funny business --"

"I'm going by what Crystal says," Max said with massive innocence. "And Mrs. Lawson. I'm paying her husband to find the diamonds. He's the expert."

Shadowy figures were walking around the towering mound of debris, pouring kerosene on the outer fringe. The pungent smell of the volatile liquid filled the night. Suddenly a tall figure appeared "Ah, we're all here at last," Praw Lawson said. "Then we can bring this case to a conclusion."

"I wish you would," Max Trelawny said. "What's happening?"

"I am about to return to you the suit in question. Not only the suit but the diamonds. I checked the lining myself and they were there."

There was no mistaking the disbelief in Trelawny's voice. "Then where is the suit?"

"Halfway up the bonfire," Lawson said, pointing to the mound which was built of old packing cases, broken civil service desks, and pieces of used lumber. It included a number of ragged effigies of Guy Fawkes. "There it is -- the one in the middle." Men with torches were beginning to light the base of the mound. "Good Lord," Lawson said, "I may have waited too long!"

Then he was gone, breaking through the crowd and running across the open space to the mound, where he leaped upon it and clambered his way upward. Men in the crowd began to shout, women screamed. It was too late to do anything about the flames -- they were beginning to flash upward.

Lawson could be seen struggling with a Guy, then he seemed to slip inside the form of the wooden pile, and disappeared from view. Within seconds the bonfire was well and truly burning and lighting up the park with flames towering well over 50 feet.

"Harry!" Lola screamed. "Somebody put out the fire!"

Even had there been a fire engine on the scene, it would have been too late. The heat and the flames were intense as the Guy Fawkes bonfire became Professor Harry Lawson's funeral pyre.

Sunday afternoons were never Lola's favorite time of the week. Now she sat at Crystal Trelawny's kitchen table and tried to rise above her mood. "I'm sorry," she said. "Every time I think I've finished crying, I start again."

"You go ahead and cry," Crystal said. "You've had a terrible shock."

Dickie Kirk was in charge of the whiskey bottle. He poured a shot into Lola's glass and another into his own. He also seemed to be in charge of comforting the Widow Lawson. "Drink up, honey," he said huskily. Kirk was a sucker for a beautiful woman, especially one of generous size. "You aren't alone. Old Dickie is going to take care of you."

"It was nice of you to let me stay the night," Lola said to the Trelawnys. "Especially since my brother had to go back and attend to business in London."

"Pleasure," Max said. He had an unfinished-business look about him.

"And that's the trouble," Lola went on. "I'm alone in the world now. I had Harry, but he's gone. And Al has his own life to pursue. So what's to become of me?"

"We'll think of something," Kirk said, wondering how much time had to pass before he could decently suggest romance to a woman whose husband had just been consumed in a bonfire.

"What really bothers me," Lola went on, "is I don't understand what it was all about. My husband didn't understand either and he went to his death not knowing. Not knowing if there were any diamonds, and if there are, then where they came from. It's all so mysterious, and so pointless, I'd give anything if it could just be explained to me."

At that moment Max Trelawny's face cleared like the sun breaking through on a cloudy day. "Listen," he said. "I've got a confession to make. Don't get mad, Dickie, everything's going to be okay now. I admit I was trying something wicked. But I'm levelling now, and we're all going to be winners."

Kirk sat straight up. "I knew there was something going on. I never believed that those diamonds were given away in the suit."

"They weren't," Max said.

"But you told me they were," Crystal said. "And ordered me not to identify the suit if he found it. You got me so confused."

"I know, I know," Max said. "But here's what happened."

"Excuse me, let me get another tissue," Lola said. She fumbled in her handbag, found a tissue, then left the bag on the table between her and Max.

"First of all, "he said, "the diamonds weren't bequeathed to me by my father. They were stolen from a house up in the Village six months ago by my good friend, Thieving Dickie Kirk."

"All right," Kirk said modestly.

"We suspected this much," Lola said.

"My job was to help dispose of the diamonds through connections I have," Max continued, "and I was sitting on them till they cooled off. Then I got an idea. It came to me when Crystal told me she'd given away my old suit. I thought, what if I *had* sewn the jewels into the lining? If I could convince Dickie they were gone, I could wait a year or so and then take off for America, sell them there, and keep all the money."

"You greedy villain," Kirk snarled.

"But why hire us?" Lola asked.

"To convince Dickie they were really lost and that I was making a major effort to get them back. Actually they are now in a safety-deposit box at my bank."

"And the reason I snatched Max off the street," Kirk said, his lips tight, "was because I only partly believed him. I figured I'd hold onto him in case something funny was going to happen."

"Then when you rang Crystal yesterday and said your husband was going to produce the suit and the diamonds at the bonfire in the park," Max said, " she got in touch with Dickie through his answering service. I knew it had to be phony but I couldn't let on. We had to show up as if the diamonds really were in the suit."

"But if they weren't there," Chrystal said, "why did Mr. Lawson say they were? Why did he run into the fire to save the missing Guy?"

"My husband was a strange man," Lola said. "He could become obsessed with a case and convince himself something was true in order not to face failure." She sighed. "But he died in vain and now I'm all alone."

"You're never," Dickie Kirk said.

"What about it, then?" Trelawny asked. "Shall we follow my plan?"

"Which is?"

"The diamonds will sell in America for enough to keep us all for a while. Then we can go on from there. You and me, Crystal. And Dickie and Lola"

All the animosity drained out of Kirk's eyes. He smiled warmly at Trelawny, then at Lola. "What do you say, honey?"

"I say yes," she said.

There was some mild rejoicing, more drinks were poured, and Lola excused herself to telephone her brother Al. When she came back to the kitchen, Trelawny had the atlas out and they were arguing about which town in America should become their new home. Being an American, Lola spoke with authority, so her vote on behalf of New Orleans was decisive. They were listening to her describe a boat cruise on the bayous when an ominously loud knock sounded at the front door.

As Crystal went to answer it, Kirk cast an alert glance at Max and got up from the table. He flung open the back door and would have stepped out had not a massive man blocked the way. The man had a lot of black hair oiled and parted in the middle and swept in two waves across his forehead, giving him the appearance of a water buffalo.

"Achilles Healey," Lola said. "Am I glad to see you!"

She was also glad to see Praw Lawson who thundered down the hall followed by brother Al and three policemen, two in uniform, one in plain clothes.

The cops were angry because they had already been told that their concern over the madman who immolated himself last night and their search for his bones through the hot ashes this morning had all been for nothing. But their mood improved when Lola produced a small tape recorder from her handbag and replayed Max Trelawny's account of the jewel theft. They had suspected Dickey Kirk and now they had him.

Crystal Trelawny was still looking confused. "But we saw you get burned up in the fire last night," she said.

The Praw was in his element. "You only *thought* you saw me get burned up." The master of illusion looked down on his audience as if from a stage. "What you actually saw was me running to the mound and climbing halfway up. I moved some of the debris and then I disappeared."

"But how --"

"Simple enough. Risky but simple. The previous night, when the park was deserted, my muscular friend and I went there with certain materials obtained in advance. We cleared away part of the debris so the ground was exposed near the center of the pile. Then with pick and shovel, Achilles dug a pit about eight feet deep. Into this pit we place a short ladder, an oxygen tank, and a face mask. We covered the top of the pit with an iron plate that had a ring in it and on top of this we replaced earth and sod to a depth of three inches."

Al had a curious look on his face. "Wait a minute," he began. "That sounds like --"

"You're right, brother Al. I got the idea from you and your potted palm." Lawson turned back to the others. "All that remained was for us to use some lumber we had brought with us to construct a sort of channel, a shaft, leading from the pit to a point halfway up the mound. This was invisible once we put all the debris back in place. All I had to do once I was on the pile was throw aside a strategically placed crate, slip inside and down the shaft, lift the lid by the ring, and climb down the ladder, closing the lid above me. At that depth I kept cool enough and I breathed oxygen through the mask."

Trelawny began to laugh. "It's incredible. It's almost worth going to jail."

"Speak for yourself," said Dickie Kirk.

"Like all successful illusions," Lawson said modestly, "it required quick execution and bold diversion."

"And you did all that," Kirk said, "just so your wife could come here with a recording machine and get us to talk?"

"Do you know any other way?" Lawson asked.

Back at the pub, Helmut sensed the mood of celebration and delivered a magnum of claret on the house. Lola smoked a cigarillo, something she did only on special occasions. Searching her handbag for a match, she came across a sealed envelope bright with stamps and airmail stickers.

"I'm sorry, Praw. This letter came for you in the Saturday post. I forgot all about it."

Lawson opened the letter and read it with a studious frown. "That's interesting," he said.

"What is?"

"Remember when we were touring America, we always wanted to play Montreal but never got there? Looks like we have the chance at last."

"Does it mean a new case?" Lola asked.

"Let's not concern ourselves tonight," Praw Lawson said. "Let's relax and enjoy our latest triumph." But as he sat back and drank the good red wine, his thoughts were already drifting away across the ocean.

A magician, he knew, is only as good as his next trick.

Alfred Hitchcock Mystery Magazine, January, 1980

MAKING A KILLING
WITH MAMA CASS

"Why weren't you at the airport?" Gary Prime said to his wife Anitra as she let herself into the apartment. "The car would have made sense. Instead I was stuck with an eight-dollar taxi." This was about as much anger as Gary ever expressed.

"I got your wire but Lee had important clients in the screening room. I had to be there." Anitra glanced at herself in a mirror, wondering if her adventure had made any visible difference. Gary back a day early was all she needed. She could have used more time to compose herself, to decide where they were all going from here -- herself and Gary and Lee Cosford.

"Busy while I was away?" Gary asked.

"As usual. How was London?"

"I enjoyed it." This was not the whole truth. Gary was a good mixer -- his job demanded it. As a salesman for a Montreal engraving house, calling on the production departments of ad agencies, he got on well with the men who could discuss the advantages of offset reproduction versus letterpress. But throw him in with the clever boys from the creative department and it wasn't the same.

He was grateful for his free trip to England even though he knew he'd been asked only because somebody dropped out at the last minute. His engravings were the backbone of the prize-winning campaign, therefore some Samaritan had suggested filling the vacant seat with good old Gary. He had asked Anitra to come along but she refused, pleading too much going on at Lee Cosford Productions.

"I enjoyed London," Gary repeated, "except for some of the brilliant conversation. My idea of hell is to be locked up for twenty-four hours with two copywriters, an art director, and an unlimited supply of booze. --The drunker they get, the more they laugh. Only I can't see the joke half the time." Gary

suspected that sometimes they derived their amusement from
him. Not that he was a clod: his suit cost two hundred dollars,
his shoes were shined, and he kept his hair trimmed. Maybe it
was the haircut. The creative types either let their heads go
altogether or had it styled and sprayed so they looked like
Glen Campbell.

"Pay no attention to them," Anitra said. She was pouring
herself some coffee from the pot Gary had made when he came
in. She looked good against the counter in slim denims made
stylish by a gold belt. "Agency guys are all the same. They think
they're some kind of elite."

"Elite. That's the word. Everything is a put-down. You
don't dare tell them you enjoyed a movie--they'll say it was
commercial and leave you feeling stupid. To hear them, the
girls going by are all dogs or hustlers, the food in the restaurant
contains the 'permissable level' of rodent hairs, and the wine is
sulphuric acid."

"Kill-joys."

"That's the word for them. Kill-joys. If you have a sincere
feeling you have to hide it or they'll make it into a joke."

"So you had a lousy time. At least it was free." Anitra
studied her husband. Something was on his mind. He could
never conceal enthusiasm -- it shone from the large square face,
the jaw set firm, the thick black hair neatly combed and
gleaming with Vitalis.

"It was only two days and apart from the meals I was
usually on my own." He was getting ready to tell her. "But there
was a thing happened --I'm excited about it. It's as if..."

When Gary finished talking, Anitra could not understand
what he was so worked up about. He had been watching late-
night television in his hotel room and had turned on a talk
show. The guest was the English actress Donna Dean, the sex
symbol from the sixties, who was still pretty today but hugely
overweight.

Anitra said, "And your idea is what? You want to ask her
to be in a film about Mama Cass?"

"Not me. I can't ask her. A film producer has to ask her.
But she'd be perfect -- if you saw her you'd know what I mean.

She's blonde, of course, so she'd need a dark wig. But she has the same baby face as Mama Cass and that majestic build. She was even wearing one of those big tent dresses Cass used to wear --"

Anitra found it difficult to become interested. Years ago, she had enjoyed listening to The Mamas and The Papas and she had agreed with Gary in those days that the bell-like voice of Cass Elliott had a lot to do with the group's success. More recently, she had heard something about the young woman's untimely death, but nothing much about it had registered. "O.K., there could be a film in it," Anitra said. "What's it got to do with you?"

"I'm the one to make it happen. I've got to do it."

After watching the Donna Dean interview, Gary had left the hotel and gone for a walk along Bayswater Avenue. It was midnight. Hyde Park was on his right, substantial white Edwardian buildings on his left. Ahead loomed Marble Arch and Park Lane with its lineup of hotels far posher than the one he was inhabiting. Noisy little cars, square black taxis, and an occasional red double-decker bus kept up a continuous roar beside him, but Gary hardly heard the traffic.

His mind was filled with music from the cassettes he used to play till they nearly fell apart, the songs of dreams and of young girls coming to the canyon.

According to the newspapers, Cass Elliott had died in a hotel somewhere near there. They said she choked to death on a sandwich alone in her room.

"I have to get the film going," Gary told his wife. "And now. Something tells me it's important."

"If you say so."

"Your boss said once that a feature film will never happen unless somebody puts all his energy behind it. There are too many other ideas competing for the funds and the facilities."

"Lee should know."

"Right. So I thought you might lay it on him tomorrow."

"Me? It's your idea." The last two days at Lee's place had given Anitra a shaking up. Some change in the relationship had been coming for a long time. But now she felt uncertain about her future and the sensation was distasteful to her. From the time eight years ago when she organized her marriage to Gary, Anitra had kept uncertainties to a minimum. The false pregnancy was a cheat but it got her out of a dismal situation at home. And it had done Gary no harm; he was forever testifying that the unexpected marriage had stabilized his life.

Now, for the sake of some excitement, she had gone with Lee Cosford. The event was satisfying enough as it was happening, but when they parted there had been a distant look in Lee's pale eyes and Anitra was no fool.

"You'd better describe the idea to Lee yourself," she said. "I wouldn't do it justice." It would kill her to approach him with this loony request, as if she thought he owed her something.

"Just mention it. Set it up for me."

"You're a big boy, Gary. You know his number. Call him and tell him you've got a business proposition. Lee Cosford would rather talk business than anything."

Lee Cosford, rotund and dynamic, rolled out into the waiting room and took Gary by the arm. "Stranger," he said laughing, eyeing Prime anxiously, "where've you been keeping yourself? Come in and sit down. Stephie, make us a couple of coffees, will you?"

The idea sounded even better to Gary as he described it in Lee Cosford's panelled office, taking pulls at a huge mug of coffee, squinting against sunlight streaming through the window past the spire of a church on lower Mountain Street. Cosford lay back in his leather recliner, boots on the glass desk, eyes closed like a man in a barber chair. As Gary finished, the bells in the tower across the street began to peal. He thought it was a good omen.

Cosford opened one eye. "Is that it?"

"That's it Lee."

The film producer sat up. "I think it's a sensational idea."

"Really?"

"Fabulous. And you've probably heard Anitra mention I want to get into feature films. You can't know how soul-destroying it is producing thirty-second pieces of film to sell detergent or sausages. Or maybe you *do* know. You have the same assignment in print."

"I know what you mean." Actually, Gary was proud of the engravings his firm produced.

"The trouble is," Cosford said, "there are too many good film ideas chasing too little money. You just can't get the financing."

"I thought there was this Canadian Film Development Council. Don't they put up money?"

"That's right." Cosford put his knees under the desk and folded his arms precisely on the cold glass. This square individual in the overpressed suit had managed to brief himself. "The CFDC will, on occasion, back a good idea."

"And this is more than a good idea, Lee. It's a great idea."

"Right." Cosford's mind was working fast. He was more than ready to see the last of Gary Prime. "But there's only one way to approach the Council. They have to see a treatment."

"Treatment?"

"Right." Cosford picked up his telephone, consulted a page of names and numbers, and began to dial. "A scenario - an outline of what the film is going to be about."

"Can't we just put the idea down in a letter?"

"No, it has to be professionally done. And I've got just the man to do it." Cosford straightened up and smiled into the phone. "Hello, Lucas? Did I wake you? Lee Cosford. Fine, how are you? Luke, facing me across my desk is a bright-eyed, bushy-tailed fellow named Gary Prime who happens to have a sensational idea for a feature film. The idea is so good, the only person to do the treatment is Lucas Pennington."

After Gary Prime went away with an appointment to see Pennington at his apartment that afternoon, Lee Cosford wandered through a maze of corridors till he came to a small room where his film editor was seated at a Steenbeck machine with Anitra Prime at his shoulder. They were peering into the frosted glass screen at the image of a child holding a doll. The editor spun the film backward, then forward again so that the child kissed the doll while Anitra clicked her stopwatch.

"I just had your husband in. Thanks for not warning me."

"I would have guessed next week. He's quick off the mark all of a sudden."

"Never mind. I got rid of him."

"He's sincere about the idea."

"I have twenty-five sincere ideas for feature films. Nine of them are my own." Cosford opened a window and spat out into a laneway three floors below. He watched the spittle float down to disappear onto grey pavement. "I sent him to Lucas Pennington to get a treatment done."

The bald-headed man at the editing machine laughed.

"Who's Lucas Pennington?" Anitra asked.

"Before your era. Once a good copywriter, now a professional drunk. He's a freelance with loads of free time. Which is another way of saying the agencies are tired of Pennington missing deadlines."

Anitra said, "It sounds like a dirty trick, Lee." She frowned at her stopwatch; she was having no end of trouble making the product shot time out properly.

"It's dirty but effective. It gets Gary off my back while he and poor old Luke use up a year pretending they're writing a movie."

It was half past two when Gary showed up at Lucas Pennington's place on Bleury Street. The apartment was located up a flight of uncarpeted stairs above a tavern and a shop that sold sneezing powder and rubber excrement. When he heard the knock, Pennington put the gin bottle and his glass out of sight--not because he was an inhospitable man, but because there was barely enough for himself. He left magazines, newspapers, open books, soiled clothing, empty food tins and soft-drink bottles where they were and went to the door.

With his guest inside and seated, Pennington performed a humanitarian act; he opened a window.

Gary looked at the man who was supposed to write his Mama Cass treatment. To recommend this one, Lee Cosford had to be crazy. Pennington managed to be gaunt and sloppy at the same time. He seemed somewhere in his fifties -- large head, patchy grey hair on a scalp that was scabby in places, apologetic eyes, and a smile that was choreographed to cover bad teeth. He had shaved a couple of days ago and had cut himself doing it.

"O.K. All right now. Right." He was rummaging around the room, not looking at Gary, sounding like a nervous infielder at the start of his final season. "Tell me about this picture of yours."

As Gary described his visit to London, his television glimpse of Donna Dean, and the flash of inspiration that led him to cast her in the role of his favorite singer, Pennington, who had discovered a notebook and a pen, lay on the floor with his head and shoulders against the baseboard, his eyes closed.

"So if Dean would agree to do it, and if we could get the right to use the original recordings for her to mime, the way the singers all do on TV these days," Gary concluded, "I think we could have a good film."

Pennington rolled sideways onto his elbow cupping his cheek in one hand. He bit the cover off the felt tipped pen he was holding, spat it away, and began flipping the pages of the notebook to find a clean one. They were all filled with indecipherable scrawl. At last he settled for half of the inside back cover. "Brilliant. Solid gold," he said as he tried to make marks with the pen. "Put me in, coach. Let me work on this one."

"You mean it?"

The writer turned his eyes up to Gary and they looked different -- they looked angry and hungry, the apologetic wetness all gone. Pennington was feeling an old, almost - forgotten sensation, the one he used to experience in his first agency job when the new assignments came in and he couldn't wait to dazzle the copy chief and the account supervisor and the client with another brilliant idea. Quite often he would deliver a winner. Then it was cover the table with beer and how about a little more money for young Luke before Y&R lures him away with shares.

"I mean it all right," Pennington said. "You're onto a sure thing, my son. Mama Cass -- that voice, the way she used to raise her hand and give that little half-salute as the song began to swing...I want to weep." The pen refused to write and, after tearing holes in the cover, he threw pen and notebook against the wall, struggling to his feet like a crippled, pregnant camel.

"The tragedy of her death." Pennington was pulling magazines and files from a buried tabletop, uncovering a typewriter. He used an ankle to drag a wooden chair into place, sat down, and cranked a crumpled letter around the roller, using two fingers to begin typing on the back of the paper. "What a career she had. Cass Elliott -- there *has* to be a movie about her. And I know what you mean about the English broad to play the role. She's almost Cass's double. And she'll do a hell of a good job -- never mind the silly parts they gave her in the sixties. She's a pro, a trained actress."

Pennington's typing was erratic. The keys kept sticking together in bunches and he cursed as he clawed them away from the paper. He squinted at what he had done. "This ribbon is dead. It's a ghost. Can you read that?"

Gary leaned over his shoulder, holding his breath. "Just barely."

"Never mind, it's coming, old son, the words are coming and I'll hammer the bastards down. Cosford knows my situation. He'll make a dark photostat of this and enlarge it three times." Pennington managed to hit several keys without an overlap and he laughed out loud. "The old rhythm," he said. "Once you've got it, you never lose it."

"Can I do anything to help?' Gary asked, delighted with this crazy old writer's reaction to his idea.

"Yes. Get out of here and let me work."

Two days later, Lucas Pennington showed up in the reception room of Lee Cosford Productions. The girl behind the board blinked at the sight of the very tall man in his dusty suit. It was a three-piece blue serge -- not this year's model, not this decade's. At the top of it, above the frayed grey collar and badly knotted tie, was a wet, crimson face looking as if the man had just shaved it with a broken bottle. At the bottom, stepping forward awkwardly across the deep-pile carpet, were astonishing leather thong sandals over patterned socks.

Lee Cosford came out to claim his visitor. In the office he offered gin and Pennington accepted, saying, "First since day before yesterday. How about that, temperance fans?"

Cosford knew this had to be about the Gary Prime project. He believed he had heard the end of it but now here was the top writer from a generation ago looking as if he had just seen a vision on the road to Ste. Anne de Beaupré. Cosford reached out and took the glass away from his guest and said, "Tell me, Luke. Before you dive back into the sauce. Is there a feature film in this Mama Cass thing?"

"Academy Awards. Cannes Festival. The idea is solid gold, my dear. I've been working for two days on the treatment without anything to drink but coffee and grapefruit juice. It's in this brown envelope, Lee old buddy, and what you had better do is line up tons of money and hire your cast and your director because *somewhere* there's a lucky man who is going to make the film of the year from this here scenario of mine."

Cosford handed back the drink. "I just wanted to hear you say it." He took the envelope and went to sit behind his desk. To himself he said, always trust a sober Pennington. He drew a thick sheaf of typewritten pages from the envelope. "Wow, what did you do, write a shooting script?"

"Almost. I had to force myself not to. I even went out and invested in a ribbon and a box of paper." Pennington drew on the drink, then set it aside and looked out of the window at the church spire.

Cosford studied the title page. It said, *"Blues for Mama Cass* -- a film drama with interpolated music. A Lee Cosford Production written by Lucas Pennington." The script had weight in Cosford's hands; it felt crisp and substantial -- he knew the heft of valuable work. He flicked the title page over and saw the beginning of the treatment. The writing flowed. It was vintage Pennington.

The producer glanced up, wondering whether he should mention the fact that Gary Prime's name did not appear on the script. He decided to let it go for the moment.

"Do you want up-front money, Luke," he asked, "or would you rather take a share of the gross?"

Pennington made growling noises in his throat as he rubbed his hands together. "Some of each, please," he said and, out in the reception area, Stephie heard through the wall the deep, nasty sounds of her boss and his visitor laughing.

Gary told Anitra how his project was going. He enthused over the meeting with Lucas Pennington, describing what a wash-out the man seemed to be, then how he came alight when the idea was explained. Aware of Pennington's bad reputation, knowing it was all a ploy to fob Gary off with a loser, Anitra was tempted to warn her husband not to expect too much. But why come on as a pessimist? Let the man have his dream for a while longer. Besides, you never could tell -- something *might* come of it.

It was only by accident that she discovered a few weeks later that something was indeed coming of the Mama Cass project. Anitra encountered Stephie at the photocopy machine and happened to see that she was running off several copies of what looked like a shooting script. A glance at the title page and Anitra was off to see Lee Cosford almost at a run.

Then she slowed down, thinking, and stopped. The film business ground on at a steady pace at the best of times. No mad rush. She would wait and see what was going to happen next.

What happened was that Lee announced he was flying to London on business at the beginning of the week. He asked Stephie to book a couple of seats on the Air Canada flight for Sunday evening. If the other seat was for Gary, Anitra told herself, her husband would have been crowing before now. If it was for her, Lee would have said something. Instead, he was keeping his head down these days, acting as if he had done a lousy job of picking her pocket and hoped she wouldn't mention it.

Anitra decided to bring up the subject as she sat in the front seat of Lee's car driving back from the Eastern Townships where they had been filming a butter commercial. She was never so grateful for a safety belt as when she drove with Lee

Cosford. The highway was fairly clear and he kept pushing the accelerator. The needle edged past eighty-five, ninety.

Suddenly the steering wheel began to shudder in Lee's hands. He straightened his arms, reducing speed. "Second time it's done that." He swore a couple of times but his eyes were bright. He was enjoying himself. "Something is wrong with this car, my dear. Anything over ninety and she tries to run away from me."

Anitra stopped bracing her feet against the floor and tried to relax, her heart still racing. "Lee," she said, "what the hell are you up to?"

"I like to drive fast," he said.

"I mean with Gary's idea. I saw the treatment Pennington wrote. You're getting ready to run with it."

"Luke says it has potential. He may be a lush but Pennington has judgment."

"But why isn't Gary's name on the front page? Why doesn't he even know you're going ahead?"

"He will, he will -- don't worry about it. As soon as I get my financing organized I'll write Gary a nice check."

"Thanks very much. Good thing I brought it up."

Cosford glanced at her and back at the road. The speedometer crept upwards and a feathery vibration in the steering wheel tickled his fingers. "Anitra, you know the film business. Let's face it, your husband is just an engraver's rep. What does he know from films? This is a Lee Cosford Production. It has to be if it's going to work." He glanced over again and this time he encountered her eyes staring straight at him. It was a frightening sight. "Come on! Gary fluked an idea that happens to have possibilities. O.K., we're going to pay him for it. But the business of making it into a film is for me and Luke Pennington. And for you -- you can be part of this too."

They drove a mile or two in silence.

Then he said breezily, "Want to come to London? Lucas and I are flying out on Sunday night to see the agent of this actress. Come along if you want. We could have some fun." He took a hand from the wheel and reached for hers.

Anitra drew her hand away and busied herself finding her lipstick and a small mirror in her purse. She concentrated on touching up her mouth. "I don't think so, Lee." She drew neat outlines with a tiny brush. "And don't pretend you'll miss me. Shacking up was fun, wasn't it? But I guess once was enough." She snapped her purse shut and turned to look at him coldly. "Right?"

He drew his shoulders up like a man in a hailstorm. "Whatever you say," he said patiently.

Gary came home that night in a mellow frame of mind. One of the agencies had been saying goodbye to a retiring account supervisor and good old Smitty had invited the representative of his favorite engraving house to stay for a drink. Gary let himself in at seven o'clock and was genuinely surprised to find Anitra in the living room with an empty salad plate beside her, a wine glass in her hand, and a news analysis program on television with the sound turned off. "Hello," he said. "No editing tonight? No answerprints? No emergency at the lab?" He said this without malice.

"You sound happy."

"We just put Elgar Smith out to pasture. They made nice advertising men in those days."

"There's a salad plate for you in the fridge."

"Thanks." His smile was that of a man who's been told his lottery ticket is a winner for the third consecutive week. He came back from the kitchen with his plate and a wine glass. Anitra poured Riesling for him as he peeled off the cling-film. "Hey, you made tuna with onions" He began eating hungrily.

Anitra reached forward and switched off the TV picture. "What's the word on your film idea?" she asked.

"Early days. I suppose Pennington's working on the treatment."

She set the glass down dead center on a coaster on the broad arm of the sofa. "Luke Pennington has delivered a thirty-page outline to Lee Cosford. They're very excited about it. They have an appointment with an agent in London for next Monday."

Gary beamed and raised his glass. "Fabulous. Thanks for telling me."

"You might well thank me. I don't think Lee was going to mention it." When her husband went on eating, she said, "I saw the script. Your name isn't on it."

"So?"

"So Lee Cosford is running away with your idea, Gary. He fobbed you off on Pennington to get rid of you, and now that Luke says the idea's solid gold, Lee has adopted it."

"That's what I wanted."

"I don't believe this. Lee told me he's going to write you a check once the financing is arranged."

"All donations gratefully received." Gary looked closely at his wife and for the first time saw the extent of her rage. "It's what I wanted," he repeated. "A film about Mama Cass-- something to really do her justice. The idea hit me in London when I was walking at night, as if she was still there, her spirit...I know that sounds stupid. But an idea is something from your soul, isn't it? That's all it is and who knows what makes the idea spring into your mind?"

"Gary, come down to earth."

"The film is all that matters. If it's going to be done, I'm delighted. No big deal if my name isn't connected with it."

"But it's your concept, damn it! You've got to be credited! Call a lawyer tomorrow and explain what's happening. Have a stop put on Lee before he goes any further." Her husband's satisfied face enraged her. "At least get mad! They're ripping you off, they're treating you like a retarded child."

"I can't get mad. I'm too happy."

Anitra picked up the wine bottle but her hands were shaking so hard she could not pour. Her empty glass toppled over. She left it rolling on the carpet. Gary was staring at her now, one cheek full. "Then maybe you'll get mad at this," she said. "While you were over in London falling in love with the ghost of Cass Elliott, I was back here in bed with Lee Cosford. Yes, that's right." She got up and said over her shoulder as she left the room, "Now will you come back into *this* world, Gary?"

Anitra found it easy to make her decision the next day. Her mind was influenced by the way the men around her seemed determined to conduct business as usual. Gary did his typical early-morning flit to work, leaving one of his screwy notes on the kitchen counter. Years ago he had played with the idea of being a cartoonist; now the talent had mostly evaporated, leaving a residue of doodled heads and neat printing. Today's note referred only obliquely to last night in a speech balloon that said, "Don't blame yourself. We'll talk."

At the studio, Cosford scurried around in his characterization as Laughing Lee the benign executive. He had everybody around the place grinning, but the best Anitra could give him was a sour, knowing smile. His only direct communication with her was when he whipped into her office and said, "Do me a favor, will you, Anitra? Stephie is away sick or I'd ask her. Drive the car around to the garage and have them check the steering. Tell him about the shudder around ninety. And I'll need it by Sunday."

"I'll call and see if they can do it now," Anitra said curtly. She picked up the phone and dialed for an outside line. But when Lee left the office she set the phone down again without making the call. The suggestion in her mind was unthinkable, but she had to consider it. She did so and came to the conclusion that Cosford had something coming. Not that an accident would happen. But if it did there would be justice in it.

Later, Cosford had to go to a luncheon meeting at the Queen Elizabeth Hotel, so he took a taxi. He telephoned from there to say that he was accepting a lift with his dairy client down to the farm in the Eastern Townships. He would be there for the weekend, returning Sunday at midday to get the car and the film scenario from his office and then to drive Luke Pennington to the airport. Would Anitra be able to come in for an hour on Sunday to discuss taking over the reins during his absence?

"Of course." She pursued her curt manner, words at a premium. "They kept the car at the garage but promised the steering will be fixed by Saturday afternoon. I'll see that it's here."

"You're a gem." Lee was expansive after his lunch. "I'll bring you back something nice from Bond Street."

On Sunday morning as Anitra was leaving for the studio, Gary came out of the guest room where he had been sleeping for a couple of nights. "Have you got a minute to talk?" he said.

"I'm in a hurry."

"I've decided you're right, I'm going to see a lawyer next week. As long as the film is being made, I might as well get some credit."

He was not looking directly at her, so she was able to observe the veiled look on his face. "You still aren't mad, Gary. You're just saying what you think I want to hear."

His voice became petulant. "Well, how the hell am I supposed to please you?"

"Nobody's asking you for that. Just grow up. When somebody walks all over you, be a man -- get mad."

He followed her to the door. "Are you going to see Lee?"

"I'm going to the studio. There's work to be done before he leaves for London."

When she was gone, Gary went into the living room and pressed the palms of his hands together. He looked around. Nothing like Sunday morning light to show the dust on everything. Anitra liked to go about with a spray can and a cloth, making everything shine and smell of lemon. Lately there had been other things on her mind.

He took down the most-played cassette in his collection and slipped it into the tape deck. He turned on the amplifier, pressed START, heard a moment's silence and then the familiar harmony flowing from the speakers on the top shelf on either side of the fireplace -- Mama Cass's huge, pure voice soaring over the others like a silver-belled horn.

At last he understood why Anitra was angry with him. It was a matter of expressing himself as unselfconsciously as the beautiful, natural woman he was listening to. Gary knew how he felt; he had to tell Lee Cosford how he felt.

By one o'clock, Anitra had made two big drinks each for Cosford and Pennington. She had poured on the whiskey for her boss and stinted the ginger. He was rolling with self-importance. She was glad when he looked at his watch.

"Time to hit the road," he said. "Where's the car, Anitra?"

"Around back." She had moved it there herself on Saturday. "The guy from the garage couldn't find any place else to park."

"Then we're off. Come on, young Lucas -- Daddy is going to show you the world. So long, Mrs. Prime."

When the door closed behind them Anitra poured herself a small drink and took it to Lee's desk where she sat down and rummaged till she found a copy of the Mama Cass scenario. Then she began to sip and read. As she turned the pages the realization dawned on her that this would make a great film. Gary was dead right. If things worked out, she and he would take it to another producer and have a go themselves.

Lee   Cosford drove aggressively to the corner and stamped on the brake pedal, throwing Pennington forward so that he had to catch himself against the padded dashboard.

"Ride 'em, cowboy," Lucas said.

"Haven't lost a passenger in years." Cosford craned his neck. "Isn't that Gary Prime?"

"It sure looks like him."

"Roll your window down. Call him over."

"Are you sure? We don't need him at the moment."

"It's Sunday -- I'm feeling Christian. Call him."

Gary saw the face at the car window, wandered over, and bent himself to look inside. "Hello, Lee. I was coming to see you."

"I'm glad. I've been meaning to talk to you about your film. We're just off to the airport. Can you drive out with us and have a drink in the lounge? Don't hesitate, my boy -- it's to your benefit. Get in."

As Gary went to open the back door, Lee whispered quickly to Pennington, "Let's give the guy a small credit and one or two percent. It's little enough and may save us litigation later on."

By two-thirty, Anitra had read the script twice and finished a second drink. When the telephone rang, she jumped. It was a police officer. There had been a crash on the highway near Dorval Airport. A car left the road and ran at top speed into a concrete abutment. The license number had been put through the computer which printed out Lee Cosford Productions as owner of the car.

"That was my boss," Anitra said, sounding disturbed. "He was on his way to catch a plane. Is there any --"

"I'm sorry. He must have been going ninety. We haven't been able to get into the car yet, but there can't be anybody alive."

Anitra telephoned him but Gary was either out or not answering. She drove from downtown in twenty minutes, thinking about the accident she had programmed. If it wasn't murder it was certainly manslaughter. Not that Lee or Pennington were any great loss to the world, but she had better not let on to Gary that she had sent her boss out with two doubles on an empty stomach and with faulty steering. Gary lacked the imagination to do anything but call the police.

The apartment was empty. Anitra checked the TV guide and saw that the Expos were on Channel Six in a doubleheader against the Phillies. That meant Gary would be down at the Mount Royal in the television lounge, drinking beer and eating peanuts. No supper required tonight. But perhaps they could have that talk he'd suggested this morning. No need for lawyers now -- no bitterness, but a fresh start with an exciting project they could share.

The reaction set in as Anitra made tea. She was trembling so much as she carried it into the living room that she arrived with a brimming saucer. She set it down with both hands, went to turn on the radio, and noticed a cassette inside the deck. She pressed the proper switches and out came the voice Gary had been raving about for the past few weeks, the cause of all the excitement and the manoeuvering and of her deadly intervention.

Now, as never before, she could understand what turned her husband on when this woman sang. Mama Cass was solo on this track, so vibrant and alive she might have been here in the room.

Anitra listened to the entire cassette -- both sides -- before she realized she was feeling impatient for Gary's return. She began willing him to abandon his precious baseball telecast and get in touch with her. And so when the telephone rang she ran to answer it eagerly.

Ellery Queen Mystery Magazine, June, 1980

EVENTS AT
HEADLAND COTTAGE

When Alexander Hewson arrived at the cottage unexpectedly from Canada, Derek Jennings was delighted. He remembered the fun they had shared back in Montreal when they attended McGill University. In those days Sandy Hewson was known as "Two Lunch" because of the way he would go a second time through the cafeteria line. The extra food did not cause a weight problem. On summer afternoons on the lawn fronting Sherbrooke Street, in the shade of the new library building, Hewson tossed and caught a football, looking lean and handsome in dark blue shorts and a tank top.

Derek's twin sister Lottie was always around. At age 19, more adventurous than her brother, Lottie had moved away from home and established her own apartment on Durocher, not far from the University. It was to this somewhat rundown but well-stocked hideaway that she and Sandy Hewson would go when he became tired of football and felt the need of a shower.

"You off then, Two Lunch?" Derek would call to his friend's departing back.

"Catch you later at the Pam-Pam," Hewson would reply across his shoulder, making for the slender figure of Lottie Jennings stationed like a silhouette in a landscape beyond the campus fence.

It was no surprise to anyone when Hewson and Lottie decided to be married. It happened a couple of years after graduation when he was an assistant professor of English at Sir George Williams, Montreal's smaller and less-prestigious college, and she was working as a sub-editor for a publishing firm which was part of their father's commercial empire.

Derek was still in town at the time pretending to be dedicated to the aims and objectives of the clients he served at an advertising agency that employed him as a copywriter. The job was a sinecure since Jennings Electronics was the agency's largest account. So life went on for Derek and Lottie and Sandy during these post-school years with no problem more pressing than whether to drink two wines with their dinner of homemade lasagna or only one.

The event that changed everything was the death of the old man. The Jennings twins had never lacked for money; now they had more than they would ever spend. Derek threw in his job at the agency, gave a month of farewell parties in his 16th floor flat overlooking the city and the river, then set sail for Southampton. It was a good move. Seeing England for the first time, he fell in love with every aspect of it from the graffiti anarchy of the London Underground to the hiss of the waves on Brighton beach. He spent day after day on British Rail trains travelling across the green and yellow counties to one city after another, and he adored them all -- Oxford, Canterbury, Winchester, Bath, Norwich, even Liverpool.

His favorite part of the country turned out to be Cornwall and here he settled near a village with the picturesque name of Mousehole (on the first afternoon he was taught to say Mowsle). It was a lucky day for a local estate agent when Derek Jennings came in looking for a house and ready to pay cash. Headland Cottage had been on the books for three years and seemed destined to stay there with property prices sky-high and mortgage money hard to find.

But here out of the blue was this courteous Canadian with stars in his eyes and a limitless supply of dollars. Moreover, all the disadvantages of Headland Cottage such as archaic plumbing and inadequate heating and something Derek had never heard of called "rising damp" were to the prospective owner simply opportunities for improvement. He signed the papers, made out a few checks, moved in, and began hiring builders from Penzance down the road.

Inside of a year -- fast going by English standards--the cottage was restored with central heating, three modern bathrooms and ceramic cylinders in the foundation to cure the rising damp. The new squire settled down to enjoy the quiet life with walks on the moors, much staring at the sea, pints every day in the snug at The Turk's Head, and a weekly trans-Atlantic telephone call to Lottie back in Montreal.

For a month or two, after the responsibilities of the cottage conversion were off his back, Derek enjoyed his carefree existence. Then he began to experience boredom and he said as much to Old Crowther, his drinking companion at the pub.

"What you need is a little shop to look after," Crowther said. "A place to go, days."

Derek had never considered becoming a shopkeeper. "I never thought of a shop," he said.

"Quiet this time of year. Busy in tourist season." Old Crowther put his nose into his dark ale and took it out again. "Get somebody to look after it for you. Come and go when you feel the need."

Two days later Derek asked his companion if he knew of such a place. Old Crowther did -- a shop specializing in pottery and ceramics made by local craftsmen, and the owner willing to sell. Located a cough and a spit from the harbor. And yes, Old Crowther himself would take on the job of tending it.

The arrangements were made within three months, Derek operating once again with his astonishing North American speed. Old Crowther established himself behind the counter and kept the place full of his cronies who came for their daily chats.

So Derek Jennings was settled and satisfied in the southwest of England. But what of sister Lottie, living with Two Lunch Hewson back in Montreal? The regular telephone calls made it clear that all was not well. "I think he actually had a fist fight with a first-year student in an early English class. They were discussing Beowulf and the kid disagreed with Sandy's interpretation and then they were on the floor pounding each other."

"I don't like the sound of that."

A month went by and the telephone bulletins did not bring better news. "He isn't here," Lottie informed her brother. "He hasn't been here for two nights."

"I *certainly* don't like the sound of that," Derek said.

"Actually it's okay," Lottie said. "Sandy has been so disruptive this past year. Now that he's staying away, I've begun working again and I love it. I'm putting together a book of Canadian birds. All those lovely Lansdowne water colors."

It was against this setting of marital imperfection at home that Sandy Hewson appeared unexpectedly in Cornwall. He drove up to the door of Headland Cottage in a rented car and began unloading baggage as Derek came outside.

"Hey, Two Lunch, what a great surprise!"

"Decided to change my life, old sod. Thought I'd expose you to the metamorphic Alexander Hewson. You can watch me struggle free of the chrysalis, protect me as my new wings spread and dry, and then cheer like hell as I fly away."

The tragedy was that Sandy Hewson could not write as well as he spoke. His new scenario was, he said, based on the development of a breakthrough in English poetry. Instead of wasting his juices trying to pound the Canterbury Tales into concrete skulls, he was now going to relax, stop resisting his impulses, and allow the volcano within him to erupt and fill pages with spectacular images.

Derek put Hewson in the corner room with its view of the ocean. They stood at the window on the first day. "Why the barrier?" Hewson asked. He was looking down at the trestles and striped yellow and black boards arranged across the grass near the point of the promontory. "It looks like a police operation down there."

"A safety precaution," Derek said. "What you can't see from this angle is the drop of a hundred feet to the rocks below. It worries me. I'm getting ready to have a permanent wall erected. But I suppose I'm putting it off because I hate to spoil the lawn."

Hewson made immediate use of the headland. He found a wicker chair on the back porch and he carried it to the grassy oval near the overhang. Here he sat on fine mornings with notebook on knee and pen in hand, writing poetry. It was terrible stuff. By midday, when he finished working and came in to eat lunch and drink a bottle of wine, Derek would be back from his morning stint at the shop near the harbor.

"Take a look at that," Hewson would say, spreading the scrawled pages of his notebook before his host. "Tell me what you think."

Derek thought it was rubbish. It was nothing but paragraphs of tedious description broken into uneven lines of three or four words each. If this was poetry, then Dylan Thomas was scrum half of the Welsh national rugby team.

Derek stared at the pages, letting time elapse before he spoke. "This is interesting stuff, Two Lunch," he said. "You get a bang out of writing this, I can tell."

At first, perhaps, yes. But gradually Alexander Hewson's state of mind deteriorated. Just as he had arrived, a beefy bearded parody of the handsome athlete Derek remembered, so now his former merry personality went through a disturbing change. Derek watched as his sister's husband became increasingly sullen while the weeks went on.

The nadir was reached when a publisher sent back a hefty batch of Hewson's work with negative comments attached. "What do they know?" the aspiring poet ranted. "I give them pearls and they expect pig feed. They aren't ready for me."

After his wine Hewson turned depressive. "It's no use. I don't know why I bother. I've wasted my life."

"Come on, Two Lunch," Derek said. "Let's go out on the lawn and throw a football."

"Why don't you go out on the lawn and throw yourself into the ocean?" Hewson said.

Derek was able to roll with this sort of punch. He had decided in the time since Sandy's arrival that the old friendship belonged to the university days and should be forgotten. Hewson was now just another house guest and a difficult one at that. Besides, Derek was so happy with the cottage, the sea view, the shop, and with his comfortable evenings in the company of Old Crowther, that he was prepared to abide Hewson until he decided to go away.

"How are things at the cottage?" Crowther asked one night as they sat at their tiny table in The Turk's Head. The curtains were drawn and because of a night chill the electric fire was turned on. Gulls cried above the roof.

"You mean my guest?" Derek acknowledged his companion's perceptive glance. "He's becoming a bit of a pain."

"Guests are like fish," Crowther said. "After three days they start to smell. This one is going on three months."

"Yes. If it were not for the fact that he's my sister's husband, I'd ask him to leave."

"Some husband, staying away all this time."

"I think my sister prefers it," Derek said.

Lottie certainly did prefer it. Her telephone conversations were full of animation these days. She was putting more work in hand, seeing new friends. "Whatever you do, Derek," she concluded, "don't let Sandy come back, please."

This fervent request posed a problem for Derek Jennings. He took his sister at her word; to send Hewson back to her would be a betrayal. But at the same time Sandy was becoming more than just a bore around Headland Cottage. His temper became increasingly foul as the list of publishers not interested in his work grew longer. Still he spent mornings in the wicker chair beyond the barrier, notebook on his lap, eyes turned to the gray horizon. But the few lines he managed to put down gave him no joy.

He blundered into the kitchen one lunchtime, banging the screen door behind him, throwing his notebook on the table where Derek was sprinkling watercress on cucumber sandwiches. "Read that!" he snapped, his voice thick with outrage.

Derek read the half-dozen fragmented lines, found no meaning in them, and was not quick enough at disguising his reaction. "Interesting stuff," he said. "Are you going to do more with it?"

"Yes. I'm going to crumple it and ram it down your interesting throat."

"Sandy, if you've had a bad morning, don't take it out on me."

"Well, why don't you say what you think when I show you something?"

"I'm not a critic. You expect too much."

Hewson slouched out of the room, playing the defeated man. He reappeared moments later, fired with fresh anger. "I've had it," he yelled. "I'm going to pack it in. I'm going back to Lottie in Montreal."

It was the declaration Derek feared most of all. He recalled Lottie's descriptions of Sandy's disruptive presence, and more recently, her delight at the progress of her life without him. Please don't let him come back -- that had been her latest appeal. And now the Hewson threatening to return would be an uglier man than the one who had abandoned her.

That evening at The Turk's Head, Derek drank his first pint far more quickly than usual, then stalled on his second, staring into the collapsing foam. Old Crowther thumbed his pipe and assessed this abnormal behavior. "How's the visitor?" he asked at last.

"Getting set to leave. Or so he says."

"Good riddance."

"Not exactly. He's going back to my sister in Montreal." Derek went on to explain the details of the situation.

"I see," the old shop assistant said. "A quandary. You don't want him here and your sister doesn't want him back home."

"That's it. If Alexander Hewson did not exist, it would not be necessary to invent him."

Much later, when last orders had been called and Derek brought the pints from the bar, Old Crowther said, "The answer, of course, is an accident."

"To what?"

"The answer to the Hewson problem."

"He's free to have an accident any time he wants." The hours of beer and conversation had put the two men on a plane of understanding where they enjoyed an uninhibited sharing of ideas that would have been unacceptable to both of them when sober.

"You can't wait," the old man said. "It wants to happen now."

Derek put his head close enough to feel on his nose the warmth of Crowther's pipe. "Are you hinting at murder, my friend?"

"Call it an assisted misadventure."

"Impossible, but what kind?"

"He sits every day on the headland in that wicker chair. I've see him from the road." Crowther reduced his pint to the last inch. "A few feet closer and he'd be over the edge."

"But he'd never go any closer."

"Unless there was mist and he couldn't see." The final draft went down. "We're expecting misty mornings any day now."

As they left the pub, Derek said, "You're a terrible man, Crowther, putting temptation in my way."

"It's the precipice that's the temptation. With a pest like Hewson sitting by the edge of it every day, I don't know how you can resist it."

As he approached the cottage that night, Derek heard Hewson's voice shouting inside. He went in and found his guest using the telephone. "It's my home as much as yours," he was bellowing. "I can come back if I want to. You're my wife. You'll damn well behave like it."

Derek took the telephone from Hewson's hand. "Lottie?"

She was crying. "Oh, Derek I rang expecting to get you. He sounds worse than ever."

"I know."

"Don't let him come back. Do something, do anything. Give him money to go away but don't let him come back here. I'll do something desperate if I have to live with him again."

"Don't worry, Lottie. You won't have to." The twins were so close that Derek could feel the panic Lottie was experiencing. He put down the phone and it was as if a living connection had been severed -- he felt that sort of pain.

Hewson was back in front of the television set where he spent most evenings.

Derek approached him from behind. "Enjoying your uninterrupted viewing?" he asked.

"Yes. Did you enjoy your uninterrupted drinking?" Hewson ignored the fact that there was a whiskey glass beside his chair.

"Sandy," Derek said, "let's not argue. This visit isn't working. Why don't you give your writing a chance in new surroundings? Ever tried Italy? I can let you have some money and you could be in Florence by the weekend."

Hewson laughed. "The Jennings twins are doing nothing but offering me cash tonight. No, I'm going back to Montreal. I think what I need is Lottie, and lots of her." He leaned forward and switched channels from the middle of a Shakespeare drama to the middle of a political broadcast. "Give me a few days to get my head together and I'll be on my way."

The following evening at The Turk's Head, Derek waited for old Crowther. When his friend came and settled himself, Derek said, "I'm at the crunch. He is definitely going back to plague my sister."

"Heard the weather forecast?" The question was not inappropriate. "Heavy mist tonight, not clearing before midday tomorrow."

Derek could hardly believe he was considering the idea. But he heard himself saying, "How can I persuade him to go out there in a heavy mist?"

"Think of something. Tell him the view as the mist lifts off the water is a sight every poet must see."

"Mmmmm." Derek pondered. "But there's twenty feet of ground between the barrier and the lip of the precipice. He'll just climb over, carry his chair forward, set it down, and wait for the mist to clear."

"He's *accustomed* to twenty feet of ground," Crowther said. "If you go out tonight and quietly move the barrier forward, say, ten feet, he'll carry his chair into thin air."

For a while Derek's resolve seemed to harden but by the end of the evening his attitude had turned 180 degrees. "I can't do it. He deserves it, and I want my sister to be free of him. But still..."

Old Crowther was looking very wise. "The Lord's Prayer says, 'Lead us not into temptation.' Yet here you are, living at Headland Cottage, as if Fate brought you here for some purpose. Your brother-in-law arrives uninvited, and without guidance from you he begins frequenting the edge of the precipice. And now, just as his behavior is at its most unendurable, the mist falls." Crowther shrugged. "I would say you have been led most flagrantly into temptation."

"I concede all that," Derek said. "But I could never take a man's life."

The mist was heavy when he arrived home. There were no lights burning in the cottage -- Hewson had gone to bed deliberately leaving the place dark. Perhaps it was this callous gesture that tipped the balance of Derek Jennings' resolve. He would shift the barrier and let Fate take its course.

Walking carefully across the shrouded lawn, he came to the first trestle. It was the work of only a few minutes to move it and the others and the yellow and black striped planks a distance of ten feet closer to the edge. Far below, the sea whispered in its sleep.

In the morning there was pale light in the sky but the cottage was wrapped in cotton wool. Hewson made himself eggs and bacon and ate them standing up at the kitchen window. "Can't see a damn thing," he said.

"Not now," Derek said from the table. "But one thing you must not miss while you're still here. That's the moment when the mist rises from the ocean."

"Have you seen it?"

"Yes, and it's unearthly. You really must take your chair out and be waiting for it. You'll never see a sight like it again." Derek paused. "It could start happening at any minute."

Hewson said no more. He left the greasy plate and fork in the sink, as always, went out onto the porch and found his wicker chair. The last Derek saw of Sandy Hewson, he was trudging into the fog with the chair over his shoulder.

Expecting to hear some sort of cry, Derek waited by the window. He heard nothing. Had the plot failed? Had the sound been muffled by the moisture in the air? Quickly, Derek struggled into a raincoat and went out onto the lawn, hurrying toward the barrier. When he reached it, he peered into the murk and called, "Sandy?"

There was no reply.

He had to make sure, in case Hewson was sitting there invisible, stubbornly refusing to answer. Derek clambered over the boards, walked cautiously two steps forward into the mist, stepped into space, and felt his heart seize as the cold air rushed upward at him...

The bodies were found at the base of the cliff trapped among the protruding rocks where, at high tide, the Atlantic rushes in and scours the crescent beach. Even by midday the mist refused to clear, its persistence making recovery operations difficult. When at last a boat could get in and the bodies were claimed and identified, the police were left with a case of deaths by misadventure. But the villagers were suspicious and always would be. Only Old Crowther could have shed some light on what happened up at Headland Cottage, but he remained silent as the grave.

What puzzled the old man in the last lonely years of his life was how the barrier could have been so close to the edge of the precipice. When he went there in the small hours to do his reluctant friend a favor, he intended to shift it forward a little less than ten feet. Yet when he came back at lunchtime to return it to its original position, the clearing mist revealed the barrier standing within a yard of the edge.

The discrepancy suggested to Crowther that his judgment of distances, even allowing for darkness and heavy fog, was not what it should be. The old man blamed this on the beer and resolved to reduce his nightly intake by a couple of pints.

Alfred Hitchcock Mystery Magazine, June, 1980

THE CHOIRBOY

The musicians had taped their tracks and departed the studio, heading for wherever musicians go in Toronto on a July morning. Now Barry Latchford was alone in the soundproof room, adding his voice to the prerecorded background.

In the control room, Norman Inch pressed the intercom button. "You're a disappointment, Barry," he said.

Latchford was a sinewy man in his thirties with shoulder length blond hair and a sinister-looking mustache. Padded earphones gripped his head. He wore a striped freight-engineer's cap to go with his vagabond outfit of leather vest and stovepipe jeans. His boots were army surplus -- parachute corps.

Barry Latchford resembled more a villain out of a spaghetti western than the best singer of TV and radio commercial music in Canada. The drummer on the gig had been awarded the laugh of the morning when he said Latchford looked like a tall angry Muppet.

When the producer from the advertising agency told him he was a disappointment, Latchford sat erect while a jolt of fear emptied his eyes. "What's the problem?" He was perfectionist enough to believe that criticism was always justified. Once, years ago, he had become a hermit for weeks, practicing his scales and breathing to be ready for the December night when the choir would perform the *Messiah*.

Behind the glass, Inch put a hand on the shoulder of his companion, Steve Pullman, the copywriter. "We were hoping we could stretch this session into an extra day," he said, his voice booming through the speaker. "But if you keep delivering the goods on the first take, we'll be on our way back to Montreal tonight."

Latchford relaxed. He slipped off the stool, eased the "cans" from his head, and hung them on the music stand.

"My wife complains about the same thing," he said. "I'm fabulous but I'm a little too quick."

"We'll hear a playback of everything so far," Inch proclaimed, "then we'll buy you a drink."

They went into a place near the studio. After drinking and talking baseball for a few minutes, Pullman said to Inch, "Tell Barry the idea. Let's not waste time."

"Mysterioso," Latchford said, taking an invisible sip of whisky.

"We write songs," Inch said dogmatically. "You've never heard of us because our commercial success to date has been the square root of nothing at all."

"Welcome to the club."

"Come on, you were in the charts with 'Apple Dreams' a couple of years ago."

"The Canadian charts -- and even that was a struggle. I've never made it with a pop single in the U.S."

"So let's get together and create some prosperity," Pullman said. "Tell him the idea, Norman."

"The idea is you come down to Montreal and record one of our songs."

Latchford could feel remorse rising about him like ground mist in a horror film. God protect him from amateur songwriters. "Cutting a side is an expensive business," he said in the gloomy voice of a businessman.

Pullman's impatience was beginning to peak. "Will you tell him the idea, Norman?"

"We do it through my company, Inchworm Productions. The recording studio will be Carlo's -- he owes us a couple of favors, so there'll be no studio charges. As for musicians, we do it on half scale. If the song takes off, everybody gets paid."

Latchford looked for a way out. "I'll have to check it out with Carol. My wife -- she's my business manager."

"Do it and let us know as soon as you can." Inch directed glances around the room like a marked man watching out for assassins.

"Even if you make the record and it's okay," Latchford persisted, "you're only half way there. If the stations won't play it, you're dead."

"Leave that to me," Pullman said. "I worked for three years as a DJ at CBAY."

"Baytown?" Years ago, on vacation, Latchford had spent an eventful thirty seconds driving through the town.

"The voice of Crystal Bay," Pullman intoned, cupping his ear pseudo-professionally. "I know how the hit parade can be rigged."

"Providing it's a good song," Latchford said. "You can't sell garbage."

"We won't give you garbage to record," Inch said patiently. "Be a good boy and check with your wife."

Carol Latchford sat at the kitchen table in one of the old cinema seats Barry had bought when the neighborhood Palace gave up and became a block of shops. Four maroon-plush recliners were now bolted to the vinyl floor, two on either side of the low pine table.

"I think you should record their song," Carol said. She was drinking beer from a bottle and smoking a thin brown cigarette.

Latchford was playing around with a wok on the gas stove, throwing in green peppers and mushrooms and slivers of chicken, being a virtuoso chef. "These are two little businessmen from the minor leagues," he said. "The writer is from Baytown -- do you believe that? It's amateur night."

"What are you doing otherwise that's so important?" Carol was a short plump woman in her late twenties. She had a pussycat mouth, a turned-up nose, and green eyes with brows that arched in permanent astonishment. If faces had to be assigned countries, hers was Irish. "Something may come of it. You never can tell."

"You don't know these guys," Latchford insisted.

"Take me to meet them then," she said, finishing her beer, dropping the empty bottle into the case on the floor at her feet and flicking out a full one with a deft backhand movement.

Latchford frowned at the hiss of the bottlecap. "Could you manage to be sober if I did?"

"I can't remember the last time you took me somewhere."

"That's where you have the advantage. I can remember."

"Loosen up then. Have a drink with me -- we'll have some fun."

"You call this fun?"

Steve Pullman was setting out a meager bar in Inch's hotel room: a bottle of Scotch, a bottle of gin, some tonic, four glasses, and a bucket of ice. "Why couldn't they ask us up to their place?" he whined. He felt poor, as if he was back in his parents' shabby house near the bay.

"His wife probably wanted to come out," Inch said. He was accustomed to pacifying his partner. Writers were all the same -- if they weren't bitching about how terrible everything was, they were going over the top with enthusiasm over some minor success.

"I don't think he likes our idea," Pullman said.

"Then we'll sell it to him."

"Maybe we should line up another singer."

"Latchford's the best. We agreed we'd start with the best."

"I'm worried about how we finish," Pullman said grimly.

The Latchfords arrived in a mood of manufactured euphoria. Carol was wearing a crimson-silk jersey dress and charcoal nylons above plastic shoes without backs. Pullman fell in love with her legs immediately. He ordered the beer she requested and, when it came and he had opened one, placed himself where he could see every one of the frequent crossings of those smooth, shiny legs.

Everybody except Latchford drank a lot and the party was a reasonable success. By midnight when they were devouring room-service sandwiches and Carol was into her seventh pint of beer, Pullman was referring to her as the small-town girl. She was like the girls he remembered from the tea dances in the gymnasium at Baytown High School. Carol was flattered. "Let this guy write your lyrics, Barry," she said. "He's a magician with words."

Latchford tossed his head back, pretending to laugh without actually producing any sound.

In the taxi on the way home he grumbled, "I should go see a psychiatrist, agreeing to do this."

"We'll go to Montreal. We'll have some fun for a few days," Carol said. Her head was back on the upholstery, her eyes closed. "What can you lose?"

"*You'll* have fun. I saw you encouraging that bush-league lover. I should put you across my knee."

"Right now, I'd be grateful for even that."

Flora Inch, Norman's wife, selected the song that Latchford would record. She came out of her study in the bungalow across the river in St. Lambert with the portable cassette player in one hand and a page of notes in the other. "Here's my choice," she said.

" 'Summer Silence,' " Norman read from the list. He tried not to look too pleased. "I like that one too."

Flora moved a flower pot so she could perch on a window ledge. Her broad shape obscured most of the view of the Montreal highrise panorama in the distance. Richelieu, a tiny dog of indeterminate breed, limped from the kitchen, saw the woman he loved, took a skittering run, and leaped onto a lap that barely existed. Flora saved the dog from falling and cuddled it to her tank-topped bosom. She had the shoulders of a Channel swimmer, the cropped hair of a woman who wants a rest. Her face was as pretty as a doll's.

"Richie, Richie," she crooned. Then, after a pause in which her eyes went out of focus, "The lyric could use a little fixing. Would you like me to do it?"

"I don't want a hassle with Steve."

"You want a good lyric. Steve Pullman has blind spots. I know -- I wrote copy in the next office for three years."

"You may be right, but leave it alone. We have a delicate operation here. Stay home and write your novel."

"God help me, I've written it three times. Let me up."

"You're the one who cried out for artistic freedom. Write the book."

"I'm coming to that recording session. I'm not going to miss the rematch between Latchford's wife and our little Stevie!"

Carlo's Recording Center was a compact set of rooms engineered and hand-built by the owner. Carlo sat at the console, straight-backed, Spanish eyes alert, watching Barry Latchford through the glass partition as if the singer might fly at any minute and it would be his responsibility to trap him in a net. Norman Inch lounged beside Carlo in the producer's chair.

Steve Pullman and the two women were crowded onto the visitors' settee. Flora Inch had always been like a sister to Steve, taking him under her wing on his first day at the ad agency. She sat on his left now, bending occasionally to feed a chocolate tidbit to the carpet remnant she called a dog. "This is your best work, Steve," she commented after the first take. "Be proud of this song."

On his right, Carol Latchford crossed her legs, bringing a stiletto heel down across Pullman's trousers. "Sorry," she said, brushing her hand firmly and repeatedly over his calf.

By the third take, everybody agreed Latchford had done his best. Carlo had a paying client coming in, so the session had to end. "Everybody come over to St. Lambert," Flora said briskly, scooping up Richelieu. "Can we all squeeze into my car?"

They straggled out of the control room. "Looks like you're on my lap, Carol," Pullman said.

Inch directed a weak grin at Barry Latchford, who looked right through him as he unwrapped two sticks of gum and stuffed them into his mouth.

Flora Inch's food was late but meanwhile the wine flowed and the house filled with the aroma of roasting beef and salad dressing spiked with garlic and dry mustard. When the inebriated guests sat down at the table and fell on the meal, they all told the hostess it was the most delicious they had ever eaten.

"Have some more beef, Steve," Flora said. She was
drifting to and from the kitchen beyond a waist-high divider
lined with a cherry cheesecake and a pecan pie. "I don't want
to end up feeding sirloin to that piggy Richelieu."

"You aren't eating, Barry," Inch scolded the singer.

"I'm always down after a session," Latchford mumbled,
looking into space. "Don't mind me."

"Don't mind him," Carol echoed. "Barry-baby will retire
to the wilderness shortly and communicate with his inner spirit.
One Magnificat, two Te Deums, and a fast chorus of Panis
Angelicus, and he'll be as good as new."

"Don't give that lady any more to drink," Latchford said
with a false smile.

"Are you a choirboy?" Flora asked. "I used to pipe away
with the altos at St. James the Apostle on Ste. Catherine Street.
If this was Saturday night, we could drive over tomorrow
morning for matins."

"I wouldn't mind that," Latchford said, his pale eyes
staring through the window into the twinkling black mass of
the Montreal skyline.

In the weeks that followed, after the Barry Latchford
recording of "Summer Silence" was released, some of the
euphoria began to wear off. They had a good song, but
pessimism arose as they listened to it for the 150th time. Inch
lifted the tone arm. "Where do we go from here?" he said. They
were using the agency studio for their private business.

"To church," Pullman said drily, "like your wife keeps
saying. Only we go to pray, not to sing."

"Pray, hell. The whole idea, *your* idea, is that we don't
leave things to chance."

"It's in the lap of the gods."

"You were going to rig the charts. Line up a crowd of
little girls to phone the stations all day asking for Barry
Latchford's new single."

"It isn't that easy. Latchford's nobody to these kids. They
only request what everybody else is requesting -- Michael
Jackson, the Bee Gees."

"Pay them then."

"It gets complicated. What if some parents wonder where the kids are getting the money? Our involvement comes out, Latchford looks terrible, and so do Inch and Pullman."

"Why didn't you think of this in the beginning?"

"I was being optimistic. Forgive me."

The telephone rang beside Inch. He picked it up. "Studio."

"A call from Toronto, Mr. Inch. Barry Latchford."

"Put him on." He said to Pullman, "It's Russ Columbo. Our troubles are just beginning."

Pullman closed his eyes and sighed.

"We were just talking about you, Barry. Did you get the record I sent you?" Inch listened for half a minute. "Feel free to do whatever you can to promote it up there. Meanwhile, we're going ahead as discussed." When the call was finished, Inch let the telephone drop into its cradle as if it was something wet.

"He's over the moon," he said. "We'd better produce some evidence that we're trying to sell his song."

In Toronto, Barry Latchford went through the house looking for Carol. He found her in the television room. The set was playing with the sound off. She was placed in a chair in viewing position, trying to read a newspaper by the light from the screen. Her knitting rested on the carpet. Beside it was an ashtray full of cigarette ends and an empty beer bottle.

"Your trouble is you don't have anything to do," he said.

"Wrong," she said. "It says here Imperial Tobacco and Molson's Brewery have increased production. I'll never catch up."

He sat on the floor. "That sounds like an unhappy woman."

"You always had a good ear."

He took the newspaper from her and snapped off the television, leaving only one source of light -- the lamp in the hall outside the open door. "I really don't like to see you unhappy."

"I'm sorry. I can't please you with satisfaction I don't possess." She lit another cigarette. "It probably isn't your fault.

Different things make us happy. I like dance halls -- they call them discos now -- and I hardly ever see the inside of one. I'd like to wear some of those wild leather clothes the kids are into, but you'd think I was crazy."

He looked away, hoping she wouldn't go on. If she turned herself into one of those freaks he couldn't imagine how he'd react.

"You fooled me. First time I saw you singing in the club I thought you were a swinger. We should never have got married." She blew a fierce shaft of smoke.

"Are you in love with that writer character?"

Carol picked up her knitting, held the needles poised, and stared at the particle of space between their tips. "Steve Pullman? Am I in love with him? Not quite."

"He never takes his eyes off you."

"Better not say that. You're making me all excited."

"He wants to take you away to Baytown or wherever the hell he comes from."

"Small-town bliss. Now there's a dream."

Latchford put a firm hand on his wife's knee. "Don't leave me, Carol."

"Message noted," she said, and the knitting needles began to click like a machine.

The Montreal promotion never did get off the ground. But as things turned out Pullman's failure to deliver didn't matter. Latchford took his copy of "Summer Silence" to a DJ friend at the top station in Toronto. He loved it, played it three times on one morning show, and the telephone began to ring. The process didn't stop for two months as the song reached the top of the charts and stayed there. The distributor told the factory to press another 50,000, and began spreading the word to radio stations and dealers across Canada. He also telephoned a connection in New York. They had a phenomenon on their hands -- a song that couldn't fail to make it big.

Indian summer is always a special time in Montreal. Bonfires send pungent smoke trailing upward into hazy blue skies. The bittersweet afternoons are silent in memory of the days of warmth and comfort that are gone forever.

Barry and Carol Latchford came down for the celebration at the Inch residence on the south shore. It was clearly time to open the champagne; the record was now the top-selling single in the history of Canadian pop music. Better still, a deal was set for distribution in the States. Latchford's dream had come true.

The party was one of those Saturday affairs where the few people not invited turn up anyway, bringing bottles as admission. Every room was crowded, as were the back garden, the front lawn, the stairs, the garage, even the cars parked in the driveway. All the doors were open, the music system was on full volume; the sophisticated party dominated the entire neighborhood.

Norman Inch finally managed to manoeuvre his wife out of the kitchen and into a quiet corner. "I'm worried about Steve," he said.

"I told him not to follow wine with beer."

"I mean the way he keeps after Carol Latchford. Barry's starting to look at him."

Flora's eyes grew large and innocent. "So?"

"So all we need is a fistfight between the guest of honor and the lyricist."

"It might be just what the party needs."

"I don't know why I bother talking to you."

"People should be allowed to go where their actions take them. It helps the plot develop."

"These are not characters in your bloody novel."

"Real people can live or die just like fictional characters." Flora blinked at her husband. "And I don't like your tone of voice. My novel one day will surpass any of your so-called successes with chintzy songs about summer love."

By two o'clock on Sunday morning the police had paid two polite visits, the music was now turned low, most of the guests had gone home, and those few who remained were caged inside the house. The Latchfords had come with luggage for a long weekend. Barry had removed his turtleneck sweater and suede jacket some time after midnight and was now wearing his pajama top. He was sitting on a couch beside his hostess, swallowing cognac from a tumbler.

"We've got to do it, Barry," Flora said. She crossed her legs and Richelieu repositioned himself on her lap without opening his eyes.

"Do what?" Latchford was looking through a doorway at his wife dancing with Pullman in the next room. Carol was a lot shorter than Steve; her cheek was pressed against his chest, her skirt riding up in back, showing plenty of rounded calf. Pullman's chin rested on the top of her curly head. He saw Latchford watching them and gave him a sleepy grin.

"We have to go to St. James the Apostle tomorrow morning," Flora said. "We have to show them how to sing."

"I haven't been to church in ten years," he said.

Latchford and his brothers had been the foundation of the choir for a long time. When they matured and went professional, their gospel quartet was good enough to hold a radio series on the Dominion Network. They even did a summer series on television. His chance to go single, to do club dates, had seemed like the beginning of a fabulous career. Now, even with the U.S. hit in the pipeline, he found himself longing for the uncomplicated delight of standing around the piano with his brothers rehearsing "This Little Light of Mine."

"You haven't been to church in ten years? I haven't been in twenty. I'd say we're both overdue." Flora followed Barry's gaze to see what was distracting him. She raised her glass and her voice. "Yoo-hoo, Stevie! Here's to young love!"

Later, Inch was unloading a tray of glasses in the kitchen. The party had gone quiet. Suddenly Latchford's voice rang out in a tone heavy with warning. *"Steve!"*

The command was so threatening Inch's heart began to pound. He moved quickly from the kitchen into the room that had been cleared for dancing. Nobody was there. Through the door way he could see a tableau at the couch in the front room. Latchford had risen, his glass in one hand, his eyes focused on the French doors leading to the garden. Flora was holding a restraining hand on his wrist while she pressed Richelieu down on her lap. The dog's ears were up -- he was tense, alert.

After this frozen moment, things began to move quickly. Latchford broke away, dropping the glass on the carpet and vanishing swiftly through the French doors. Flora struggled up and the dog went scampering.

"What's happening?"

"Steve and Carol stopped dancing and went out back."

Inch showed his wife a hopeless face. "I'm not happy stopping fights."

"Steve has it coming. He's been socking it in with that little slut all evening."

Carol Latchford's voice rang out in the garden. "Don't you start, Barry -- I'm warning you!" Then she screamed "Stop! Somebody stop him!"

When Inch reached the end of the garden he could hardly see in the darkness. He could faintly make out Latchford's pajama clad arm rising and falling as he knelt across Steve Pullman. Forcing himself to intervene, he put a hand on Barry's shoulder. It was like touching a button on a machine. The beating ended abruptly and Latchford sat back on his haunches.

"Call the police," Carol said. Her voice was outraged, like that of a parent who has seen a child go too far.

Inch's eyes were accustomed to the darkness now. He leaned down and looked at what had been Steve Pullman's face. "We need an ambulance," he said.

Latchford got up and walked away. He discovered he was holding a rock in his hand. He let it fall. Behind him he could hear the panic, the excitement, people running into each other, voices shouting, somebody trying to start a car and calling a girl to come on because he wanted to get going.

His arms ached. He remembered the day when he was ten years old and he tried to walk home from the supermarket carrying two paper bags of groceries against this chest. The bags seemed light enough at the start but before he was halfway home he knew he couldn't support them longer than another few seconds. There was no place to set them down and he felt such a sense of failure and embarrassment he began to cry. When he finally made it to the house, after spilling the contents of one of the bags in the gutter, his arms throbbed for the rest of the afternoon.

The lights of Inch's house were getting farther away. Latchford turned and blundered back through a low hedge, across a flower bed. He went inside and hurried up the stairs to the guest room, where he stripped off the blood-spattered pajama top and changed into a shirt. He paused, then felt impelled to put on a necktie and his suede jacket.

As he was leaving the house by the front door, he was confronted by Carol. Her face was streaked with tears and dirt. "Where are you going? The police are coming."

"Bye-bye, Carol."

"You're crazy."

"I told you to stop fooling around."

"Why did you keep hitting him? Once was enough."

"Why did you drink so much?"

She held him by the arm as he tried to walk away. He twisted free, feeling skin from his forearm collecting under her fingernails as he released himself. "Feel better?"

"Where are you going?"

Latchford had no idea.

He followed curving streets and found himself close to the river. The metropolis lay on the other side, humming, vibrating like a starship just landed after a voyage across the universe. To his right, a gigantic bridge connected the south shore with the city. He began walking in that direction.

Halfway across the bridge, he stopped and stared out at the night past a barrier of steel struts and girders. He was like a prisoner in a cage, but he felt safe, protected rather than confined. The considerable amount of alcohol he had consumed was beginning to wear off. Latchford realized now, for the first time, that he had deliberately killed Steve Pullman, beaten him to death, murdered him. He tried to recall the event but it wasn't clear in his mind. He had a suspicion he had enjoyed it.

Carol's question had been "Why did you keep hitting him?" Latchford stood in his cage and tried to think of an answer. Hardly a day went by in which he was not tense as a spring, racing from here to there, doing what everybody else wanted, singing their nonsensical jingles, taking their money and their praise when he knew he was guilty of conspiring to produce rubbish.

What should he be doing then? What sort of life would have converted him into a satisfied man who did not beat rivals to death at parties? The days of singing with his brothers -- were those not happy times? Latchford tried to recapture the feeling that went with standing around the piano in the family living room, harmonizing gospel hymns --"Throw Out The Lifeline," "What a Friend We Have in Jesus." The memory of the music brought tears to his eyes but he could identify no sense of inner peace from that faraway life.

Perhaps he had always been driven to go further and try new things. Maybe that was why he'd left the quartet and pursued a commercial career. Latchford didn't really understand why he did what he did. For as long as he could remember, he had been carrying a giant rage. Maybe he deserved credit for containing it till now. The question was not really why he had killed but how everybody else kept the blood off their hands.

A giant bus frightened him as it hissed its brakes going past on the road behind him. With his heart pounding, Latchford began walking toward the city.

The police arrived at the Inch residence promptly and were disturbed to learn that the assailant had been allowed to walk away from the scene. They took a description and spent half an hour checking out the neighborhood gardens with flashlights.

"He's miles away by now," one of them said with satisfaction as they slammed the doors of the police car and followed the ambulance carrying Pullman's body.

Nobody slept. By nine-thirty in the morning Flora had washed three loads of dishes. Carol was drying and stacking. Norman was sitting at the table, smoking, staring out the window at the glorious morning, shaking his head solemnly every now and then, like a baseball pitcher shrugging off his catcher's signals. They were all waiting for the phone to ring.

At last Carol said, "Can we have the radio on?"

Norman reached out and snapped the switch of the transistor. An announcer read the weather, gave the time, then an organ played an introduction and a lugubrious male voice began to sing.

"Sweet hour of prayer, sweet hour of prayer
That calls us from a world of care..."

Flora raised her head from the detergent bubbles. "I know where Barry is," she said. "He's at church."

"He hasn't gone since we've been married," Carol said.

"I told him last night about St. James the Apostle." She began drying her hands.

"I'll get the car out," Norman said.

"No, I'll drive myself. You haven't shaved."

"Wouldn't it be better to call the police?" Carol said.

Flora stared at her, then turned to the door. "Wash your face, child. We're going to find your husband and bring him home."

In the car, Carol said, "I guess I sounded inhuman back there."

"My husband has never killed anybody," Flora said, "so I don't know how I'd behave in your place." She gunned illegally past a line of cars on the bridge. "As far as I *know* he's never killed anybody."

"It can't get any worse for me. I've been misrable for most of the last six years. Barry is bound to go to jail for a long time and I know I'll be happier without him." They were off the bridge now, moving through the narrow streets of east Montreal. "I'm a bitch, eh?"

Flora gave Carol a speculative glance. "Yes, I'd say a bitch."

Parking spaces were plentiful on a Sunday morning. Flora stopped on Crescent Street, locked the car, then led the way at a fast pace toward the gray-stone church. The fine weather showed no signs of breaking. Flora's cream straw hat sparkled in the sunlight. She had offered to lend a hat to Carol but the Torontonian declined and wrapped her head in a scarf. Small-town girl, was Flora's assessment of that decision.

They were just in time for the service. The church was filled. An usher helped them cram into a pew near the back. Flora, a choir-trained Anglican, genuflected and said a silent prayer, then sat back. In every direction she saw massed heads and shoulders. Carol leaned close to whisper, "We'll never find him, even if he *is* here."

"Don't worry, he's here."

The service began with the choir chanting what to Flora were familiar notes, but there was no response from the congregation so she remained silent. Then the minister announced the opening hymn and as the organ played the seventeenth-century tune, "Nun Danket," the congregation and choir rose, shuffling and coughing.

> *"Now thank we all our God,*
> *With heart and hands and voices...."*

It was at the beginning of the second verse that she realized something unusual was happening. The congregation had fallen silent and many of the choir members had their eyes raised to the balcony. Above her, out of Flora's sight, Barry Latchford was singing as if it had been rehearsed this way.

> *"Oh, may this bounteous God*
> *Through all our life be near us..."*

Gradually the choir stopped singing until, by the last quatrain, it was Barry alone accompanied by the organ. His tone was fuller than anything Flora had heard in Carlo's studio all those months ago. She felt she was listening to a different voice.

"And keep us in His grace,
And guide us when perplexed,
And free us from all ills
In this world and the next."

The women waited for Latchford in the sunlight outside the church. He made no attempt to walk away. He was unshaven and red-eyed but he was smiling. This boyish smile was different from the cynical one Flora had come to think of as typically Latchford. Carol didn't move to him nor did he approach her.

Flora watched them for a few seconds, squinting into the sun. "Let's go home," she said at last.

"Are the police there?"

"No. I thought we'd have lunch, you can clean up and rest for a while, then we'll call them."

He nodded. In the car he said, "Not a bad ending."

"What ending?" Flora said. "You won't be in forever. You'll come out and start singing the proper music, the way you sang this morning."

"I don't think so."

"Why not?"

"I killed that man. All he did was play a little game with Carol and I took his life. That can't be right."

The police took Latchford away at four. By five, Carol had departed in a taxi for the airport, refusing a lift. The house was tidy -- Norman had been busy. He came into Flora's study carrying two drinks; she was in her swivel chair, staring at the typewriter.

Norman handed her a glass and sat down. "I wouldn't want to go through that again," he said.

"You won't. Not with Steve, anyway."

"I could do without the smart answers. He was my partner."

"You'll find somebody better. Carol will settle down with a small-town boy who suits her. Latchford will sing the roof off the prison chapel. Everybody's ahead."

"Except Steven Pullman."

The telephone rang and Norman went down the hall to answer it. When he came back a couple of minutes later, the glass in his hand was empty. "That was somebody from the police. Latchford is dead."

"I don't believe it." Flora looked stunned. "What happened?"

"They didn't handcuff him because he was so quiet, the way he gave himself up. In the station he knocked over a cop, managed to get hold of his gun, and turned it on himself."

Flora reached under the desk and lifted Richelieu from the basket. She cradled him on her lap, rocking back and forth in the swivel chair.

"That's how right you were about Latchford," Norman said bitterly. "I wonder about the rest of us."

Ellery Queen Mystery Magazine, July, 1983

CHILD OF
ANOTHER TIME

Their eyes met and Blake Metcalfe felt as if he had been kicked in the stomach. She couldn't be older than seventeen, young enough to be his daughter. But she held out her glass, and as he filled it with red wine she said: "Hi, my name's Tina Flanagan. I'm the new girl in town."

He introduced himself and heard that she was just down from Toronto. Her father had used influence to get her a job in a Montreal ad agency. It had been her wish to get away from home.

They stood side by side at the drinks table, watching couples dancing in the area occupied by desks and drawing boards during the working day. "I've been watching you," she said. "Do you work here?"

Metcalfe nodded. "I'm one of the old originals. The oldest," he added, providing emphasis that was hardly necessary. At forty-eight, he was going heavy, trousers rolling at the waist, cheekbones covered by a mask of fat. Life was good these days, life was easy. Apex Art Studio was charging clients a premium for his illustrations and he was collecting part of that money. He ate big lunches, drank out of habit, went home and made love with Laura as often as most men might with a wife of twenty-five years' standing. Having his ailing mother-in-law in the house was a problem, but then.

Metcalfe found himself looking down at Tina's hair. It was chestnut, thick and wavy, and the way it grew and glistened reminded him of somebody -- yes, his daughter Maggie. Good thing Maggie had not made it to the party or she would have been casting sarcastic glances his way, seeing him chatting up the young talent like this. Still only twenty-three, Maggie Metcalfe was fast becoming one of the better illustrators in the advertising department at Rambeau's.

"I have to say it." Tina looked up at him. "I go for older men. I hope you don't mind."

"I'd be lying if I said I mind." There was something so attractive about this plump, pretty kid. Metcalfe couldn't express it other than to admit he felt inclined to pick her up and hold her in his arms. And although there was an element of lust, the attraction was not totally sexual. No, he felt an overpowering affection for her, a disturbing urge to nuzzle her big, smooth face, to tuck his nose into the dimple in her cheek, to inhale whatever soapy fragrance he might find clinging to her.

"It's because I never had a father," she confessed. "I was adopted. My parents levelled with me when I was twelve. I think that's a good idea, don't you? They told me I was chosen because they love me so much." She sipped some wine. "My father is Horace Flanagan, the real-estate man. You must have heard of him."

"Who hasn't. He's the cover story this month in *Locus* magazine.

"See how clever I am." She gave Metcalfe a smile that interrupted his heartbeat. "If you're going to be adopted, choose somebody like Horace Flanagan."

Some of the party left to go to the baseball game, where they would be guests in the Apex box at the Olympic Stadium. The reduced crowd seemed to be settling in for heavy drinking and close dancing. Metcalfe looked at his watch. He had told Laura to expect him around nine. He never stayed till the end at company parties.

"If you're getting ready to go, I'd appreciate a lift," Tina said.

They walked from the building along Notre Dame Street through a cool summer night. The girl fell into step, matching his stride naturally. Not many people did this -- most of them asked him where the fire was.

In the car, he asked her where she lived. She told him she had an apartment on Durocher Street. "But I don't want to go home yet. Can we go somewhere for coffee?"

Metcalfe avoided the restaurants where he was known, drove to a place down east where he took late nourishment after his occasional solo debaucheries in the strip clubs on The Main. Tina seemed fascinated, listening to the foreign hum of the place, flashing a friendly smile at their French-Canadian waitress.

"This is so nice of you to take me out."

"My pleasure." Had she really forgotten it was her suggestion? He felt like nothing more than coffee and pie but Tina ordered barbecue chicken, fries, roll, and a vanilla milkshake. As she tucked in, she said:

"I love Montreal. For some reason it feels like home to me. Maybe I was born here -- my parents have never said where I came from when they adopted me. Is it possible I feel something in my soul, like a salmon that goes back to where it was spawned?"

"It's possible."

"Talk to me while I eat. Tell me about yourself."

Metcalfe seldom opened up to anybody but now he found himself telling this child everything, eager to describe his life to her. He spoke of his early dreams of becoming a fine artist, of having a studio in Paris -- a city he had never even visited. He explained his acceptance of the security in the illustrator's life, where he was usually bored, never stretched, by the assignments.

He glowed when he spoke of Maggie and her burgeoning career at the department store. "She's better than I am already." He produced a snapshot from his wallet.

"Looks like somebody I know," Tina said, frowning, dipping a french-fry into a pot of spicy sauce.

Metcalfe went on to talk about his wife, who had resumed her career teaching languages until her mother's illness became so far advanced that the old lady had to be taken into the house where Laura could devote full time to looking after her.

"What is Parkinson's disease?" Tina asked. "I've never come across it.'

"I hope you never do. The victim shakes constantly, can't do much of anything for herself, wastes away but very slowly. It can go on for years and years."

"No cure?"

"Sometimes a very tricky brain operation can help if they get to it soon enough. Laura's mum is too late for that." Thinking of the old lady with her hideous life sentence and Laura trapped at home as nurse, Metcalfe felt impotent rage.

When they were finished, Tina went to the ladies room. As Metcalfe gave money to the waitress she said: "Your daughter is a chip off the old block. I can see the family resemblance. She looks like you."

Metcalfe felt weak in the legs. Seventeen years fell away and he was back in the waiting room of the maternity hospital facing a troubled Dr. Fox, trying to understand what the man was saying. "Something is the matter with the baby. She's having trouble breathing. We'll do everything we can, but I think you should prepare yourself. No, we won't say anything yet to Mrs. Metcalfe."

So the baby they had planned to call Angela came and went in one shocking weekend in October. Metcalfe called the department store and managed to get rid of the new crib before Laura came home from the hospital. Somehow they recovered, concentrated on six-year-old Maggie, but the wound never healed completely. To this day, when he remembered the death of Angela, Metcalfe wept.

"Are you all right?" Tina searched his face as she joined him at the restaurant entrance.

"Come on, I'll drive you home."

The suspicion was no more than a whisper in Metcalfe's mind. It was the most incredible nonsense but he listened to it. She was the right age. There was this instant rapport between them, which was much more than an ordinary physical attraction. And now the waitress had said they were father and daughter, she emphasized the resemblance.

Saying goodnight outside Tina's apartment building, he was deluged by clues. That laugh -- it was like Maggie's. When she turned her eyes down, they were Laura's eyes. The broad

forehead was his own -- and the overlapping teeth in the
bottom row, why hadn't he noticed them before? That was the
Metcalfe bite, his dentist would recognize it.

He drove home at twenty-five miles an hour. The
suspicion was right or it was wrong. If wrong, Tina's
appearance here, her very existence, was an incredible
coincidence. If the suspicion was right, the explanation was
even more overwhelming. It would suggest a crime that
hardly bore thinking about. Had Dr. Stanley Fox deliberately
lied about the baby's condition? Did he, somehow, fake
Angela's death, present to Metcalfe through the undertaker a
small white coffin -- empty -- then provide a healthy baby to
the millionaire Toronto realtor, Horace Flanagan? It could be
done. Anything could be done with money and Flanagan
had plenty of money. But why?

"Why my baby?" Metcalfe said aloud, sitting parked in
front of his house.

"Are you staying out there all night?" Laura called in a
stage whisper from the open front door.

He went in and pretended he was sick to his stomach to
cover his shell-shocked condition. He drank a bromo, then
took a cup of black coffee. There was no way he could breathe
a word of this theory to Laura. Seventeen years ago, losing the
baby had almost wiped her out. To this day, the subject could
hardly be discussed.

"How's your mum?"

"She had one of her bad spells this afternoon."

"You should have called me."

"I knew you had the party. I called the doctor, I explained
she was getting violent -- it's the depression. She brought my
silver hand mirror down, cracked the glass top on the dresser."

"And you were here alone." He had stopped suggesting
they institutionalize the old lady. Laura wouldn't consider the
provincial hospital -- it was a nightmare, the wards and
corridors populated with pitiful human wreckage out of an
engraving from the Middle Ages. The acceptable alternative
was a private nursing home, but this would cost the world.

"The doctor told me to increase her medication. I don't
think she'll act up again." Laura's face was showing new

creases, her mouth set in the familiar determined line. She lowered her eyes and Metcalfe saw for a fraction of a second the expression that had crossed Tina Flanagan's face. "Will you go in and speak to her before we go to bed? She looks forward to seeing you."

Metcalfe pulled a chair close to the bed and turned the lamp so his cheery face was illuminated. "Evening, Mum," he said. "I've come from a drunken party. Don't worry, I drank your share too."

The pale, drugged eyes looked up at him. Her lips parted as she tried to smile and the palsied hand crept towards him across the blanket. Leaning forward to give her a kiss on the cheek, Metcalfe kept smiling but he closed his eyes and held his breath.

For two days, Metcalfe carried the fantastic theory around. It did not evaporate, made ludicrous by the passage of time. It hardened into reality, like an excavated relic of some ancient war. He was going to have to dig in order to verify his suspicion or to dispel the delusion. But he would need help and there was only one place where he could find it. One man who would go along without trying to talk him out of it.

Metcalfe took Tuesday afternoon off and drove to the apartment building on Decelles Avenue. The building looked sadly familiar -- red brick, three tiers of iron balconies, an entrance decorated with curved concrete like something out of an Alexander Korda film. This was the doorway through which he and Laura carried baby Maggie on the proud return from the hospital twenty-three years ago. Six years later they had crept in alone, empty-handed, guilty, nothing to show.

On the first occasion, Alphonse Ferrier had been coming up from his basement apartment. Al was the building superintendent, a former policeman expelled for drinking and insubordination. When he saw Maggie, his Indian features produced a proud smile -- she might have been his baby.

After the loss of Angela, while Laura was still in the hospital, Metcalfe had wandered into the Texas Tavern around the corner for a few beers to help him sleep. Alphonse Ferrier was alone at a table near the door. He must have heard the news. When Metcalfe sat down, Ferrier pushed one of three glasses of beer toward him and said: "Not very good, is it." There was something stoical, an acceptance of bad luck, in the understatement that reinforced Metcalfe more than all the effusions of sympathy poured over him in the past two days. He relaxed, relieved of the hideous embarrassment.

"Thanks, Al," he said. "Cheers." He drank the glass of beer at one draft and ordered four more. He and the super closed the tavern that night. After that, they drank together once a week until Laura suggested a year later that they get out of the apartment with its melancholy nursery and move closer into the city. Since then, he only managed drinks with Ferrier at Christmas.

Metcalfe parked the car. Ferrier was washing the glass in the front doors. He looked a few pounds heavier. The glossy black hair fell in a thick curtain as he bent to his work.

"Time for a beer, Al."

He stood up with a chamois in one hand, the dark Iroquois eyes finding out everything there was to know about his former tenant who had come back so unexpectedly. "What's the matter?"

"I've got big trouble."

"What can I do?"

"Come and listen to me. Tell me if you think I'm crazy."

"I can tell you that right now. But I could use a beer."

The tavern wasn't crowded. They took a table by the door, said nothing till the beer came and they had tasted the first one. "You're getting fat, Al."

"I had to stop running." Ferrier used to walk every day to the steps leading up to Beaver Lake. He used to go there, fair weather or foul, and run for miles over pathways covering the mountain. "I did something to a bone in my foot. It's getting better -- I'll get back to it."

Metcalfe finished the first glass, drew the next one to him. "Remember when Angela died the day after she was born? Well. You aren't going to believe this. I don't think she died. I think I've seen her."

Ferrier did not look surprised. He never looked surprised. "She'd be a big girl by now. Seventeen years?"

"That's right. I've met a girl that age. From Toronto. She told me she was adopted. A waitress saw us together in a restaurant and said my daughter looks just like me. But, Al, it's more than that. I had a feeling about her right from the start. Before I knew any of this."

Ferrier looked through the doorway, far away down the street. "How could it be?"

"I don't know. The doctor would have had to take my baby out of the hospital somehow. Convince people she died. I don't know why he'd do that."

"Are you going to ask him?"

"Not yet. He'd say I'm crazy, he'd simply deny it. For all I know, he'd be telling the truth. No, Al, I have to do something"

During their drinking sessions, Ferrier had always been able to read Metcalfe's mind. Now he drew lines with a fingertip in the condensation from the beer glasses, traced the shape of a cross on the table top. "Will you be able to do that?" he asked. "Look in your own baby's grave?"

The weather was good, the risks would never be less. Ferrier took Metcalfe back to the apartment building and fitted them both out with gardener's overalls. He found two pairs of grass clippers, a rake, a spade, and a large canvas bag. With the tools in the bag, they went back to Metcalfe's car and drove to the base of the steps at the side of the mountain.

"If we go in through the cemetery gate," Ferrier said, "they'll ask us what we want. But there's another way in."

They climbed the steps, Ferrier carrying the bag, walked past Beaver Lake and the chalet, then continued up a grassy slope until they came to a bluff overlooking the cemetery.

"This is the hard part. Follow me." Ferrier began to scramble down the steep face, clutching at shrubs and rocks, sending a cascade of gravel ahead of them. Halfway down, the slope began to level out and the passage became easier. Soon they were on grass, moving through a stand of young birch trees, then they were on a path between marble gravestones.

"You know the way from here?" Ferrier asked.

'I visited once or twice years ago. There's an area set aside for the children."

It was a quiet time of afternoon, the cemetery almost deserted. Metcalfe led the way past rows of monuments, the larger ones casting shadows over the path. They moved into an area where the stones were smaller and beyond to where the graves were marked only by rectangular plaques. "This is it." He was occupying his mind with extraneous details, the length of the grass, the number of lace holes in Ferrier's boot. If he thought about what they were about to do, he knew he would not be able to proceed.

"People over there," Ferrier said, handing his companion a pair of clippers. They bent to the edge of the path and began trimming grass.

Ferrier stood up a while later and made a few passes with the rake. "Okay," he said. "Let's make it fast." He took the spade and went to work, Metcalfe more than willing to leave him to it. The spade was sharp; it cut the turf into neat squares Ferrier dragged to one side. Now he was into dark earth.

Metcalfe had not come with the undertaker to the cemetery. The ceremony in the funeral parlor was enough; he had listened to the prayers and watched them take the small white casket away, then he had gone up to the hospital to sit with Laura.

Ferrier's spade struck something solid. He scraped away the earth to reveal crumbling wood. "Want to leave it to me?"

"Yes, go ahead." Metcalfe turned away, bent to examine a patch of clover, tugged at tendrils of weed twisted through the roots of grass. Ferrier's call brought him around.

"You were right my friend."

"What?"

"This is an empty casket." He stirred some fragments of wood as Metcalfe peered over his shoulder. "There was never anything in this box but the lining."

The building had once been somebody's home. Now it was a suite of offices. The automatic switchboard, the telex terminal, the massive electric typewriter all looked expensive. The girl at the reception desk appeared a bit pricey as well. She had been talking on the telephone when Metcalfe came in. Now she set down the phone, picked up a glitter earring, and fastened it to a shell-like lobe.

"Can I help you?"

"I'd like to speak to Mr. Fox. I rang earlier."

"Mr. Metcalfe? Yes, go on through, I'll buzz and tell him you're on the way."

The former Dr. Fox had put on weight. Metcalfe remembered him as a nervous young man with the build of a hungry schoolboy. Now that frame was concealed inside a suitful of flesh. When he stood to greet his visitor, the fat on Fox's chest kept his arms from touching his sides.

"What can I do for you?"

Metcalfe sat down. He could see by Fox's eyes that the man had decided not to remember him. The gun he had borrowed from Alphonse Ferrier felt heavy in his jacket pocket. "When did you stop being a doctor?"

"Quite some time ago. I decided real estate was better for me. After all those years of study, too." Fox made a coarse sound between a cough and a laugh. "Ain't it a bitch!"

Metcalfe decided to get on with it. "Seventeen years ago, you delivered my daughter Angela. You told me she had hyaline membrane, couldn't breathe properly, you said she died the next day. Recently I met a seventeen-year-old girl from Toronto who could be my daughter. I've been told we have a strong resemblance. She's adopted. What do you say, Dr. Fox?"

The heavy face was like damp clay. Mottled patches suggested worms below the surface. "I remember the case, of course. Very tragic. But this girl -- you mustn't let something like that play on your imagination."

"I agree. That's why I went to the cemetery and opened the grave. I've just come from there." Metcalfe held onto the gun butt as if he would fall without it. "It's an empty coffin. As you well know."

"Oh, God." Fox buried his face in two bunches of fleshy fingers. A couple of gaudy rings stared at Metcalfe. "What are you going to do?"

It was time to show the gun. Metcalfe took it out and let the barrel rest on the edge of the desk to keep it from waving like a baton. "I haven't made up my mind. I may shoot you in the gut. But first I want to know what happened. I want to know who. And why."

"It was Horace Flanagan. He offered me money -- so much money I couldn't let it go. Can you imagine somebody putting a quarter of a million dollars in front of you -- tax free? He wanted a baby. He and his wife couldn't conceive. They couldn't adopt, either -- not in Quebec because they were different religions."

"I don't see the problem. These things happen underground all the time. Girls are in trouble, they have babies and they farm them out."

"Flanagan is a crackpot. He believes the infant from an unwed mother carries bad blood. It wasn't good enough for him. He came to me and told me what he wanted, a child of good parents, cultivated people, talented people, he was ready to buy that baby. I told him no way, but then he named this incredible sum of money. I wanted out -- medical practice was killing me, I owed people from my years in college. Flanagan had found this out."

Hearing his suspicion confirmed was almost beyond Metcalfe's belief. "How did you get away with it?"

Fox explained. The maternity hospital was a small place with only a few patients. He had arranged to have Laura Metcalfe induced so the baby would arrive on a Sunday night when a young, inexperienced nurse was on duty. He convinced the nurse the infant needed emergency treatment, said he would drive it to Montreal General himself. He took the newborn child to the Flanagan residence, where a private nurse took over the post-natal care. It was a healthy girl, there were no complications.

"But the undertaker? He staged a funeral service."

"Staged is right. I gave him twenty thousand dollars. Only one man knew about it. I said I performed an autopsy so the coffin was sealed, nobody would want to look inside." Fox took his hands away from his face. "I did a terrible thing."

Metcalfe got up and went to the door. "I'm not sure what I'm going to do with you. I may bring in the police. I may kill you myself." He put the gun in his pocket. "First I want to go and see Flanagan."

Incredibly, Fox tried to mitigate his crime. "Babies do die. It happens all the time. It's a terrible thing for the parents but they get over it. Life goes on."

"There's only one thing wrong with that," Metcalfe said. "My baby *didn't* die."

In the days that followed, Metcalfe tried to decide what to do. He was bricked up, he realized, like a frog in a cornerstone. He couldn't tell Laura about his discovery -- she would go out of her mind. Nor could he go to Tina Flanagan and explain that he was her real father. The revelation might turn the girl upside down. He had observed during their time together that she had a crush on him. Sexual fantasies had probably taken place in her mind. To learn he was her father...

On the other hand, if he went to Toronto, looked up Horace Flanagan, and faced him with his outrage, the tycoon would surely have him killed. How could the holder of such a threatening secret be allowed to live?

What if Metcalfe were to kill Flanagan? If he did it precipitately and was caught, then the secret would be revealed with Laura and Maggie and Tina left to live with it. And he himself would spend the rest of his life in prison.

What if he took care, murdered Flanagan and managed to go undetected? It would be a shocking loss for Tina, who obviously loved her adoptive father. How could he do that to her?

There was no direction in which Metcalfe could turn, and yet the urge for revenge was so overpowering he could taste it like a mouthful of copper coins.

A further chilling thought was the realization that Dr. Fox must have telephoned Flanagan the same day and told him about Metcalfe's discovery. The millionaire, a great believer in insurance, could well have set the wheels in motion by this time to have the threat eliminated. So whether Metcalfe took action or not, fate, having shown him the truth about a devastating aspect of his past, might now be about to sort out his future.

"I'd like to have you guys down to the loft for supper in a couple of weeks," Maggie said. She had come for a meal and a visit and was now playing stud poker with her father at the dining-room table, using matches for chips. Laura was in a deep chair marking French papers, a job she did freelance for one of her former colleagues at the school. Her face lit up.

"Sounds lovely," she said. The evenings at Maggie's place were always entertaining. Odd friends dropped in, there was wine and much spontaneous laughter. The loft was part of a converted clothing factory -- spacious, mattress on the floor, painted bricks hung with bright, original work. "Let's make it soon."

"I may have to go to Toronto," Metcalfe said in a tone that cancelled all other plans.

"What does it take to raise a smile around here?" Maggie complained. She shuffled the cards. "New game. Seven-card stud. Deuces, treys, one-eyed Jacks, and low-in-the-hole wild. Everybody prospers."

Two days later, Metcalfe was at the drawing board in his private room at the art studio. The telephone rang. "Metcalfe?" said a resonant voice. "This is Horace Flanagan. Can you come out and talk to me? I'm outside the building."

Metcalfe tried to visualize the tycoon in a telephone booth. "Why not come in here?"

"Better we not be seen together. For both of us. And for Tina."

That was direct enough. Metcalfe felt reassured, as if now the matter was on the table and this man, whose career was built on problem-solving, would do something to make Metcalfe's agony go away. "I'll be right out."

Flanagan had not been calling from a booth. The telephone was in a grey limousine stationed outside the building like a slab of polished glacial rock. The back door opened and Metcalfe climbed into an upholstered interior that resembled a corner of the lobby in an expensive hotel. Horace Flanagan blended into the grey-plush fabric. Only his face emerged-pink-and-white skin, sea-green eyes, sparse white hair, a long upper lip curved in a mild smile, a dimple in a plump, square jaw. This is the man Tina accepts as her father, Metcalfe thought, understanding how it could be so. She loves him. She looks forward to seeing him.

"Thanks for coming out." The car began to roll. "It's after eleven. Have a drink?"

"Rye and water." Metcalfe watched Flanagan open a cherrywood panel and measure whisky into crystal glasses. Here is the man who did this unspeakable thing to me, he thought. Why aren't I at his throat?

"Cheers." Was it actually the best booze he had ever tasted or was it the influence of the experience -- drifting silently with a gentle surging movement through surroundings tinted green by glass that was probably bulletproof? If the gods went about the world, this was how they did it.

"To the point," Flanagan said. "A terrible coincidence has taken place. I should never have allowed Tina to move to Montreal. But the chance that she would encounter her father, or that you would recognize her, seemed infinitely remote."

"She encountered me," Metcalfe intoned with a hint of mockery. "I recognized her."

"And you went further, Dr. Fox tells me. You opened the grave and established the case. Well, I give you credit, Mr. Metcalfe, for not running amok. I can't say I would have been as controlled. In your position, I reckon I'd have grabbed a gun. There would have been bodies, Tina would have lost two fathers. She would be the ultimate loser."

"And her mother. My wife."

"Of course." The millionaire put his hand on a black despatch case beside him. "But you didn't do that. You have kept the secret, which means there is still a chance for a happy ending."

"I doubt it." Metcalfe's sense of outrage was rising as Flanagan talked on about civilized behavior.

"We can't turn back the clock. I can't give you back your baby. She doesn't exist. She's a young woman and she accepts me and my wife as her parents. We have a sound relationship -- we love each other."

"You'd better let me out of the car."

"No, listen. We have only two courses of action open to us. This case contains a lot of money. Half a million dollars. It may sound crass, Metcalfe, but what else can I offer you as compensation? Believe me, money does buy happiness. A lot of people achieve it in no other way."

Metcalfe was thinking of Ferrier's gun. It was in his desk at the office, in a bottom drawer buried under a couple of art pads. "You said two courses of action."

Flanagan looked genuinely troubled. "If you refuse to cooperate, I'll have to take steps to protect my own position and the contentment of my family." He glanced through the glass panel at the back of the chauffeur's neck. The driver was not a large man. Narrow shoulders, tendons in the neck, and signs of a scaly scalp suggested an impatient individual, one who took pleasure in carrying out antisocial assignments under the protection of a wealthy patron.

When Metcalfe said nothing, Flanagan snapped the catches of the despatch case, opened the lid, and placed it on his passenger's knees. The money was real, it was half a million dollars. The sick old lady could be installed in a proper home where she would receive the best of care. Freed from her slavery, Laura could pursue her teaching career, could return to McGill to obtain a better degree. Or why not the Sorbonne- while Metcalfe took that studio within sight of the Seine and gave himself a real chance to develop the talent that had come down to him through the generations? It wasn't too late.

"What's to stop me taking the money," he heard himself saying, "and then going to the police with the story about you and Dr. Fox?"

"Your common sense. Imagine what such an action would do to Tina. I know you love her, she's your daughter. But the man she accepts as her father -- and she loves me, believe it -- would be involved in a nasty court case. Think of the publicity and how it would affect her."

"At least you'd be in prison where you belong."

"Never. I could buy the Canadian prison system and turn it into a chain of holiday camps. No, I'd suffer from the exposure, but I'd keep my freedom. You, on the other hand, would lose your life in some sort of accident. So your wife would be a widow, your daughter would be fatherless, Tina's life would be a shambles, and you'd be dead. While against that--" Flanagan passed his hand over the case of money.

They were back outside the studio building. By closing the case himself, Metcalfe took possession of the payoff. Clasping the door handle, he said, "Just so you don't think you hold all the cards, I wasn't alone when I opened the grave. A friend was with me. An influential friend. If anything should happen to me, he could tell the whole story."

Flanagan looked respectful. "Who is this influential friend?"

"If you think I'd tell you his name," Metcalfe said as he opened the door, "you must believe I'm suicidal. And homicidal."

Metcalfe spent the afternoon working, then carried the despatch case home with him. He was afraid to let it out of his sight. "It's part of a job I'm working on," he told Laura.

"Al Ferrier telephoned you."

"When?"

"This morning, just after you left for work."

"I'd better see what he wants." He dialed the number on the kitchen phone. "Al, it's me."

"I thought you'd like to know I'm helping you." The former policeman sounded pleased with himself. "Early this morning I went around to the house of that Dr. Fox. I put a little fear into him, showed him my old department identification. How was he to know it's no longer valid? Anyway, I told him he better cooperate with you."

"Thanks, Al. But I'm not sure that was such a wise thing to do."

"Why not? He looked shook up."

"I can't talk about it. I'm coming to see you, are you home?"

At the door, Laura said, "What's the mysterious business with Al Ferrier?"

"He's getting involved in a betting thing and I'm trying to talk him out of it. I won't be long."

Metcalfe drove to the apartment building on Decelles Avenue. He went inside and hurried down the marble steps to the superintendent's apartment on the basement level. Reaching for the bell, he noticed the crack of the open door. A cold wind seemed to flow from the place though when he stepped inside he discovered the apartment was stuffy and there was an unfamiliar musky smell in the air.

He stumbled over Ferrier's body in the kitchen. His throat had been cut and a lake of blood had collected at the low end of the uneven floor. Metcalfe stood over his friend for a full minute. Then he went upstairs and out of the building and drove to the nearest public telephone from which he placed an anonymous call to the police.

Throughout the whole procedure, Metcalfe now realized, he had been carrying the despatch case. He opened it on the car seat beside him and stared at the money. It seemed to be the only thing of value in his life, including the life itself. Because of him, Alphonse Ferrier was dead. Had he not involved him in his morbid investigation, Al would be alive.

But it was *not* morbid. His own Angela had made her way back into his life. There were many clues to her identity. Naturally, he had followed it up.

There seemed to be a message here for bereaved parents: don't go searching for your dead children -- they may prove to be alive.

He switched on and drove to Maggie's address on Crescent Street. She was up in the loft, propped on her mattress with a bottle of chianti and a slab of cheese, watching a movie she'd seen four times. "It's a good thing I love you more than Robert Redford," she snarled, turning off the set and pouring her father some wine.

"Maggie, you have to do something for me. Hold onto your hat." He opened the case.

"New bills for the Sunday-afternoon Monopoly game," she said in a subdued tone.

"It's real. There's half a million there."

"When do the cops start firing through the windows?"

"I promise you, this is legal money. It's ours. You can smile if you want. You're the oldest unmarried daughter of a wealthy father."

"Where did you get it?"

"I can't tell you at the moment. It's a thing I've become involved in."

"You're not in trouble."

"Not yet. But if it turns out that way, you'll have to take over. I want you to hire a safety-deposit box tomorrow and stow the money in it. Tonight, I want you to go and see your mother."

Maggie sensed what was coming. "Why can't you see her? Daddy, what's happening?" Her hands gripped his hard enough so he would have to struggle to free himself.

"I have to go away for a while. You know your mum -- if I start to tell her this, there'll be a big scene. Believe me, Maggie, I'm doing the only thing I can."

Metcalfe stopped off at the office and collected Ferrier's gun. Then he drove to the building on Durocher where Tina Flanagan lived. He hadn't seen her since the night he dropped her off after the party. He felt he had to have a word with her though he had no idea what he would say.

Her name was hand-lettered on a card over the doorbell. Metcalfe's heart turned over as he studied the printing -- it could have been done by Maggie or himself. He rang four times and was turning to go when a woman came out of a ground-floor apartment and smiled at him.

"The Flanagan girl? She's gone for a while. But she's keeping the place. She paid two months in advance."

Metcalfe drove up Decarie Boulevard, put the car on Highway 401, and aimed it at Toronto. He was halfway there when his mind began to emerge from the shock of discovering Al's body. It was almost midnight. At this rate, he would arrive in Flanagan's city in the small hours of the morning. He might better try to get some sleep.

Finding a motel with a vacancy sign, he checked in and lay between chilly sheets in a room that smelled of damp plaster and emulsion paint. What alternative did he have now that the mistakes had been made?

The first and worst one was to have let his imagination loose on the identity of Tina. Another drink and home early to bed that night could have saved all this. But he had taken her to eat, had watched her, listened to her, accepted the idle comment of a waitress who was simply being flattering. Crazy little accidents like that could make the world come to an end.

The other serious mistake was involving Al Ferrier, and then telling Flanagan he had an accomplice.

Al had, of course, contributed to his own fate by running to Dr. Fox and identifying himself.

Metcalfe turned over on sagging springs. If he did nothing, if he went home and pretended he had spent a night out drinking, would all end well? Never. Having killed Ferrier, Flanagan was committed now to doing away with the only man who could connect him with the crime.

No, he was doing the best thing, the only thing he could do. In his childhood Metcalfe had listened to Foster Hewitt broadcasting NHL hockey from Toronto on the radio. One of the commentator's favorite clichés was, "The best defense is a good offense." This was what Metcalfe was doing -- defending himself. By four o'clock, he was up and shaved and back on the road.

The current issue of *Locus* magazine supplied a photograph of the Flanagan mansion as well as an indication of its location. Metcalfe knew the city well enough to find the district. Then he cruised the early-morning streets until he came across the house, a colonial front set back behind an iron fence, trees, and a curving gravel road. The sleek grey limousine was parked opposite the entrance.

Driving half a block ahead, Metcalfe parked in a position where he could watch the front of the house. There was no point in going up and ringing the bell. A man in Flanagan's position would have layers of people between himself and the public. The time to make the move would be when he came out to get into the car. But it would have to be done quickly.

At eight o'clock, the chauffeur appeared from the side of the house and opened the limousine door by the driver's seat. He took a chamois and began polishing a fender. This was the warning Metcalfe needed. He left his car quietly and hurried to a position where he was hidden by a clump of shrubbery.

Footsteps on gravel. The chauffeur was approaching. Metcalfe's hand tightened on the gun in his pocket. A squeal of iron hinges as the man swung open the gates. Then retreating footsteps. Metcalfe's luck was holding. The rich man worked to a schedule and he was about to leave for the office.

Metcalfe peered between branches at the door of the house. The chauffeur was yawning, looking at his watch. The chamois was at the ready -- like an old soldier, he wanted to be occupied when the colonel appeared.

The door opened, the chauffeur turned to his polishing, and Metcalfe darted from his place through the gateway and over thirty yards of cropped lawn. Horace Flanagan, splendid in a white suit and straw hat, saw the running man and saw the gun but only as Metcalfe raised it and aimed from a range of five yards.

"Just a minute," the millionaire said.

"It's all I can do!" Metcalfe called. The chauffeur was reaching inside his jacket but Metcalfe wasn't worried. He would have time for them both.

Then Tina Flanagan came through the open doorway. She saw Metcalfe and the gun. "What is it?" she said. "What are you doing here?"

Her eyes and Metcalfe's eyes came together. She was smiling, as if at a performance. Then she sensed something and her brow lowered, her mouth formed a silent question. In far less than a second, information flowed between them, not all the questions, not all the answers, but a flood of near-understanding, enough for her to work on for the rest of her life.

Metcalfe's gun wavered as the chauffeur's gun appeared. Flanagan observed the indecision on his assailant's face and called out to his bodyguard, but he was too late. The chauffeur fired twice and Metcalfe fell.

"Daddy, what's going on?" Tina cried, "I know him! He works in Montreal!"

"Don't go there, Tina. Come with me. Come inside."

"Why was he going to shoot you?"

"People do crazy things. Leave it, come inside."

Metcalfe had only seconds left for considering what had happened. He was not in pain. He was slipping into a condition that was not unpleasant. It was a good ending. Laura and Maggie would be well off. Laura's mother would be cared for properly. His own life was finished but it had to be, it was the only way. This was far better than if he had killed Flanagan and been left to cope with the aftermath.

The chauffeur was kneeling over him, observing him with neutral eyes."The truth doesn't set you free," Metcalfe said, puzzling the man who had shot him. "You have to set yourself free."

Ellery Queen Mystery Magazine, November, 1983

GUNFIGHT AT THE
O'SHEA CHORALE

"She did it to me again," Gertie O'Shea said, coming into the kitchen from the rehearsal hall and tossing her folder of music on the table, where her husband sat stringing a guitar and waiting for his coffee to cool.

"Beverly Luxton?" Griff O'Shea said. He knew it was Luxton. Only the bell-voiced soloist of the O'Shea Chorale could get so far up Gertie's nose.

Gertie took up Griff's coffee and drank half of it. In her late forties, she was built like a jockey and had the stance of a good bantam-weight. Her blond perm recalled the mute Marx Brother. Her miniskirt and boots were from the era of Mary Quant.

"It never fails. She waits until the rehearsal has started and then she telephones. Sorry, bad throat. Sorry, the washer overflowed. Sorry, I've got extra papers to mark." Gertie set down Griff's mug, empty. "Feel like a coffee?"

"I did, yes." Griffith O'Shea was handsome, bearded, and overweight. Once upon a time he was Griffith Gorman. Years ago, when he fled Montreal and hid in Baytown, it made sense for him to marry Gertie and assume her name. For one thing, the Gertrude O'Shea School of Music was long established at No. 1 Footbridge Lane, the name synonymous with singing, tap-dancing, elocution, and deportment. The other reason Griff was happy to adopt the alias was because he owed money to so many Montrealers his persona had ceased to be grata.

Escaping to Baytown, Griff brought with him his ability to play any musical instrument. He was a one-man band. In fact, he had earned many a capful of quarters keeping bass drum, cymbals, guitar and harmonica all going at once on busy pavements along Ste. Catherine Street. At the O'Shea School, he gave lessons on anything from bugle to zither.

Now, as his wife poured two fresh coffees, Griff said: "I don't know why you tolerate Bev Luxton. I'd tell her to take a hike."

"I can't. She's the best singer in the chorale. The rest of them are crows compared to her. She's only a pain when she's playing hard to get. When she sings, she's an angel."

"Can't you replace her?"

"Some nights," Gertie mused grimly, "I feel like taking her out onto the parking lot and beating the stuffing out of her and throwing her into the river."

"I'll help you."

"She's safe and she knows it. With the Kiwanis Karnival coming up next month and us programmed to do three numbers."

"What you need," Griff said, "is for a stranger to ride into town, tie up his horse to the footbridge railing, and start singing with full-throated ease."

"Not *his* horse, *her* horse. I've got tenors. I need a soprano."

The front doorbell chimed. Griff left the kitchen, crossed the darkened rehearsal hall, and opened the door. The visitor had retreated to the footbridge entrance, dark river below, twin lines of streetlamps arching behind him to the grimy brick backs of the Front Street shops.

"What a pleasing setting," he said. "How fortunate you are to live here." His accent was English.

Inside, with coffee in front of him, he was revealed as a twenty-five-year-old six-footer with a cameo face, an expensive suit, and the name of Desmond Smaile. "I'm a newcomer, as you've probably gathered," he said. "Born in Durham, grew up in London, been in Canada only three weeks, the last four days in Baytown. I like it here and I'm thinking of staying. I like to sing and they tell me at the Baytown Banner, where I've just become employed, that yours is the best choir around."

The late-night audition of Desmond Smaile took place there and then. Griff led the way to the rehearsal-hall piano and asked what their visitor would like to sing. "My repertoire is not large," Smaile said. "Do you know 'Who is Sylvia?' " Griff knew enough to fake it, and after some introductory chords the Englishman began to sing the famous Shakespeare lyric. And Gertie O'Shea's heart stood still.

The sound being produced by Desmond Smaile was higher than a tenor and clearer than a soprano. Devoid of vibrato, it was like a shaft of moonlight through a cathedral window. When the song ended she said quietly: "Bless my soul, a counter tenor."

"Yes, I hope it's all right. I know you don't run into them much on this side of the Atlantic. But in England, some of us boy sopranos continue to produce this falsetto sound -- anyway, it's the way I sing."

"Mr. Smaile," Gertie said, and Griff joined her in the heartfelt response, "you go right on singing that way."

At the next rehearsal of the O'Shea Chorale, Beverly Luxton arrived holding a tissue to her lips and surrounded by the pungent odor of menthol. "Forgive me, Gertie," she whispered, "my throat is acting up. I've been to the pharmacy to see Sylvester Cartwright and he's given me something for the symptoms."

"Poor thing."

"I'll wheeze along in the choruses but I'm afraid I can't do my solo parts tonight." Beverly smiled her brave, tubercular smile. She was tall and dark, with the robust good health of a dairymaid. She taught a class of ten-year-olds at Pine Street School, maintaining discipline through love and fear. But she liked to pretend she was frail. "Sorry," kaff, wheeze.

"I wouldn't dream of putting a strain on you." Gertie turned to the singers assembled in curved rows of collapsible chairs in the rehearsal hall. "All right, everybody, let's begin. Kiwanis Karnival is only a month away, so concentrate, please. First we'll do 'Where E'er You Walk.' And the solo part -- Mr. Smaile, would you try it, please?"

There was a craning of necks as curious choristers turned to see the stranger to whom Gertie O'Shea had just assigned one of Beverly Luxton's solos. When he began to sing, it was all they could do to sustain their own parts at first. Then they responded to the crystal clear voice that lifted them up and drew them along to a far, far better performance than they had ever done.

Beverly Luxton excused herself and went home early, snuffling into the night and letting the door slam behind her. This Snail or Quail or whoever he was was going to be a problem. He was a good singer, that was for sure. But who was he? Where did he come from? He was alien all the way from his elegant suit and the cut of his silky hair to that incredible voice that reminded Bev of a silver cornet in a Salvation Army band. How come he had suddenly popped up in Baytown to interfere with her well ordered life?

Beverly would not have ordered her life any other way had she been handed a menu. True, she was twenty-eight years old and she lived alone, but that was by choice. It was not the usual thing for a Baytown girl to move out of the house unless she was getting married, but Beverly was not your usual girl. Mum and Dad were on her side and she could afford her own place, so good luck to her. As for proposals of marriage, there had been enough of these and all of them suitably unsuitable that she felt confirmed in her single status.

But here was a threat. Her role as soprano soloist in the O'Shea Chorale was important to Beverly, and had been taken for granted since high school graduation. No smooth-voiced interloper was going to drift into town and knock Bev Luxton off her perch. Not without a fight.

Step one was to discover all she could about Desmond Smaile. That meant having coffee with the young proprietor of Cartwright's Pharmacy, so Beverly went there after school the next afternoon. They sat at the counter and she probed Sylvester Cartwright, pharmacist, amateur magician, and town gossip. After high school, when a number of boys opted for medicine at Queen's University, Sylvester took the quicker, easier road to becoming a druggist. Magic was his hobby. Not real legerdemain but a hokey, hilarious sort of act in which he stumbled about the stage, breaking his props, in a constant state of terror and surprise. The audience loved it and "The Great Sylvestro" appeared at all town functions, including the Kiwanis Karnival.

Cartwright was a natural gossip. He had always got on with women -- they told him everything. Men liked him for his readiness to take a joke as well as to perform one. He sat now at the marble counter in his white jacket with the high collar buttoned at one side. It gave him an innocent appearance that was not misleading. Round face, button eyes behind glasses with thick rims, short black hair combed flat with a wide-toothed comb, Cartwright raised and lowered his coffee mug as he recited his dossier on Desmond Smaile.

"He answered an ad and came to work for the Banner, selling space. He never did it before, apparently, but his accent and appearance make it easy for him. He's English all right -- came over a few weeks ago, spent some time in Montreal, then wandered down here."

"Where do you get all this?"

"I ask. The staff from the newspaper come in here, too."

"What's he doing here, anyway? How many people do you know of who come to Baytown from another city, let alone a foreign country?"

"I'm with you." Sylvester looked puzzled, as if the rabbit in the hat had appeared as a rubber chicken. "Whoever that man left behind," the magician theorized, "is wondering where the hell he's got to."

This was the incentive Beverly required. She would get close to the mysterious singer, this tenor without a past, and she would probe him -- not in any vicious way, but just to persuade him to move along. Let him take his pear-shaped tones to Vancouver or points west and leave the O'Shea Chorale to its soloist in residence.

Beverly said goodbye to Sylvester Cartwright and hurried down Front Street to where the *Baytown Banner* editorial offices shared a building with the Coronet Hotel. She inquired after Mr. Smaile and was directed to an office at the end of a lopsided corridor. She knocked once and entered a cubbyhole packed with a desk, a chair, a filing cabinet, and a telephone.

Dim light seeped through a window last washed just before it left the glazier's. Smaile was on the telephone. He looked at his visitor but did not see her.

"If I may say so with respect, Mr. Little," he intoned, "I think you ought to reconsider. A firm held in such high esteem as yours must have its name in the Banner's special Karnival issue. This is why I persist, sir. If the issue were to appear and your company not represented, then you'd think me to have been less than conscientious for not persuading you to take part. So I come back at you once again, sir. Yes? A quarter page is only two hundred dollars and it qualifies you for a frequency discount should you choose to run the ad again in the next thirteen weeks --"

Leaning against the wall -- there was no other chair -- Beverly closed her eyes and almost went under. The mellifluous voice was as hypnotic as Billie Holiday blues. When the phone went down at last and he came to stand beside her, she still could not feel the ground beneath her feet.

"You're the girl from the rehearsal last night," he said. "The one who went home early."

"Beverly Luxton. Where did you learn to sell like that?"

The reference to business displeased him -- his voice became abrupt. "Oh, that. Survival. One does what one must do."

The reference to survival brought Beverly back to earth. She had a career as choir soloist to protect. "I felt terrible not being able to stay last night," she said. "I wanted to come and tell you how beautifully you sang."

"Most kind of you."

Beverly felt herself back in a tiny front porch years ago, squeezed in beside a perspiring boy she had delivered home from a Sadie Hawkins dance. She began to panic. "And how about dinner?" she heard herself say.

"How about that?" Smaile agreed, opening the door and gallantly offering her the freedom to the corridor.

"Can you believe what's happening with Beverly?" Gertie O'Shea asked her husband. The little boy packing up his trombone was permitted to listen. He was only nine years old and half deafened from an hour of making harsh noises.

"What's happening?" Griff asked, pocketing a five-dollar bill. Junior students paid cash.

"She's spending all her spare time with Desmond Smaile."

"How do you know?"

"Sylvester Cartwright just rang to ask how much time he has on stage at the Karnival. I told him and then he got onto Bev and Des. He says they've been dining, dancing -- the works."

"He must be speculating about the works."

"Does it make sense? This English character has been in town two weeks. She hated him from day one. Now here they are, thick as thieves."

"Tell you one thing," Griff said, blowing a scale on his piccolo, getting ready for the next student. "Beverly's up to something."

And she was. Convinced that Desmond Smaile was concealing some dark secret, she played the role of Mata Hari, setting up her victim to make him talk about himself. So far she had learned nothing useful. His childhood in Durham, lower middle class; his acquisition of a fine education -- and the proper accent -- through scholarship; his career as opening batsman with Surrey County Cricket Club -- all good stuff but no reason to bring in the police.

"What baffles me," Beverly said, carrying a second bottle of wine from her apartment kitchen, "is how come an attractive man like you isn't married."

"Nobody will have me."

"Stop fishing for compliments." She refilled his glass. "There must be a lady back in London. At least one. Tell me," she said, sitting beside him with one silky leg tucked under her, "I want to know."

"That face --" he said, kissing her gently on one side of the nose she thought was too prominent. "Very Lauren Bacall. All right, there is a woman. And if you'll hold me close and smother my anxiety, I'll tell you all about Mercia Challenfont and her hideous father, Hugo -- and why I had to get away."

The letter arrived addressed to Miss Mercia Challenfont care of Challenfont Enterprises, City of London. The anonymous correspondent apparently did not know the street address. After a second reading, Mercia perused the envelope, saw a Canadian stamp and the words PERSONAL AND CONFIDENTIAL. It certainly was.

But why? Why had somebody in a place called Baytown taken the trouble to inform her as to the whereabouts of her escaped fiancé. Only a woman could be so vindictive. On the other hand, a man might do it if Desmond was lording it about, breaking the hearts of the local talent.

Mercia rode downstairs on the platform installed to lift her father's bulk without undue strain on the old man's heart. The machine moved with the speed of the Mendenhall Glacier but Mercia had always been prankish, a child in a woman's body. Lover of hitchhiking, of vaulting a narrow stream on a pole. Of throwing a punch when angry.

The body she inhabited was that of a peasant girl, thick in the wrists and ankles, plump of calf and of cheek. Her health was robust, her appetites where keen. She had close-cropped red hair and green eyes that could perject two moods only -- boredom and mischief. She was as single-minded as a hungry cat and boisterous as a victorious basketball team.

The real Mercia Challenfont was camouflaged behind that magic name and a wardrobe of clothes made for her by designers in London, Paris, and Rome. It was only after he had seen the young lady under the influence of a few tantrums that Desmond Smaile decided to vanish. Mercia was taken by surprise. All she knew was that one day Desmond was talking marriage, then he became silent for a few weeks, then he was gone.

Mercia stepped from the platform at the foot of the staircase and went in search of her father, tapping the pages of the letter against her cherry lips, blowing across their edges a buzzing rendition of the march from *The Bridge on the River Kwai*. She found Hugo Challenfont in the kitchen, drinking ale from a mug the size of a chamber pot and eating a couple of pounds of Cape grapes.

"Daddy daddy daddy," she said, spreading the emphasis equally, "guess who's turned up?"

The old man's mind produced the name of a British Secret Service bloke who had gone missing decades ago while snooping around the hull of a new Italian naval vessel in a frogman's suit. "Commander Crabbe?" he volunteered.

"Daddy, you're always so stupid. No! Desmond Smaile. He's over in Canada, some little place in Ontario called Baytown."

"Who says so?" Challenfont had been glad when the Smaile character absconded, was even happy about the ten thousand pounds he had managed to steal from the company's current account. It had meant he would never be seen again and the ten thousand was a reasonable price to pay for a future devoid of Desmond Smaile.

"The letter is unsigned."

"Never believe an anonymous letter. It's a hoax. Throw it away."

Mercia threaded her finger into her father's hair and twisted the silvery blue strands until the old man roared with pain, most of it mock. "Daddy, you're such a liar. You always hated Desmond. I'm going to go and find him and bring him back."

"You do and I'll slap a theft charge on him. You'll end up visiting him in Wormwood Scrubs."

Mercia did not bother responding to this hollow threat. "Desmond Smaile is the handsomest man I ever went out with. Why don't you like him, Daddy?"

Challenfont couldn't admit the real reason, the fact that the arrogant young man had loved his daughter and then left her. True, Hugo had made things difficult for the prospective son-in-law while he was learning the brokerage business, had missed no opportunity to act the tyrant. But why didn't the boy fight back? The old man would have respected Smaile had he stood up and said, "I'm marrying your daughter, sir, and you can go to hell." But it was obvious the boy didn't care much for Mercia. He would rather have his freedom and ten thousand pounds.

But Hugo Challenfont could say none of this to the girl sitting opposite him in a silk mother hubbard with her bare feet resting on his lap. "I'll tell you why I don't like him," he responded to his daughter's question. "I can't stand a man who sings like a bloody eunuch!"

As Desmond's voice soared through the rehearsal hall, Beverly escaped into the washroom. She felt strangely affected -- not with envy as in the earlier days. It was another sensation, almost unpleasant but not quite, and she had to flee that sound. In the cubicle, she sat and smoked a cigarette -- bad for her throat, but since she was doing fewer solos these days she was abandoning her regimen of voice care and training.

There had been no response yet to her letter. Perhaps it had never been delivered.

Desmond had told her enough about Mercia for Beverly to feel she knew the girl. She was headstrong, spoiled, accustomed to having her way. That was why he had cut and run -- and why Beverly had persuaded herself that information as to his whereabouts would bring the wealthy English girl on the next plane. Followed by the destruction on the ground of Desmond Smaile and the return of Bev Luxton to her rightful position as soprano soloist with the O'Shea Chorale.

But nothing was happening. Beverly's glazed eyes focused through drifting smoke on words she had been staring at for some time. They formed a four-line verse scrawled on the painted metal door in ballpoint pen.

> Here comes Gertie,
> Mean and dirty,
> And closer to sixty
> Then she is to thirty.

Charming. Obviously the management never used this washroom. The handwriting was familiar -- she had seen it somewhere recently. Scrounging through her purse, Beverly came up with a receipt written out for her by Griff O'Shea when she paid her choir fee. She held the paper near the graffito -- a perfect match.

She felt sad. Griff and Gertie. All those years married and so close to each other. There was no such thing, apparently, as a perfect relationship. The mean feelings had to come out somewhere.

The couple went back to Desmond's place after rehearsal and Beverly carried her despondency with her. The apartment belonged to the newspaper and was rented out cheap to the sort of employee who came and went on notice too short to justify a decent place in a proper part of town.

"Are you all right?" Desmond asked as he prepared drinks at a bare table furnished with one bottle and two glasses.

"I'm fine," she said with assumed gaiety. She was looking down from a window at a deserted parking lot behind the hotel next door and, beyond its stone parapet, the broad darkness that was the river. There was a newspaper clipping mounted askew in a shabby frame suspended on the wall beside the window. It was front-page material from an ancient edition of the Baytown Banner. Beverly recalled the event from her childhood. There were men in a boat on a flooded Front Street with ice floes forcing their way through the main doors of the Coronet Hotel. The caption was headed: THE MIGHTY EDNA OVERFLOWS ITS BANKS.

"You don't sound all right to me." Desmond handed her a drink.

"I've done a terrible thing." Beverly sipped her whisky. The confession was on her lips and there was no way she could take it back. She spilled the whole thing -- her jealousy of his singing, her resentment at losing her position with the O'Shea Chorale, her campaign to discover some damaging secret from his past, and finally, her letter to Mercia designed to lead to his departure from Baytown. "But I don't want you to go now," she wailed. "I love you, Des. I don't care about the solos, we can sing duets, I want you to stay."

They embraced and her panic was dispelled. "I'm not going anywhere. But one thing is beyond dispute." He was looking at the picture of the flooded street and the ice floes. "If Mercia comes here and checks into the Coronet, we'll have a job and a half getting her out again."

"She can't come tomorrow," Beverly said. "It's Saturday, the day of the Kiwanis Karnival." That meant field events all afternoon on the Baytown High School campus with a tea table and a bar under a marquee. In the evening the Chorale was to appear as part of the stage show in the auditorium. This would be followed by dancing in the gymnasium to the local swing band, the Serenaders, playing stock arrangements of Dorsey, Goodman, and Brown. "Nothing can stop the Karnival."

But the Fates, with their keen sense of the dramatic, chose just that Saturday to have Mercia Challenfont arrive at noon in a hired car, having flown in to Montreal hours before. She barged through the brass-plated hotel doors with such presence that the manager altered his reservation list and assigned her room 212, the one with the good mattress.

By asking questions, Mercia discovered the where-abouts that day of Desmond Smaile. At one-thirty, she telephoned him at the school, where he was rehearsing with the choir. Beverly came with him to the Principal's office to hear him take his call. The moment he was paged she had known the worst had happened. He confirmed her fears when he put down the phone.

"She's here. Registered at the hotel. Wants to see me."

"Don't go there," Beverly pleaded. "You'll never come back."

"I have to go. If there's ever going to be a peaceful life for you and me, I have to face her."

Beverly played her last card. "If you go to that hotel, don't expect me to be here when you get back." It seemed a good line when used by movie heroines. But after he hurried out of the office and she heard his footsteps echo down the corridor and out of the school, she saw the weakness of it. "Where am I supposed to go?" was her futile plea.

In Mercia's room at the Coronet Hotel, Desmond Smaile did as he was told. He sat on the edge of the bed and listened to what she had to say. The firmness of the mattress surprised him; clapped-out hotels like this one usually had shattered mattresses.

"You look wonderful, Des. I've missed you beyond telling. I've forgotten how much tonic you take in your gin."

"Just a splash."

She brought the drink and sat down beside him. Her hand rested on his thigh. Given a damp cloth, she could have pressed his trousers without an iron. "I'll never forgive you for running away from me. But I've found you now and I'm not letting you escape again."

"It's nice to be wanted, my dear. But I'm not coming back to London."

"You must be joking. I've been in this town for three hours and I'm bored already."

"It's not the same for me. I have a job. I've joined a choral society." Desmond took a drink. "I've made friends."

Mercia stiffened, her voice hardened. "There's another woman."

"Yes, but it's more than that. I've got a new life here."

Mercia got up and went to the dresser. She opened her handbag and took out a revolver. Facing Desmond, holding the gun firmly, she said: "Don't blame me, then, if somebody gets hurt."

"I won't let you harm Beverly." Desmond put his drink aside and stood up.

"Is that her name?" Mercia said in the cultured tones grafted onto her by the school that provides BBC radio with an unending supply of plummy-voiced newscasters. "I may not shoot her -- I may do you right now and have done with it."

"You can't shoot me, Mercia." They both knew she could.

"Why on earth not?"

"Because I have to sing 'Roses of Picardy' at the Kiwanis Karnival tonight."

It was such a preposterous excuse that she let him go. But she promised to be in the audience, ready to claim him when the performance was over -- at gunpoint if necessary.

Back at the school, helping to decorate the stage in the auditorium, Desmond told Beverly about his dangerous interview. "She's a woman scorned," he concluded.

Beverly was reconnoitering the problem for a way out. "Is the gun real?'

"Indeed. Mercia comes from a wealthy English family-- they grow up with guns. They kill animals the way you play dominoes."

Beverly leaned against the cabinet used by Sylvester Cartwright in his hilariously abortive attempt to saw a woman in half. "Then there's only one thing to do. We'll have to call in the police."

"We can't. There's something I haven't told you." He went on to explain how, before he fled London and the employ of Hugo Challenfont, he had stolen ten thousand pounds from company funds. It was partly travelling and setting-up money, partly insurance to guarantee the family could never take him back. "Failing all else, Mercia may blow the whistle. They'd extradite me. I'd never see the green, green grass of Baytown again."

Beverly was thinking. "Then the police are out. But there must be another way." She was staring at Sylvester's table of magical props when the idea came to her. "Of course! And it's so easy! Listen..."

More than any disc jockey, Sylvester Cartwright was unable to refuse a request. Let a friend ask him to do something and he would do it. He might do it even if a friend didn't ask him. So when Beverly Luxton took him aside before he went onstage to do his act, he listened quietly nodding his head. When she finished her briefing, she called to Desmond, "Take Sylvester to the peephole and show him where your friend is sitting."

Desmond did so. Sylvester spent a long time staring. When he drew back, he said thoughtfully: "She looks sort of --"

"Formidable?"

"That. But something else, too. I don't know --"

"Will you help us?'

"I'll help you, I'll help you."

After four hours at games on campus in hazy sunshine that afternoon the Baytowners were in a mood to be entertained. They responded to the first set of numbers by the O'Shea Chorale. They were receptive to a couple of renderings on the musical saw by a member of the town council billed as "the only man who can play 'Trees' and cut them down at the same time." And when the Great Sylvestro was announced, there was quick applause followed by an expectant hush as the curtains opened to reveal a rickety table piled with the tools of the magician's trade. His timing was superb. In the wings, Sylvester gave the audience about fifteen seconds to gaze at this forlorn tableau while nothing happened. Then, just as the nervous giggles began, he yanked on a thread attached to the front left leg, the table collapsed with boxes, rabbits, bells and balloons scattering everywhere and this was his entrance. The Great Sylvestro, improperly prepared, a loser who could only win in a contest to choose the worst loser, was going into his act.

He fanned cards -- they littered the floor. He palmed a coin -- it rolled off the stage into the pit. Sylvester cracked eggs and poured milk into a top hat, stirred it with his magic wand and presto! -- out came a glutinous mess of uncooked omelet. Checking his wrist for the time, he drew the metal strip from what was, in fact, a tape measure. "Hmmmm," he said, "nine inches after eight."

Scanning the hall, the magician announced: "I need a volunteer. You. Yes, you -- the young lady with the dramatic hair." As Mercia Challenfont approached the steps at the side of the stage, he went on: "The Great Sylvestro reads minds. I'm getting the word 'Bobby'. You have a husband named Bobby. No, it's a London bobby -- a policeman. You are from London."

Beside him now, she confirmed this fact and the crowd applauded their pharmacist's transparent achievement. "Have we ever seen each other before?"

"No, but I'm glad we have now," Mercia said. "You're cute."

This statement, combining boldness and sincerity, knocked The Great Sylvestro off stride. For a moment he fell out of character, became himself, stuttered and turned noticeably pink. Louts in the audience whistled. Mercia loved it.

"And now for my piece of resistance," Sylvester said, mastering himself with effort. "The famous set-fire-to-the-purse trick. May I have your purse, please. Back home, you call it a handbag."

Mercia passed it over, a large burgundy-leather creation with more pockets than a regiment of Guards. Sylvester took it, raised it over his head like a pagan offering, held it behind his back, and it fell onto the stage. "Sorry about that," he said. Bending to pick it up, he kicked it against the hem of the curtain. Waiting hands snatched it out of sight, to the delight of the watchers. Moments later, another purse was pushed forward from beneath the curtain.

Sylvester picked it up. It was a cheap cloth bag with a drawstring top, clearly so unlike the one the volunteer had given him that the trick became hilarious. He produced a metal tray, set the bag on it, and doused it with lighter fluid. He touched it off with a match, making reassuring noises to the girl beside him, then losing confidence and retreating to a book of magic -- through which he leafed despairingly as the bag was reduced to a charred mound.

"I have it here," he cried at last. "It's all in the magic words! " Raising his voice, he called out: "Ashes to ashes, dust to dust, come back, handbag -- you must, you must!" With that, he back-heeled the tray and its contents through the curtain behind him. Back it came with Mercia's bag on it, good as new.

Had she been given time to think, the girl from London would have realized her bag seemed lighter in weight than before. But the three-piece band was playing, the crowd was applauding, this vulnerable young man was bundling her offstage, and as they parted he said something to her. He said: "I'm really sorry, dear -- this wasn't my idea."

Back in her seat, Mercia thought about the cryptic apology. Why did the man say such a thing? She had her property back, no harm done. What idea was not his? The curtains opened to reveal the chorus on stage fronted by Desmond and a dark-haired girl singing "Come, come, I love you only..." And Mercia's investigative thinking was submerged in a blood-red tide of anger.

When the show ended, the auditorium became a gentle shoving match of bemused people all in a hurry to get where they were going. Mercia had decided by this time to take the situation in hand. She stopped somebody and put her question: "Could you please tell me how to get backstage?"

The members of the O'Shea Chorale never attended the public functions that followed their appearances. Instead they returned to the rehearsal hall at No. 1 Footbridge Lane, where there was food and drink laid on and there was space and music for dancing. This elitist practice was Gertrude O'Shea's idea. Gertie had always believed she was one of the brightest and best from the day she went alone as a teenager on the train to Toronto, found her way to a CBC radio studio, auditioned for and later won the competition known as "Opportunity Knocks." Nobody from Baytown had ever done that before.

Now she stood at the front window with many of her current flock and watched her husband ignite the ceremonial skyrockets. Griff always marked a choral success by sending up three bright rockets from the center of the bridge. As their starbursts lit up the sky, Desmond brought Beverly a drink. "The duet worked," he said.

Her mind was somewhere else. "She'll retaliate, won't she? When she discovers the gun is gone"

"Don't worry about Mercia Challenfont."

"She's come all this way to get you. Taking that gun isn't going to stop her."

"I'll go to the hotel tomorrow," Desmond said. "I'll talk sense to her. She'll go back to England and leave us alone." He took Bev's glass and set it down beside his own. "Let's dance."

"Lord help me," Bev said as she put her head on his shoulder, "I remember when Baytown used to be a peaceful place."

It was hours later and most of the choristers had gone home when rifle fire began outside the O'Shea Chorale. Griff switched off the record player. Gertie turned off the overhead light. They and the only dancing couple left, Desmond and Beverly, crouched at the window, looking out into the parking lot.

"What is it?" Gertie asked.

"Somebody took a pot-shot from behind that car."

A cultured female voice rang through the darkness. "Come on out Desmond! We know you're in there!"

"Mercia Challenfont," Beverly said.

"No," Griff corrected her. "It's a Ford Capri."

Desmond took from his pocket the pistol he had stolen from Mercia's handbag during the magic trick. Beverly saw it. "You can't use that!"

"Maybe just to scare her off --"

The popping sound was heard again. Something whizzed through the open window, struck the back of a chair, and rattled on the floor. Griff groped and found it. "Just as I thought," he said. "BB shot." He began to snicker.

"It's no laughing matter," Beverly snapped. "They could put somebody's eye out."

In the darkness, Mercia was having doubts about the effectiveness of the rifle. "Are you sure this thing is dangerous?"

Sylvester Cartwright was pouring from a thermos jug into a plastic cup. "My mother always said it could put somebody's eye out." He passed the cup to the girl beside him. Her power had mesmerized him from the start. When she came backstage and lit into him for his part in the theft, he heard few words but felt every wave of her personality. When she seized him by the arm and forced him to leave the school and drive to his house, he hoped she would never let go. She was demanding a replacement weapon and his old BB rifle was all he could offer.

He spent an hour pretending to look for it while he fed her drinks. What a difference she made to his sitting room -- he kept looking in on her, catching her from various angles, surprising himself. By the time they drove off for the hall she was in a calmer mood, perhaps because of the booze.

Now, hiding behind the car, he continued the alcohol therapy. "Here," he said, "drink your vodka and orange."

"I wish they hadn't turned the light out," Mercia mumbled. "I can't see the window."

Sylvester put his head close because he was enjoying her fragrance. "You must really hate Desmond Smaile."

"Hate him? The bastard stole my father's money, thousands and thousands. Used it to run away. Left me at the altar. Well, near enough. Nobody does that to Mercia Challenfont." She cocked the rifle and sent another pellet to rattle off clapboard. "No, not hate. Resentment is more like it. How bloody dare he!"

Maybe it was the vodka. Something was bringing up from deep inside Sylvester Cartwright a sense of adventure he usually experienced only on stage. Maybe it was this woman. "I'm glad it's only resentment," he said. "Hate is the other side of love. If you had feelings that strong about Desmond, I wouldn't like it."

Mercia's response was a kiss delivered with fair accuracy under difficult conditions. "Portable bar," she said. "A gun you don't mind lending. What's a prince like you doing in a diabolical little town like this?"

"I've got an idea," Sylvester said. "Everything's going to be all right." He drank a cup of courage and stood up. "Keep me covered."

The parking lot was deserted. No light showed inside the O'Shea Chorale. Cartwright planted his feet and tried to keep his balance. A gust of wind sent a tumbleweed of crumpled newspaper scuttling across the pavement. On the other side of the bridge, a horse whinnied in the stables of Baytown Pony Rental. "Hey, inside the house!" he called. "I'm coming in!"

Behind him, the rifle popped. He felt a pellet strike the back of his leather jacket and drop to the ground. Mercia's whisper was apologetic. "Sorry!"

Sylvester approached the screen doors in character, pace measured, hands held a few inches from his thighs. His boots clumped on the porch floor. He repeated his announcement: "I'm coming in!" Then, using both hands to fling open the pair of doors, he strode into the rehearsal hall.

People mobbed him. Out of the babble of hoarse questions he selected that of Gertie O'Shea, who asked: "What the hell is going on out there?"

"I'll explain later. Everything's going to be okay. Just do as I tell you. Have you got that gun you stole from Mercia's purse?"

"I'm holding it," Desmond said.

"Is it loaded?"

"Afraid so."

"Good. Where do you want the bullet, Gertie -- in your ceiling or in your floor?"

Outside, behind the parked car, Mercia Challenfont was becoming restless. She poured some more vodka and orange. This was all most unusual to say the least -- squatting on damp pavement of a cool evening, no supper, not a friend in sight, her own gun probably aiming at her at his very moment. But being an upper-class Englishwoman, she was accustomed to discomfort. Her father's house -- centuries old, worth millions -- had worse plumbing than the average hotel. She was enjoying herself thoroughly.

End of the vodka. Perhaps Sylvester had more at home. What an interesting fellow -- a wild man on stage yet such a governable child in the relationship they had established.

A shot rang out. Mercia's head came up and she stared at the drab building across the yard. The screen doors burst open and Sylvester Cartwright stumbled out backward, took three steps across the wooden porch, then fell spread-eagled on the pavement.

"Sylvester!" Mercia dropped the rifle and ran to his side. She arrived at the same time as the party from the house but she might have been alone as she knelt beside the fallen man. "I never wanted this," she moaned.

"It had to happen," Sylvester croaked. "It was the only way."

"Don't try to talk." She cradled his head.

"I must. You've got to hear this --" Sylvester coughed hoarsely.

"Get water," Gertie improvised and Griff hurried inside.

"I'm glad it happened, Mercia, because now at least we've met."

"I'm glad, too. You're the sweetest man ever." She looked up. "You can keep Desmond Smaile, whoever you are. You're welcome to him, and all the misery that goes with him."

Desmond and Beverly, holding their breath, looked down at the prostrate chemist. He spoke again. "Say you love me, Mercia."

"I do. I love you, Sylvester."

"After so little time?"

"What does time matter?"

"I'm afraid it matters quite a lot." Sylvester got to his feet smartly and brushed himself off. "I have to open the store at nine o'clock. We'd better get going."

"You beast!" Mercia gasped. "You aren't even hurt!"

"Yes, I am. When Desmond fired that shot into the ceiling and I lost my balance and fell on the ground, I gave my back a heck of a jolt."

"I'll show you what a jolt really is." Mercia began pursuing Sylvester around the parking lot and had yet to catch him when the police car pulled in, blue light flashing.

The officer who got out was a patient man. "Have a heart, Gertie," he said. "We can put up with sky rockets off the bridge when it isn't even the Queen's birthday. But gunfire in the night is something else."

"Sorry," Gertie said. "We need a gun shot in our next concert. We were singing 'Pistol Packin' Momma.' It was only a sound effect."

"What's this, then?" The officer, prowling the darkness, came back with the BB rifle.

"That's mine," Sylvester said.

"We'll be using it onstage for a prop," Gertie ad-libbed "For presenting arms when the flags come on."

"Be careful," the officer said. "You could put somebody's eye out with that."

Weeks later, when a bright-eyed Sylvester Cartwright announced he was going to sell his pharmacy and move to England, his friends were astounded.

"This is your home town," Gertie said. "You're thirty-two years old. How can you do such a thing?"

"We know you have a crush on Mercia," Griff said, "but how can you leave Baytown?"

"That's the whole point," Sylvester said. "Baytown. There are nice people here, old friends, new ones like Desmond. I'm staying for his wedding to Beverly but as soon as they're married, I'm off. Pleasant as it is, Baytown can drive you crazy with boredom. Nothing ever happens here."

"You're right about that," Griff said. He finished adding water to a bucketful of cement, stirred it a few more times, then pressed Mercia's revolver into the mixture as far as it would go. "Let's have a drink while that mess hardens. Then you can come with me while we sink it in the bay."

Ellery Queen Mystery Magazine, January, 1984

SILENTLY, IN THE
DEAD OF NIGHT

The telephone rang on the bedside table and jarred Birtles awake. He picked it up and listened.

"Norman?"

"What time is it?" The dryness in his mouth was not unpleasant. He had taken just the right amount of whisky but not enough sleep.

"Almost eight. I thought you'd be up."

"I don't go in till one. Charlie opens the place today." He stared at the window and the grey autumn light. "It's as if I'm still delivering the mail."

"I'm sorry." But she didn't sound sorry. She sounded as bright as her lacquered hair. Birtles could imagine Anitra Colahan dressed and groomed as for a tango competition, earrings sparkling, short skirt flaring over several crinolines. "I missed you last night," she said. "I thought you were coming over."

"We had trouble balancing the cash after we closed. And then Charlie offered me a lift home." Only partly a lie. The cash had been a problem but he ended up taking a cab from the rank outside Wimbledon Station.

"I would have driven you home."

"I don't want you on the roads at that time of night." What Birtles really didn't want was to be stuck in the death seat speeding along London streets after midnight. Anitra had taken the driving test three times before passing. Her style at the wheel was risky and spectacular, much like her performance on the dance floor.

"Can you come by the studio tonight?" she asked. "I have something to tell you. Something nice."

"O.K. I finish at six."

"Lovely. We can go to the Taj. It's good news, Norman."

Birtles checked the bathroom window-ledge but found no note. When Barbie wanted to be called in the morning, she would leave a page from her notebook pinned under the talcum-powder tin and the breezy words, the erratic left-handed scrawl always gave Birtles a lift. The absence of a note probably meant his daughter would be sleeping till noon. Which meant he wouldn't see her before he went to the poolroom. One more day gone from the diminishing week before she took off for Canada.

Birtles went downstairs and along the hall toward the kitchen, passing Barbie's bedroom on the way. The door was open. What he saw stopped him cold. The room was empty, the backpack gone, her makeup, brush, and comb vanished from the dresser. The bed was in disarray but that was normal -- he couldn't tell if she had slept here last night.

Perhaps she'd left a note somewhere in the room. Birtles looked around but found no message among the clutter of pop-music magazines, soft-drink tins, overloaded ashtrays, and the accumulation of discarded clothing.

There was a coffee mug on the bedside table. Birtles picked it up carefully -- sometimes they were half full of murky liquid. This one was dry but there was a crumpled envelope tucked inside it.

He unfolded the envelope, found it unaddressed. Some greenish-brown grains of leaf fell into the palm of his hand. They looked like something from one of his spice jars. Printed in the corner of the envelope was: Hotel Candide, Inverness Avenue, London W2.

Carrying his discovery into the kitchen, Birtles put the kettle on, made toast, made coffee, ate and drank standing while he tried to handle his feelings. The sight of Barbie's room deserted had shaken him. He was not looking forward to her going away. When his wife died six years ago, he had kept going, for Barbie's sake. Part of him had wanted to convert what little he had into cash and head off to some hot country where his main duty would have been to keep himself drunk.

Instead, he had become a meal-maker and housekeeper. Well, it was an achievement, something to be proud of, and Barbie's confident character was the result. His example had taught her how to soldier on. Now, apparently, she had packed up her possessions in her old kit bag and hit the long, long trail. Without even saying goodbye.

No, that wasn't possible. Barbie with her curly head and the sweet baby face and her silent understanding of what he was going through in losing her would never do a moonlight flit. Fear hit Birtles in the stomach like a draught of acid. Something had happened to her. She was in trouble.

It was early to ring Jeremy but Birtles couldn't wait. The boy came on the phone coughing like a veteran. "Sorry to disturb you but I was wondering if you saw Barbie last night."

"We didn't, Mr. Birtles. The band was playing at the Ploughman. If she'd been in, I'd have known about it."

"O.K. Sorry to wake you."

"Barbie hasn't come around much the last few months. She's saving her money."

"I know. I've had to put up with her almost every night. Like an old married couple." Birtles kept two trays handy and produced supper regularly in front of the TV. They watched everything, not reacting much, in comforting balance there side by side in the upholstered chairs drawn round to face the screen.

"If you see her, ask her to call home."

At the poolroom, only three of the nineteen tables were in use. It was too nice a day for people to be inside shooting snooker. Charlie was behind the counter serving the occasional beer or Coke, answering the phone, reading a tabloid of few words and many pictures. It was pointless for two of them to be on duty on such a quiet afternoon, so Birtles suggested Charlie take off.

"I'll go in a minute." Charlie went on reading. Birtles strode back and forth, his rangy figure looming large over the counter. When he had been employed by the Post Office, before the economy cuts made him redundant, more than one customer told him they always knew when the mail was on the way, he was so easy to spot coming up the street. Now he mopped clean a spotless surface, snapped his fingers, opened and closed the refrigerator cabinet.

"You're giving me the creeps, Norman. Settle down."

Suddenly, at the end of the room where the card table was situated, a chair was kicked back, players were on their feet, arms extended across the table grabbing shirtfronts. Without a word, Birtles reached for the light panel and snapped the switch controlling the lamp over the table. He raised the counter gate and strode to the scene, head on one side, arms loose, the picture of a man with his patience exhausted. He recognized the troublemaker and faced him.

"You! Out!" Said while pointing at the door.

"This geezer's won all the money and now he wants to quit."

"I said when I sat down I'd have to leave -- "

Birtles cut through the argument. "Walk to the door. If I have to say it again, you won't touch many steps on the way down."

Back behind the counter, his hands trembled as he tried to open a box of pool chalk. The cubes went all over the counter, some on the floor. Charlie watched him. "Are you all right?"

"A little nervous."

"You were awfully rough for a first offense."

"A little nervous today."

Charlie folded his paper and took the afternoon off. When he reported back at six, Birtles washed up and then walked on down the Broadway to the dance salon. He climbed more stairs and emerged in the ballroom. Anitra was on the floor with her client, taking him through the basic movements of the cha-cha. As they vamped across acres of polished hardwood, their images were reflected in a series of mirrors.

Birtles took a chair against the wall. The client had the grace of a piano mover but Anitra managed to make him look competent. She glistened in her freshly done peach hair, her swirling skirt, those shiny tapered legs ending in blue sequined high-heeled pumps. "One and two, cha-cha-cha," she commanded while the recording of a brassy Latin band played "Tea For Two." She spotted Birtles and blew him a kiss.

The client left at last after an exchange of money and a flurry of cheek-kissing. Anitra came and sat beside Birtles, kicking off her shoes and slipping into a pair that looked less like they had been built by a custom-car maker. "Bless his heart," she said, "he'll never be a dancer but it keeps me working."

"What's your good news?" Birtles asked, putting on a smile.

"You look tired. Are you all right?"

"You said it was special."

"They're making me manager here. That means I'll get a regular salary in addition to the fees for my lessons."

"Congratulations." She was expecting to be kissed. He leaned towards that rouged cheek, inhaled the lilac scent, kissed her. That was the trouble -- she was warm and soft and if he wasn't careful she would become a part of him and then she would leave or die and that part would be torn out without benefit of anaesthetic.

"I think you should let me treat you to dinner," she said.

"Never refuse a free meal."

They went next door to the Taj Mahal and ordered onion bahjis, Madras curry and chapatis, and a bottle of white wine. Late in the meal, Birtles found the courage to say: "Barbie wasn't there this morning. Her room was empty, everything gone as if she'd moved out. But she'd never do that without telling me."

"I knew something was the matter. When is she supposed to leave for Canada?"

"End of next week."

"No note in her room? Nothing?"

Birtles took the crumpled envelope out of his pocket and put it on the table. "I found this."

"Hotel Candide." Anitra studied the few grains of leaf. "Looks like something the kids smoke."

"I suppose so. They tell me it's no worse than this." He drank some wine. "I'm wondering if it's a clue to where she might have gone. The envelope, I mean."

"Are you thinking of calling the police?"

"They wouldn't want to know. A girl Barbie's age, they'd assume she's gone off with friends. Especially since she's saved up a pile of money and had a trip planned."

"How much has she saved?"

"Over six hundred pounds. It was all in traveller's checks. She was ready to go."

Anitra poured the grains back into the envelope. "Where do you suppose she got this?"

"I'm not sure. There was a girl came to see her the other day but she didn't stay long. A girl from up the hill in the village. Barbie told me her name -- Lucy Feather."

Birtles remembered the girl's arrival at the front door one morning a couple of days ago. Barbie was still in bed. "I'm Lucy Feather. Did Barbie tell you I'd be coming by? She has a book I'd like to borrow."

"Yes, she mentioned you. Come in, you may have to wake her up. It's the door at the end of the hall." Birtles watched the movement of her skintight jeans. She was a solid girl with hair three shades of blonde. Her tweed jacket was expensive; she was not one of the dole-queue layabouts who comprised most of Barbie's list of friends.

Birtles went into the kitchen. Through the wall he heard their voices but not their words. The conversation was not exactly amicable. Barbie's final statement sounded like an invitation for Lucy Feather to get the hell out of there.

The bedroom door slammed. Birtles hurried into the hall and accompanied the visitor to the front door. "Got it, thanks." She waved a paperback at him -- he recognized it as an in-depth report on a psychopath named Eric Merlot who had drugged and murdered a dozen young travelers in the Far East over a period of years.

When she was gone, Birtles had rapped on Barbie's door and put his head inside the stuffy room.

"Everything O.K.?"

The curly head turned on the pillow and Barbie gave Birtles that reassuring, almost patronizing smile that reminded him of his mother. Who was forty-eight and who was nineteen here? "She wants me to go to India with her instead of Canada. I told her no thanks."

"I heard you."

"All right, I told her to get stuffed. I don't get my kicks from catching dysentery."

"I though she was a friend."

"She's crazy. Her parents threw her out of the house and she came back when they were out and set fire to her room. I can do without friends like her."

Anitra spooned up syrup from her dish of lychees as she listened to Birtles' account of the Lucy Feather visit. At the end, she said: "Is it possible she persuaded Barbie to go with her after all?"

"I doubt it."

"Kids are impulsive. They might have got high last night and decided to head east. Maybe there was a coach leaving late, or somebody with a car. Barbie didn't want to wake you, so she got her stuff and took off. As soon as they come to a phone, she'll get through to you."

"It's a theory. But it doesn't sound like my daughter." Birtles smoothed the envelope and studied the hotel address by the light of the small candle in its red globe.

"All right," Anitra said, "I know what's on your mind. Come on, I'll drive you to Inverness Avenue..."

Thanks to some fine defensive driving by other motorists, Anitra Colahan made the trip safely. She controlled her second-hand Mini like a rally driver, shoulders up, hands locked on the wheel at the "ten minutes to two" position, and the choreography of her feet on and off the pedals was constant. Birtles braced himself, one hand on the door handle, the other flat against the dash.

"Relax," Anitra said. "Everything's under control."

"Let me out at the traffic lights. I'll get a taxi."

"All right, I'll slow down." She sulked for a few blocks but couldn't contain her aggression any longer than that. Soon she was cutting in and out again, carving up the passive drivers.

Inverness Avenue turned out to be a short street of Edwardian houses not far from Kensington Gardens. Almost without exception, the buildings had been converted into hotels. Anitra found the Candide and parked across the road.

"What do we do now?"

"I'm going to go in and ask a few questions."

"O.K., I'll wait."

"Thanks, but there's no point. If I get no joy from the desk clerk, I'm going to hang around and watch the place."

"More fun for two to watch than one."

"No, really, I'd rather wait alone." He had an idea how to persuade her. He took his key from his pocket and handed it to her. "Go home to my place and wait for me. If Barbie phones like you said, you'll be there to take the message."

He watched the Mini gun down the street and swing abruptly onto Bayswater Road, then he crossed over to the hotel, pushed open the glass door, and went inside. The lobby was simply the former living room with a narrow reception desk added. The rest of the furniture looked like the original pieces. Through a doorway he could see a bar in the adjoining room.

The desk clerk was a young Asian in a pale-blue suit, white shirt, and maroon bow tie. "Sir?"

"I'm looking for a Miss Barbara Birtles. Could you tell me if she's registered?" He spelled the name while the clerk ran down the guest list. When they drew a blank, he asked for Lucy Feather but she wasn't staying at the hotel, either.

"Is it all right if I buy a drink in your bar?"

"We welcome the public, sir."

Birtles went next door, ordered a large whisky, and took it to a seat where he could watch the foot of the staircase in the lobby. His mind began to wander -- so far that he almost missed the girl when she appeared. It was the splendid thighs in tight, expensive denim that caught his attention. Lucy Feather was in the lobby, holding out her hand, waiting for someone to come down the stairs and join her.

The companion turned out to be a Eurasian, one of the most handsome men Birtles had ever seen. He was in his early thirties, lean and muscular in white slacks and an open-necked shirt. His black hair swept in a wave across his broad forehead above widely spaced almond eyes.

It was the color of the eyes that shook Birtles. In that creamy coffee face, they were a pale, transparent blue. Birtles could have believed they were contact lenses worn for some spectacular stage effect. The man clasped hands with Lucy and they went out into the gathering darkness.

His heart pounding, Birtles tossed back his drink and hurried after them. They were walking not far ahead, the Feather girl in flat shoes, her hips rolling provocatively, her loose-limbed companion padding beside her like some jungle animal. He stopped an approaching stranger, an American-looking youth, and said something. The young man produced a lighter and put a flame to the Eurasian's cigarette. Birtles noticed the American's face as he continued on and thought he looked dazed, as if he had been spoken to by a movie star. It must have been those eyes.

The couple went into a pub on the corner. Birtles gave them a minute to settle themselves, then followed them in. They were still at the bar. He worked his way through at the far end and ordered a pint. By the time it had been pulled and paid for, they were sitting on an upholstered bench, part of an island arrangement in the middle of the room.

Birtles was able to find a place to sit where his back was to them. He could make out only part of what was being said. The Eurasian had a quiet voice; his remarks to Lucy Feather came across as those of a patient father handling a difficult child. "It can be done," he said at one point. "Anything can be done." And later: "Isn't it enough just to go and let them wonder?"

Lucy's voice rose after a few minutes. "No, I can't. I was riding her a couple of days ago. You'll have to."

He felt his stomach tighten. A few days ago she was in his daughter's room, he had heard the hectoring voices through the wall. Was that what Lucy was referring to -- had she been riding Barbie, nagging her about going to India? If so, what was it her companion would have to do?

Birtles stood and carried his glass on a wide circle so that he approached them from the bar. He managed to look surprised when his eyes met Lucy's, and before anything was said he slipped onto the bench beside her.

"Hello, Lucy. You don't recognize me. I'm Norman Birtle's, Barbie's father."

"Yes, of course." She was nervous. Her big, moist lips grimaced over perfect teeth. She tossed her head and her bound-up hair shook like a horse's mane. "This is my friend, Ezra Monty."

Monty gave Birtles a warm handshake. The blue crystal eyes met his and Birtles felt penetrated. He felt studied and stripped down and emptied out, but the surprising part of it was he didn't mind. A lot of casual conversation was going on and he couldn't have remembered a word of it.

"Well," Lucy was saying as he began to emerge from his stupor, "funny to run into you here. Quite a coincidence."

"I used to live around here," Birtles improvised. "I come back sometimes to see the old neighbourhood." They knew he was lying. There was an attentiveness around the table and Birtles imagined heads lifting in the jungle, nostrils sniffing the air.

"I'm worried about Barbie," he said to Lucy. "She left home the other night. I woke up in the morning and she was gone. With all her stuff."

"I understood she was leaving for Canada."

"Not till next week. And she'd never go without saying goodbye."

"Maybe she changed her mind. Maybe she just decided to go."

"Silently?" Birtles demanded. "In the dead of night?" He implied it was the sort of thing Lucy Feather might do to her parents, but not his daughter.

Monty leaned across Lucy and touched Birtles on the arm. "I understand your concern," he said. "I have many contacts in all sorts of places, I travel a good deal. Barbara Birtles -- Lucy will give me a description. I'll put out the word. Don't worry, sir. We'll find your daughter."

It was an incredible sensation -- Birtles felt as if a heavy load had been lifted from him. Ezra Monty was in charge and everything was going to be all right.

"And now" -- Monty glanced at a sliver of gold in his wrist -- "we have something we must attend to. Lucy?"

They were on their way out the door when the spell wore off and Birtles realized he mustn't lose them. More than ever, he sensed there was a link here with Barbara. He tried to drink some beer, almost choked on it, got up, and hurried out onto the dark street.

The couple were climbing into a car a short distance up Inverness Avenue. Birtles lurked in the pub entrance and watched them drive away with Lucy at the wheel. When they turned onto Bayswater Road and headed west, he began looking for a taxi. A car horn tooted, attracted his attention. It was Anitra in the Mini, cruising slowly toward him.

He climbed in beside her and slammed the door. "Bless your heart, I told you to go home."

"I thought you might need help."

"Turn right." She turned, causing a double-decker bus to brake and sound its horn. "There's a black Volvo ahead, can you see it?"

"In this traffic?"

"It's Lucy Feather and her boy friend. I talked to them in the pub. I have a feeling they're hiding something."

After driving as far as Notting Hill, Anitra said, "They could have gone anywhere. They might be on the way to the airport."

"I didn't see any luggage. They may be going to her place. Stop here." Birtles ran to a call box and checked the telephone directory. He found a Feather listed on Southside Common in Wimbledon. Back in the car, he gave Anitra the address and she took off. "Do me a favor," he said. "Keep me alive for a while longer."

Anitra's ability to cover the ground brought them to the Feather residence in record time. It was a three-storey gabled house that bespoke generations of money, probably starting with dividends from the East India Company. There was no black Volvo in sight.

"It was Heathrow like I said," Anitra predicted.

"Once around the Green," Birtles told her.

She took it easy and when they turned back onto Southside the Volvo was there. Anitra pulled over, engine off, lights out. Lucy got out of the car ahead and Ezra Monty followed, both easing the doors shut.

"Why are they acting like that? Isn't it her house?"

"It could be anything," Birtles said. Their movements as they left the car and crept down a laneway beside the house filled him with fear. They were like a military patrol out to silence an enemy position. During the drive he had told Anitra about the conversation in the pub. Now he said: "They might even have Barbie locked up here."

"Kidnapping? Is that possible? How would they have got her out of your place at night without your hearing them?"

Several minutes went by. Through the open window, Birtles could smell the delicious freshness from the Common, all those trees breathing in the night. Now there was movement at the entrance to the lane. Lucy ran out, turned and beckoned -- she seemed impatient, in a state of high excitement. Monty followed and stood in front of the girl, put his hands on her shoulders, and shook her gently.

Her head fell back, and in the streetlight Birtles saw her eyes closed, her mouth open. If she had just inhaled some intoxicating substance, this would have been her reaction.

Monty fed her into the car and closed the door. He ran around and got in at the driver's side, switched on, and drove away. Birtles touched Anitra's shoulder and she began to drive ahead slowly. As they passed the laneway, he noticed something on the pavement. "Stop!" he told her and when she did he jumped out. By the time she parked and joined him, he was examining a dark wet smear on the concrete. He touched it and lifted his stained finger. "Blood," he said.

"Oh, God, get the police."

"I have to know. Have you got a flashlight in the car?" She ran away and brought it to him. He aimed its dim light at the ground and walked down the lane. Anitra kept close enough to touch a hand to his back every now and then.

They came to an out-building. The main house was a dark mass to the right. He saw grass, a concrete birdbath, rose bushes. The door was open in the shed beside him. As Birtles moved into the doorway, he smelled the pungent odor of a stable. He flashed the light over the board partitions of a stall, a leather harness on a hook, brass fittings, a saddle -- then, on the stone floor, the body of a horse lying on its side. The animal was not quite dead -- a leg kicked convulsively.

"Stay back." Birtles moved in closer, felt beneath his feet the pool of blood that Monty had tracked to the street, saw the gaping opening where the broad chestnut neck had been cut through. "Insane," he whispered. They're both insane..."

When they were driving again, he told Anitra to take him back to the hotel. She wanted to get the police but he said he was only concerned about his daughter and if they wasted one minute they might lose Feather and Monty. "I think they came out here to do this and now they'll be on their way."

"That must have been her own horse. Why would she kill it?"

"I don't know. In the pub she said, 'I was riding her a couple of days ago.' I thought she meant arguing with Barbie." Birtles nursed his fear as Anitra gunned down quiet roads.

When they arrived at the Candide, they found the Volvo parked outside. Anitra pulled in and idled. "The police?" she said plaintively. "Can we have the police now, please?"

"O.K. I'll get out and watch. You drive to the police station -- there must be one near here. If you see a cop on the street, stop and tell him."

Birtles got out and positioned himself where he could watch the hotel entrance. The Mini wheeled down the street and turned the corner. Almost immediately, the glass door was pushed open by Monty carrying a couple of expensive-looking suitcases. Lucy Feather followed with a zippered flight bag.

Monty loaded the luggage expertly, closed the trunk, and went to join Lucy in the front seat.

Birtles had to make up his mind. He ran forward, opened the back door, and slid inside just as the car pulled away.

Lucy glanced at him in the rearview mirror as she moved into traffic. "You again! What gives?"

"That's what I intend to find out. Why did you kill your horse?"

Her voice hardened. "Take care of him."

Monty turned and gave Birtles a look of admiration. "Were you out *there* tonight?"

"I'm looking for my daughter. I'm convinced you two know where she is."

"Why do you think that?"

"Because I found a Candide Hotel envelope in her room with some pot in it. And when I came down here I ran into you and Lucy. Lucy visited Barbara a few days ago -- I heard them arguing in her room."

"He's quite a detective, Lucy. He's a determined man. I like that."

"All right," Lucy said. "I gave Barbara some stuff when I went to pick up the book. We argued because I wanted her to come with us but she wouldn't."

"End of story," Monty said. "We know nothing about your daughter, Mr. Birtles."

"I think you do. Anyway, we're going to have it out. My girl friend went to get the police."

Lucy gave him a contemptuous glance. "That's pathetic. Do you know who this is? I told you Ezra Monty -- his real name is Eric Merlot. You know the book I got from Barbara? It's about him."

Birtles had read the book, had glanced at a couple of badly reproduced photos in the centerfold. This could be the man.

"He's killed eleven people already. You mean nothing to him. He'll blow you away as soon as look at you. Where shall we go, Eric? Out in the country?"

Merlot laughed and patted her shoulder. "She's my greatest admirer. When she heard there was a book about me, she had to get a copy right away." He became serious. "Nobody's killed anybody here and nobody's going to. This is England, not India. I said I like you, Mr. Birtles. Barbara's a lucky girl to have a father who cares about her as much as you do -- I can tell you that from experience. And I can see the same qualities in you that I like in her."

"You've seen her then."

"Of course I have. I was keeping quiet because she asked me to. She's agreed to come east and work for me. I provide a service for young people traveling out there and Barbara would be ideal."

Birtles looked at the handsome face watching him across the upholstered seat. Those pale eyes caught what little light there was -- all he could see was intelligent, honest, friendly eyes. "She never said anything to me."

"She wouldn't. She cares about your feelings. I'm offering her glamour, excitement, her own apartment in one of the nicer hotels in Singapore. That beats a cubbyhole bedroom with Daddy listening through the kitchen wall."

Nobody spoke for a few seconds. Then Birtles said: "You've been in my house, Mr. Merlot. When was that?"

"Eric, you're going to have to kill him. This is getting worse."

"Just drive the car. Mr. Birtles is an intelligent man. Sir, I'll admit I was there. We came in the other night using Barbara's key. She sent us to get her backpack. She'd decided to come with me. O.K.? I've told you the truth."

"And her traveller's checks. You got those too?"

"Of course. She said not to forget her traveller's checks."

"But one thing still doesn't fit. Even if Barbara had decided to go with you she would have told me. But she hasn't, and that means something's wrong."

"Eric?" Lucy said in a voice that combined a supplication and a warning.

"And if she's going with you to Singapore, how come you two are driving away without her?"

Merlot laughed. The laugh announced that Birtles was the most entertaining company he'd encountered in a long time. "I'm going to have to give you the rest of it. Barbara wanted your feelings spared -- that's why you haven't heard from her. The fact is, she and I met through Lucy and there was this physical thing between us. Can you understand that? She moved in at the hotel and all she cared about was -- well, *two* things. She also loved what I gave her to smoke. She's been stoned out of her mind for the past three days."

Birtles waited. Yes, he could believe any woman might become infatuated with Eric Merlot. He hated the idea of Barbie falling into that existence. But right now all he wanted was to find her and see that she was all right.

"I decided," Merlot continued, "that the best thing for me to do was disappear. Since she's so young. So I left her in the room at the Candide -- I paid for another couple of days in advance. When she wakes up and sorts herself out, she'll come home. And, Mr. Birtles, please don't tell her where I've gone."

The car slowed down and halted at a traffic light. "I've been told so many things," Birtles said. "First, you were taking her to Singapore. Now you've left her and she doesn't know you've gone. It could all be lies."

"Shut up," Lucy snapped. "Just shut your mouth and get out of the car." She pulled on the hand brake, leaving herself free to sprawl back over the seat and open the back door. "Just get out and go away. And consider yourself lucky."

Birtles got out. He slammed the back door and opened the front door beside Merlot. He put an arm lock on the younger man's head and dragged him from the car. "You're going, too," he said. "I want you with me until I find my daughter."

The light changed. They were in one of the middle lanes and Birtles had to dodge cars as traffic began to move. Lucy had no choice but to drive on. When they reached the sidewalk, Merlot laughed in a high shrill voice. "Fabulous!" he screamed. "You incredible sonofabitch, that's the sort of thing I'd do!"

He was still laughing when they reached an Underground station. As they went down the steps, Merlot's arm firmly held by Birtles, the Eurasian said: "That's how I got away from the police in Rajasthan. Impulse. A window was open, so I climbed through and ran across a yard and out the gate. You keep your eyes open and you take quick, decisive action."

They missed a Central Line train heading east and had to wait on a deserted platform. Merlot glanced at the hand locked onto his upper arm. "Getting tired?" he asked. "I know how hard it is to hold somebody who doesn't want to be held. That's why I use a lot of drugs. You should buy me a coffee and put a few capsules in it."

Birtles pushed Merlot onto a bench and knelt before him. He took his right foot in both hands and twisted sharply. "Oh, Christ, no --" Merlot groaned. The bone snapped and Birtles released the foot.

"Now you won't run," he said. "Not on a broken ankle."

Merlot threw his head back so hard it hit the tiled wall. His eyes were glazed. "Sadistic bastard, you didn't have to do that."

"I think I did. Anyway, you killed that horse, don't talk to me about sadism."

Merlot struggled to get a handkerchief from his pocket. He wiped his eyes and blew his nose. "Want to know why we killed the horse? It was Lucy's idea. She's worse than both of us put together."

A train was approaching. Birtles drew Merlot up and supported him on the lame side. They boarded the train and the doors closed. They sat on a double seat.

"The horse," Merlot said. "I needed money and Lucy got it for me by selling some of her parents' things. Her father threatened to sell her horse to recoup the money. That was what made up her mind to come away with me. Before we left, she decided to kill the horse so they couldn't sell it."

"I think you two deserve each other," Birtles said grimly. "But God help the world if you should spawn."

Merlot laughed. "You think I'd marry or have children? Put more life into this rotten world? Have no fear."

When the train arrived at Queensway Station, Merlot's eyes were closed. As Birtles helped him onto the escalator, he asked: "How's the ankle?"

Merlot seemed still to be thinking of the absurdity of his marrying Lucy Feather. "She's just a contact for me in London -- a source of money while I hide. A gang of English kids in Katmandu gave me her name. When I broke jail the last time, it gave me a place to come and stay."

The three-block walk to the hotel took time. Merlot gritted his teeth and limped on. His weight was light but his slender, supple frame reminded Birtles of the aluminum tent poles he used to erect on camping trips. They were practically unbreakable.

Approaching the Candide, he kept a lookout for a police presence. There was no sign of vehicles or uniformed men. Of course, Merlot had been gone for some time -- Anitra would have returned with the police to be told their man had checked out. By now she and the police would be on the way to the airport.

Inside the hotel, on the stairs to his first-floor room, Merlot said: "Your daughter is O.K., I promise you that. When you're satisfied, will you let me go?"

"All I care about is Barbie," Birtles said. But did he mean that? The man on his shoulder was a murderer, escaped from police custody. He was a psychopath, capable of killing a horse with a knife. How could he be let free? He was smug and confident, holding in contempt the laws and the society that Birtles had supported all his life. "I don't care about you," he added.

"Then we understand each other," Merlot said in a quiet voice with just a trace of an edge.

Merlot had kept his key. As he unlocked the door of his room he glanced at Birtles and read the inquiry in his eyes. "There was no way Lucy was getting on that plane. I was going to give her the key and send her back to take care of Barbara. O.K.?"

They went inside where Merlot snapped on a light and closed the door. It turned out to be a small suite. He indicated a closed door. "She's in the bedroom."

"You, too," Birtles said, pulling Merlot with him.

Merlot opened the door and Birtles went into the bedroom. He saw a familiar shape in the bed, recognized the curly head on the pillow even in near darkness. He left the limping man and hurried to the bed. As he bent over her, Merlot turned on a lamp. The light fell on Barbie's face, undamaged but passive as a sculpture.

"Barbie? Love?" Birtles touched her cheek. There was warmth. "Are you all right?"

Her eyelids flickered, raised -- she saw him and immediately there were tears. "Oh, it's you," she slurred. "Daddy, I was hoping you'd come --"

"I'm here now. You'll be O.K."

"They gave me drugs. They wanted my money. I couldn't phone, I couldn't move or do anything."

"I'll get a doctor for you. We'll have you home in no time."

"Daddy, I'm not going away. I'm going to stay with you --"

"Shhhh." She had reverted to the school girl who used to feign illness so she could stay home in bed where he would bring her lunch on a tray and the deck of cards for a game of rummy. "We'll talk about it when you're better."

He heard the bedroom door close, heard the snap of a key in the lock. He got up and ran to the door. "Merlot, don't be crazy!"

"She's O.K., right? That's my side of the bargain. I don't trust you, Mr. Birtles -- I'm off."

"You'll get nowhere on that ankle."

"Pain is all in the mind. I've turned off worse than this when I had to."

Birtles hit the door with his fist. It was old-fashioned, a solid, heavy panel. "Merlot!"

"I've been in three jails and got out every time. You never had a hope of holding me." His voice drew away. "Goodbye, Mr. Birtles, you'll never see me again. Too bad -- I like you." The outer door closed.

Birtles went back to the bed. "Barbie, I'm going to make some noise. I have to break the door. Don't worry, I'll be back soon."

She gave him the wise, mature smile -- his mother encouraging him to do his best. He went back to the door and balanced himself. It took five lunges to put his boot through the panel. A minute later, he was outside and running for the stairs.

The lobby was deserted, nobody on duty at the desk. Merlot was crafty enough to be hiding somewhere inside, but Birtles decided to have a quick look on the street. Self-hypnosis or whatever, he couldn't be covering the ground very quickly.

Outside, he saw a crowd gathering at the corner of Bayswater Road. He stared and could hardly believe his eyes when he made out what looked to be the familiar blue Mini. Running in that direction, he picked out Anitra Colahan's peach coiffure glistening under the street lamp in the midst of the crowd.

He reached her and when she saw him she took his arm for support. "Oh, God, he ran right in front of the car! You weren't here when I got back with the police. I was cruising the neighborhood looking for you. I turned the corner and he was running across -- not running, limping."

"It's O.K." Birtles looked down, saw the pale-blue eyes staring. Somebody would have to close them for him now. "That's Merlot, the man who was holding Barbara. They drugged her to rob her. He's killed a lot of people."

Anitra turned away. A police car was pulling up. "Here they come," she said grimly. "Three tries to get my license and now I'm going to lose it."

Birtles looked from her to the dead man and back at her angry face. All right, so there were signs all around that it was indeed the selfish, imperfect world Merlot believed it to be. Not so long ago it was a jungle and people were eating each other.

"When you've given the cops your statement," he said, "come back to the hotel. I'll be with Barbie, waiting for the doctor. When she's taken care of, you can drive me home."

As he walked away, Birtles realized he'd just told Anitra that he loved her.

Ellery Queen Mystery Magazine, February, 1984

HER VOICE ON THE
PHONE WAS MAGIC

Seebold walked five paces this way, five paces that way, trying to imagine what the woman would look like. Thank goodness it was dark. He could picture friends in cars driving by and saying: "Isn't that Martin Seebold hanging around the telephone building?" Earlier that evening he had spoken with an operator while placing a call to his wife who was visiting their son in Newcastle. The operator's voice did something to him -- and here he was. Blame it on the evening, Seebold told himself, excusing his behavior.

The weather was a plausible defense. Days of such quality happen rarely in an English summer. The sky had remained clear since morning. Now there was a sprinkling of stars and the breeze seemed to be coming in off a warm sea.

The door at the top of the steps opened and a girl appeared. She came down awkwardly on chunky heels, lugging a shoulder bag and a plastic carryall. Incredibly, she wore a hat.

"Fay?" Seebold said. "Fay Blore?"

"948-1090?" They shook hands and teetered off balance, sharing a suspicion that the best part of this affair might have been those flirtatious words exchanged across the romantic anonymity of a telephone connection.

"How about a drink, then?" he said. She was not ugly, only plain. No style to her brown hair, no feminine appeal in the moist, pale eyes, the heavy jaw. She was short, but not petite. "Do you mind the Alex?"

"The Alex is fine."

They walked to the Alexandra Pub and found a quiet corner. She asked for dry sherry and Seebold brought her a large one along with his double whisky. He imagined his wife criticizing him: "The doctor would be thrilled to see you into the strong stuff." But Sylvia was with Gary in Newcastle and would be there for the rest of the week. So Martin Seebold was free to forget he was fifty-six and to behave like an adolescent down here in Wimbledon.

"I've been a telephone operator for ten years," she informed him. Before then, she had sold shoes in a local department store. Went to school in the borough. Born in a house not far from where they were drinking. Parents retired, probably watching television in the old sitting-room at that very moment. A brother named Reg was drifting about someplace or other -- getting himself into trouble, like as not.

"I'm local, too," Seebold responded. But their origins were not the same. Born up the hill in the Village, the only son of professional parents, Seebold had elevated himself further by marrying Sylvia and settling in her centuries-old family property on the edge of Wimbledon Common. He skated over this information, concentrating on his two years in the RAF at the end of the war. "I was lucky. I was posted to India with the pay corps. Marvellous."

An hour later the pub bell rang and they were chivvied out onto the pavement. "Care for a burger?" Seebold intended to see the situation through to the end.

"Lovely," she said, taking his arm and heading for the McDonald's sign with choppy steps as if they were crossing a ploughed field. There was safety in the crowded restaurant. If he should encounter a friend, Seebold could fob Fay Blore off as an innocent acquaintance.

"You don't have to see me home," she told him when they were outside again.

"Don't be silly. It's a lovely night."

Her flat was not far -- down a laneway off the Kingston Road. Seebold found himself, surprisingly, in no hurry to say goodbye. It was like making small talk with the dentist after the session is over. "You live up there?" he said, observing the iron steps and the narrow landing at the top. "It's like something designed to go on a stage."

"Do you want to come in?" She had expected him to be gone like a thief in the night.

"See you to the door anyway." The adventure had turned out fine. He would enjoy describing it to Lionel Henning next time they played gin rummy.

The steps rose beside the glass-roofed kitchen of a fish-and-chips shop. Seebold followed her to the landing, looked down over a railing at peaks of opaque glass, heard the clatter of plates, the roar of boiling oil as a new basket of potatoes went in, saw steam venting from a grating under the eaves. He felt he was in the engine room of a giant ship, a passenger embarked upon a mysterious voyage.

"No, not again..."

Seebold turned and saw Fay at her front door. It was hanging ajar, the room in darkness behind it. "Have you been robbed?"

"I know who did this," she said. She moved inside and switched on a light.

Seebold followed her, saw the room disarranged but not as destructively as some he had read about. No slashing of upholstery, no daubing of walls. "Don't touch anything," he said. "Call the police."

She went to a drawer that hung open, knitting-magazines dragged out and scattered on the floor. She found a battered envelope, checked that it was empty. "Forty pounds gone."

"Ring the police now, Fay."

"I haven't a phone." The operator's wry smile acknowledged the irony. "We don't need the police," she said, moving to the door and closing Seebold in. "I know who did this. It was Reg, my brother. He needed money and he knows where I keep it."

"Couldn't he ask?"

"If I'd been here, he would have asked."

Seebold's euphoria evaporated. Here he was keeping late hours with an uninspiring woman who had a criminal psychopath for a brother. "I'll help you clear up."

"I'll put on some coffee."

With the books back on the shelves, they sat at the kitchen table drinking coffee and sipping brandy. She had put on a recording of somebody playing the piano. It sounded to

Seebold like underground trains but Fay's eyes sparkled when she announced: "Pinetop Smith!" so apparently it was something special.

"What puzzles me," he said, "is why throw down the books and toss the other things around? If it's your brother and he knows where you keep your money."

"I know. Maybe he was drunk." She swallowed some brandy and compressed her lips so thin they disappeared.

Rain began falling a few minutes later. The drops hammered on the glass roof of the fish-and-chips shop. "When that stops, I'd better be off," Seebold said.

After half an hour, they were standing in the doorway watching what was clearly going to be an all-night rain. "You'd better sleep here," she said. He couldn't conceal his dismay. "I mean on the settee. Come on, I won't attack you in the night. Have another brandy while I make up some kind of a bed."

Her sheets were fresh. Tucked in with the remains of his third brandy on the table beside him, Seebold began to enjoy himself. Who could predict what was going to happen to a man on a given day? He grinned to himself as he took another swallow of brandy. He could hardly wait to tell Lionel Henning about his adventure with the spooky telephone operator.

"You all right?" She was in the bedroom doorway wearing a robe of some fuzzy brown material. Her hand was on the light switch.

"Like a bug in a rug." He raised his glass, she blew him a sisterly kiss and the room went dark.

Seebold had no trouble falling asleep. The drinks and the hypnotic drumming of rain on the glass roof overcame the discomfort of the settee. He couldn't tell what time it was when he drifted awake. The room was pitch black, no sign of dawn's early light. His watch was on the coffee table but he couldn't see the luminous dial for some reason. He put out his hand and touched warm, naked flesh.

"It's all right," she whispered. "Do you mind being woken up?"

"What is it?"

"I was lonely." A little girl's voice trying to be sexy in the dark. "I thought I'd come and see if you were lonely, too."

The approach was so transparent it annoyed Seebold. Or was it something else that made his skin grow cold? He was being put on the spot, asked to perform. He had never enjoyed responding to overtures. Not just physical demands but anything at all, a request from Sylvia for him to attend the theatre would leave him rigid with annoyance. Because it was not his idea.

"I was asleep."

"Sorry."

At last she had to speak again. "I don't please you do I? I could tell when you saw me for the first time outside the building. It's one of those things, either it works or it doesn't."

"Don't blame yourself too much." Seebold was calming down. Since he would never see this woman again, he could afford to say something reassuring. He had never revealed this before to anyone, not even Sylvia. Now it was as if it had to be said -- he was in the dark confessional and the truth would cleanse his soul. "Sex has never been important to me. I'm not gay, don't get the wrong idea, I just don't care all that much about making love."

"I see." She didn't sound convinced.

"What I am is romantic. The part I go for is the companionship."

"That's the best part." She placed her head on the pillow beside his for a moment. But their breathing never fell into rhythm. Soon she said: "Good night," and left the room silently.

In the morning they sat at the kitchen table in pale sunlight eating muffins and drinking tea. Seebold was reminded of uncomfortable breakfasts with his landlady years ago when he was at the university before he gave it up and settled for accountancy.

"Looks nice for my day off," she said, indicating the out-of-doors with an awkward movement of her head.

"Clouding up later I think I heard it said." She was inviting him to spend the day with her and all Seebold wanted was to get away.

"Will you walk home from here?"

"Yes. Up the hill to the Village. The white cottage on the corner of the High Street, facing the Common." He enjoyed flaunting Sylvia's house.

Fay had left the front door propped open when she brought in the milk. Now a tall young man came through and stood close to the kitchen table. He had inherited the same sort of head as his sister -- shaped by a potter with a lot to learn-- but his body was well-proportioned. "Too late for breakfast?" He extended a hand to the older man who shook it, half rising.

"This is Martin Seebold. He got caught by the rain last night. My brother Reg. You've got a hell of a nerve showing your face around here this morning."

"What's the matter?"

"You know damn well."

"I don't."

"Forty pounds taken out of my drawer last night. When I came home the place was in a shambles." She watched Reg's reaction as he turned and surveyed the sitting-room. "We put it back together."

Reg ambled into the other room. He opened the drawer where the knitting-magazines were kept, closed it, and walked back into the kitchen looking thoughtful. "Why do you think it was me?"

"Who else?"

"Last time I only took twenty. I borrowed it."

"The way they borrow from Barclay's Bank in the middle of the night."

"I'd never toss your place. You know me better than that."

"Unless you wanted me to think it was somebody else."

"I have an idea who did it." Reg made a helpless gesture. "Why don't you have a telephone like decent people?"

"Do you want coffee?"

"I have to go and see somebody."

"Have some coffee first."

"No, thanks. My sister thinks I robbed her."

Seebold walked up Wimbledon Hill to the Village. He began to feel better when he reached the top, the High Street shops aligned ahead of him with their pricey merchandise and well designed fronts. There was a physical difference between down the hill and up the hill, he was convinced of it. The air-pressure up here allowed his blood to flow more easily, or perhaps ozone from the trees in the Common was a tonic for his lungs. He always felt safer and happier up here -- just as down in the town there was excitement, but danger among a different kind of people.

He let himself in, carried the morning mail upstairs to his office, and sat at his desk, looking out across the road at the giant chestnut tree and the pond in the middle distance. He still thought of this room as an office although he did not work here. When he took early retirement last year, Seebold had spoken in terms of doing a little freelance. But nobody had offered him any such work and he had not pursued it. His redundancy settlement had been generous and Sylvia's resources were considerable. All Seebold had to do was take it easy and grow as old as possible with maximum grace. The famous heart attack two years ago provided justification for a degree of idleness.

Seebold's head was nodding, his mind filled with images of Fay and Reg on rope-ladders scaling the side of a ship, when the telephone rang beside him. It was Sylvia calling from Newcastle.

"Where were you?"

"Where was I when?" After a long separation it took only this brief exchange to reestablish their relationship.

"I rang three times last night and twice earlier this morning. It is now eleven-fifteen."

"I wasn't here. I was playing gin with Lionel Henning. Then we watched the late film. When it started to rain I camped out on his settee."

"Oh yes."

"My neck feels as if it contains a hot poker."

"I suppose I believe you. With your medical history, I can't imagine you chasing the girls while your wife is away."

"Very funny."

"Promise me you won't end up dead in the bed of some teenaged tart."

"Even funnier."

She fell silent and Seebold occupied the time watching the ducks and coots on the pond. It interested him that a belligerent coot chased only other coots. Ducks, much of a size, were left alone.

"I rang to say I've decided to stay another few days."

"Having a good time, then?"

"Good time has nothing to do with it. I'm helping Gary and Rose, doing the things a mother does for her son and his wife. It happens to be more difficult at a distance of several hundred miles."

"I know."

"They could be living somewhere in London, if you were a normal father."

"I did nothing --"

"If you'd done nothing, Gary wouldn't have taken Rose this far away."

Seebold remembered the moment in Cannizaro Park when Gary came upon the two of them. On a Sunday afternoon, he had led Rose through a tunnel of rhododendrons to show her the view from his secret lookout. In tight jeans and cotton blouse, she was like a muscular young boy. Drugged by the droning afternoon and the waves of fragrant greenery breaking around them, he had put his arm around her slender waist and drawn her to him. Her hair smelled of shampoo. He had kissed the part in her hair.

"Fortunately," Sylvia was going on, "Gary has never told me what you were up to."

"There was nothing."

"So you say. But he and Rose live in Newcastle now, in a very ordinary little house. So don't talk to me about having a good time in Newcastle."

Seebold considered putting down the phone, pretending they had been cut off. But she would only get through again, more disturbed than ever. Like taking the cane, trousers down, gritting his teeth across the headmaster's desk, Seebold had to absorb his wife's telephone call.

"I'm putting an envelope of photographs in the post. Gary and Rose and the baby. When I get back, we'll decide which ones to have framed."

"So I'll see you when? Saturday?"

She laughed and for just a second or two the buoyant sound made him feel secure. "Don't worry, I'll confirm my estimated time of arrival. Give you time to wash the perfume off the pillowcases."

Seebold put down the phone. Then he picked it up and dialed Lionel Henning. His old friend was ready to provide an alibi. "What have you been up to, naughty boy?"

"I'll explain when next I see you. An incredible story, full of moral significance. Never become involved with the common people. They'll drop you in it, plunge you straight down into the roaring fires of hell."

Seebold, after a lunch of cheese and granary bread and a shapely bosc pear, was napping on top of the bedspread when the doorbell chimed downstairs. The noise dragged him out of a half sleep in which he had been grinding his teeth. A casement window was open. Sunlight across the end of the bed warmed his feet and the fragrance of mock orange permeated the room.

The bell chimed again.

When he opened the door, Seebold did not recognize Fay Blore for a couple of seconds. She stood there enjoying his discomfiture. Her cheeks were burned from hours spent in the sun. She had put aside the trappings of premature middle-age to appear now in velvet slacks, open sandals, a stylish blouse, and a tiny scarf knotted at the neck. Her brown hair was pulled around and clipped at one side -- an improvement -- but starry pencilled eyelashes could not save the mismatched eyes.

"You were having a nap!"

"It's all right. Come in."

He sat her down in the living room under the sloping ceiling, the dark beams, all of it centuries old. She stared about her like a tourist in a museum. "I've come to take you out. I owe you for last night."

"You took a chance."

"You said your wife is away."

"A few more days. We were on the telephone a while ago."

"Did you tell her about me?"

"I told her I was out last night with my old friend Lionel. Playing gin rummy."

"Good old Lionel."

He brought the Waterford decanter to the Jacobean table and poured her a glass of Australian sherry. In crystal, it looks as Spanish as they come. He went upstairs and changed, shaving in five minutes. He pattered down the winding stairs like a schoolboy, smelling of lemon cologne.

Outside, she said: "I'll leave the choice to you -- this is your territory. But remember, it's my treat."

Seebold wanted to get out of the neighborhood. A bus was laboring up the hill in the distance. He guided her to the stop and they boarded the bus for Putney. "There's a lovely little place near the bridge," he said.

The giant proprietor was bellowing down the telephone in Italian. After five minutes, he presented himself to Seebold and took the order repeating the word "Signor" after each item with mock obsequiousness. But the veal was tender and the sauce of lemon and white wine was delicious.

When they left the restaurant, there was still an hour's light in the sky. The tide was in, the grey water high against the embankment protecting the Lower Richmond Road. Seebold led Fay along the footpath towards the brick facade of The Star and Garter. They sat at a table by the window, watching cruise boats heading up to Teddington or down to Greenwich. Conversation was easy and once, when she lowered her head against his shoulder laughing at one of his jokes, he kissed the part in her hair.

Later, they caught a bus on the south end of the bridge. It was dark now. Talked out from the pub session, they travelled along the Parkside in silence, holding hands. Seebold had time to think. She must not come inside with him. Her presence in the house would last forever. Nor could he go home with her a second time. That way lay disaster.

As the bus approached the turn onto Wimbledon High Street, he got up and put a hand on her shoulder. "I'd better say goodnight."

She was so experienced at being rebuffed that she took it with an approving smile. "Keep in touch," she said as the bus stopped and he escaped onto the pavement.

Seebold took his time walking past the cenotaph, past the pond and the chestnut tree. Inside his iron gate, he studied the silhouette of the hydrangea. They looked as if they could use a drink. Tomorrow. He searched for the front-door lock, and before he could insert his key the door swung inward. He stood listening. After half a minute, he reached through and switched on the light. He noticed a mark on the doorframe where the jimmy had gone in.

The place had not been ransacked, but he was able to inventory the missing articles immediately. The carriage-clock from the mantel, several pieces of silver from the cabinet. Suddenly, as sure as death and tax-evasion, Seebold knew who had robbed his house. Reg Blore. While he was out for a couple of hours, escorted by the sister. For all Seebold knew, Fay was in on it.

The police. He had the telephone up, had dialed the first two nines, when he changed his mind. To cause trouble for Fay without giving her a chance to say something was not right. Instead, Seebold dialed a taxi number. The cab came and he had the driver take him down the hill to the Kingston Road and drop him a hundred yards from the fish-and-chips shop. Taking deep breaths, he walked down the laneway and climbed the iron steps. Below him, the crash and hiss of deep-frying on a massive scale went on, hidden beneath the glass roof.

Seebold knocked at Fay's door and stood waiting in the dark. If she was willing to get hold of Reg and make him return the stolen goods now, this night, he would forget the matter. Otherwise...

Fay was taking a long time coming to the door. He knocked again, sharply. A light went on somewhere inside, not in the sitting-room. He knocked a third time. Voices began whispering on the other side of the panel. Seebold began to feel unsure of himself. If Reg was in there and he wanted to make an issue of the accusation...

Another light came on and the door swung open. A girl Seebold had never seen stood to one side in jeans and bare feet and a pajama top. Behind her stood another stranger, a bleached-blond young man, also wearing tight jeans, bare-chested, tanned. These people, Seebold told himself, have climbed out of bed to open this door.

"I'm looking for Fay Blore."

"Hello. Come in. My name is Annie Wickersham." Her manner was airline-hostess-friendly but her voice was public school. "This is Bjorn Lindgren. We're friends of Fay's brother. She should be along soon."

He came inside and accepted Bjorn's handshake. The boy looked and sounded like middle-class money in Sweden. "I won't stay if Fay isn't going to be around."

Annie's self-assurance was overpowering. "Please sit down, Fay would want you to." She sat after he did and faced him with her hands draped languidly across her knees. "We used a key Reg gave us -- with Fay's permission, of course. I expect she's stalling now to give us time."

Bjorn stood confidently, hands in pockets. All the pose needed was sand and sun. "We're just back from Greece," he said.

"Crete, actually," Annie confirmed. "I've been touring for the past six months -- India, Nepal. I ended up in Crete, where I ran out of money. The only thing I could do was take work picking cucumbers and tomatoes." She stared at her roughened hands. "Then along came Bjorn and rescued me. Air fair home." The boy's hand hung close enough for her to take it and press it against her cheek.

Footsteps approached on the iron stairs. Seebold got to his feet. So did Annie Wickersham. "The wanderer returns," she said.

Fay tapped with one knuckle, opened the door, and allowed Reg to enter ahead of her. Seebold's presence stopped them in their tracks. "What are you doing here?"

"I have to talk to you. Alone."

"We're just on our way," Annie said. She took Bjorn by the hand and led him into the bedroom. They were back dressed and out the door before the tension had time to escalate.

When the front door closed and their footsteps began retreating down the iron stairs, Fay said: "Well?"

"My house was broken into this evening. While you and I were together."

"That's terrible. Did they take much?'

"A few valuables."

Reg said bluntly: "Why come here? Why tell us?"

Seebold thought, let the confrontation begin. "Because I think you did it."

"Me?"

"The coincidence is too much. I've never had robbers in my life. Last night I came here with Fay and her place had been ripped off. She said it was you. Tonight she and I went out -- which you must have known -- and somebody entered my house." Seebold was getting into a fine swing. "Too much!"

"You bastard. I was with friends. I never left -- they'll vouch for that."

"I'm sure they will. Let them tell the police."

Reg made a move and Fay intercepted him. "Get out of here, Reg. I'm not having a fight in here."

"This old creep says I robbed his house."

"Go." She managed to open the door while restraining her brother. "Go home. There won't be any police."

When they were alone, Seebold, feeling easier now because he had done his job as a man, said: "I'm sorry, Fay, but you must see my point. It has to have been Reg."

"He has an alibi."

"Of course he has."

She tossed her shoulder bag onto the settee and turned to face him, not on his side at all. "Have you any idea how many break-ins there are in London? I saw some figures. Five hundred a day. Something like forty here in the borough. Your number came up."

"That's not how it feels to me."

"What have you got to go on besides your hunch?"

"He didn't leave his name on the wall -- a hunch is all there is. But I know it was Reg, it had to be him."

"Then call the police."

"I don't want to."

"Well, what *do* you want, Martin? You're starting to drive me up the wall. I don't know why I bother with you."

She looked helples, on the verge of tears. He kept his distance. "I want back the things he took. Tell him to return my stuff and that will be the end of it."

She watched him for a few seconds, then turned away. "I'm going to take a shower," she said as she left the room. "We'll talk after."

"I'm not going to hang around."

"Stay or don't stay. I'm having a shower."

He was still standing there as the drizzle of water began hitting a plastic curtain. His sense of outrage was mounting. He was being taken advantage of, right, left, and center. His house had been burgled, almost certainly by Reg, and Fay could not care less.

Seebold looked around the room. He would collect payment in kind. Something to hold against the return of his stolen goods. Not that there would be anything in this firetrap worth taking.

Then he saw it on a shelf near the bricked-up fireplace -- a brass peppermill. It was obviously an antique, in need of a polish but a fine piece; cylindrical, ten inches high, with a jointed handle on top fitted with a wooden knob. The mill was in two sections. He tried separating them, but the joint was tight and he didn't want to damage it.

Feeling a mixture of terror and triumph, Seebold slipped the peppermill into his pocket, left Fay Blore's flat and took a cab home.

As he placed the peppermill on the mantle piece where the stolen carriage-clock used to sit, Seebold was feeling a sense of destiny. Fay's presence in his life was very different from tedious debits and credits that balanced at the end of the day. He had been let in on a mild form of anarchy. Truth be told, he was enjoying himself.

Pajama-clad, slumped in a wingback chair, his slippered feet propped on a needlepoint hassock, Seebold sipped a drink. It would be a bad thing, he realized, to bring in the police and implicate Reg Blore. If they made a case of it, Seebold would end up on the witness stand explaining how he happened to know Reg and, more to the point, his sister Fay. Sylvia would ask questions and his comfortable life here in the cottage on the High Street might be threatened.

The telephone rang. Seebold put out a hand and took up the receiver. Speak of the devil...but it was not Sylvia.

"I was thinking about you while I took my shower. You've had nothing but grief from me."

Her voice on the phone was magic. Seebold closed his eyes and curled up inside himself like a boy being told a bedtime story. "Not to worry."

"I do worry. I'd like us to start again."

"Listen. I've decided you're right about my robbery. It could have been anybody. I'll bring in the police tomorrow just so there'll be a report for the insurance. But I won't mention Reg."

"That's sweet, I'll tell him. He and Annie are there now. I'm at a call-box. Bjorn's coming soon with Chinese food."

He imagined the scene in Fay's apartment -- plates, glasses, muffled words -- the tribe back from hunting, safe for the night. He felt left out. "By the way," he boasted, "I took your brass peppermill. To make up for the stuff I lost."

"Peppermill?"

"It looks good on my mantel. Of course, if my things turn up, I'll discuss giving it back."

"I didn't even notice it was gone." She sounded anxious. "It belongs to Bjorn. He brought it back from Greece."

"Fine taste, these Swedes."

"He wants to sell it to a dealer. He only left it here for safekeeping."

"There's no such thing as a safe place any more."

"Bjorn will be upset."

"You can tell him I'm chairman of that club."

Seebold did not sleep well. Lying cheek down, he could feel each beat of his heart. How much longer would the old pump carry on? And why was he not more afraid? Was this final section of his life such a bore that he could anticipate the end with no more interest than he felt during the credits of a bad television film?

He heard a thump below. His eyes opened, focused on the green clock-dial. Almost four o'clock -- he must have been sleeping, after all. More noise downstairs. The front door juddered open and hit the wall. Then silence. He knew who was down there.

Quickly he rose and found his robe. He pulled his arms through the sleeves as he crept downstairs, past the bend and into the darkened living room. His hand found the switch and turned on the overhead light.

Annie Wickersham was at the mantelpiece, the peppermill in both hands. Reg was at the door, close enough for Seebold to touch him -- or be touched. He felt no fear. It was as if he was father and had come upon the children engaged in some naughty prank. He moved to the girl, his hand extended.

"Where's Bjorn?" he asked. "Does he always use you to do his dirty work?"

"He's outside in the car," Annie said. Obediently, she handed Seebold the peppermill.

"Annie," Reg groaned, "don't give him that."

She reached for the peppermill. Seebold fended her off. They grappled. She was beefy under the blouse, nothing soft about her. He was enjoying her weight against him, but he was falling off balance. The fire irons went over with a crash and, as he sank to the floor, Seebold saw fit to raise his voice in a ferocious cry.

Reg's eyes were wild. "Come on. Let's *go!*" He moved back into the doorway.

When Annie followed, Seebold flung the peppermill at her back as hard as he could. It missed her, struck the doorframe, and fell to the floor in two pieces. Reg bent and retrieved the pieces in an odd, scooping motion. Then he was gone. Moments later, car doors slammed, an engine revved and retreated into the distance.

Seebold lay still. Strange, he thought, how his heart could hold up through this kind of stress. Had the doctors been wrong? Or had he experienced some sort of remission? The vital organ seemed, apparently, to be mending itself.

A forgotten episode from his childhood entered Seebold's mind. Seven years old, he stood on the school stage in front of an audience of parents. A female schoolmate faced him, holding two pieces of a heart made of red paper. To a piano accompaniment, she sang: "Are you a tinker?"

"That am I," the young Seebold sang in response.

"Can you mend my heart...?"

"I'll try," he volunteered.

Focusing on the open doorway, Seebold could see white powder on the carpet where the halves of the peppermill had fallen. He crawled over and stared at the powder. In television dramas about drug-trafficking, a police officer -- a narc? -- would dip his finger into the powder, taste it, and know what sort of dope he was dealing with.

But Martin Seebold would not have known what taste to expect. And, anyway, he was afraid to try.

In the morning, a pair of policemen came around. Seebold allowed last night's forced entry to account for his loss from earlier in the day. He listed what had been taken, with estimated values. He didn't refer to Reg or Annie or Bjorn. The officers went away, bored as tourists.

Jaundiced thoughts, like dregs of stale wine, collected in Seebold's mind as he shaved. But he felt better when he left the house and walked down the hill to visit his friend Lionel Henning. They lunched on Henning's patio, then went inside for a game of gin rummy. Seebold lost two quid. He was concentrating less on the cards and more on his recounting of the Fay Blore saga. It was all fine, self-deprecating stuff -- her glamorous voice, her appearance as a dowdy dwarf, that hat which must have been her mother's...

There was a film he wanted to see at the Odeon down the Broadway, so he went there alone at three o'clock and sat in the dark, filling his mouth with chocolate-coated caramels while admiring the way Jack Nicholson attacked a door with an axe.

The pubs were open when the film let out, so he wandered back to the Alex for a couple of drinks while he read the paper. Then up the hill for a light supper, an hour watching the box, and early bed.

Nobody broke in that night. The telephone did not ring. In the morning, the postman dropped a large brown envelope through the slot. Seebold opened it and found, protected by squares of shirt cardboard, several beautiful photographs of his son Gary, his wife and the cherubic grandson. A handwritten note was folded between the photos.

Back at the kitchen table, Seebold sipped apple juice and read the familiar script. Sylvia would be back on Monday. He was not to come all the way to King's Cross. She would ring when the train arrived, then she would take the District Line to Wimbledon. Seebold could time himself to meet her there and help with bags and a taxi.

His holiday was coming to an end. Too soon, the bad old routine would begin again. It was difficult for him to pin down just what was bad about his existence here with Sylvia. Never mind. He felt grim and justification was not required.

The day was sunny again, no mention of rain in the forecast. Seebold took out the hose and watered the plants in the back garden. Then he went up to the flat roof outside his study. The potted marigolds lining the eaves looked tired. He scooped water from the rain barrel and gave them a drink.

Next he unfolded a deck chair and reclined facing the sun. After an hour, his face felt crisp so he took himself inside. The last thing he wanted was to get himself fried.

He would have to see Fay one more time before Sylvia came back. This idea occurred to Seebold at four in the afternoon as he was working a crossword puzzle. It made sense for him to let the girl know that, as of Monday, she must not ring up or appear at the cottage for any reason.

He put on the expensive maroon corduroy trousers Sylvia had bought for him a year ago when she thought he ought to try dressing young. He slipped his feet into black patent-leather loafers and drew over his head a white knitted shirt with a tiny gold crown on the pocket. Seebold decided to consider himself a well preserved man heading out to keep some mysterious appointment.

With a bottle of claret wrapped in a Harrod's plastic bag, he set out down the hill. He was anxious to arrive at Fay's place, to see her, even to run into the three kids again. He missed them all -- the room, Fay's loud music, the whole atmosphere of their young lives. They were so far behind him on the road, it seemed a sensible thing for him to go back and meet them.

He was in the lane, approaching the iron stairs, when it occurred to him she might not be home. If there was no response when he knocked at the door, he would simply wander away, find a pub, have a couple, and come back.

The door was ajar when he reached the iron landing. Fay's door seemed to spend more time open that shut. Voices murmured within. His rap brought Reg to the doorway. "Fay, come here," he said as if Seebold was an exhibit. "Look at this."

She appeared at her brother's side wearing a flowered shift, barefoot, her eyes wide and bright. "Martin! How lovely, we're having a celebration."

He allowed her to lead him into the dusky room. Bjorn was lying on the settee, a clear place beside him where Fay must have been. He was pinching the stub of a thin cigarette. Annie Wickersham lay on the carpet, her head on a pillow. Reg went to her and lay down. He took the cigarette she offered and drew on it deeply.

"What's the occasion?" Seebold asked, his confidence ebbing.

"We're celebrating a deal," Annie said. "An arrangement."

Bjorn spoke up. "Annie flies to Greece. Annie flies back. With her good clothes and accent, Annie flies through customs."

"Then everybody gets high," Reg said and they all laughed for a long time.

Finally Seebold said: "I brought some wine."

Fay left the settee and came to receive the bottle. As she took it, she put a wrist around his neck, drew his head down, and applied a wet kiss to his lips.

With a glass of wine in his stomach and a second one in his hand, Seebold's personal pendulum took an upward swing. He sat with his legs extended, shoes making a glittering V. "So this is how you lot enjoy yourselves," he commented, a tolerant judge.

"One of the ways," Bjorn said.

"How do I love thee?" Annie recited. "Let me count the ways."

"You can't count that high," Reg said.

Seebold felt an urge to get closer to the life they led, to show some sophistication, "By the way," he said, "what was the white powder that ended up on my carpet the other night when the peppermill came apart?"

The response was silence. Bjorn sat up and put his feet on the floor. He looked from Seebold to Reg to Annie. "What the hell happened in there? You never told me."

"He threw the mill," Reg said. "It broke apart."

"How much is lost? That stuff sells by the gram."

"Hardly anything," Annie whispered.

Bjorn climbed to his feet. "And this bugger knows?"

Fay came in from the kitchen. "It's all right," she said.

"It isn't all right! This guy can do us if he feels like it."

"I don't feel like doing anybody," Seebold said. "Except maybe Fay if the rest of you would disappear."

Fay took Bjorn's arm and turned him. She moved him towards the door. "Go to the off-licence, love. I feel like another nice bottle of wine."

Bjorn was trying to turn back. "We've got to do something about this guy."

"We'll talk when you come back. Reg, go with Bjorn. You know the wine I like."

When the young men were gone, Fay came to Seebold. "You'd better go. He can be terrible when he gets mad."

"I don't want to go," Seebold said.

"She's right," Annie said. "Bjorn goes crazy. In Crete, in the greenhouse, a man got on his nerves. Bjorn cut him with a trowel. He would have killed him."

"All right." Seebold moved away from the door. There was wine in his glass. "May I finish this?"

"Quickly, please."

He took his time drinking the wine while Fay stood in the center of the room and Annie went to look out the window. Setting down the empty glass, he said: "Okay if I go to the bathroom?"

"Hurry, for God's sake."

He took his time and when he came out, Annie said: "They'll be here any minute."

The door was open. Fay propelled him through and stood, wanting to close it. "I'll ring you."

"You can't ring me after Monday."

"All right, tomorrow. Go now."

They heard the clang of heavy steps on the iron stairs. Fay said something Seebold missed and Annie made a moaning noise in her throat. Bjorn appeared first, Reg behind him carrying the supplies.

"What's this?" Bjorn faced Seebold.

"Going home."

"To ring the police?"

"No, I just want to go home." Now, when he could have used courage to bluff his way out in front of the women, Seebold was swamped with fear. This young man could thump him nine ways. He took a breath and felt his heart miss a beat, stutter, and catch up.

"You're not going anywhere," Bjorn said. "Not till I make sure about you."

As Seebold made a move to pass the young Swede, Bjorn grappled with him. The weakness in Seebold's arms was ridiculous. For heaven's sake, he could lift a filing cabinet if he had to. He struggled to break free and Bjorn threw a punch he managed to avoid.

Fay called: "Let him go!" but she remained in the doorway. Annie was a face behind the curtains. Seebold managed to get loose and tried again to pass Bjorn on the railing side. Bjorn caught him by the shoulder, swung him around with his back to the railing, and aimed another punch. This one landed, driving Seebold against the railing which gave way, letting him step back into space.

He heard Fay's scream as he fell. The glass roof of the restaurant kitchen shattered and Seebold burst through into heat and light, seeing white tile, stainless-steel shelves, red floor, startled upturned faces. Life does end unexpectedly, he realized. There is a hell and we descend into it literally.

And for Seebold hell was a cauldron of cooking oil heated to a temperature of almost 400 degrees.

Ellery Queen Mystery Magazine, August, 1984

THE COLLABORATORS

"Have you been taking your medication?" Mariette asked and the question converted Luke Adams' righteous anger into outrage.

"Stick to the bloody point!" he yelled. He kicked the bedroom wastebasket against the wall and it spewed its load of her multicolored tissues. "You're going off to Paris for two months leaving me alone in London!"

"You love London. I wish we'd never left Montreal." She turned on him the black brows and square jaw her ancestors had brought to Canada from Brittany centuries ago. On her the features were pretty and sexy much of the time, but not now. Now Adams was punishing objects to keep himself from having a shot at her.

"My job brought me to London," he reminded his wife. "Head of the U.K. office, a *promotion*. Lisa has made the adjustment -- she's well in at the film studio. We're supposed to be a family!"

"In Montreal, I could breathe, I could think. My friends are all there. Listen, I'll tell you what it is, I'm French, okay? I want some time in Paris. Jacqueline and Jean-Claude will put me up."

"I have three presentations next week. Two here and one in Sheffield. Don't do this to me, Mariette."

She was putting the wastebasket explosion back together. "When is your next appointment with Dr. Farrow?"

"Dr. Farrow has no magic. We have to sort this out between ourselves."

"My ticket on the channel ferry is for tomorrow. Do you want me to tell Lisa?"

Adams told Lisa. She was his girl, compact with sandy hair cut short like his and the same perfect little three-quarter nose. Heads turned as they entered the restaurant and people smiled at this obvious father-daughter combination. He coated the pill for her, but she caught a faint taste of the truth.

"We decided Mama could do with some French ambience. She's beginning to wilt here among the Anglos."

"But you'll be alone in the house, Dad. Are you going to be all right?"

"Not to worry. I've got so much going on at work these days I'll hardly be home anyway. Besides, it's only a temporary adjustment. The petite peasoup will soon miss her old porridge-eater and she'll come racing back to London." He was afraid to say how much he missed her. As a youth, Adams had been a good marathon swimmer, had come third in an all-day crawl across Lake Ontario. Now he was almost ready to swim the channel to be with his wife again.

"I could lock up my flat and come for you." Lisa's suggestion scored high for good intentions.

"Never!" Her independent streak was as strong as his own. When she moved out last year, Adams missed her daily presence but he basked in the prestige of the phrase, "digs in Chelsea." It rolled proudly from his tongue whenever he spoke of his daughter. Her job at Arpy Productions was no great thing; she was a gopher -- gopher coffee, gopher the mail. But she was learning film editing and one day she would climb. "How are things at work?" he asked her.

"Wait'll I tell you! They came in last week to shoot part of a commercial for Air Scotland..." Lisa's belly laugh, exactly like her father's in the days when Adams used to laugh, made everybody in the restaurant look up.

Back at the agency, Adams, whose relationship with the staff was matey, made a big thing out of his wife's departure. He would rather they heard it from him. His arrival two years ago as the new broom from the Canadian head office had filled them with dread. But they soon discovered he was an anglophile and that he led from the front. And that he was a former copywriter, which made him a human being. With their new boss working all the hours God sent, the writers and artists and account people began to drop their lazy ways and imitate this man who demonstrated the art of being professional and enjoying life, too. Now they told him poor thing, poor thing, when they learned he was to be a summer bachelor.

"You'll never go home now," said Gareth Lloyd, the creative director. "I hope you'll remember the rest of us still have families." The young Welshman had been worried lately by Adams' intensity. He knew the boss was on some kind of medication and that he attended therapy sessions at St. Antony's.

"Don't worry," Adams said, "all I'll expect from anybody is the usual hundred and ten percent." Then he broke down to this extent. "I'm worried about her going away. Mariette. She's more French than she is Canadian. These friends of hers may drag her into the Paris life and she'll never come back."

Gareth offered a suggestion. "How would you like to move in for a while with me and Bronwyn? We've got a spare room. Think of the satisfaction -- you could talk shop day *and* night."

"It's good of you, Gareth --"

"And after a while you'll be so sick of leek soup your empty house will seem like heaven on earth."

The house was so big and so empty the night after Mariette went away that Adams almost wished he had accepted Gareth's invitation. Even in early summer the wind cut across Wimbledon Common and rattled the leaded windows in his Eighteenth Century cottage. He had to go outside into the pine scented darkness where he could see traffic passing on the Parkside to reassure himself he wasn't trapped on Wuthering Heights. Set back from the road on landscaped ground, the house was the envy of his colleagues because it was that little bit of England which few Englishmen can afford to own. Adams had arrived with a sizable stake realized when he sold his Montreal dwelling. When he saw the cottage advertised, he decided to have it. Especially since so much of the mortgage interest could be deducted from taxable income.

But he was isolated up here on the edge of the village. So on his first night alone, he asked himself if he would have been better off buying a terraced house in Chelsea, where a street of shops with a pub at either end was never more than five minutes' walk from your front door.

Adams went inside and dialed Dr. Farrow's night number. The hospital operator took his name and said Dr. Farrow would ring him back as soon as possible. When the telephone rang, he felt immensely reassured.

"How are you, Luke?"

"I'd like to come and see you, Milt. Tomorrow, if possible. I know my regular visit to check the medication isn't for a couple of weeks --"

"Tomorrow, tomorrow..." Farrow intoned as if he was about to deliver a soliloquy. "Yes, I can fit you in at three-thirty. Will you be all right this evening?"

"Yes, I'm fine. Just making the appointment eased the panic. See you tomorrow afternoon."

St. Antony's Hospital is located on an area of parkland in Wandsworth within sight and scent of a brewery. Its plant is a combination of Victorian buildings in burgundy brick and an escort of low, prefab structures put up after the war as a temporary measure to house the expanded services of the National Health. Decades later, with money scarce and socialism struggling against a swing to the right of the political pendulum, these huts have about them the shabby inevitability of the hospital of the future.

Adams drove in through the main gateway and turned sharp right to where Adult Psychiatry was located in a couple of the tall brick cottages. He parked and went inside, announced himself to the daft old soul who kept track of appointments, then went to a table in a corner and bought a plastic cup of watery coffee from the convalescent lady in charge of the silex and the biscuit tin.

As he sat on a damaged chair and sipped his hot brown water, Adams watched the comings and goings of maintenance staff and a few people in suits who might have been doctors. They all looked half out of it, as if they were patients whose treatment included being given a few simple duties. This evidence of the inmates running the asylum had troubled him at first, but now, after more than a year's attendance at Dr. Farrow's clinic, Adams accepted the eccentric establishment because it worked. Perhaps it was England itself in microcosm, this collection of limping misfits making do in a clapped-out building as if there could be nothing any better in the world.

Milton Farrow appeared in his doorway and smiled. He stood aside as Adams went through, and the Canadian experienced, as always, the sheer physical presence of the giant doctor. Six and a half feet tall, heavy, slope-shouldered, barrel-chested, Farrow always presented an apologetic smile as if to say: "Forgive me, I never intended to grow this big."

He sat at his desk and shifted a few papers. Adams occupied the wooden chair beside the desk. Against the opposite wall of the tiny office, a hospital cot with made-up sheets and blanket and a pillow came as close as the state institution could manage to the leather couch of Dr. Freud.

"Well," Farrow said, turning to his patient, and Adams said: "Well," and they both smiled because they always began their session with this breezy, down-to-business echo.

"I have the results of your last blood sample," Farrow said, running a blunt finger down a page. "Your lithium level is still well within the limit. Are you feeling okay?"

"Fine. I'm not clinically depressed." Years ago, Adams had been diagnosed as a manic-depressive, and to control the condition, to level out his highs and lows, he had been given tablets of lithium carbonate to take. Nobody really understands why lithium can help a lot of manic-depressive people remain on a more even keel, but it does.

"The thing is, at the moment," he went on, "my wife has gone away to Paris. For the summer. She has friends there -- I told you she's French-Canadian, she can't really talk to people here. So --" Adams let it come out as simply as he could. "I'm all alone and I don't like it."

"Mmmm." The doctor sat like a man waiting to see if the tap will extrude another drop of water.

"My daughter has said she'll come and stay with me but I know she doesn't really want to move back home. She's got her own flat and a nice life going."

"Yes."

"And this good bloke I work with, Gareth. He's invited me to stay with him and his wife. But that wouldn't be right." Adams looked through his hands at the floor, feeling Farrow's presence. "So last night, alone in the house, suddenly I felt this panic. That's when I rang you."

"You seem calm now."

"Don't let it fool you."

"Yes?"

Ideas were bubbling up in Adams the way they often did in the presence of the doctor. "I thought of myself the other day," he said, "as a Mediterranean person inside. On the outside I'm this calm, civilized Luke Adams. But maybe I should rage a lot more, wave my arms at people, even let myself weep."

"Why don't you?"

"Because you guys would put me away if I did."

The session went on easily for the usual half hour, which was all the clinic could allow per patient. Adams and Farrow never had a problem talking to each other. As always, the doctor found an opportunity to introduce the subject of the book he was writing. Adams had been able to suggest some useful alterations in the Farrow volume of case histories. Today, he offered another tip and the doctor made a note on the manuscript.

"You're nobody in the medical establishment here unless you're published," he said. Farrow was an American, recently graduated from a university in Florida. In an early chat with Adams, he had admitted the reason for his moving to England was an awareness that he was not up to competing in America -- his qualifications were not good enough. But here in England, where everything was low key, where the treatment of mental illness was still seen by many as a matter of the patient pulling himself together and soldiering on, Farrow felt he would fit in. When Adams first showed up at the clinic, referred by his general practitioner, Dr. Sharma, to have his lithium level checked, he was passed along to Farrow because it was felt the two North Americans might make a match.

"I have a suggestion to offer," the doctor said as the session ended. "You're my last patient today. If you can put up with me, why don't I invite myself to your place for dinner? I can bring my manuscript and pick your brains a little more. We can watch the final episode of *I, Claudius* on BBC2." Farrow's face produced an engaging smile "Before I was psychoanalyzed, I could never have invited myself like that."

Adams laughed. "It's a great idea. Can you leave now?"

"Let me have five minutes to make a couple of telephone calls. I'll meet you in the waiting room..."

They drove to the Wimbledon cottage in convoy, Adams proceeding slowly and keeping Farrow's rusty MG sportscar visible in the rearview mirror. The stylish, battered little vehicle enclosed the giant medical man like a capsule.

When both cars pulled into the gravel lane beside the cottage, Farrow climbed out, inspected the trees and shrubs and the handsome building, and said: "Advertising is the career to choose."

"The rewards are there," Adams admitted. "But you're always having to persuade people that a campaign is superlative when your true belief is that it is no better than fairly good. It can rot your soul."

Preparing supper turned out to be fun. Milton Farrow emerged as an enthusiastic amateur chef. While Adams poured drinks, the doctor went into the kitchen and rattled the pots and pans. Busy with chopping-board and skillet, he produced a massive Spanish omelette, which he cut in half and served on warmed plates along with steamed brussels sprouts in a mustard-and-lemon sauce and a bowl of salad in which the ingredients, cut in large chunks, glistened in a tangy garlic dressing.

"Crudites," he said as he doled it out, "straight from the French quarter of Fort Lauderdale."

Adams enjoyed the meal and the convivial evening that followed, during which the absence of Mariette never entered his mind. When the prestige television drama ended and they finished the brandy, he yawned without embarrassment and said: "Me for bed. Big meeting tomorrow."

"How are you feeling?"

"Better than I thought possible this afternoon."

Farrow did not celebrate. "You'll feel a reaction tomorrow. Your anxieties over the absence of your wife have only been suppressed."

"Well. This has been a useful visit anyway, Milt, and I thank you for coming."

Farrow glanced at his watch and winced. "Long drive back to my place after all the booze."

"Listen, I'm silly, forgive me. Stay here, use the spare bedroom."

"Will it be a lot of trouble?"

"None at all. I should have suggested it earlier."

When Adams came into the spare room carrying fresh towels, Farrow was stretched out on the bed with his ankles crossed, his shoes carefully extended clear of the spread. "I always think of my brother Dave," he said. "Did I ever tell you about him?"

"Not that I recall." It seemed inhospitable to stand over his guest. Adams drew a chair close and sat near the head of the bed.

"We had four sisters, so Dave and I always had to share a room. We were close. He wasn't overgrown like I am, he was normal size. All through school, Dave got top marks while I had trouble getting through. They made me play football, not because I'm an athlete but because it took two guys from the other team to move me. The girls loved Dave, he could choose anybody he wanted." Farrow fell silent for a few moments. Then: "I remember --"

Adams waited, then heard himself prompting in the same neutral tone used by the doctor during their sessions. "Yes?"

"One Saturday, my parents took all the girls in the car on a shopping trip for clothes. There was a place about a hundred miles away where my father knew the owner and could get a discount. So the house was empty all day because I had football practice and Dave -- I wasn't sure what Dave was doing.

"When I came home I didn't expect to find anybody there, so I threw down my gear and went upstairs. I was tired,

I was going to flake out on my bed. But when I went in our room, there was Dave with this girl. It was quite a scene. I froze. I just stood there, staring at them. It was a hot afternoon and they didn't have any covers over them. After what seemed a hell of a long time, Dave said: "What are you going to do, Milt? Are you getting in with us, or what?" I ran out of there and as I went down the stairs I heard the two of them laughing."

In the silence that followed, Adams noticed the way Farrow's fingers gripped the bedspread as though he anticipated a sharp movement that would fling him into space.

"Hell, it was my bedroom, too," Farrow concluded.

Adams knew he wasn't required to comment on this event. He said, in an attempt to bring his guest back from the past: "Where is your brother now?"

"He's an important man in computers." Farrow sat up and wiped both hands over his face. "Out west, in Silicone Valley."

"And you're an important psychiatrist in London, England."

"Not very."

"Important to me."

Now the big face shone with boyish gratitude. "Thanks for that, Luke."

In the morning, Adams quietly organized himself through breakfast and getting dressed. Before leaving, he tapped on the guestroom door. "Do you need a call this morning, Milt?"

"No patients this morning," the muffled voice responded.

"Lucky for some. I'm off."

It was one of those days during which Adams had, literally, no time to look at the clock. He was astonished to find himself at six thirty driving back across Putney Bridge, along the crowded high street, then up the long hill to the Parkside and home. As he drove in between the chestnut and the elm, he was surprised to discover Milton Farrow's car still in the yard, though parked differently than it had been that morning.

Inside, the house smelled deliciously of home cooking. Farrow emerged from the kitchen carrying a gin and tonic. He took Adams' briefcase from his hand and gave him the glass. "How was your day? I went out and did some shopping. You are about to taste Mother Farrow's Oven Beef Casserole -- stew with a crust on top. Drink that, I'm ahead of you."

Adams experienced a mixture of annoyance, embarrassment, and amusement. "You didn't have to stay and make me supper."

"I wanted to. Look. Give a glance in here." He led Adams into the library and indicated papers spread on the desk. "My manuscript, sorely in need of a collaborator. I thought after supper we could spend an hour getting chapter five in shape. After which there is pro basketball on Channel 4. Crystal Palace versus Sunderland."

Adams sipped his drink and wandered into the kitchen. The pie smelled heavenly and it came out of the oven ready for the photographer. Luke was surrounded with tender loving care substantially above the level he received when Mariette was at home. But, damn it, none of this was his idea. It was being done to him.

The delayed reaction had been learned during a long course of therapy back home. Adams swallowed his urge to respond with irritation and decided to wait until after dinner. The meal went well -- Farrow had purchased a fat bottle of wine on his shopping trip -- but as coffee was served, Adams still felt put upon.

"Milt," he said, "that was delicious. But you didn't have to."

"I wanted to."

"I mean I'm okay now. I've absorbed the impact of Mariette's departure."

"Let me be the judge of that." Farrow finished his coffee. "Shall we have a go at the manuscript?"

"No. I'm sorry to be blunt, but you give me no choice. I've been working all day. I don't want to take on your book."

"Never mind. We can set it aside till tomorrow."

There was silence in the room while Adams absorbed the implications of what had just been said. "I can't work on it tomorrow, either. And what about your patients?"

"I have a month's leave of absence pending. I rang in today and said I was taking the time to work on my book. They don't expect me at the clinic till this time in August."

Adams began to understand the scope of his problem. He chose his words carefully. "Milt, I don't know if I said something to give you the wrong impression -- either about the help I need or about my willingness to help you. Either way, let's get it straight. I'm okay. I was upset about my wife leaving for the summer but it's not the end of the world -- I can cope by myself. So you go on home and work on your book. I'll be available for telephone consultation if you run into a bad patch. And next month I'll come and see you, as always, to check on my lithium level."

Adams got up and carried his dishes to the sink. When he turned, Farrow was watching him with a triumphant expression on his face.

"It's worse that I thought," he said.

"What is?"

"Believe me, Luke, you don't see yourself. As a doctor, I recognize in you a man close to the end of his tether. You've been working too hard for months. We both know that. Now, without much notice, your wife abandons you. When you came to see me the other day, you were about to disappear over the edge. Even now, I'm not sure I can drag you back."

Adams had to laugh. "You must be talking about some other patient. Milt, listen to yourself -- this is preposterous. I'm beginning to think *you're* the one who needs treatment."

"As I feared," the doctor murmured, shaking his head.

"In any case, I refuse to go along with this any longer. I don't like to be impolite, but you force me to be. Finish up, please, and then leave."

Farrow stood up, towering over Adams in the kitchen which had gone dark as the sun went down. He snapped on the light over the sink. "You go and relax," he said in a subdued tone of voice. "I'll wash up these dishes, then I'll bring us both another coffee."

"And then you'll go, Milt. I have to get back to normal."

"Normal?" The doctor squirted liquid detergent into a stream of hot water running into the sink. "Where the hell is that?"

Adams sat by the front window where he could see both cars parked on the gravel yard. He switched on a lamp and spread the evening paper across his knees but he couldn't concentrate on the news. A plan occurred to him -- he would arrange time off work, pleading fatigue, then hop a plane to Paris and join Mariette. Tell her the truth -- that he was lost without her and that anything might be possible, not excluding a voluntary posting back to the Montreal office where it all began. Those had been good years, both of them young and full of enthusiasm, feasts at fine restaurants, roaring with the hockey crowd in the forum, vivid colors, bodies against the boards, the frantic organ urging them on -- *"Les Canadiens sont la!"*

Farrow brought in two steaming mugs. "I put in the last of the brandy," he said. "Drink up and then I'll go."

Adams sipped -- it tasted good. "No hard feelings, Milt."

"If you don't need me, what's the point?"

"I need your services as before, but not here day after day."

"I understand. I promise to be around when you need me."

They finished their coffee and Farrow got up to go. He stood over Adams."Are you all right?" Your eyes look heavy."

"I'm fine." Adams stood up and fell sideways, catching himself with a hand on the doctor's arm. "Hey, my legs are numb."

"It's a reaction. I was afraid of this."

"My head is floating--"

"You're a sicker man than you've been willing to admit. Let's get you to bed."

Tucked in and with Farrow looming over him, Adams said: "I don't believe this. Why should it hit me all of a sudden?"

"You've been repressing a lot of anxiety, pretending it was business as usual. Don't worry, I'll stay and we'll see how you are in the morning."

Adams slept with an awareness of the passage of time. When he opened his eyes, the room was bright. Farrow moved into his line of vision. "How do you feel?"

"As if I've been drinking lead." He got up to go to the bathroom and the doctor had to help him through the doorway. He seemed to be wrapped in thick material. When he was back in bed, Farrow presented him with two pills and a glass of water.

"What are they?"

"Good for what ails you. Do as the doctor says."

He swallowed the pills and sank back onto the pillow. Then his swampy mind heaved and something solid floated to the surface. "Work," he said. "I've got meeting."

"I telephoned at half past nine. They send their love and you're not to worry, somebody named Gareth is covering for you."

"I want Lisa to know. My daughter. Ask her to come and see me tonight. Her number is in the little book by the phone."

"I'll take care of it. You rest."

Adams did not exactly sleep, he fell unconscious. When he surfaced again, the room was dark. He reached for the bedside lamp and knocked it off the table. The overhead light came on and Farrow was bending over, helping him. "What the hell is happening to me?"

"Don't be frightened. It's a breakdown. I've seen it coming for a long time."

"I was going along fine."

"You'd be the last one to know. Your wife spotted it and she didn't want to be here when it happened. She got away. But I'm here to help as long as you need me, Luke. You'll get past this crisis and then we'll take our time easing you back."

"Farrow went away and came back with a tray. "Time you ate something."

"No sale."

"Drink the juice, anyway. Doctor's orders."

He sipped and set the acid down. "I'll take it after."

"Lisa looked in. She brings you love." He produced a paperback book. "She thought you might like to read this." He set the book on the bedside table. "I'm working on my manuscript. Boy, am I in need of a healthy Luke Adams to assist me. Back soon."

Adams lay gazing at the ceiling. He managed to turn his head and focus on Lisa's gift. The book looked familiar. He remembered the title from the newsstand in his office building. He had bought it and read a third of the way in before losing interest. He managed to pick it up now and turn the pages. There was the dog-ear at page ninety. Lisa had not brought him this book. This was a book he had bought himself. He lay breathing deeply, rising out of his semi-coma, putting it all together.

If Lisa had not been to see him -- and he was certain now that she had not been in the house -- why was Milt Farrow pretending she had been? He had not telephoned her, clearly, or Lisa would have arrived in a taxi and would have sat by his bed until he woke up, however many days it took.

Things were not as they seemed. Farrow had not called Lisa because Adams was not sick, but he *felt* sick -- he felt shattered. Why? The answer was so obvious, he began to grin. He was drugged! The farewell coffee and brandy the other night. Next day, the pills. Right. Adams would avoid all food and drink from now on. No more juice for a start.

He managed to pull his legs up, turn, and put his feet on the carpet. Still shaky, but better. The early dose must have been a real Mickey Finn. Now, if he rested for a moment, Adams felt he could walk. Why was Farrow doing this? The man had tried to move in with his terrible book project when he learned his patient's wife had gone away. Perhaps he just needed companionship, he was lonely. No, it was worse than that. He was not behaving in a rational way.

So? Whoever said psychiatrists were immune from emotional disorders? Adams had read somewhere that the suicide rate was high among members of the medical profession.

He got up and held his balance. He went to the door and turned the handle. It turned, but the door did not move. Something was different. He peered through the crack and saw a dark shaft. Farrow had mounted a bolt on the other side! He was locked in, a prisoner in his own bedroom!

He could hear classical music playing on the kitchen radio down the hall. Dishes clashed in a sinkful of water, a deceptively domestic sound. Adams went back to the bed and sat down. The locked door could be a blessing in disguise; it forced him to think before acting. Farrow was twice his size. To confront him and accuse him of this crazy kidnapping might be to invite a broken jaw, or worse.

Adams needed help. Professional help. To bring in the police was not the answer. For one thing, Farrow would probably dazzle them with technical language. Besides, Adams wasn't interested in getting the doctor in trouble with the law. The poor man was pathetic. No, somebody had to come who could understand a quiet explanation, who could sense in Farrow the workings of a troubled mind.

Dr. Sharma. As his general practitioner, she had set Adams up with the referral that led to his relationship with Farrow. Call Dr. Sharma, have her come around and observe them both.

Adams began to get dressed. It turned out to be a laborious process. He settled for shoes without socks, jacket over pajama top. He pocketed his booklet of personal telephone numbers and went to the window, raising it quietly. The drop to the ground was no more than five feet. He landed in soil he had turned himself only a week ago when one of his greatest problems had been weeds among the marigolds.

There was a telephone booth on a corner three blocks away. His watch had stopped. He estimated the time to be near midnight, judging by the infrequency of the traffic. The call box was in sight. He wouldn't call Dr. Sharma directly. It was difficult at the best of times to speak to a particular physician. And in this case, it had to be Sharma. He would ring Gareth Lloyd and explain the problem to him. Gareth would understand, and then, however long it took, efficient Gareth would get through to Sharma and persuade her to come to the house and rescue him.

It worked well. Gareth was watching a late film, only a little drunk. For a minute or so, he insisted on believing that his colleague was sending him up. When the truth got through, he settled down and played back exactly what he was to do and say.

"Hold on, old sod," he concluded. "We'll soon have this straightened out. Sure you don't want me to whiz around and beat this man to a pulp?"

"Just get me Dr. Sharma."

Adams was leaving the booth when a police car pulled up, blue light flashing. Two young officers climbed out and approached him warily, keeping their distance, one either side. "Evening, sir. You all right?"

"I'm just going home."

They noticed his bare feet inside his shoes, the striped pajama collar at his neck. "Climb in, sir. We'll run you there."

"It's all right, I prefer to walk."

"No trouble, sir. Mr. Adams, is it?"

In the end, he got into the car. Farrow was waiting at the side door as they rolled onto the gravel square. Adams' mind had been working, he knew what not to do. A wild scene in front of the police with him accusing the doctor of holding him prisoner would play into Farrow's hand. He need only shrug his big shoulders and raise his eyebrows and Adams might end up in a straitjacket.

So he went in without a word, proceeded to his room, undressed down to his pyjamas, and got into bed. After all, help was on the way later tonight or in the morning. Dr. Sharma was on the way.

Farrow stood over him. "Silly thing to do. You're establishing a colorful case history for yourself."

"I wanted to ring Lisa. She wasn't home." Let him find out about Sharma when she arrived at the door.

"There doesn't have to be war between us, Luke."

"Why put a lock on my door?"

"For your own protection, and mine. Don't you remember what you did the other night? I found you in the kitchen at three o'clock -- you were getting out knives."

"I don't believe that." But he went to sleep wondering if it could be true. He felt now as if he needed some kind of weapon in this unfair fight against Milton Farrow.

Adams slept late again and was awakened by the sound of voices in the hall. They murmured on for some time as he sat up, rubbed his face awake, combed his hair with his fingers, and propped a couple of pillows behind his back.

The door opened and they came into the room together, Farrow leading the way, Dr. Sharma following, her waist-length braid of coarse black hair swaying, her dusky face solemn behind neat gold spectacles.

"Here's our patient," Farrow said. "How are we this morning?"

"Let's take a vote," Adams said, then regretted his flippancy. "I feel fine."

"I didn't realize you'd made contact with Dr. Sharma through your friend last night. But a check-up is a good idea."

"Can I talk to you alone, Dr. Sharma?" Adams said.

As she drew up a chair and set the bag on the floor, Farrow was moving out of the room. "I was just leaving," he said. "Give a shout if you need any help," he added as he closed the door.

"So," Dr. Sharma said. The owl eyes observed him compassionately. He had always liked visiting Shipra Sharma. He was a healthy man, his visits had always to do with minor problems, and whenever they talked at her desk in the surgery Adams always felt as if he was moments away from asking her out for a drink. Now he watched as she unpacked the narrow metal box, wrapped the rubber bag around his arm, pumped it up, and read his blood pressure.

"It isn't me," he said, "it's Dr. Farrow, I think he's gone around the bend."

"Why do you say that?

"Because he's got me here and he won't let me out. He's giving me drugs to sedate me."

"Did the police collect you in your pyjamas last night?"

"I had to go out the window to use the phone. He's put a lock on my door."

"He showed me the lock. He says you don't remember taking out the knives."

"That's all lies!" Adams heard the outrage in his voice, but he couldn't control it. "I didn't go *into* the kitchen! I can't even walk!"

"You walked to the phone booth."

"That was last night. I've stopped eating and drinking so he can't give me any more drugs." Adams searched the calm, dark eyes. "Christ, you're supposed to help me!"

She repacked the blood-pressure apparatus. "I understand your wife has gone away."

"For the summer, that's all. She's visiting friends in Paris."

"How do you feel about that?"

"I wish she was here. But it isn't a catastrophe -- I can cope. I have my work."

"I believe you work very hard."

"You're saying what he says. You've swallowed everything he's told you."

She got to her feet. "I don't think there is anything physically wrong with you. You need lots of rest. Can you let things go and stay in bed for a week?"

"He's moved in, damn it! He invited himself here and he tried to stay and when I eased him out he gave me a knock-out drug and made up this story about how I'm sick and need his supervision! He wants me to help him with his goddamn book! I'm his prisoner, Dr. Sharma, can't you see that?"

"Why would he do that to you?" she asked quietly.

Adams brought out the only answer he could think of. *"Because he's lonely!"* he shouted so loudly that Farrow thudded down the corridor and opened the door.

Dr. Sharma left the room with him and through the closed door he heard their murmuring conversation again. After the front door closed, Farrow returned to the bedroom. "I could have told you she would side with me. You don't know much about the medical profession."

Adams forced himself to be calm. This lunatic was in charge and nothing was to be gained by calling him mad. "Why are you doing this to me, Milt?"

He sat down. "Because when you told me your wife had gone to France, I saw my summer working out in a certain way."

"Staying here."

"Why not? I didn't realize my presence would be anathema to you. I'm a good cook. I can feed you better than she ever did. I have plenty of leave, I could use the time off. And you could help me with my book. I'm sorry I ever started the damn thing -- I can't finish it myself."

"But you're forcing yourself on me! I have my own life!"

"I know." Farrow stared at the floor and his face was so sad it was ugly. "I've always been the unwanted party." He got up and slammed out of the room.

Ten minutes later, he was back. "I've gone too far to stop now," he said. "You'll have to cooperate with me. No drugs, I promise -- nothing in your food or drink. As for you, don't try to get away or call anybody else. The police have a report on you and Dr. Sharma has seen you. Any more erratic behavior and I can certify you. All right?"

"You're the one who's crazy. Do you understand that?"

"I'll cut down my time. Two weeks only, a fortnight. That should allow us to get the book in shape. Then I'll go back to the clinic and you can go back to work."

The telephone rang. Farrow went to answer it. He came back carrying the extension phone, which he plugged in beside the bed. "It's your daughter." He lifted the receiver and handed it to Adams.

"Lisa, hi!"

"What's up with you? I called the office and they said you aren't well."

Adams realized how cleverly Farrow was behaving in letting him speak to his daughter. If he tried to tell her the truth, he would upset her. If he began raging against his imprisonment, he would end up having to contend with the police and Dr. Sharma. So here he was, playing Farrow's game while the doctor looked on, smiling. "It's nothing serious, love. A slight case of overwork. I'm fortunate in having Milt Farrow staying here with me."

"The shrink? How do you rate him?"

"He has some leave of absence coming, so he's going to bunk in here for the next fortnight. I'll repay him by helping him with a book of case histories he's writing."

"It's called, *Where the Bodies Are Buried,*" he concluded and all three of them ended up laughing.

For a week, the routine was developed. Adams let his colleagues at the office know that he needed a fortnight's rest. They seemed pleased that he was going to look after himself. He decided this, too, would pass and settled in to make the best of it. The food was excellent. Work on Farrow's book was no duller than most of what he did for a living. They even began to relax and have a laugh or two as in the old sessions at the clinic.

By the beginning of the second week, the situation was so calm that Adams sensed he could probably walk out of there, go back to work, and let Farrow do his worst. But if the man was vindictive enough, it could mean policemen in the office. For the sake of a few more days, he decided not to make waves.

On Thursday evening, as they were having a nightcap, the doctor said: "I propose a holiday weekend. A final reward for all the hard work we've both been doing."

Into Adam's mind floated a view of Paris and himself at a candlelit table with Mariette. "The good places are crowded right now," he said.

"Not where I have in mind. A friend of mine owns an island off the south coast. He and his family are in Greece this summer. He gave me the key and told me to go over any time I want to."

"I'm not sure--"

"Don't be so negative, Luke. Dr. Farrow prescribes."

It might be a nice ending to a painful experience. "All right," he said. "But leave your manuscript here."

"Agreed." Farrow shook his patient by the hand. "No work for three whole days."

In the morning they took a taxi to Victoria Station and boarded a train for the coast. A bus carried them to the coastal village from where Adams could see the island lying a couple of miles offshore. Farrow had telephoned ahead to lay on a man with a powerboat. Adams stood by the boat while his companion entered a shop to buy supplies. He was surprised when Farrow showed up with two assistants laden with boxes. "I thought this was a weekend," he said.

"I've been coming and going for the past month and a half," the doctor explained. "I owe it to my friend to replenish his stocks."

The trip across into choppy water was not pleasant. They were soaked with spray. Even though all three of them in the boat had put on life-jackets, Adams noticed that Farrow was gripping the seat and his knuckles were white. When they entered calmer water near the island, he said: "I'm glad that's over."

"Don't you swim?"

"Two lengths of the Y pool."

Adams said nothing. He looked back at the mainland and judged his marathon swims as a young man to have been much farther. Here, of course, there might be tides and currents.

The weekend passed quickly. Adams enjoyed the sea air, Farrow's well-cooked meals, the breezy hours on the shingle soaking up the sun. Late on Sunday afternoon, he asked: "When does the boat come back for us?"

Farrow had surrounded himself with a low rampart built of stones gathered from the beach. He was putting up flags made from match-sticks and cigarette papers. He said: "I told the man next week."

"You told me three days! Don't play around, Milt, I'm due back at work tomorrow!"

"Relax. Isn't this a nice place?"

"Are you telling me we're trapped here? What if somebody has a heart attack?"

"There's a skiff in the boathouse." He glanced up. "It's locked and the key is put away."

Adams got to his feet. "You're crazy, Farrow! And when I get back, I'm going to make it known! What are we supposed to do here for a week?"

"I brought the manuscript. I thought we might press on with chapter twelve."

"Not me!" Adams kicked Farrow's construction, scattering stones along the beach. "If I find your bloody manuscript, I'll set fire to it!" He strode away toward the house.

"And you say I'm crazy!" the doctor called after him in a jubilant tone of voice.

From the front-room window, Adams could see the wind had dropped at the end of the afternoon. The water between the island and the mainland was calm. Although he hadn't done any marathon swimming in years, he had kept himself in shape and he felt certain the distance was within his capabilities.

Quickly, Adams stripped down to his shorts and left the house at a trot. Once past Farrow and into the water, he would be safe. The doctor was no swimmer -- he had said so and Adams believed him.

It worked. Farrow looked up from his stone repairs as Adams splashed into the shallows. "What are you doing?"

"Going home."

"You're crazy! It's farther than it looks!"

Farrow moved to the water's edge and watched his prisoner striking away into deep water. "Okay!" he called. "You win! Come back -- we'll row home tonight in the skiff!"

"I believe you," Adams said, and he kept on swimming.

Farrow's next cry planted the idea in Adams' mind. "If you get in trouble," the doctor called, "I won't be able to help you!"

Almost without thinking, Adams took a few more strokes, then he turned onto his back and began to thrash the water. "Help!"

"What's wrong?"

"Cramp! Oh, God -- help!"

"Swim back!" Farrow, fully dressed, blundered into the water up to his knees.

"I can't make it! Help me, Milt -- help!"

The doctor plunged forward and began to swim, producing a ponderous overhead stroke, all wasted energy and very little progress. Treading water, Adams watched his approach. As he came close, Adams moved himself away, staying just beyond Farrow's reach.

"I'm too -- too far out." Farrow turned his head, saw the beach in the distance, looked back at Adams, his face split with panic. "Help me, Luke --"

Adams said nothing. He had stopped struggling. He paddled himself easily away, maintaining the distance between them. Farrow began lashing the water. His head went under and he came up choking, spitting out. "Luke -- I'm drowning!"

Adams moved away again. Their eyes met and at last Farrow understood what had happened, what was going to happen. There was one calm moment when he stopped fighting. "Was it that bad?" he asked.

Adams turned and began to develop his most powerful free-style. He felt driven to get away. He counted to one hundred strokes and when he looked back, the sea behind him was calm.

Mariette came back from Paris a couple of weeks early, bored with her friends and ready to give London a chance. Lisa became engaged to the film editor at the studio. The agency landed two big accounts. Adams decided he needed help and shifted half of the executive responsibility to Gareth Lloyd.

"You look well", Dr. Sharma said when he went to see her about mysterious spots on his ankles. They turned out to be flea-bites, a byproduct of the cat they'd acquired as company for Mariette.

"I'm working less and enjoying it more," Adams explained.

The doctor wrote a prescription for a soothing ointment. "Are things all right for you at the clinic?" she asked.

"Yes, I'm seeing one of the junior doctors. It's only every three months to check my lithium level."

She handed over the prescription. "I'm sorry I didn't listen to you last summer. We might have arranged some help for Dr. Farrow instead of leaving a sick man to wander into the sea."

"Don't blame yourself," Adams said. "I was there, I should have saved him."

That night, after dinner, he went into his study and sat down again, facing the almost-completed manuscript. Editing it into publishable shape was turning into the hardest job he had ever tackled. There was no guarantee he would persuade a publisher to accept it, either. For all he knew, he would sweat over this project throughout eternity -- he was the ancient mariner and Farrow's book was his albatross.

He went back to the beginning and turned the first page. The dedication fascinated him -- he read it again while his heart beat faster:

> "To my dear friend Luke Adams,
> without whose devoted assistance
> this project would never have been completed."

Ellery Queen Mystery Magazine, October, 1986

THE PRIZE IN
THE PACK

Here was Casey Dolan trying to prepare his six o'clock sports broadcast and there was Carmen's big brother Alvin, waiting for her to finish work and giving Dolan the evil eye from the outer office.

Clement Foy's sonorous voice poured out of the monitor speaker. "A reminder that in fifteen minutes the old catcher will be along with your early-evening sports show. In the meantime, more rolling-home music here on CBAY, the voice of Baytown, as Les Brown and the Band of Renown offer some musical reassurance, 'I've Got My Love To Keep Me Warm.' "

Foy was stuck in the big-band era, which Dolan could stand. At forty-eight, he was five years older than the program director and he liked the bouncy sound. His two-finger typing of tonight's script rattled along almost in time with the rhythm. The age problem, if he had one, was in relation to Carmen Hopkins, who was only nineteen. This was a gap that had seemed unbridgeable six months ago when she came on staff. Now that they had made love, there turned out to be no gap. Dolan had been surprised and gratified but soon learned he was exchanging the fear of inadequacy for that of an early death at the hands of big brother Alvin. He had always suspected there was a trace of Indian in the Hopkins genetic pool. Now those Iroquois eyes watched him from beyond the front desk. Did Alvin know? How could he know? Should Dolan give him a smile?

"I'm on my way," Carmen said, leaving her desk at the back of the room, passing Dolan's chair, letting her fingers brush the back of his neck. "Any problems with continuity, talk to my lawyer." That was a laugh. In six months, she had mastered the job better than anybody the radio station had ever employed. She was good. Too good for such routine work,

Dolan kept telling her. "You take it easy now, young lady," he said in an avuncular tone. It was the voice he had used when he was catching for the Redmen and a young pitcher needed reassurance out there on the mound.

"I always try," she said, riveting him with her mischievous stare, "though I don't always succeed." She swaggered away to join her brother. Dolan feasted his eyes on her. She still carried some babyfat he had discovered. Heart-shaped face, lips a bit on the heavy side but perfectly shaped, cheeks forever blushing. Her hair was glossy toffee, tied in twin braids with green ribbons. She had skin that drove Dolan mad, arms, legs, shoulders -- she was packaged in this slightly textured, almost café-au-lait material and keeping his hands off it was for the over-the-hill but lately reborn athlete a severe exercise in self-discipline.

"Let's go, Carmen," Alvin said as he opened the door, towering over her, pretending to be out of patience with her instead of her slave, as even Dolan with his deteriorating vision could see. "I want to pick up some beer before the store closes."

"If you're getting drunk tonight," she said, "I'm going out."

Dolan got the message and the typewriter keys jammed. His heart was still pounding like a teenager's when he went on the air ten minutes later. "Good evening, sports fans. First place changed hands last night in the Baytown Fastball League as --"

After he signed off, Dolan drove home and showered and washed what was left of his hair. He was still using Anna's shampoo. A few drops was all he needed, so three months after his wife's departure for Centralia the big plastic bottle was holding out. The smell still reminded him of her. So did the bath itself, oddly and sadly. In early years, when David was still a baby, they sometimes performed what seemed in those days an adventurous act -- they got into the shower together. Soaping each other, they laughed a lot and he called her his seal. Now -- it seemed no more than a few weeks later -- David was in charge of the science department at Centralia

Polytechnic while his mother had opened a shop in the same city selling coordinated paints and wallpapers. And Dad was making it on his own.

Dolan rubbed himself dry with a rough towel. He faced the mirror at an angle that showed the least paunch, the fewest veins. Carmen seemed to like him. Mind you, it was always lights off and after a couple of drinks. He got dressed in the coordinated green-and-grey outfit, a modified track suit. The store manager had said he looked twenty years younger. Anna would laugh. She had forever been after Dolan to smarten himself up, buy new clothes. All she had to do to get her wish was leave him.

She hasn't really left me, Dolan said to himself as he pocketed money and keys and went outside into a balmy summer night. After twenty-six years together, we're trying it apart. A little freedom, room to move.

He knew he'd find Carmen in the back lounge of the Coronet Hotel. It was her idea to conduct their meetings in the public eye. "If we sneak around and drive out to The Cedars like you're suggesting, somebody is bound to see us and say those two are up to something. But here in the heart of town, how bad can it be? We're fellow employees having a drink together."

"My problem will be keeping my hands off you," he said.

"I have the cure. Think of you touching me, and then Alvin walking in."

The blind jazz pianist was at the keyboard when Dolan entered the lounge. His dog lay at his feet, head down, barely tolerant of what was going on. Jack Danforth, owner of the Coronet, sat at the end of the bar. Dolan placed himself at a corner table, distributed a few waves, and ordered a large brandy-and-soda. He was halfway through it when Carmen appeared, spotted him, hugged the wall on her way to the table, and slipped furtively onto a chair.

"Are you all right?" he asked her.

"Do I look all right?"

He studied her face. It might have been called a swelling on the jaw. "There's no light in here. Have you been hit?"

The music climaxed, lots of applause, end of set. Pianist and seeing-eye dog filed out behind Danforth to sit in his office. Carmen was at her most rebellious, a sailor on leave. "I came so close to putting a knife in him, Casey --"

"Tell me."

"It's one thing when he nags me. That's what a big brother is for. But when he started in on Peter, I went for him."

"Calm down."

"All right. All right. Get me a beer."

He ordered a Molson and another brandy. The drinks came and they started in on them but she was still taking deep breaths through her nostrils. In this mood, she was more attractive than ever to Dolan.

"Did he know you were coming out to meet me?"

"No. I don't know. I don't care. Do you care?"

"I don't care."

"Stop worrying about my brother. I'm over eighteen, I can do whatever I want. There's not a damn thing Alvin can do about it."

Dolan tried to put from his mind thoughts of Alvin Hopkins doing something about it and then being punished for it by a life sentence, with Dolan no longer around to appreciate justice being done. "What made you so mad?" he asked.

"He said I'm not a responsible person. Without him to look after me, I'd go down the drain. He thinks I should still be at university."

Dolan thought so, too, but knew better than to tell the headstrong girl. She was a classic under-achiever. Born with brains to spare and limitless energy, she refused ever to do more than just enough to get by. In Baytown High School, she got top grades while hardly cracking a book. Her brother Alvin, with no encouragement from Carmen, borrowed the money to pay for her first year in an arts course at Queen's University in

Kingston, sixty miles down the road, past Centralia. He bullied her into registering and moving there and attending some lectures. But she only stayed three weeks, arriving back home on the bus, her trunk showing up, rail freight, a few days later.

The debacle cost Alvin a good part of the money he paid. And when his clever little sister got a job selling dresses at Artistic Ladies Wear, it was almost more than he could bear. The new job writing continuity (whatever *that* was) at CBAY was an improvement. But still she seemed more interested in going through the motions and having fun than in getting ahead. For a man who used all his limited ability to work his way up through the yards to a job behind a ticket window at the CN station, Carmen's behavior was calculated to drive him up the wall.

Dolan said to her, "What did he say about Pete?" Carmen Hopkins' other brother Peter, known to his friends as Hophead, had killed himself two years ago in a road accident involving his pickup truck and a steel power pylon.

"He said I'm not just bad for myself, I'm a bad influence on other people. That's a laugh. Pete was drunk when he showed up that night."

"I know."

"I couldn't ask him to stay. It was a girls' party. And he kept grabbing hold of people, it wasn't funny. Vera didn't like him and he kept grabbing hold of Vera."

Dolan had heard the story before. "So you ordered him out," he said gloomily.

"I whacked him and pushed him out the door and locked it. Then when I went after him, it was too late. He was driving away."

Dolan stared into the battered-baby eyes, hoping it was over. "Carmen," he said softly, "it was not your fault."

After a minute or so, she became calm. "You've had a normal life, eh, Case?" she said. "Good family. Lots of success."

"Yeah, sure." He gave her the grin that usually worked. "The only reason the Redmen kept old Casey Dolan behind the plate was I didn't mind being hit by bouncing baseballs." He took a drink. "And with our pitching we had a lot of bouncing baseballs." He showed her his collection of broken fingers.

"It explains a lot," he said.

They went off for a drive later, across the Bay Bridge and into the county. The windows were down and there was a lot of clover in the air. On the radio, Clem Foy was doing his night show, ignoring the musical tastes of his audience, playing a selection of 78s from his own library. He thanked Lionel Hampton for rendering "Midnight Sun," then introduced Louie singing "A Kiss To Build a Dream On."

As they approached the colored lights of a roadhouse, Carmen said she was hungry. Dolan drove in and parked in darkness on the farthest patch of gravel and went inside to get takeaway, leaving her in the car.

"That really cheeses me off," she said when he came back with hamburgers and shakes. He could feel the vibrations, so he switched on and got rolling again, heading farther into farmland. "You won't even take me inside," she complained with her mouth full. "I feel like some kind of cheap whore."

Half an hour later, he parked off the road on a headland with a view of the bay where it becomes part of Lake Ontario. Her mood was sweet again. Dolan kissed her, and his advancing years faded, leaving him feeling strong, not worried for the moment about anything. He knew it was only nature trying to get him to propagate the race, but he didn't care. Her mouth was soft, she smelled of soap and lipstick.

On the way home, she was buoyant. Her window was down, her eyes narrowed against the rush of air. "If you and I were married, there'd be no problem," she said. "Alvin would have to shut up."

"I'm already married. Did you forget?"

"She's left you. Get a divorce."

"What's the rush to get married? You're a kid, you've got your whole life. You're a talented girl, you can write up a storm. I'm just a stupid ball player but I can recognize what you've got."

"Here we go."

"You sit at that desk bashing out promotion announcements and program scripts with one brain tied behind your back. Work, damn it. Write." He glanced at her face, saw the down-turned mouth. "Develop the talent God gave you."

"Who asked Him?" she said. Then after half a mile of slipstream, she said, "Would you marry me if I said I was pregnant? I'm not, but if I told you I was?" She was smiling now. "You wouldn't believe me, would you?"

"Not in the nineteen-eighties." He shrugged. "I believed it in the fifties."

Carmen passed Dolan's desk one afternoon in the following week and dropped a sheaf of folded typewritten pages in front of him. "Read it and weep," she said and wandered away. He glanced at page one, saw "*Nor Iron Bars* by Carmen Hopkins.*"* He was so excited by the manuscript, he couldn't get on with his work. He took it to the washroom and read it in the privacy of a cubicle.

She had written a story about a young girl in love with an older man. They both worked in a small-town radio station. There was practically no invention in it, the plot was his experience and hers, but it read like a house afire. At the end, the sports announcer was still with his wife and the girl was floating face-down in the bay.

He emerged into the office and went to her desk, where she was elaborately turning the pages of a newspaper. "Come for coffee," he said, handing her the manuscript.

"You like?" It was the only time she had appeared nervous in front of him.

"Come for coffee."

They went around the corner to the Paragon Cafe, where he ordered two coffees and the slab of cream pie she asked for. A kid. "Your story is brilliant," he said. "Exactly what I wanted you to do. Keep it up."

"What for?"

"Because you can."

"I tried it and now I know how easy it is. Big deal."

"You want to be infuriating, don't you? Who are you trying to provoke, your father?"

"The great prospector?" She laughed. "All he ever did was search for uranium that wasn't there and come back once in a while to get my mother pregnant."

"Succeed for yourself," Dolan pontificated. "Not for anybody else."

Carmen finished her pie, gave him the mischievous smile with her mouth half full. "I forget," she said. "Did you promise the other night to marry me if you got me pregnant?"

He knew she was teasing him, but his heart turned over anyway. "One of these days, kid -- over my knee."

"Ready when you are," she said.

The Redmen were batting in the bottom of the third against the Napanee Oilers. The sun was setting behind the canning factory. Seated at the microphone in the press box under the grandstand roof, Dolan called the balls and strikes and kept up a flow of anecdote and description. He was feeling at peace with the world, almost smug, hoping Management never discovered that he would broadcast baseball for nothing. In the bleachers, several hundred fans in shirtsleeves watched and ate and drank and yelled at the players and the umpires.

Around eight o'clock, Carmen made her way up the ladder and took a seat not far from Dolan. Perhaps to make her entry legal, she had put on her CBAY T-shirt. She was munching caramel corn from the famous narrow red box. When they cut back to the studio for a commercial she extended the package in his direction.

"Thanks, I can't. Gets in my throat."

"Is it all right for me to be here?"

He looked at the scrubbed healthy face, the glistening braids, the ripe body in a shirt one size too small. "It is absolutely perfect for you to be here." Then, encouraged by her glow, and just before his cue from the engineer, he said to her, "Carmen dear, life is a box of Cracker Jack and you are the prize in the pack."

She stirred the air above her head with a finger. "Hoopdedoo!" she said.

After the game, they walked to his car in the parking lot behind the dance pavilion. The Clem Foy Five was playing inside, and through screened windows colored lights glowed behind the movement of dancing couples. They watched in silence holding hands. It was a big regret for Dolan that he couldn't take the girl inside and hold her for a while to music. Now he drew her to him. She must have been reading his mind because she angled her cheek against his shoulder, rested her hand on his collar, pressed herself against him, and moving hardly at all, unsteady on gravel, they danced part of a chorus of "Moonglow."

"Come here often?" she said to lighten the atmosphere. He said nothing, unlocked the car, let her in, slammed the door, and strode around to the driver's side. As he switched on, backed away, gunned a ferocious turn, and raced out of the fair grounds, she said, "You can come home with me tonight."

He said, "What?"

"Alvin has gone away for few days. A friend of his called and asked him to go up to Montreal for some stag thing. A guy they know is getting married. He got on the train this afternoon."

Dolan drove in silence.

"On the other hand, if you don't want to -- I just thought it would be nice to get in bed and not have to worry about rushing off."

He thought of what she had written. The young girl dead by her own hand. The possessive brother. The old athlete trying to squeeze a few more drops of flavor out of a desiccated life. She called it *Nor Iron Bars*. "I want to," he said as he made the turn to take them down the hill toward Station Street. "I just can't believe my luck." In his mind, cutting through the confusion, Dolan heard a sound that was not hard to identify. It was the door of a cage slamming shut behind him...

Her house reminded Dolan of vacation cottages he had inhabited in wilderness country. It was of frame construction, ramshackle, okay in summer as long as it didn't rain. The furnishings were lightweight, carpets worn through, woodwork covered in paint faded years since to the color of an ancient keyboard. The telephone (only once had Dolan dared speak to her on this vulnerable line) hung on the kitchen wall. For a yard around it, the wallpaper was peppered with a buckshot explosion of scrawled numbers and messages.

She found a bottle of gin and gave him a drink he did not want. "Relax," she said, bouncing into place beside him on the sprung settee, tucking a leg under her where he could not miss seeing the plump, shiny curve where calf met thigh.

She surveyed him with delight. "You're among friends, Casey. Don't look so mournful."

She gave him butterfly kisses with her eyelashes. He let his hand rest on that smooth leg. His anxiety evaporated and he began to share her excitement. The feeling reminded him of a time when he and some of the kids went into Woolworth's on Front Street and lifted a few lead soldiers. It was wrong and he knew he would hate himself later, but the urge had been irresistible.

Her bedroom was through a curtained doorway off the sitting room. She said, "Give me a minute," and went in there. Dolan sat, glass in both hands, elbows on knees, staring at the floor. Strange, he thought. The room smelled of decay, it showed no evidence of maintenance and yet he sensed there was a stability about the place as if it would still be here, sheltering the Hopkins tribe in a hundred years, long after his tidy bungalow had been bulldozed and built over.

"Ready!"

He went to her in the silent bedroom, saw a small cot with the covers turned back, inviting in pink light from a tiny lamp. She was naked under a flimsy gown, torn at the hip. He embraced her and was so overpowered that he lost his balance and they did a struggling dance, laughing at themselves. "You'd better lie down," she said, "before you fall down."

The front door opened, then closed with a slam. Alvin's voice was bored. "Carmen? You home?"

Dolan went ice cold. He stepped away from her and faced the curtain. Footsteps in the other room. The brother's boots showed in the light at the hem of the curtain. "You decent, kid?"

"Yes," she said in a tone of great weariness.

"What is it?"

"You may as well come in."

Alvin drew the curtain aside. He saw Dolan, saw his sister sitting on the edge of the bed. "What the hell?" He stayed where he was but raised his arm and pointed a finger at Dolan's face. "You bastard!"

"Alvin, calm down. He's here because I asked him. I work, I bring in money --"

"Shut your mouth."

"You don't own me!"

"Shut up!" Alvin's voice rose. He moved toward Dolan.

"Listen! Listen to me!" Carmen ran at her brother, grabbed his arm, and used her strength to turn him. "You touch him, you lay a hand on him --" her finger was in his face now " -- and I'll be gone so far from here you'll never see me again!"

Dolan felt as if he had been tied hand and foot and set on fire. He was due to die horribly and could do nothing about it. Shock numbed him. "I don't want any trouble," he said lamely, able to feel embarrassment through his panic at the weakness of his response.

"Just go, Casey." Carmen put her back against her brother, making way for Dolan's departure. "Don't say anything, get out, I'll take care of this." As he fled, she told him, "I'll talk to you tomorrow."

Seated in his car where he had parked it on the next street, Dolan had to wait a good minute before his fingers could fit the key to the ignition lock. As he drove away, he assured himself of one good thing emerging from the debacle -- he would certainly not be spending any more time with that dangerous little bitch.

Carmen was waiting for Dolan in the Coronet lounge. She had telephoned in sick to the radio station, taking a day's leave. At four in the afternoon, with his evening broadcast mostly prepared, he had responded to her call and come down to see her. She was halfway through a beer. Soon due on the air, Dolan ordered coffee.

"Can you believe it?" she opened. "That whole business about the stag in Montreal was a put-on. He suspected us. He set it up to catch you with me."

Dolan could believe anything of Alvin and he said so.

"You don't have to worry," she said. "I'm sorry I put you through it."

"Not your fault," he said bleakly. But he thought it was -- why couldn't she just leave him alone? He was old enough to be her father. Why all the provocative attention?

"We talked for a long time after you left. Alvin can be sweet when you approach him the right way. At first he didn't want to know but I kept on and finally he understood. We love each other."

"Carmen, did you see his face?"

"He was all right later. I told him you want to marry me."

"Carmen --"

"Don't you? Are you just in this for what you can get?"

"You know better."

"Well?"

He tried to be patient with this stubborn child. "I *have* a wife."

"You talk as if you've got cancer. Millions of men get cured of wives. It's called divorce."

"It takes two to get a divorce."

"Have you asked her? She doesn't even live with you. She's over in Centralia having a ball running her store. She's probably waiting for you to bring up the subject."

It was all so complicated. What had happened to the quiet life he used to think was boring? A divorce would cost money. A wedding would cost money. Carmen would get pregnant. Babies cost money. He would be the oldest daddy in Baytown -- laughter in the beverage rooms, to say the least.

He drank his coffee doggedly, aware that she was watching him across her beer.

"Okay," he said at last. "I'll drive over to Centralia and put the question to her."

Dolan waited until Sunday when he had no program to do and then drove down the Bayshore Road through a region of dairy farms and acres of half-grown corn, reaching the concrete towers of Centralia at five o'clock in the afternoon.

He had always hated the big city. Years ago, the Redmen had come up against Centralia in a sudden-death semifinal leading to the Southern Ontario Baseball League championship. Baytown lost the game eleven to four and Dolan, besides going hitless, had allowed the ball to get past him twice and each time a run scored while he was scrambling around twenty feet behind homeplate, trying to find the handle.

Warned by his telephone call the day before, Anna was waiting for him in the back garden when he walked around the side of the house. It was bigger than his place back home but she was only renting it, furnished. Reclining in a folding chair, an empty one beside her, she raised her sunglasses and studied him as he shambled across the grass.

"You've lost weight," she said.

"Pining away without you."

"You look younger." Her voice and her frown conveyed suspicion. "What's her name?"

There was a pitcher of lemonade and a couple of glasses on a table between the chairs. He poured himself a splash and sat down. "You're a mindreader."

"Why else would you ask to come and see me?"

"Maybe I miss you."

"Maybe, but you don't." She had not taken her eyes from his face. "Don't look so pathetic. I wrote us off a long time ago."

"I hate it when you say that."

"Stop clinging to a finished thing. Move on, Case."

He set down his empty glass on the tin table. It rang like the signal for the start of round one. "Funny you should say that, Annie. I need a divorce."

"So. What's her name?"

"Carmen Hopkins."

Anna turned her head.

"Is that the fat little teenager I met the last time I came into the station? You must be joking."

"She's a clever young woman."

"She's a bloody genius if she's trapped you." Her face was pale, she looked her age. "Is she pregnant?"

"Not that I've heard."

"She's saving her trump card. Casey, listen to me, I'm about to do you a favor."

"I'm listening."

"No way will I ever grant you a divorce to marry that carnivorous high-school dropout. If you were to come to me with some mature, intelligent, decent woman -- " She watched his face for a few minutes while he counted blooms on hollyhocks. Then she got up and carried the pitcher and her glass to the house. "Crazy," she threw back at him. "Out of sight."

Dolan came in a few minutes later and heard the shower drumming. He wandered through rooms he had seen only once before. He used to believe, like a kid, that he and Anna in the house in Baytown were permanent because nothing else could ever contain their relationship. He was wrong. There was always another way.

She joined him as he was exploring the bedroom. It was a new robe, soft towelling in a shade of blue he liked, and she smelled of the lilac soap she had brought into his life decades ago. She stood beside him; there was no place for his arm except across her hip. They slipped easily into a familiar embrace. As they kissed, she whispered, "I was hoping you hadn't driven all this way just to argue."

"Seems I didn't," he said.

In the next hour, the light in the room diminished slowly as afternoon became evening. Casey lay at ease with Anna tucked close against his side. The occasional things she said buzzed against his ear. He was falling asleep. The trip had solved nothing. All it proved was that he and Anna could still get it on, but that had never been in doubt. They could not live together, and she would never, clearly, release him to marry Carmen.

"No divorce?"

"No divorce."

"You're a bitch," he said.

"I'm the best friend you ever had."

They ate something at nine o'clock. By then, he was outside unlocking the car, making his escape from boredom, the nagging that was beginning to emerge -- not all hers, he was dishing out his share. The car smelled strange inside, but he cranked down the window, switched on, and began to roll. Then Alvin Hopkins got up off the floor behind the driver's seat and put a knife against his neck.

"Hey!" The car swerved before Casey got control and stepped on the brake, easing to a stop fifty yards from Anna's house.

"Keep driving."

"How the hell did you get in here?"

"You shouldn't have given Carmen your spare key. She doesn't even have a license."

"She told me she does."

"She tells you lots of things. Like I was going to Montreal for a friend's wedding."

"She made that up?'

"That's right. My sister is crazy, don't you know that? After Pete crashed his truck and died, she went out of the house one night and put her head on the mainline track, waiting for the Toronto express. I think she knew I'd find her and bring her back but I'm not sure."

"So the whole story about she'd be alone in the house for a couple of days was to get me found there by you."

"She likes excitement."

They drove slowly in silence, down empty streets. At last Dolan said, "Where are we going?"

"*I'm* going back to Baytown. By bus, the way I came."

Dolan felt, at last, the cold tide of fear. It filled his gut, loosened his muscles, his foot relaxed on the accelerator.

"Don't do anything crazy."

"Keep driving. Turn left at the corner."

They drove into an area with trees and shrubs on either side of the road. Streetlamps cast pools of brilliance which only emphasized the black distances beyond.

"Slow down. Pull off over there, between the lights. Here."

Dolan switched off and sat, trembling, sweating ice-water. "If you want me to stay away from Carmen, you've got it. I was just with my wife -- we're planning on getting back together."

"It's Carmen staying away from you. She'll never do it, no matter what I tell her. She's a bad little girl. It's vital that I prevent her having her own way. The kid is spoiled rotten." Alvin leaned forward. "Now look at this. I want you to see something." He held the knife blade in front of Dolan's face. The thick fist, the muscular wrist formed an unbreakable grip that trembled slightly. The blade itself gleamed -- at least seven inches long, a streak of oil on the honed edge. "If you yell. If you run. If you do anything but as I say, this goes into your gut and I turn it."

"Oh, Jesus," Dolan whimpered."Jesus."

"Get out of the car. Slowly."

Hopkins was out and waiting for him on the pavement, took his arm as he slammed the door and led the old ballplayer away from the light and down a pathway smelling of ripe earth. Furtive movement occurred at intervals in the shadows. "This is where the Gays hang out," Alvin said. "We're not alone."

They came to a silent clearing. Dolan could make out the surroundings, could see the shape of Alvin Hopkins as he was forced around to face him. "You'll be robbed and stabbed a lot. They have these crazy killings here all the time. But you've behaved, so I'm not going to hurt you. This blade is razor-sharp. I'll cut your throat -- you won't even feel it. Then I'll do the rest. Believe me, it won't hurt."

Casey Dolan found the desperate courage to raise his voice "Not going to hurt me?" he screamed. "Bloody hell, you're *killing* me!"

Alvin moved swiftly, turned Dolan, lifted his chin, and swung the knife. And he was right about that important thing -- Dolan didn't even feel it.

Six months passed, during which Carmen Hopkins stayed late every night at the radio station. She told her brother she was writing a novel. He didn't believe her, he thought she was messing around with Dolan's replacement. But try as he would, however often he popped in unexpectedly, he always found her at the old typewriter, knocking hell out of the keys.

Then it was finished and she began coming home after work, eating whatever he put in front of her, then watching television until signoff. It was agreeable in a way, a nice routine which Alvin appreciated. But she was putting on weight and had stopped doing anything with her hair, which gave him an uneasy feeling. In fact, by the end of the year she was looking more like a fat sloven than his sexy little sister.

"You should take a look at yourself in the mirror," he said to her one evening.

"You should burn in hell," was her calm response.

The letter from Toronto came one Saturday morning while Carmen was still in bed. She received little mail, but whatever arrived with her name on it, Alvin opened and read. This one was first-class, typewritten envelope, a company name in the corner -- Tandem Publishing Ltd. The letter was brief. It said:

"Dear Miss Hopkins:

Thank you for letting us see your novel, *Hey, Don't You Remember?* It needs a bit of tightening but it is a powerful work and we would like to publish it. Is it autobiographical? The character of the psychopathic brother, Al, is particularly well drawn, while the doomed love affair between the young girl and the broadcaster is poignant, to say the least.

Can you come to Toronto and talk to us? I'll look forward to an early reply --"

Holding letter and envelope in one hand, Alvin shuffled across the room in his broken slippers, drew back the curtain, and went through into the musty cave where Carmen lay asleep on her cot. She was breathing slowly, a hand resting below her chin, wrinkled thumb not far from her open mouth. When it used to be his job to watch her as a child, Alvin had repeatedly dragged the wet thumb free, trying to break her of the habit. Another failure.

Now he had a new problem. His little sister was going to become a published author. She would be rich and famous and a guest on TV chat shows, where she would discuss the background of her book. Or not. It was up to him and he would have to make up his mind soon.

Counting her shallow breaths, eyeing the pillow on the floor beside the cot, Alvin smiled with deep affection. "Carmen, Carmen," he said softly, "What in the world am I going to do with you?"

Ellery Queen Mystery Magazine, December, 1986

FEAR IS A KILLER

With his heart pounding, Walter Wingbeat sat at the boardroom table half listening to what Clay Fetterson was telling the client. "Nor do we usually formulate an advertising plan before the product is developed and tested. But in this case, at your request --"

As the head of R&B Advertising continued his preamble, Wingbeat glanced from face to face around the mahogany oval. The client, Norman Imrie, president of Metro Distillers, was looking noble. Sensing Wingbeat's attention, Imrie returned an encouraging smile. Tough, but fair and decent -- that was Mr. Imrie.

"So -- we have prepared, among other exhibits," Fetterson continued, "a media plan. But before I ask our media manager to take us through it, may I voice anxiety over the name of the new product. A liqueur distilled in America is a great idea. Using the flowers of an indigenous desert plant gives us something to talk about in the advertising. But for a drink, the name Yucca..."

Wingbeat was turning his pages. He remembered what it was to breathe deeply but the technique had escaped him for the moment. The imaginary iron strapping around his chest was at maximum clamp. Pinprick bubbles of light fizzed around the periphery of his vision.

A hand touched his. A voice murmured, "Are you all right?" It was Penelope Good, the girl from England. He had hired her as his assistant three months ago. The department was in need of people but Wingbeat was afraid to hire. What if he chose the wrong person? In Miss Good, it looked as if he had brought in somebody very good indeed. And now he was a afraid of *that*.

He managed a smile, glazed eyes and sick lips that would have stampeded nurses in an intensive-care unit. "Butterflies," he whispered, fluttering a flat hand. "Okay once I start."

She made a kissing face at him. It was way out of line, he hadn't even taken her to lunch yet. Her honey hair was much too smart for the money she earned. How did she manage? Her suit looked expensive. Her blue eyes were calm. Penelope Good fitted in around the executive table like the maroon-leather armchairs themselves.

"Not to worry," she mouthed silently, "I'm with you."

Apprehension about the new brand-name had been expressed to Norman Imrie before. "Be assured, gentlemen and lady," he said, "the name Yucca has been thoroughly tested. I went around my office and spoke to twenty people. Told them my wife had come up with a concept and a name for a new liqueur. Yucca. What did they think? Not one negative reaction. One hundred percent in favor."

Clay Fetterson's grin became brighter than a thousand suns.Wingbeat had to avert his eyes as the boss said, "Can't argue with research as conclusive as that. On we go. Let's take a look at the media plan. Everybody got a copy? Fine. Wally, will you lead us through this?"

"Uh, sure, Clay." Wingbeat was alone, terrified. "These are rough figures, guesstimates, because I was told I wouldn't see budget until after the taste-testing, which I understand is not happening until --"

"Could you just take us through it, Wally?"

"Sure, Clay. Uh, page one is a summary of the major markets, with some additional weighting in --" The iron bands tightened. Wingbeat's breath was reduced to a flutter. "Oh, wow," he said, as panic took over.

"Everything okay, Wally?"

Elbows on the table, Wingbeat put a flat hand on either side of his face, shutting out witnesses to his humiliation. To die like this in public -- Trouble breathing. Just a minute."

"Is there pain?" The observers were riveted. They were not callous people but if the media manager went in mid-presentation -- would *that* be a story to dominate drinks this evening.

"Not a lot of pain," Wingbeat said. He was coming out of it. It was stress, tension. "Have to get my breath."

"Should the man try to continue?" Norman Imrie asked. He was less entertained than the others. "Give him a rest."

"Exactly right," Fetterson said. "Can you take over, Miss Good? Wally, slide over to the couch. Put your feet up."

As Wingbeat left the table, Penelope Good unbuttoned her jacket to reveal a nicely rounded white silk blouse. Placing a fist on her hip authoritatively, she said in a voice worthy of the Royal Shakespeare Company, "The summary requires less than a glance at this time. May I direct your attention to the following pages, where, market by market, we see the media breakdown. Forgive the word 'breakdown', Walter," she said and everybody laughed, including Wingbeat.

As was his habit, Wingbeat worked a couple of extra hours after closing to give the Friday-evening traffic a chance to clear. By the time he drove home and parked his car in the driveway that separated his cedar-and-stone bungalow from the brick-and-stucco cottage next door, his wife and son had finished their supper. Corliss was in a deckchair on the back lawn under one of the stately poplars, holding a depleted glass of gin and tonic in her hand. A glow and babble from the television room showed where young Philip was hiding.

"Cold plate in the fridge," Corliss said as she accepted her evening kiss. There was a book opened face-down on her lap, something heavy from the non-fiction bestsellers list. Corliss Wingbeat was never seen without a book, but she seldom read anything clear through. Her last conquest dated back several years -- *Jonathon Livingston Seagull.*

Wingbeat ate his salad standing up in the kitchen. Taking food out-of-doors in view of the neighbors gave him a queasy feeling. After rinsing and stacking his plate, he wandered through to change this clothes. On the way past the TV room, he looked in on Philip, who smiled tenderly at him as he reduced the sound.

"Evening, Pip," Walter said to his eleven-year-old. "Shouldn't you be outside enjoying the glorious fresh air?"

"Same air in here, Father." The boy indicated the open window.

"You have a point." Wingbeat lingered.

"Is everything all right?" Pip was watching his father's face.

"Just fine! It's the weekend!" The distressed adman clapped his hands and executed a buck-and-wing. The step was not badly done. A generation ago, he had sparkled as one of the policemen in a high school production of *The Pirates of Penzance*.

"You look sad, Father."

"The mature face in repose, my son. Nothing to be alarmed about. How's this?" Wingbeat hooked an index finger in either side of his mouth and dragged his lips upwards into a manic smile. At the same time he let his eyes go crossed. Philip fell over, laughing and rolling on the carpet and Wingbeat walked away feeling good for the first time in days.

When he appeared on the back lawn ten minutes later, dressed in slacks and T-shirt and his recently whited tennis shoes, the sun was setting. Its last rays picked out the awkwardly sporty figure and made him glow. The raucous voice of Wingbeat's neighbor, Larry Boxer, filled the silence.

"Hey, Wally," he bellowed, "dim your shoes!"

As Wingbeat dragged a chair across the grass and sat close to his wife, she muttered, "Why don't you tell that oaf to shut his big mouth?"

"He's only kidding."

"You let people push you around, Walter. It isn't good for you. What are you afraid of?"

"I'm not afraid."

"You *are*." Corliss raised her voice just enough. "You reek fear."

"I've never seen the sense in contention. Why argue with people? Cooperation is more productive." He had not played his trump card in months. Tonight it seemed risky but he threw it down anyway. "It works for me. I'm the head of media in one of Canada's leading ad agencies." Secretly, Wingbeat knew why they kept him in the job. Because he worked all the hours God sends, not employing extra staff, keeping the department budget low. He would never say this to his wife. He was afraid to.

Corliss finished her third drink. She was feeling comfortably aggressive. "How is the smarmy limey?" she asked.

He knew she was referring to Penelope Good. There had been bad blood between the two women since an office party a couple of months ago at which the English newcomer mistook Corliss Wingbeat for catering staff, handing her an empty glass. "Who?"

"You know who. Penelope Put-down. I'd keep an eye on her. She wants your job. And God help her if she takes it." Corliss modified her threat. "God help *you.*"

"We can help each other," Penelope said, glancing at Clay Fetterson for confirmation. The hotel dining room was medium busy for two o'clock. It was unusual for Walter Wingbeat to be lunching in such surroundings at such an hour. His normal lunch was tuna salad on whole wheat taken at his desk along with yet another mug of company coffee.

"My idea exactly," the managing director said. "You obviously need relief, Wally. We don't want a repetition of the seizure episode last week. Bad impression in front of the client. I know it's illogical but it could make him think R&B Advertising is not healthy."

"It hasn't happened before," Wingbeat said. "Shouldn't happen again." Fear flooded his belly.

"We're seeing to that," the boss said. "Penny will take on the executive responsibilities. She will confront ferocious clients in their dens. Meanwhile, the wealth of Wingbeat experience will still be ours to tap when and as we need it."

Penelope could only repeat what she had said before. "We can help each other." But her grin was tight and she swallowed without drinking or eating anything.

"And now," Fetterson said, "we'd better get back to the office. At four-thirty, we taste-test Metro Distillers' newest product, Yucca Liqueur."

"Yeeuch!" Penelope said, pretending to recoil as the managing director landed a playful punch on her arm.

Testing a client's product was almost like being let out of school. Opinions were so widely sought that every member of the agency staff, from Clay Fetterson himself on down to the lowliest filing clerk, was welcomed into the boardroom to join the party and put forward an opinion. This product being made with alcohol, the session was scheduled for late in the working day. By five o'clock closing time the room looked and sounded something like happy hour at a neighborhood bar.

Several bottles of Yucca stood open on the mahogany table, protected now with a linen cover. Almost everyone punctuated the first sip of the liqueur with the spontaneous reaction -- "Yeeuch!"

"That name has got to go," a copywriter on the account would say and the crowd would laugh.

But the sober truth was, the stuff did taste vile. Nobody wanted a second glass of it--except for Penelope Good. The English import swilled the liqueur down and became merrier by the minute. "Jolly nice," she commented. "Not finishing your sample, love? Waste not, want not, I'll just tip your glass into mine."

Wingbeat was among those who abominated the mickey-mouse booze. But, a solid agency man, he appreciated the fact that Yucca was the brainchild of the client's wife and he knew they would have to sell it.

Wife. Watching Penelope getting high, he brooded. Here was his replacement as head of the department. Soon it would be made public and Corliss would have to know. Staff might accept the change and forget about it but his wife would not take it easily.

"Cheer up, Wally," Fetterson said, his overfed face florid with good-fellowship. "It may never happen."

"It already has."

"You hate presenting to clients. You'll be happier out of the rat-race."

"There are others involved."

Fetterson, a married man, knew what his former media chief was getting at. "Explain to Corliss. Tell her the job was killing you."

Wingbeat left the session. He fled to the safety of his desk, lost himself in pages of figures which demanded nothing of him except that he arrange them in columns that added up. Never mind the job killing him. Robbed of her prestige as wife of a manager, deprived of the extra money that went with the responsibility, Corliss would make his life not worth living.

The idea entered Wingbeat's troubled mind without preamble. Kill or be killed. It was preposterous, but perhaps it was the only way. Not Corliss -- he would never murder his wife. But if he could find some safe way to terminate Penelope Good's stay on the planet, his problem would disappear.

Wingbeat was so shaken by the possibility that he left the office earlier than usual and drove home in rush-hour traffic. His street looked different at a quarter to six, with men getting out of cars and wives greeting them. Larry Boxer was opening his front door, jacket off, shirt sleeves rolled, bulging briefcase hinting at problems the jovial salesman faced like anybody else.

"What happened, Wally?" he called. "Fired at last?"

"Not yet, Larry." Wingbeat was so harassed, he let fly an answering salvo. "But when they drop me, I'm coming over to live off you."

Inside the house, he took his wife and son by surprise. They were playing dominos at the kitchen table. Corliss had her first gin and tonic beside her. Philip was getting through milk and cookies.

"Good Lord," Corliss said, as if a game-show host had climbed out of the television set.. "What are you doing here?"

"I live here. Hello, dear." He kissed her and ruffled the cornsilk hair on his son's giant head. "Evening, Pip." As he moved off to change his clothes, he said, "Think I'll do a little gardening. Not hungry yet."

"Have you been drinking?"

"Taste-testing. Metro's new liqueur."

"Is it as bad as it smells?"

Ten minutes later, wearing an R&B sweatshirt and the trousers he was proud of because of their grass-stained knees, Wingbeat hurried down to the gardening shed and brought out clippers, rake, work-gloves, and a plastic bag for rubbish. The tin of weed-killer was almost full. He took it to the light and began reading the copy on the label. It certainly carried enough warnings about the danger of swallowing the stuff.

"Father?" Philip was watching him.

"Hello again, Pip." He felt uncomfortable, caught in the act. "Nothing on the box just now? Aren't they rerunning *Dr. Who?*"

"Can I help you? I want to help."

"Take the clippers and go up to the rock garden. Trim the grass between the rocks."

"What are you going to be doing?"

"Finishing reading this." Empathy between father and son was intense. Wingbeat had to turn away as his eyes filled up. "Get on with it, son," he said. "Dad needs to be alone."

Early next morning, briefcase in hand, Wingbeat left the breakfast table and walked not to his car but across the back lawn to the gardening shed. Inside, he opened the briefcase, took up the tin of weed-killer, fitted it carefully inside between files, then closed the case.

"What gives?" Corliss called from the doorway as he came back and let himself into the car. Pip's calm face watched from the kitchen window.

"Left my watch on the shelf last night," he said, raising his wrist as an exhibit. It was no lie. Anticipating such a question, he had taken off his watch and left it in the shed before going after dandelions last night with a rusty knife.

Penelope Good paid him a short visit at half past nine, perching on his spare chair, crossing her shiny legs and swallowing coffee from a mug with "Carnaby Street" silk-screened on it. Then, "Must run, love," she said. Penny called everybody love, or ducks. "The idiot in the corner office wants to pick my brains about a new-business presentation."

Her irreverence about Fetterson only made Wingbeat wonder how she talked about *him* in front of others. "All right, love," he said. "Did you enjoy the Yucca tasting?"

"Fabulous. I can't understand why the others were putting it down."

Wingbeat had smuggled a full bottle out of the boardroom. He opened his bottom drawer and lifted the jug into view. "Play your cards right --" he hinted.

"Yummy-yum," the girl said, rounding her eyes.

"You never know your luck in a big city," he told her. "This could be the day!"

When she was gone, he closed his door. He found a sheet of clean paper and folded it crisply. He twisted open the cap on the bottle and removed it. He took the tin of weed-killer from his briefcase and poured a quantity of the white powder into the V of the folded paper. Then he funneled the poison carefully into the bottle, tapping the paper to expedite the flow. Last of all, he capped the bottle, turning it a few times to disperse the powder. The bottle stored away, he opened the door, went back to his chair, and lost himself in a forest of numbers.

At four-thirty, Wingbeat wrapped the bottle in a brown-paper bag left over from one of his frugal lunches. Then he got into his jacket, took hold of his briefcase in one hand and the bag in the other, and walked down the hall to Penelope's office. She was on the telephone, shoes tumbled on the carpet, stocking-feet propped on her desk. As she spoke and listened, she read her visitor in the doorway, his face, his briefcase, the rounded paper bag. The silky toes crimped and flexed.

"Is this an imposition?" Wingbeat asked when, at last, she terminated her call. "I know it isn't closing time yet, but this bottle needs drinking. And you *do* enjoy the stuff. And I used to be manager of this department and you soon will be, so between the two of us we ought to be free to --"

"Say no more, say no more." The girl got up and slipped her feet into the alligator high-heels. She put on a Charles Boyer voice... "Come wiz me to ze Casbah. I have cheese to go wiz de booze!"

The receptionist performed not a double, but a triple-take as she saw the unlikely couple vanish into an elevator. "Strategy conference," Penelope called as the door slid shut.

Home from school, Philip Wingbeat raised suspicion in his mother's mind by not raiding the refrigerator directly. "Are you all right?" she asked him.

"Worried."

"What about? Damn it, you've been sleeping in class again, I'm going to have to pay yet another boring visit to placate the principal."

"Worried about Father. He seems depressed."

"He enjoys it. If it wasn't for me pushing him, he'd be shining shoes at Central Station."

Philip could not bring himself to mention the weed-killer. His silence on the subject had something to do with preserving his father's dignity. But he was determined to sound a warning. After that, he would have done everything in his power.

"Mother, it isn't like other times. I think he may try something. Father needs help."

Corliss Wingbeat heard something in her son's voice. An alarm rang inside her head. Walter had come home on time from work the other night. That was definitely odd. The boy's rapport with his father was close. "You may be right," she said. Leaving her chair, she went and found her purse, throwing in wallet and car keys. It was one thing to tease Walter in a casual way, but she wanted him secure for quite a few years yet. "I'll collect your father at the office. We'll have supper out. I'll talk to him. Feed yourself from the fridge, darling."

Corliss drove in the opposite direction to the main flow of traffic, arriving at the R&B offices just as the receptionist was putting things away. "I'm sorry, you've missed him, Mrs. Wingbeat," the girl said. She could hardly believe her luck. Wingbeat's wife never came to get him. And tonight of all nights!

"I can't have missed him. It's barely five o'clock."

"He left early." The smile came easily. "Along with Penny Good. They said they were going for a strategy conference."

By a heroic effort, Corliss managed to conceal most of her fury from this twerpy girl. "Have you any idea where they're holding their conference?"

"Penny's apartment isn't far from here." The receptionist checked a list in a rare display of efficiency. She recited the address, adding, "It's the old converted building around the corner."

Walter Wingbeat was surprised at the smart interior of the apartment, situated as it was in such a grotty old structure. He said so as he cracked the cap on the bottle of Yucca, pretending he was breaking a seal.

"Thanks," Penelope said. "I badgered the landlord into plastering the cracks and painting. The rest I did myself. But the exterior is not to be believed. I shudder at the thought of a fire." She produced two tumblers. "Sorry I don't have liqueur glasses."

"You'll buy a nice set of crystal," Walter confided, pouring a generous measure of the ruby liquid into one of the tumblers," out of your first pay as department head. Listen, have you got any juice or mineral water? I'm not as keen on this stuff as you are."

"Hurray, more for me!" She brought him a bottle of fizzy orange. "You're awfully good about this job change," she said. "Some men would be homicidal."

"Truth is, the stress was killing me. You've done me a favor, you and Fetterson." He poured his orange, toasted her, drank as heartily as she did. The important thing, the reason for his being here, would be to get rid of the remains of the poisoned liqueur after she keeled over. Then, to fake illness himself. When she was well and truly deceased, he would come around and telephone for an ambulance. Too late.

"Yeeuch!" the English girl said with delight. She poured the drink down her throat and reached for the bottle. "I don't care if the public laughs at the name and hates the product. I shall drink all they can produce."

Nearly an hour had passed and half the bottle of cactus liqueur was in Penelope Good's stomach when the door buzzer sounded. Wingbeat's terror had been mounting, drink by drink. He had put in enough poison to fell a rhino. His former assistant was very merry indeed, but she showed no signs even of a mild tummy upset, let alone death by weed-killer. "I'm going to answer the door," Penny slurred. "If I should return during my absence, please notify me."

Wingbeat had no place to go. The apartment was of the bed-sitting room variety with kitchenette attached. His alternatives were to hide in the bathroom or a closet or else stay put and face the visitor. When it turned out to be Corliss, with an expression on her face of curiosity mixed with repressed fury, Wingbeat panicked. He had never been so terrified in his life. His mind couldn't produce a logical assessment. All it could contribute was the idea, "Out, out, out!" His wife was blocking the doorway, flanked by Penelope Good, who was smirking from one shell-like ear to the other. The window! There was no other escape route.

Flinging aside a length of curtain, he hoisted the sash and stepped through onto the iron-barred platform of a fire escape. A paved parking lot lay three floors below.

"I wouldn't!" his hostess called.

As if to substantiate her warning, the rickety construction squealed, a couple of rusty bolts slipped out of crumbling concrete moorings, and the fire escape swung out and away from the wall. "Hey!" Walter yelled. Now he really had something to be afraid about.

Corliss and Penelope were framed in the open window. His wife did the usual -- she demanded something from him that he could not deliver. "Get back in here!" she yelled.

The English girl was shrieking with delight. "You look so funny! I love it! Your wife showed up and you actually -- This is fabulous!" And then, having spent a part of her life being pummeled and battered in an English private school, and on her holidays falling out of boats or off of mountains in Europe, the bold young woman said, "Hang on, love. I'm coming to get you."

Wingbeat watched her kick off her shoes. He stared in fascination as her nylon-clad toes took purchase on the window ledge. "Don't move," she said. She tried a step forward onto the platform. It was too far away from the wall. "Give me your hand. And hold on. We'll drag you back."

It was a moment of focus. Walter Wingbeat saw his manifold fears now combined in the person of this optimistic girl. She had taken over his job. He was afraid to pass the terrible news on to his wife. The future was unbearable. If only Penelope Good did not exist.

Her arm was extended, her hand inches away. The decision was made for him by a survivor inside, a Wingbeat of whose existence he was only dimly aware. He grasped her hand, took his tightest grip, then gave a sudden, ferocious pull. It was as if he was taking her to him and her face brightened mischievously, but only for a split second because there was no place for her to go but down. She swore, two blunt words he was surprised to discover in her vocabulary. A moment later, she was spread-eagled between cars on the pavement. The building superintendent, who had been watching the drama, ran to examine the body.

Corliss raised her eyes. They met his. The glance asked many questions as it seemed to supply some answers. No heroine, Corliss Wingbeat solved the risky problem simply. "Get in here," she snapped. And her husband obediently took a long stride forward onto the window ledge and allowed himself to be dragged inside.

The super's testimony backed up the story of the surviving couple. It was embarrassing for the Wingbeats, but there was no case against them. Fleeing husband, angry wife. Brave mistress accidentally falls to her death. Misadventure.

The Wingbeat case could not be dismissed so easily at the office, however. Norman Imrie was a bit of a prude. Such goings-on between employees of his ad agency were not acceptable. So the offending department head had to be retired early. But the liquor tycoon was nothing if not fair. The man ought not to be penalized financially. Imrie let it be known that Wingbeat should receive his full pension. And it was done.

For the first time in his life, Walter Wingbeat had nothing to be afraid of. His income was guaranteed, his pension linked to the inflation rate. He had nothing to do these days but work around the garden and spend some time handicapping the thoroughbreds at Blue Bonnets. A few days later, Corliss came to where he was sitting on a bench by the garden shed. She had a cup of coffee for him and a suspicious frown on her face. She sat down.

"Spill it, Walter. You were up to something. A philanderer you're not."

He decided to level with her. "She was about to take over my job. I wanted to get rid of her. I put weed-killer in a bottle of Yucca liqueur and gave it to her. The poison could never be tasted in that horrible stuff. The reason I went to her apartment was so that nobody else would drink some accidentally. But it had no effect, the powder must have lost its potency."

"Fortunately for you. You must have been crazy." She showed him affection over his foolish behavior. " Had she died like that, there would have been an autopsy. They'd have discovered the poison. You gave her the bottle, you'd have been hauled up in court."

Wingbeat shrugged. "I wasn't thinking straight. Anyway, it didn't happen."

Corliss Wingbeat's fond mood lasted for the rest of the day. She decided to make her husband a bowl of his favorite vanilla pudding. Nobody else liked it, he could have what was left of the nearly full box of pudding powder she had found inside the pedalbin a few days ago. She asked Pip if he'd thrown it out and he said no, but who else would have done it? Maybe he was afraid he'd be given the hated pudding for dessert one day.

The boy fled that confrontation wondering if he should have spread the weed-killer around the garden instead of substituting it for something harmless. But somebody would have noticed the powder on the ground and he might have been observed had he tried to dig it in. Trust his mother to inspect the trash. Never mind -- as long as the stuff was thrown out, it didn't matter that she suspected him of putting it there. Thus Philip Wingbeat worried the matter round and round. He had noticed that as he got older, he was more frightened of things.

In the kitchen, Corliss got out the pudding powder and the milk and a bowl and a whisk and gave herself a few minutes' exercise whipping up the mixture. When it was set, she brought it into the garden, where Walter was resting on the lounge swing with a pen and a pad and the daily racing form. "Here," she said, handing him the bowl and a spoon. "Just to let you know how I feel about you."

"Hey!" Wingbeat said. He scooped up a spoonful and swallowed it. It tasted odd -- milky and bitter -- but he was afraid to say anything that might destroy Corliss's friendly mood. So, with appropriate noises, he wolfed down the entire nasty mess while his wife watched and wondered how much longer she could survive, shackled to this irritating man.

MARQUIS
PRINTED BY
IMPRIMERIE D'ÉDITION MARQUIS
IN JUNE 1995
MONTMAGNY (QUÉBEC)